# OATHBREAKER

---

## KEEPERS OF THE ELUSIVE MYSTERIES
### BOOK 1

## MEGHAN TOMLINSON

Print ISBN 978-1-7386860-1-8

Ebook ISBN 978-1-7386860-0-1

*For all the dreamers out there*

# AUTHOR'S NOTE

Dear reader,

This book uses Canadian spelling, according to the Canadian Oxford Dictionary, 2nd Edition. You might notice some words spelled according to British usage, while other words use American spelling. This is Canadian spelling in a nutshell. We couldn't decide which spelling system to use, so we took a little from column A and a little from column B. After all, we wouldn't want to offend anyone.

You may also notice the use of the Oxford serial comma. Now that just makes good sense no matter how you spell harbour or realize.

## CONTENT NOTES

*Oathbreaker* is an adult fantasy novel with themes for mature readers. More content information can be found on my website:

www.linktr.ee/meghantomlinson

Happy reading!

Meghan T.

# CONTENTS

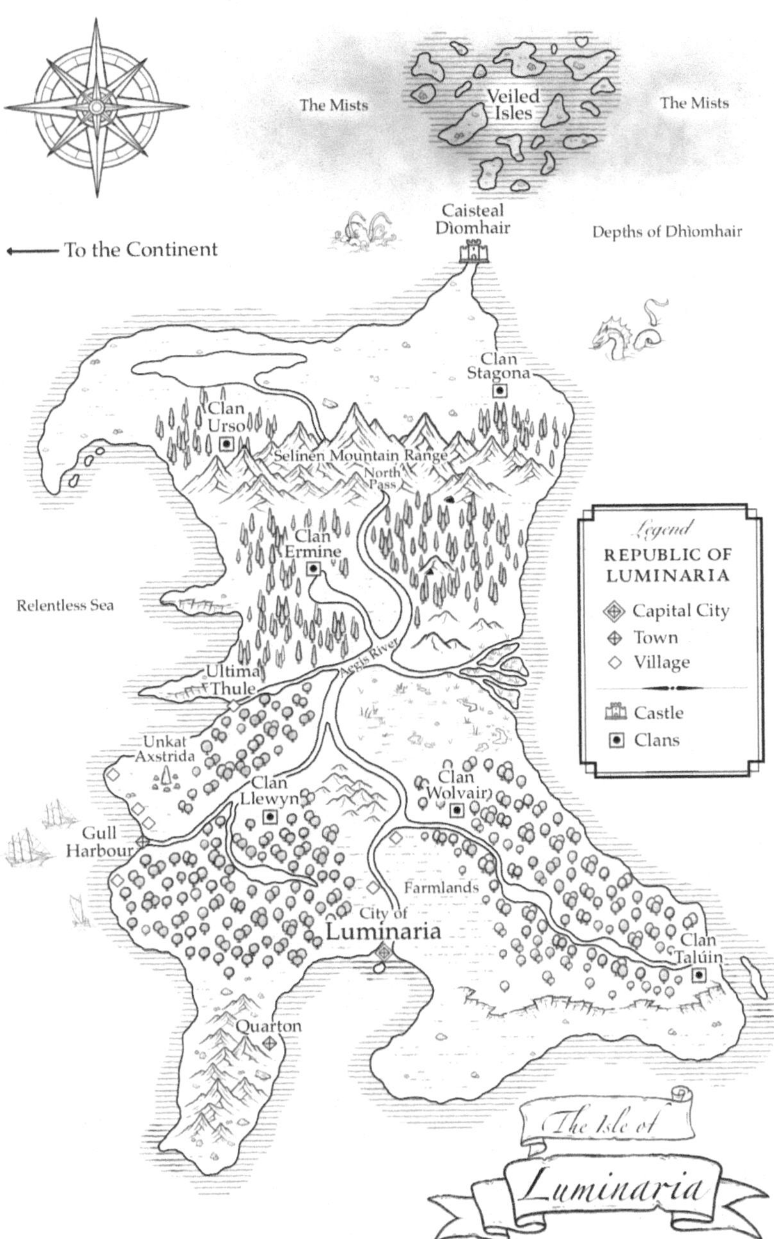
To the Continent
The Mists
Veiled Isles
The Mists
Caisteal Dìomhair
Depths of Dhìomhair
Clan Stagona
Clan Urso
Selinen Mountain Range
North Pass
Clan Ermine
Relentless Sea
Ultima Thule
Unkat Axstrida
Aegis River
Clan Llewyn
Clan Wolvair
Gull Harbour
Farmlands
City of Luminaria
Clan Talúin
Quarton
Legend
REPUBLIC OF LUMINARIA
Capital City
Town
Village
Castle
Clans
The Isle of
Luminaria

# PART I

# AN OATH TO HONOUR

**1**

———————

Over the beat of the drums and the trills of the reed pipes, Seren Moralis heard the muttered insults as though the sullen voice whispered in her ear. The source—a nob with barely a chin beard—leaned over a Conquer board at a stone table on the far side of the crowded hall. Nobs like him never thought there would be consequences for dishonouring her behind her back. It was worse than if they flung it in her face. Then, at least, she could challenge them to Aequitas.

Her fists curled at her sides, aching to do just that, and her feet altered course toward the game players. Bringing her elbows up, she pushed her way through the writhing mass of young nobilis who imitated the hip-swaying of the dancers on display. The decadence of the entertainment and the exhibitionism of her peers made her lip curl. One such nob, in plum-coloured silk and dark tight-fitting pants, made the mistake of stepping out in front of her. Clearly, he was drunk or flying, or he wouldn't dare leer at her.

"Dance with us."

*Ridiculous.* What he was doing wasn't dancing, not like

3

Master Kai had taught her. She easily sidestepped his hand—right into a serv, who had appeared out of nowhere with a tray of fluted glasses of Ambrosia. The pale honey-coloured liquid splashed over his finely embroidered tunic—special for Pledging Night—and narrowly missed her white ceremonial wrap. Glass shattered on the polished stone floor at her sandalled feet.

*Solfire.* The last thing she needed was to be publicly humiliated tonight by this spectacle.

"Clumsy lout," the decadent nob sneered, stumbling back from the drenched serv who was already on his hands and knees, picking up the shards and cutting himself in his haste. "If you injured, Mistressa—?"

He still didn't realize who she was. She lifted her chin so he could have a good look at her while she glared at him. "This is all your fault."

His shapely mouth snapped shut—or maybe the force of her scowl stole his words—and she watched as recognition stole over his arrogant face. *Fool.* She wouldn't be the centre of attention now if he hadn't gotten in her way.

Before his shock at finding himself conversing with Seren Moralis shifted into an insult she'd be unable to ignore, someone tugged at her elbow. The familiar scent of earthiness after a rainstorm, however, stopped her from striking out at the soft touch.

"Goddess, Seren, you ran off like the Amphitheatron was on fire." A teasing smile lifted the corner of her friend Valera Calissi's generous mouth before it faded. "It's not, is it? A fire would severely hamper my night."

"It could be on fire." Seren couldn't help the dourness in her tone. The phantom attacks of their enemies had grown bolder of late.

Of course, Valera hadn't overheard Chin-beard. Her friend didn't have the blood of their enemies in her veins. Blood that cursed Seren with hearing so acute and sight so keen, she never missed a taunt or a lip curled in her direction. Tonight's insults were neither new nor original, yet she'd been steps away from challenging Chin-beard to Aequitas and a moment away from ruining all her hard work for the last four years.

"Even if it is aflame, it's not your problem," Valera reminded her. "You're not a legionnaire yet." She slipped her arm through Seren's, ignoring the gawking crowd that had swallowed up both Plum Shirt and the serv. "So let's get your uncle's summons over with, and then we can make our pledges and celebrate properly."

That was where Seren had been headed, yet her feet would rather take her toward a fight than to the House Moralis rooms in the Amphitheatron. For tonight, on Pledging Night, a summons from the patrius of one's House meant nothing good.

"I don't need an escort, Valla." Or anyone to witness her shame of being forbidden to pledge to her family's House.

"Maybe I'm here for their protection. Those *buccones* behind us said something, didn't they?"

Seren sighed, unsurprised. Her friend possessed a talent for defusing altercations between Seren and their classmates. And she was more perceptive than most gave her pretty face credit for.

"Not them." Seren's gaze slid over her shoulder to where Chin-beard sat among others in the same dark green shirts. He seemed to be deliberating where to advance his miniature legion on the three-tiered gameboard. Around his mop of dark blond hair hung a blueish haze of Ashe smoke, courtesy of the pipe between his lips. She recognized him now from last year's graduating class. While he wasn't the first to call her a traitor because of her blood, he was, so far tonight, the first to say it within her hearing.

"He's not worth your dreams, Ser."

Despite that, Seren's free hand twitched by her side as he

caught her eye and laughed with his companions. How she longed to break his prominent nose, so it never sat straight again. But she couldn't.

On Pledging Night, violence of any sort was forbidden. The Consul would disqualify her from pledging her loyalty to her House. Then Uncle Tarquin would be hard-pressed not to disown her, as so many had counselled him to do over the years. The thought of him pinning two silver eagles of House Moralis to her shoulders had kept her from fights in the past. Well, most of them.

Seren flexed her right hand, feeling the split in her knuckles from the last mouth to take issue with her during the final matches. "They can defame my father all they want, but one day they won't dare insult my honour."

One day, she would have her vengeance on those who considered her lower than dirt. Pity her father was already dead.

Valera's hands swept down Seren's bare arms to squeeze her hands, interrupting her dark thoughts. "No, they won't."

The rest of their walk toward the stairs was unimpeded but not unnoticed. Valera garnered a different sort of attention from those they passed. Swathed in the traditional white linen wrap of a pledge, she was all soft curves and long sunshine tresses; the one good, true thing in Seren's life. And . . . soon to be lost. After tonight, their duties to their respective Houses would take precedence, and opportunities to see each other would be few.

As if sensing Seren's change in mood, Valera paused at the top of the steps. "Your uncle probably has a speech about the responsibilities of a pledged member of House Moralis. On the ride here, my father went on and on about my duty to House Takkakus, then recited our history, all the way back to the founding of the Republic of Primordia."

Easy for Valera to roll her eyes at her father's pomposity.

Pater Calissi hadn't been convicted of treason and executed before she was born.

"Then you best not wait for me. If Uncle Tarquin starts in about our ancestors coming to this isle, I might miss the Pledging."

The weak joke fell flat. Still, she couldn't let go of Valera just yet, and her fingers threaded through her friend's. "I'll find you after I'm done here, down on the floor?"

Valera looked like she wanted to argue about leaving, but then she nodded solemnly. "And afterwards, we'll toast each other's good fortunes to have each other, then drink to the fall of our enemies."

Seren's lips quirked upward. *Enemies?* Valera had none except the ones she took on her friend's behalf.

After another squeeze, their hands parted, and Seren hastened down the stone steps, wracking her mind for any offences she had committed recently and, of those, which ones might alter Uncle Tarquin's decision. Nothing in particular came to mind.

She'd answered the Lyceum examiner's questions as best she could. While she didn't have the flair for rhetoric that Valera did, she hadn't done poorly enough on her final examination to warrant banishment to the Detritus Quarter. And she had won honours in her matches without letting her opponents land a single strike. After years of holding back, she'd earned the right to see the looks of astonishment from her classmates when she tossed Sila, the reigning victor of their year, onto her back.

At the second tier, Seren strode down the corridor toward her House's private box. Sweet floral notes greeted her as she passed through to the open-air balcony. Here, the less youthful members of House Moralis conversed and indulged in a quiet pre-celebratory drink. None of the men in their old-fashioned robes matched Uncle Tarquin's profile, but her eyes snagged on a woman in a stunning peacock blue wrap with long auburn tresses. Seren's breath caught in her chest until the woman turned to greet another.

Not her mother. Seren dismissed her disappointment and foolish hope. It matter not that Adalyn wasn't here to celebrate her eldest daughter's pledging.

A young page in House Moralis pomegranate motioned to her to follow him into the quiet stone corridor. At each door, Seren's heart skipped a beat. Behind one of them, her uncle waited. Soon he and all the House patriuses would take a turn on the arena floor to accept new pledges. Or deny them for all the nobilis in the city to witness—a rare occurrence, as it brought dishonour to the House and the pledge. No, if Uncle Tarquin was planning on denying her pledge, he would do it in private. Like this.

The youth left her at the last door. Heart lodged in her throat, Seren knocked on the wood. After eighteen years, Uncle Tarquin surely wouldn't disown her now.

"Uncle?"

The spot between her brows prickled—it had been doing that a lot lately—and she checked the darkened corridor again for anyone who might be lurking.

Empty. No sounds came from behind the door, either. Not the beat of a heart or the breath of lungs.

Disappointment laced with relief stabbed at her. If she had to wait for him, there was no reason she had to do it skulking out here like a scolded child. With a confidence that was fading fast, she opened the door and stepped inside.

The strange tingling she'd grown accustomed to after that night four years ago assailed her now like a thousand pinpricks along her back, far more intense than ever before. And the air —was there any in this room?

Gasping for breath, Seren fumbled for her knife, hidden below her armpit in the folds of her ceremonial wrap, but her fingers were heavy and slow. Between her shoulders, her skin burned with the heat of Sol's hells as if he, the sun god himself, ran a hot iron over her spine. Her muscles spasmed, and she fell to all fours, stifling a scream by biting her tongue until a coppery tang filled her mouth.

What phantom attack was this? If the Felinae were here . . . they could be after Uncle Tarquin. But the room was empty—at least, she had heard no one before she entered.

She must alert the guards. But if she called for help, the nobilis would add cowardice to her faults.

No, she must be the one to handle her attacker. But first, she needed to clear her head of pain. Seren inhaled through her nose.

*I am stone. Stone feels nothing.*

Once, when she was little and had been blubbering over skinned knees, Uncle Tarquin had given her those words. He'd told her how House Moralis was descended from warriors who fought alongside the demigod Uttica in the founding of Primordia. That the descendants of these warriors had built the City of Luminaria after leaving the hedonistic old republic behind. That those who pledged to House Moralis had to be as strong and enduring as the stones upon which their new republic was founded.

But unlike stone, Seren felt every sensation keenly. It had always been this way, an inherent weakness of her father's ancestry that, as her uncle had explained, she must overcome.

While Master Kai would frown at such bemoaning, he would at least acknowledge her suffering after landing a brutal blow in their matches. More than once the tall, hard-faced ascetic had tapped his staff on the sandy floor of his one-room schola where he'd scratched out her lesson for the day: *Pain is life.* Her only solace now was the words he had scrawled after that: *Both shall end.*

Seren prayed the end would come soon. *The end of pain*, she clarified for any listening deities.

Then, as quickly as it had come on, the phantom pain dissipated. Seren reached for her knife. Or tried. To her horror, her hands refused to move. Panic sent her heart and thoughts racing. A poisoned dart? The cowards. Yet she hadn't felt a prick. Perhaps it was a slow-acting agent. Her attackers could be lying in wait as the poison made its way to her heart. Fear clawed at her chest where her ribs had once been broken.

*Assess the threat, Moralis.*

The room offered no hiding spots. Four wooden cradles stood in the centre of a red and white braided carpet, much like the one in the nursery at House Moralis. One cradle rocked back and forth. Had she stumbled into it during the attack?

Whoever had made the cradle had carved the phases of the moon into the headboard. For the full moon, however, there was a diagonal line through it. If she could move, she might have doubled over at the shock of recognition that hit her. For the past three years, she'd searched Luminaria high and low for a black ring of the same design.

And here it was on a cradle.

There wasn't time to contemplate the strangeness. Like a marionette controlled by an invisible puppeteer, her legs walked to the cradle of their own accord.

*Moon Goddess, what enchantment is this?*

Her head turned, forcing her to look down into the cradle. Beeswax and lemon from the oiled wood tickled her nose. Inside slept a babe, swaddled in linens, with black-brown hair and the squashed face of a newborn. One scrawny leg had kicked free and twitched, while tiny, clenched fists rested by delicate ears. Who had brought a babe to Pledging Night?

Her hand, of its own volition, slowed the cradle. Only it wasn't her hand. It was broader and bronzed with black hairs on it. As if possessed by a vengeful wraith, the hands picked up the empty bunting from another cradle, then pushed it down over the infant.

She screamed, but not a sound came out of her. In vain, she tried to wrest those strange hands of hers away from the babe, but she couldn't even look away, let alone move a finger.

"You can't exist in this world." The iron timbre that emerged from her wasn't hers either, but it was familiar.

*Goddess, no.*

Her fear was confirmed when she helplessly glanced up into a mirror on the wall. It reflected none other than her uncle, Tarquin Moralis, standing over the cradle, his jaw clenched in determination. However, his jade-black hair held no silver, and it was cut short, while the lines around his eyes had vanished. His clothing was just as odd. Instead of the legionnaire regalia of a golden breastplate and leather skirt for Pledging Night, he wore the simpler black version of it as donned by the City Patrol.

With a bang, the door flew open. A woman rushed in, her auburn tresses flying behind her while her pomegranate over wrap flapped untied about her ankles. "You brute!"

With the determination of a legionnaire, Adalyn Moralis charged her brother, but the collision didn't budge him from his task. Undaunted, she scratched at his bare arms and hands with a high-pitched screech, and Seren felt each gouge.

Even as she wished her mother victory, Seren ached to protect herself. Uncle Tarquin did more than that. He let one hand fly, backhanding Adalyn, and Seren felt her hand smash into her mother's cheek. She didn't know what shocked her more: the strike or that her mother took it solidly so she could latch onto her brother's arm. Unbalanced, Uncle Tarquin staggered back from the cradle, pulling Adalyn to the ground with him in a loud crash.

Seren didn't pay heed to the pain as Adalyn lay atop her. Had it been too long?

Then the baby took up a loud wail.

A cry of relief escaped her mother's lips. Adalyn shoved her brother back before she scrambled to the cradle. At the sight of her mother settling the squalling babe on her shoulder, Seren's relief twisted into a fit of inexplicable jealousy. Could one be jealous of oneself? For undoubtedly, this babe was her, and at this precise moment, her mother had loved her. If any of this was a true glimpse of the past.

In the commotion, a serv had slipped into the room. She stood at the head of the empty cradle, arms raised, and her eyes open but unseeing. With her grey wrap and braided dark hair, the slight woman didn't look measurably different from other servs—except for the mark upon her brow. A black circle with a slash through it. The same symbol that was on the cradle and the ring Seren searched for.

"Guards, seize the Felinae spy!" The words flew out of Seren's mouth as Uncle Tarquin got to his feet. It was astonishing to think a Felinae had infiltrated House Moralis. The Consul had banished their enemies from Luminaria before Seren's birth.

Cruel feminine laughter filled the room in the absence of the guards. "Did you forget, brother?" Adalyn held her daughter close to her chest, her cheek flaming red from his strike. "You ordered the guards elsewhere so you could murder my child."

"They wouldn't have stopped me, Adalyn. The honour of our House requires it." The clipped words tasted bitter in Seren's mouth. "Father should've never let it go this far."

If she could have, Seren would've fallen to her knees, for her entire world was collapsing under her.

"You're despicable." Unbridled hatred altered her mother's comely features. "She's innocent of our faults."

Uncle Tarquin's attention, however, had moved to the Felinae. "You're the nursemaid. Are you here for the child?"

"This child," she crooned, heedless of her impending execution, "will walk with the night and the sun, fathered by many, mothered by none. She will inherit more than the legacy of her bloodlines, for the burdens of all Times are hers."

A new urgency hummed through her uncle's body as he approached the nursemaid. "You speak of an inheritance?"

If it was from her disgraced father, Seren didn't want it.

"Nomi, what is this?" Adalyn demanded as she backed away from her brother.

"Goddess Seline," Nomi continued, eyes blank, "has favoured us with a piece of her broken soul to light our way through the darker days to come. Three futures lay before this one, represented by three souls, one for each Time, who may help or hinder her on this journey. The warrior seeks a return to a past of bloodshed. The philosopher seeks succour in a present built on illusions. The strategist seeks a future birthed in flame and ash. Whoever stands by her side will steer the course of our isle and decide the future for all the children of the moon."

The symbol on the nursemaid's forehead disappeared before she collapsed right into Uncle Tarquin's arms. Though Seren wasn't privy to his thoughts, she felt him shiver.

"How can this bastard decide the future of the Republic of Luminaria?" he demanded, shaking the unconscious woman. "Is she to inherit the Felinae Throne?"

Without warning, the phantom pain returned, overcoming her so swiftly Seren couldn't breathe. *Air.* Her mouth opened and closed futilely as she clawed at her throat. *Her* throat and *her* hands.

As the room turned black, everything was lost to her—except the tiniest sliver of hope. Uncle Tarquin had let her live. And her uncle did nothing without reason.

# 2

Air slammed into Seren's burning lungs like Uttica's legendary war hammer. Tremors twisted her body—*her body*—as she lay on the cool stones, remembering how to breathe.

A glance around the room confirmed she was alone. The rug and cradles were gone, too. In their place was the cold stone floor and a wooden divan opposite an open archway that looked out over the arena. Soon the pledging would begin.

On shaky legs she stood, grasping for explanations of how she'd been locked inside her uncle's body while he tried to smother her. A waking nightmare brought on by nerves, perhaps? She leaned on the divan. Like she needed additional torment to harry her nights. Unlike the memories that haunted her, this one couldn't be her memory. She had been but a babe.

Yet everything had been rooted in reality—the smells, the sounds, the feel of the soft linen in her uncle's hands as he pushed down. She shuddered.

But even if it were a true depiction of the past, that didn't explain the pain.

A throat cleared behind her, and she whirled, swallowing a curse for letting her guard down. In the doorway stood Tarquin Moralis, in the flesh. Unlike in her nightmare, a legionnaire's gold breastplate and leather pteruges were moulded to his compact form, which he worked to maintain. His black hair, tucked neatly behind his ears, was peppered with silver threads.

As he entered, the space in the room shrank, and Seren had to fight down the feeling of being cornered despite being slightly taller than him.

At his raised brow, she hastily saluted with two fingers in a V against her heart, then bent down on one knee. "Patrius Moralis."

"What thoughts occupy you, blood of my blood?"

"I had a strange dream," she blurted to his sandal-style boots. "More real than any memory."

"You are not given to fancy, Niece."

She chanced a glance from her bent position. His unyielding stare over his long nose made it nearly impossible to breathe. And yet, he had yielded and let her breathe. Let her live. When everyone else must have told him it was a mistake to shelter the bastard child of his sister and the disgraced Felinae prince. Why?

"I must ask, did you smother me in my cradle, Uncle?"

Without answering, he strode past her to stand at the archway, and the fading light of the sun glinted off the rubies and onyx embedded in the hilt of his sword, Magnanimous. If —no, *when*—she pledged, she'd press her lips to the steel to seal her oath.

"Do you breathe?" His tone was conversational as he looked upon the bustling arena floor below.

Feeling foolish, she dropped her gaze. "Yes, Uncle."

"Then I did not smother you, did I?"

His logic was sound, yet the spot along her back tingled as if reminding her of the pain. She hadn't imagined that. "But did you try? I saw you by my cradle—"

"What have I taught you about trying, Niece?"

She stiffened. "That the trying is inconsequential."

Silence descended upon them for so long, Seren wondered if her uncle had forgotten to dismiss her. Then he spoke, his tone curious, "In this dream was there a prophecy?"

Was it real then? "Is that what the Felinae nursemaid spoke of? My path?"

A flush of rare satisfaction filled his angular cheeks. "It seems my doubts about you were unwarranted."

Had he been about to disown her then? But she had pleased him with this strange nightmare. At his hand wave, she approached. Something akin to vindication glinted in his dark grey eyes. Seren fought to keep her knees from buckling as she joined him. Down below, a line of white had formed along the arena's walls.

"Do you know why I summoned you here, Niece?"

"No, Uncle."

"To remind you of your duty to this House. Of what honour means to a Moralis. Of the loyalty a pledge owes her patrius."

The tension building in her shoulders eased. Valla had been right. She was here for a speech. The *Duty and Honour* one had been given to her cousin Quinton so many times she knew it by heart.

"Nineteen years ago, before you were born and after your father dishonoured our House, I demanded Aequitas. I was denied the chance to face him, warrior to warrior. Instead, the Consul and Senate ruled Devan Morningstar guilty of breaking the Accord and conspiring against our new republic in a plot to assassinate the consulars. The Consul executed him for his crimes, his crown no shield from our justice. But was that the end of it?"

She inhaled sharply. This wasn't his usual rhetoric, but she knew what came next. "After the execution, the Felinae burnt our river settlements in an unquenchable fire that only exhausted itself after a mist fell upon the land, driving our survivors and legionnaires back. When it lifted, the Felinae had vanished from their castles."

For the next fifteen years, her uncle had used all his political and financial clout to locate the Felinae clans, to no avail. But, without an enemy to fight, the Consul let the issue of the vanished Felinae fade away. Out of sight, out of mind.

"Many thought the war over," she said, choosing her words carefully. Some of the nobilis had laughed at Tarquin Moralis's obsession, as they called it then. The Exilers more than most. However, Uncle Tarquin had been right. "And then the strikes began."

Mostly at night. Ships in coastal harbours and fields of crops burnt to ash. Farm wagons robbed on their way to the city. Armouries and storehouses raided.

Somehow the Felinae had allied themselves with pirates from the southern coastlines of the continent. Imports and exports were more often than not lost on the high seas. Shortages of resources less readily attainable on the island—medicines, paper, books, silks, perfumes, precious gemstones, spices, and khava—resulted in rumblings amongst the Houses.

Meanwhile, the streets coursed with resentment over the failure of Junius, the Consular of War, to end the attacks. Uncle Tarquin had forewarned this day would come when the Felinae would return to avenge their dead royals. Although his warnings had been unheeded over the years, Tarquin Moralis had risen in the Senate and attained a seat on the Consul as Consular of City Affairs.

"Just so, Niece. I swore an oath to the Goddess Lumina I'd see peace again on this island and the Felinae brought to heel." Her uncle turned his head toward her, but he was somewhere else entirely. "Each time they strike us without losses, our House's dishonour sparks anew."

So far, the Legion had failed to capture a single Felinae warrior. And they had no targets to strike. Scout ships that sailed to the north of the isle more often than not disappeared into the strange mists that whipped up the waters at a moment's notice. Still, from all accounts, the old castles of the Felinae remained empty.

Seren's chest swelled with the enormity of what she had to say, and she bent her head low. "No, Uncle, it is not the shame of House Moralis, but mine."

His hand raised her chin. "You asked if I smothered you." He paused, searching her eyes for something. "I let you live that day because another path was revealed to me. A new, unexplored path for House Moralis. For all of Luminaria."

Only his firm touch kept her jaw from dropping at his tacit admission of guilt. Did he mean the nursemaid's strange mutterings? Something about an inheritance. About three souls she was to meet in time?

Uncle Tarquin's thin lips flattened as he considered her. "You may be my greatest weapon yet."

Pride burned through her at the unexpected praise. Goddess Lumina had answered her prayers. Although they never talked about her training outside the Lyceum, Uncle Tarquin must have read reports from Master Kai about how far she'd come. And for all her tireless efforts, revenge on the Felinae would be her reward.

Impatience had her bending her knee. "Uncle, I owe you my life, my loyalty, my love. You raised me as the daughter of an honourable man when I was not. If you accept my pledge, I swear my life in loyal servitude to House Moralis and to uphold its sworn vows to seek vengeance on the Felinae." His eyes, shining dark orbs, drank in her oath, perhaps even her soul, and her lips trembled.

Magnanimous sang a sweet note as Uncle Tarquin unsheathed his sword. "House Moralis accepts your oath. Bring us honour and glory, and when your body turns to dust, your sword will fight on."

The icy steel against her lips was sweeter than a lover's kiss.

"Rise, Seren Moralis of House Moralis."

It was done. She was pledged, now and forever. Seren accepted his hand, and he pulled her to her feet. Then he straightened, his thick black brows knitting together. "Our enemies slither around our necks, Niece. House Moralis will need to stand together."

"I am your weapon, Uncle. Use me as you see fit."

He nodded, pleased, but already looking beyond her. "We will speak more later. After I meet with the Consul tonight, all will become clear."

Seren squashed her surprise at the impromptu meeting. "Do you expect the Felinae to attack?"

Uncle Tarquin hesitated at the door, one hand on the handle. "Tonight's meeting will transform our isle from an insignificant note in Primordia's great history into the sacred ground where the once-glorious republic of Uttica will be reborn." His lips twisted at the corner at some private amusement. "Albeit in an altered state. After tonight, I will set us upon a new course to defeat our enemies."

Seren wasn't certain what he had in mind, but an answer was expected. "Yes, Uncle."

"I trust what I have told you stays between us. Some within our ranks would rather let the enemy weaken us so they can skewer us from behind."

The Exilers. Was he warning her not to confide in Valera? Her House was one of the Exilers. After the Republic of Primordia had fallen into ruin fifty years ago, some Primordian Houses had fled into exile, sailing to the fledging Republic of Luminaria. Here they sought sanctuary, yet they brought with them the decadent ways of the tyrant. Although the Consul had opened their arms to the Exilers, it was no secret that Uncle Tarquin and many of the Founding Houses disdained the Exilers' influence upon the city.

She waited for her dismissal.

"Keep your exceptional eyes and ears open, Niece. And stay close tonight. Our enemies wait for any opportunity to lay me —and us—low."

Her cheeks warmed under his scrutiny. So he did expect an attack—one targeting him. Unease crept through her as she glanced at the darkened archways across the tiers of the arena. In every third archway, a legionnaire in gold stood guard, the red plumes of their helmets visible to all.

"Yes, Uncle."

A curt nod and he was gone, leaving Seren to sort through their conversation. Many Lyceum graduates would become House guards, and every graduate knew the first rule of protecting a body was to keep eyes on him at all times. Forbidden meeting or not, why else would Uncle Tarquin have confided in her? Tonight might be a test toward earning a larger role in the war. Flushed with pride at the honour, Seren stepped into the corridor, ready to prove herself.

**3**

———

Locating Uncle Tarquin on the arena floor was easy. Shadowing him was harder. A crowd of political aides, sycophants, and eligible widows and daughters surrounded him as he tried to cut through them. Her lip curled at their fawning. All around her, the nobilis of the colony, the young and the old, preened and panted after each other's power and station. Everyone except Uncle Tarquin. Such behaviour was beneath a Moralis.

Unable to watch as the widow Matrona Kaelha commandeered her uncle's reluctant notice, Seren turned her attention to the stone stairs that led up past the tiered seating to the stacked archways climbing into the starry sky. Tonight, the moon shone in her full glory on the decadence below her. How the Goddess Lumina must abhor what she saw. But Uncle Tarquin would purge the city of its failings once the threat of the Felinae was gone.

"Planning your escape so soon?"

She whirled around, one hand sliding toward her hidden knife. Instead, at the last moment, she crossed her arms.

Quinton had the gall to flash his dimpled grin at her. In his pomegranate brocade jacket, black pants, and high boots, her cousin was a dashing figure to behold. And despite his decadent reputation, the nobilis considered him a fine match for their daughters. Trouble was, he'd already slipped through most of their fingers—and their beds. Quinton never stayed caught for long.

"Oh, am I visible to you tonight?"

A curl of jet-black hair fell over his shuttered eyes as he half-bowed. From his bent position, he gazed up at her with a look that had stolen many a heart. "How can a star that burns so bright not be admired?"

It was a line and not a new one. "You tell me, Q. You've ignored my existence quite easily."

Oh, he was civil enough in front of his father. But other than awkward family dinners, he stayed clear of her. He hadn't even acknowledged their kinship when she'd entered the Lyceum. He'd been in his graduating year, and all her peers had taken their cue from him, the heir to House Moralis. If she wasn't good enough for her own cousin . . .

She glanced behind him. Wherever Quinton went, a certain tall shadow followed. But for once Tyberius Attica—Quinton's secondo in his City Patrol unit and his accomplice in scandal—was nowhere to be seen.

Quinton caught her looking. A muscle twitched in his cheek before his countenance smoothed over once again. He tossed back the rest of the Ambrosia in his fluted glass. "Allow me to seek forgiveness for all the time I've squandered?"

She frowned. "How much have you had to drink?"

His genial expression faltered, but he recovered with a wink. "Not nearly enough for tonight."

As it so often did around Quinton, the strange tingling broke out between her shoulder blades; to her relief, it was no stronger than the pricking one got in one's foot when it fell asleep.

Seren stifled a sigh. "Do you even know who I am?"

To her alarm, Quinton knelt on one knee before her and raised her hand to his lips. "I certainly do," he whispered. "You're my—"

Strong fingers clamped down on Quinton's shoulder. "There will be time for this later. Come, Quinton."

His father's presence sobered Quinton, and he stiffened to legion preciseness as he straightened. "Yes, Father."

Side by side, father and son made an attractive pair with their chiseled features and dark hair. Only Quinton had the moonlit skin and eyes of his late mother, Aiko.

Uncle Tarquin's gaze shifted to her. "Remember what I told you, Niece."

*Stay close.* She nodded at the chastisement. She shouldn't have let Quinton distract her from guarding him.

As the two men crossed the arena through the line of pledges, she trailed them. While the crowd made room for Uncle Tarquin and Quinton, it closed up in their wake, forcing Seren to weave her way through. The men passed under an archway, which led to the kitchens. By the time she navigated through the stream of servs carrying platters of peacock and lion and bear, they had disappeared.

Closing her eyes, she inhaled through her nose. Savoury smells enticed her, but she concentrated until she pulled out Quinton's over-spiced cologne and Uncle Tarquin's muted cedar undertones. Their scents led her down a set of steps into the catacombs, where she detected muffled noise about fifty paces ahead.

Silent as the moon, Seren padded through unlit passages used by the prize fighters, beasts, and condemned criminals who ordinarily entertained the nobs and the servs up above. Unlike her fellow Primordians, she didn't need torchlight to see in the dark. To her eye, the tunnels appeared almost as clear as in the daylight but in dull shades of grey. Few knew of her heightened senses. She'd learned at a young age that anything that pointed to her Felinae heritage would be used against her.

At twenty paces, her nose confirmed a whiff of cloves and cedar amongst the dampness. She followed the scent deeper into the bowels of the Amphitheatron. Thirty-odd paces down another passage, the staleness of decay and excrement assailed her, and she lost them. Bile burned in her throat as she raced forward, straining her ears for any sound. If she failed at this . . .

A low-pitched groan made her pulse leap. The noise led her to an iron door, where a lone torch burned. She had expected to find Quinton guarding the door since anyone who was not a member of the Consul would need special permission to attend, yet he must haven been invited inside. But for some reason, Uncle Tarquin wanted her present but not seen at the meeting.

While she considered what to do, footfalls sounded from down the hall, and she faded into the shadows beyond the door. A few steps back, her heel hit stone. Stairs led up to a narrow, arched doorway. She pressed herself against the wall, cursing the whiteness of her wrap, and peeked around the corner.

Two men approached silently in the circle of their burning torch. The broader was Dara Kaelha. At thirty, he was the youngest consular. Like Uncle Tarquin, he wore the breastplate and pteruges of a former legionnaire, and a sword hung at his side. This winter, he'd successfully claimed his late father's seat as Consular of Agriculture, and he often conferred with Uncle Tarquin.

The thin, grey-haired man in the silver-embroidered suit was her mother's second husband and a wealthy merchant from a mid-rank nobilis family in House Moralis. Sivio Silvestri's business acumen had swelled his and Uncle Tarquin's coffers through continental trade, enough to gain the

Consul's interest and procure him the appointment of Consular of Commerce.

Absently, she studied her stepfather's hollowed-out face as he turned to say something to Kaelha. Had he influenced her mother's decision not to attend tonight? It mattered little, Seren supposed. Where once Adalyn's absence might have sliced deep, now it was nothing but a dull twinge.

The door groaned again as Kaelha and Silvestri entered the room beyond. The irregular meeting had to be critical to interrupt the celebrations. Maybe a new plan of retaliation against the recent Felinae assaults on the farmlands outside the city? Whatever it was, Uncle Tarquin wanted her to stay close to protect him.

Muted voices trickled down the stairs to her left, revealing another entrance. It was a gallery. Four rows of empty benches overlooked a battered table and a collection of chairs, beyond which she was certain were catacombs of bones. This was a mortuary. The deep gouges in the wood were evidence that the arena's fighters weren't safe from blades even after their earthly defeat. In the middle of the table, candles burned, and the light flickered over the faces of the consulars. The grey dullness around the rest of the chamber meant anyone else would be hard-pressed to see beyond the candlelight.

At the head sat Uncle Tarquin with his fingers steepled before him as if he regularly held meetings amongst the dead. Behind him, like an obedient guard despite his lack of uniform, stood Quinton. Shadows played across his prominent cheekbones and straight nose, making him appear like one of the sculptures in the Moralis gallery.

Her ears twitched at a sound in the passageway, but then the door was groaning open. Now was her chance. Gathering the ends of her wrap over one arm, she crawled down the steps to the second row and huddled behind the first bench to gain a better view.

"My apologies for my tardiness, Consulars." Vesuvius's dulcet voice slipped over the air as lightly as they entered the room in their lavender silk wrap.

Seren dared a look over the benched seating. The Consular of the Arts and Spectacle deposited their torch in a sconce along the wall with the others, then took the last chair at the table at the other end from Uncle Tarquin. Between them sat Agrippa, the long-standing Consular of Aptitude, and Manguella, Consular of Enlightenment, in old-fashioned robes befitting their Houses. On the other side were Kaelha and Silvestri. Like a game of Conquer, all the players were lined up and waiting for the roll of the dice.

Except one. Junius, the Consular of War.

Uncle Tarquin cleared his throat, his gaze taking in all the assembled. "Consulars, I will not mince words. You have heard about last week's raids on the farmlands. But I have more concerning information. Word from the Legion's Western cohort arrived shortly before I left tonight. Two days ago, the Felinae struck Gull Harbour at dawn. Most of the port burned to ash, along with half of the nobilis and servilis quarters. Forty legionnaires were injured. Another thirty, including their centurio, are dead."

Seren gritted her teeth. That was nearly the entire Western garrison, injured or dead. Horrific, although the death toll could've been higher. Gull Harbour was the largest trade port on the west coast.

"Twenty-four nobilis injured, ten dead," Uncle Tarquin continued, each word clipped and measured. "Three hundred servs are presumed burned to death in the fire. A third were children."

Someone cursed.

"May Lumina and Lleufer see them to the Vale," Manguella murmured, his balding head lifted.

"Has Consular Junius been apprised of this?" Vesuvius asked evenly.

Uncle Tarquin's shoulders stiffened. "He was informed by messenger, as was I."

"Then why isn't he here to brief the Consul?" Agrippa demanded, echoing Seren's own sentiments.

Her uncle offered the barest acknowledgement of the question. "You must ask him. He was informed of the meeting."

"What is the extent of the damage?" Silvestri asked. By the look on his face, he was tallying the cost, coin by coin, in his head.

"Most of the wharf, seven ships, two-thirds of the serv housing, and the medica hall." Uncle Tarquin steepled his fingers before him again. "Simultaneous fires that consumed at twice the usual rate. Accelerants of some nature were used, or the Felinae—"

He broke off, and a knowing look passed around the table.

Kaelha pounded the table with his fist. "For the last two years, these attacks have made our legionnaires look like children with sticks. We cannot continue to let the Felinae strike with impunity."

"Just so, Consular." Uncle Tarquin's iron-cold stare rounded the table as if looks alone could bend them to his will. "And I possess a weapon to end the war once and for all. With it, I will restore peace and prosperity to our republic within a year, or you may hang me a traitor."

Seren forgot herself and gasped—not that she could be heard over the noise of consulars. It was an ambitious promise, but if her uncle said he could do it, he would.

A chair scraped backward. Agrippa pushed himself to his feet, the persimmon orange sleeves of his House's robe flapping about. "And how, pray tell, do you plan on accomplishing this tall order, Consular, when the Legion can't locate a single Felinae stronghold?"

"Perhaps Junius is looking in the wrong places." Kaelha looked ready to skewer the scholar with his House's sword from across the table.

"If I recall, Junius has been guilty of that failing before," Vesuvius mused. "If we are to be triumphant on this isle, we cannot rest on the laurels or tactics of our ancestors."

"And who's paying for this hunt?" Agrippa shook a pudgy finger in the air, unwilling to have his tirade interrupted. "Do you propose we raise taxes again? Or cut what paltry funding we allocated to the Librarium and Lyceum? The Legion already accounts for almost half of the annual tax intake." He drew a breath and planted both heels of his hands on the table. "Or will you be privately funding this venture by keeping a stranglehold on imports from the continent, Consular Moralis?"

The accusation of corruption hung ripe in the air.

"My ships, my imports," Uncle Tarquin said, as quiet as a Marked assassin's blade sliding into his unsuspecting target.

In the founding of Luminaria, the major industries had been divided up among the Houses who had left Primordia. When the Exiler Houses arrived fifty years ago, the industries had been adjusted by reapportioning some or establishing new ones, such as the burgeoning silk trade under House Vesuvius. But House Moralis remained the sole shipbuilder.

"Stick to supervising the city streets, Consular Moralis," Agrippa huffed, "and your son's decadent ways."

Seren gritted her teeth. How dare he. Crime was down two-fold since Uncle Tarquin became consular. And Quinton might be insufferable to her, but he'd been serving in the City Patrol and, for all appearances, staying out of trouble these last few moons. Uncle Tarquin didn't react to the affront, his silence its own rebuke of the man's bluster.

Kaelha, however, didn't take kindly to his idol being

disrespected and jumped to his feet. "Sit down, old man. We didn't come to hear you speak."

Agrippa's white-bearded double chin bobbed as he sputtered until Manguella placed a liver-spotted hand on his arm. "Consular Kaelha speaks rightly, if without tact. Let us hear Consular Moralis and then raise our objections."

The corner of Uncle Tarquin's mouth twitched in irritation at the need to explain himself—something no one in House Moralis would dare ask of him—but he nodded. "War is a series of moves, some of which are made possible by the assets one holds. We have been stuck on the defensive for far too long, our moves restricted by an unfair advantage. The lack of a target. My weapon will remedy that. Over the last nineteen years, I've honed it for this moment. With it, we will meet our enemies on the same terms. In short, my weapon will infiltrate the hidden lairs of the Felinae so we can strike them down."

Seren's heart beat loudly against her chest as her uncle's words to her earlier. *You may be my greatest weapon yet.*

"With nowhere to cower, the surviving whelp of the late queen will have no choice but surrender the Felinae Dominion to us," Uncle Tarquin finished.

The ingenuity of the plan took her breath away. Who better to infiltrate the Felinae than the bastard daughter of a late Felinae prince? It all made perfect sense, except why hadn't Uncle Tarquin mentioned it to her? Had it been a test of her skills to infiltrate this meeting?

It didn't matter, she decided. He'd manoeuvred her here to overhear his plan, and whatever Uncle Tarquin asked of her, she'd do it. That was what her oath meant. Anything to expunge the dishonour her late father, Prince Morningstar, had left on House Moralis.

Her palms tingled, and then her forehead. She tried to ignore it, but the prickling sensation spread to the spot between her shoulder blades until every nerve in her body burned with purpose. Only this time there was no pain, only a sense of rightness.

*Her destiny.*

"And you'll give us this weapon freely? If it exists, that is," Agrippa scoffed, pulling at his sleeves.

"In times such as these, is there a price we can afford not to pay for the peace of the republic?" After letting that sombre thought play upon his audience, Uncle Tarquin leaned back in his chair. "Consulars, it is not the costs we need concern ourselves with, but the conditions necessary for victory."

"What conditions are those, Consular?" Manguella asked smoothly.

Uncle Tarquin laced his hands together. "You will surrender your powers of state unto me, and as Imperator of Luminaria, I will win you this war."

**4**

———

*I*mperium.

Her blood hummed with anticipation. History was happening. The first imperator of Luminaria. What Uncle Tarquin was asking for, well, it was nothing short of absolute power. The Senate would no longer decide which issues to debate; the Consul would no longer pass or revoke laws. As imperator, Uncle Tarquin would have sole discretion to rule as he saw fit.

The measure had never been enacted in the colony's two hundred years. In the seven hundred years of the Republic of Primordia's conquest across the continent, two instances of imperium came to mind. Both times, a formidable force had threatened the security of the capital, and the imperator had marshalled the legions to defend their walls. After the invaders were vanquished, the imperator had returned power to the elected Consul.

Primordians did not stomach tyrants, at home or abroad, and the position came with a predetermined end. After all, rule by representation was one of the shining examples of Primordian superiority. One only had to look at the chaos that had swept the continent since the Republic of Primordia fell to know the truth of it.

"Our temples of Lumina's Enlightenment stand ready to support peace at any cost," Manguella said, cutting into Agrippa's blathering. "When will we be privy to the particulars of your plans, Consular Moralis?"

In the dark, Seren couldn't help but smirk as her conviction of herself as the weapon grew stronger. The Legion had no leads on where the Felinae had hidden for the last nineteen years after they'd vanished into an unearthly mist that lasted nearly a full moon cycle. But if the long-lost daughter of Prince Morningstar were to seek them out of her own volition?

As Seren rose to announce herself to the fools below, strong hands bit into her shoulders from behind, pulling her down. She snapped her elbow back, but her attacker released her. In that instant, the scent of sandalwood and lime made her go still as his breath fell on her cheek.

Why in Sol's hells was Tyberius Attica hiding in the mortuary?

"Do you court death?" he whispered harshly from behind her.

"—the less you know about my weapon," Uncle Tarquin continued, a sharp edge to his words, "the greater the chances of its success. We've long supposed rats have breached our walls."

"Some might say you are asking for the moon with naught but pretty songs to woo her," Vesuvius remarked.

"Which is why I ask for but one year to accomplish my task. My request for imperium is foremost about saving Primordian lives and preserving our republic's ideals. Rest assured, my weapon is ready to commence tomorrow." Uncle Tarquin's face was grave as he stood and gave the old republican salute—two fingers splayed in a V over his heart. "May the Great Republic of Primordia live on here in Luminaria."

While Agrippa fumed, the other consulars returned the salute. A knowing grin tugged at the corner of Kaelha's mouth for his mentor. Since Silvestri was her uncle's creature that made two votes. That left the two Exilers, Manguella and Vesuvius, and Agrippa.

Silvestri called for a vote.

"We cannot decide this without our Consular of War," Agrippa protested. His voice, however, had lost its steam in the face of his quiet colleagues. Junius's popularity had passed.

"His loss," Kaelha declared, throwing his arm in the air.

"Quorum has been met, Consular Agrippa," Vesuvius noted. "We may proceed."

In a measured manner, Silvestri raised his hand. That was three, including her uncle's vote. A tie.

Then, after a beat, Manguella's hand rose.

And just like that, Uncle Tarquin had become the most powerful man in Luminaria.

Kaelha roared in triumph and clapped Uncle Tarquin on the shoulder, who allowed himself a thin smile.

"All those against?" Silvestri asked as a matter of form.

With an air of defiance, Agrippa raised his hand, his cheeks ruddy as his robes as he glared at his colleagues. "You are fools if you think the promises of an imperator will be worth the seats upon which you sit."

Silvestri pointedly looked to the last consular. "Abstained?"

Vesuvius nodded, but it didn't matter. Four votes carried the majority.

"Long live the imperator!" Kaelha cried with a slap to the table.

There would need to be a ratifying vote in the Senate, of course, but these consulars, Silvestri excluded, were the patriuses of powerful houses. Their House senators would vote as they were told.

Quinton presented a scroll to each of the consulars to affix their seals with the wax from a purple sealing candle.

That completed, Uncle Tarquin stood. "To those who place their trust in me, I am overwhelmed and honoured. To those whose trust I must earn, I pledge myself and my House to a victorious ending to this war. Consulars, the Republic of Luminaria will need each of you and your Houses in the coming days."

The meeting adjourned, and, as the consulars filed out, Tyberius's hands came back to rest gently on her shoulders, as though she might leap out again. Once Uncle Tarquin and Quinton left, she'd see what Tyberius was up to. For now, she let his hands stay and pretended the shiver down her back was because of the dampness in the catacombs and not the way her palms tingled at his touch. It was almost as if he caused the tingling, instead of the legacy of her old injuries.

Below, Quinton held the scroll open for the wax to dry. "That went well, Father."

A raised hand from Uncle Tarquin silenced him. "It's not over yet."

Out of the darkness of the crypt emerged a cloaked figure, his face obscured by a deep hood. Where the cloak parted, gold breastplate peeked out, followed by thick, burly legs. A legionnaire—or a former one.

Beside her, Tyberius drew in a breath, in tandem with the jerk of Quinton's head toward the newcomer.

"Are we in agreement?" Uncle Tarquin asked the shadowed man.

Her shoulder muscles spasmed under increased pressure from Tyberius, and his hold immediately loosened.

"Joren will deliver the one you covet to the Observatory if our business tonight concludes satisfactorily." A languorous Exiler accent marked the low rumble. "Is Junius no longer Consular of War?"

Deliver who? And what business did her uncle have at the old tower?

"I will remove him upon my inauguration," Uncle Tarquin confirmed, "but as imperator, I'll have no need of more consulars."

The air hung still between them, neither hostile nor friendly. Finally, Uncle Tarquin nodded in Quinton's direction, and he stepped forward. The dutiful heir.

"The imperator will require someone of noble lineage, victorious in battle, to direct his Legion when it marches north into the Felinae lands," Quinton stated. "A Legate of War who shares the imperator's vision of a strong new republic."

The burly man placed two fingers in a V over his heart. "I accept then. House Takkakus will pledge our support to imperium in the senate."

Then this was Patrius Calvus Takkakus. She frowned at the thought of her uncle conspiring with Exilers. First Manguella, now Takkakus. Since Manguella oversaw the temples of Lumina and Lleufer, it made sense to deal with him. If the priestesses came out against her uncle as imperator, he would lose support amongst the populace. Perhaps the deal with Takkakus was also an unfortunate necessity for ascending to power before he reformed the city.

"And the one I seek," Uncle Tarquin reiterated, "will be delivered tonight, Legatus."

It wasn't a question.

"As you command, Imperator."

Takkakus faded back into the crypts, and after a short interval, Uncle Tarquin and Quinton left the mortuary through the door, taking the last torch with them. The pressure on Seren's shoulders disappeared, and the room plunged into greyness, as it did when there was little to no light.

She should follow Uncle Tarquin, but her mind was too awhirl with the enormity of his plans. All these years, her uncle had never said a word about what he had been preparing her for. This task must be the different path revealed to him by her nursemaid, the reason he'd let her live.

"What do you think you're doing here, Seren?"

The harsh tone had her drawing her knife from the folds under her left arm.

At the scrape of her blade against its sheath, Tyberius stumbled back in the darkness. "I'm not your enemy, Seren. But if I'd wanted to, I could've slit your throat with none of them the wiser."

The truth of that last part stung. She'd been preoccupied with the consulars and hadn't paid close enough attention— something she'd sworn never to do again. Once she focused one sense to its heightened capacity, the others faded away. It was something she'd been working with Master Kai to overcome. And the stench of the corpses had covered his scent until he was right behind her.

"You could've *tried* to slit my throat," she corrected, if only to save her pride. "You'll find I've improved since we last sparred."

Nearly four years ago, she'd thought she'd done well against the older boy of eighteen. Now, she knew he'd been humouring her that summer before she entered the Lyceum.

"Improved or not, spying on the Consul is punishable by death. Are you trying to get yourself killed?"

"No more so than you," she retorted, moving along the benches to put distance between them. "Why are you here, Tyberius? Playing Quinton's shadow again?"

As he turned toward her voice, she leaped to a higher bench, then another, moving toward the gallery's exit. It would serve him right if she left him without a torch to find his way out in the dark.

"You wouldn't believe me if I told you, Tabby."

The old nickname rankled as much as it had when she was younger. Quinton, in his first year at the Lyceum, had brought

Tyberius back to House Moralis for the autumnal break. As usual, Quinton ignored her. So she had quietly stalked the boys around the grounds until Tyberius called her out like a kitty, to her embarrassment. By rights, she should've hated him, but he was never cruel in his teasing. And when he noticed her, it forced Quinton to acknowledge her, too. So it became a game: she would stalk the boys, and Tyberius would try to catch her in the act while Quinton did his best to pretend she wasn't there. But at eighteen, she was too old for such a name or such games. Even if he had caught her in the act again.

"Try me."

"The political schemes of these men aren't friendly sparring matches." He squinted in the dark, searching for her. "If Agrippa or Takkakus learns you were here, you'll suffer worse than broken bones."

Did he think because he was four years older and Quinton's sword brother, he could lecture her? She flashed her teeth—not that he could see. "So will those who annoy me."

"Oh, I forgot you can scowl your enemies to death." The corner of his mouth lifted in a way far more dangerous to her than his knife or a scolding.

Most noticed Quinton's classical dark looks first, but Tyberius had a rough edge to him that attracted his share of admirers. A slightly crooked nose divided his lean face, but it was his ruffled coppery hair and wild green eyes that drew her in. There was a heat to him, so very different from the glacial reserve of her family.

The air seemed saturated now in the scent of his shaving soap and citrus. She inhaled deeply. Would he taste as good as he smelled? Lumina, where had that thought come from? Maybe from the fine pair of black pants that hugged his hips and his silk shirt, open at the top to hint at the firm chest beneath. Not that she was looking. Tyberius treated her more like a younger sister—someone to instruct and look out for.

Which was ironic, since Quinton wasn't her brother and had never acted as such.

"Doesn't seem to be working," she muttered, though her gaze wandered back to his mouth, which had widened into a delectable grin.

Thank Lumina the cover of darkness allowed her to look upon him unobserved.

The grin widened. "That's because you're not scowling at me."

A flush burned her cheeks as she rearranged her features appropriately. "And now?"

"Consider me chastened." He bowed, laying a hand over his heart. "The passages should be clear now. Shall we head back to the arena before I test your temper any further? If you leave me in the catacombs, I'll be doomed."

"Doomed to what? Miss the celebration?"

While Quinton had cleaned up his act, the rumour was Tyberius still caroused the illegal undergrounds for all his amusements. And while it hurt, it made sense he wanted to get far away from her.

"Well, it would be a shame to have the city's finest liqueurs go to waste. But I meant I'd be lost down here without you," he clarified, peering at her. "Though I can think of worse fates."

She rolled her eyes. "Oh, how I weep for the hardships you've endured, Tyberius."

The silence widened between them until it was as though they both stood on either side of a chasm.

"For all your spying, you've no idea, do you?" he murmured.

The rebuke stung. She had never heard him so serious. Truthfully, she knew little of his life outside of House Moralis and Quinton. It made her hesitate. "About what?"

His once-inviting mouth tightened as he pulled on his discarded jacket. "Let's get out of here before we're caught."

"Then you'll tell me why you were here."

"If you tell me why you're here." With a bow, he indicated she should go first.

That should be obvious. She was the weapon. But since time was of the essence, she held her tongue.

By unspoken agreement, they navigated the tunnels with Tyberius gripping her shoulder from behind to keep his footing in what had to be pitch dark to him. His hand was warm, except for the kiss of metal around one finger, and the warmth travelled down to her belly. Quinton must have told Tyberius about her exceptional senses at some point for him not to question how she was guiding them. Which made her wonder if Quinton had confided the secret consul meeting location to Tyberius as well.

A few rodents scurried along the edges of the tunnels as Seren retraced her steps; otherwise, it was quiet except when Tyberius stumbled against her and mumbled an apology.

"How, by Lumina's Grace, did you find your way in?" she whispered after the fourth time.

"Agrippa made enough noise for a parade to follow in his wake," he muttered just as the smells of spiced meat and briny oysters reached her. The noise of the kitchens, still a hundred paces away, grew louder with each step. So much so, she almost missed the approach of soft footsteps from that direction. Fifty paces and closing, she guessed.

She halted, and the brocade of Tyberius's jacket pressed against her bare back. When he didn't move away, her breathing hitched. He had spoken truly about the penalty for spying on the Consul. And if she failed to gather intelligence at such a meeting without being caught, Uncle Tarquin might reconsider sending her to infiltrate the Felinae.

She grabbed Tyberius by the hand and pulled him further into the dark.

"Seren, what—?"

With her forearm, she pushed him back against the wall,

then put a finger over his mouth. He stilled. Hot breath warmed her finger. Under his finery, she could feel—and hear—the rapid beating of his heart. Her own seemed to skip a beat. Did he hear the footsteps yet? Their pursuer would stumble upon them soon.

Tyberius turned her head back toward him by the chin, his mouth nearly brushing her nose. Her finger traced the dip in his upper lip. A tingle wound through her and a shocking idea along with it. There was one quasi-acceptable reason for being in the catacombs on Pledging Night.

"May I?" she murmured.

His green eyes widened. "Lleufer, yes."

Before she could think better of her recklessness, she kissed him. The taste of peach Ambrosia drew her in, and she chased the sweetness, her mouth eagerly opening as his hungrily slanted over hers. His hands slid lower, leaving a trail of fire where they caressed her over her wrap. Meanwhile, her hands had wound around the back of his neck to stroke the soft skin there. She ran her hand through his hair—longer on the top than the sides—and he shuddered against her.

*Oh, Lumina.*

She pulled back slightly for air, and, without warning, Tyberius reversed their positions, pinning her loosely against the cold stones. She gasped at the sensation. Then his hot mouth trailed desperate kisses down her throat to her collarbone until she was writhing under his touch. Yet his hands held her firmly; one at the top of her hip, the other at the base of her neck, sending exquisite shivers down to her toes as his mouth demanded everything of her.

"Seren. *Seren.*" He uttered her name between kisses like a prayer.

The respite gave her enough time to think. Had the footsteps stopped? She tried to say that one of them should listen for their pursuer, but his lips pressed against hers again, and all thinking ceased.

Someone moaned, low and deep. Goddess, she prayed it wasn't her. Then she couldn't think anymore. Still, she needed more. She slipped her hands under his jacket, under his shirt, to get closer to that delicious heat, and he answered by crushing her between his hard body and the wall. All her nerves felt as if they'd been lit on fire.

A throat cleared. Once. Twice.

The fire in her veins vanished along with the fog in her head. Their pursuer had found them.

Tyberius untangled himself, but his body blocked her from view while she hastily fixed her wrap in the sudden coolness of his absence. But when he stepped away, it wasn't a serv or a legionnaire on patrol before them. Nor even a consular.

Seren touched her swollen lips. "Quinton—"

"Is this where you've been?" Gone was his dimpled smile from earlier. Instead, accusation hung in her cousin's storm-grey eyes as his knowing gaze slid from her to Tyberius, who leaned against the wall, unrepentantly stretching his neck. Did Quinton know they had been spying on the Consul? His gaze held disapproval, yes, but there was something else. Betrayal? "The entertainment for the night is over, Attica."

"Maybe it's only begun," she retorted. Did Quinton think she was still a child? She could kiss whomever she wished. It was no concern of his. The heat of her anger cooled into a fine edge.

Tyberius shrugged as he tucked his shirt back in place around his slim hips. "Easy come, easy go, Centurio."

Seren couldn't help the flaring of her nostrils at the insouciant words. The kiss had been nothing other than an excuse to be in the catacombs, and yet it irked her that Tyberius would sluff her off as yet another one of his fleeting conquests.

"Good to hear, Secundo," Quinton said with frosted

indifference, "because we have new orders. Dust off your gold breastplate and boots, our commissions in the Legion have been reinstated. We ride out the day after tomorrow with the first three cohorts and our new legatus."

"For where?" she demanded.

"Gull Harbour," he answered. "It's been burned. The ships, the wharf—half the town is gone." Her chest loosened. Quinton wasn't acting like either of them should know about the attack, which meant Tyberius hadn't been in the mortuary gallery at Quinton's behest. "The garrison has requested reinforcements and aid."

A cleanup mission. The cohorts would help the harbour town rebuild and reassure the citizens of their safety and her uncle's care for them. She glanced at Tyberius, wondering again why he had been spying on the Consul.

"Any Felinae will be long gone by the time we arrive," Tyberius said, focused on buttoning his brocade jacket.

Out of the corner of her eye, she caught the flash of black-glass as his nimble fingers worked the last button. The smooth band had shifted around his finger to reveal a circle with a black gemstone bar bisecting it on the diagonal.

**5**

———————

"**Y**ou?"

It came out as a choked cry. One autumn evening, that ring had been the last thing she'd seen before her attackers struck her unconscious. On her jaw, there remained a small scar from it. Seeing the symbol in a nightmare on her cradle was one thing; seeing it on Tyberius's finger was quite another.

"Me?" Confusion rippled across Tyberius's face as he reached out toward her with his hand—*that hand*—and the ring came perilously close.

She flung herself back against the wall, out of reach. "Don't. Touch. Me."

His hand dropped to his side, and shame filled her. Was this why she had trained every night with Master Kai? To be incapacitated by fear? To run away? No, she'd trained so she'd be ready for the bastard when she found him.

*But Tyberius?* He might live a decadent existence, but she'd always felt safe with him. Even when Quinton ignored her, Tyberius had found some little way to notice her.

"Sol's hells," he muttered, following her gaze to the ring. He

43

twisted the design around to hide it inside his palm. "It's not what you think, Seren."

Quinton glanced between the two of them, his lip curled but not at her. "Another lover's token, Ty? Truly, you are in high demand these days."

She swallowed what she suspected was a panic-stricken laugh at Quinton's assumption of the ring's origin. Or could someone have given it to him?

"Jealousy is unworthy of you, Q," Tyberius shot back.

Quinton inclined his head toward the light at the end of the passage, high colour across his pale cheeks. "You're done here, Secundo."

Tyberius opened his mouth to argue with his centurio, then shut it. He didn't glance back as he strode out of the tunnel. She half wanted to race after him and demand answers, demand justice—or better yet, pay him back for every blow, every strike, every kick she'd endured—if he'd been the one.

While she couldn't get her revenge tonight, the moon would rise again tomorrow.

She realized Quinton was staring at her. "What are you doing here?"

"Father tasked me with collecting you," he said stiffly, "and Valera Calissi said she saw you enter the catacombs."

He shifted as if she should understand, but all she could think about was the ring and Tyberius.

"The Pledging has begun," he prompted.

*Moon above.*

He managed a tight smile, though it lacked its former brilliance, and offered her his arm. "Allow me the honour, dear cousin?"

Seren smiled back, teeth peeking out between her lips. It was far too late. "When Sol's fiery hells ice over, dear cousin."

Then she swept past him to claim her destiny as the weapon of House Moralis.

———

IF LUMINA'S High Temple was the soul of Luminaria, the Amphitheatron was the beating pulse. Here, the city cheered their favoured legionnaires as they slaughtered mercenaries from the continent, booed criminals sentenced to hang, and wept for an actor's final breath, which seemed to be the way most plays ended. Tonight, the pulse showed no signs of ebbing.

Seren leaned against the cool stone of the inner wall of the arena, taking it all in while waiting for her turn on the platform. Dinner had been served and eaten in her absence, and the laughter and babble of the satiated guests nearly drowned out the gentle refrain of the harps. Servs in gold sheaths carted picked-over platters back to the kitchens, and her stomach rumbled at the smell of the ocean—oysters. Maybe she could duck into the kitchens after pledging for a taste.

Quinton had dogged her footsteps the entire way to the Pledging line, and then he'd disappeared, to attend his duties as heir to House Moralis she supposed. The other Moralis pledges in the line gave her a wide berth. All the better, as she didn't want to make conversation. Questions and accusations crowded her mind, but interrogating Tyberius would need to wait until her eagles were pinned to her shoulders.

A serv with a tray of Ambrosia flutes wandered by—not the fellow whom she had bumped into earlier—and, though she rarely imbibed in such decadence, she snagged one. She deserved a congratulatory toast for surviving four years of gruelling physical training, dry lectures, and petty classmates. The honey-coloured beverage fizzed as she stared at it. After waiting so long for her pledging, she wanted to savour it. The sweet Ambrosia tickled her tongue. A touch of peach and summer sun.

*Like Tyberius.*

The kiss came flooding back as the bubbly wine warmed her belly. No one had ever touched her with such passion, such desire. All she could compare it to was a peck of a kiss at age ten. But she couldn't overlook the fact that Tyberius wore the ring of her attacker, evidence of his betrayal; and if Tyberius was her attacker, that meant Quinton was involved. Whatever spat they were currently embroiled in, back then Quinton hadn't sneezed without Tyberius there to wipe it, and vice versa.

Her mouth went dry at the thought of her cousin betraying her like that. Could Quinton's apathy extend to such hatred? He was for all purposes a stranger to her, and she couldn't rule out his complicity. But she also couldn't accuse the heir to House Moralis without iron-clad proof. Especially not when her uncle never discussed the attack that had almost taken her life. And with good reason.

Defeated warriors didn't deserve the acknowledgement of their patrius. So while she had lain comatose in the Lyceum's infirmary, there'd been no visits from Tarquin Moralis, uncle or not. She knew because, after waking, she'd asked the moon sister attending her. The next morning, she'd found a note wrapped around an old but well-crafted knife with a black onyx letter M inlaid into its bone-white hilt. The note told her to report to a little-known schola, where she'd met Master Kai and begun her training. Those sessions had given her hope that someday she'd earn back Uncle Tarquin's esteem and have her revenge.

And so she had anointed the blade with her blood and named it Vindicta.

Up ahead, the line for House Verilli dwindled. House Moralis would be next. Seren scanned the Takkakus private box for signs of Valera's blonde tresses. Had she pledged yet? There were too many nobs crossing the floor to afford Seren a good view. Among the darker shades, a head of coppery hair, however, blazed like a torch.

*Tyberius.*

And he was headed straight for her. She pushed herself off the wall and crossed her arms, and her fingertips brushed against the handle of Vindicta, hidden in her dress. The steel lent her some strength in the face of possibly her greatest enemy. As he neared, her gaze fell onto his ring hand, which he hid in his pant pocket.

"Let me explain, Tabby."

She didn't want to hear anything he had to say. Not here. Not now.

"Go away, Tyberius, unless you wish to dance with Vindicta tonight."

His look of incredulity at her smuggling a weapon into Pledging Night was highly satisfying.

"Is Secundo Attica bothering you, Mistressa Moralis?"

The interruption came from her right. Seren began to dismiss the nob, but a glance at his face left her speechless. Under his left eye, the skin was purple and swollen. More black bruising lined his dimpled jaw, and ugly stitches crawled over his left eye like a wriggling worm. Either he had lost a dirty fight or won a worse one.

Unlike most, his head was scraped clean by a razor in the manner of a temple penitent. He wasn't taller than her, but he was built like the First Founders of Primordia, with arms as wide as the war maces they had favoured. His tan jacket declared him for House Takkakus, and she guessed him to be older than Tyberius as she couldn't remember him from the Lyceum.

Tyberius moved to her side. He didn't touch her, though with her acute hearing she heard his heart thud against his chest. "Run along and mind your own House matters, Takkakus."

There wasn't a hint of the flippant decadent about Tyberius, nor was there any respect for Joren Takkakus, for that's who this was—Patrius Calvus Takkakus's heir, the one who was supposed to deliver someone to her uncle. While she knew of him in passing, she hadn't recognized him with his shorn head and injuries.

She raised her chin. "Secundo Attica is nothing more than a minor nuisance." If she admitted Tyberius was bothering her, then it made House Moralis look weak—made her look weak. She could handle her own battles. If nothing else, the night of her attack had taught her that she had to rely on herself. "Thank you, Centurio Takkakus."

Tyberius made a shooing motion with his hands. "That's a dismissal."

While Seren winced at the insubordination, Joren didn't react. "Perhaps you would do me the pleasure of walking through the gardens after your Pledging, Mistressa?"

"You're not wanted, Centurio." Tyberius's shoulders seemed to broaden as he stood chest to chest with the more muscular man.

The menace in Tyberius's voice startled her. Why did he care if she joined Joren? He'd made it clear she didn't mean anything to him in the tunnels.

Joren tapped his bruised jaw. "So you've made abundantly clear, Secundo."

"Tyberius did that?" An ache spread through her jaw in sympathy. Striking a superior was a serious offence, the punishment for which was at minimum ten lashes. Joren must not have reported the insubordination, however, or Tyberius would still be recovering.

But why should she be surprised at such audacity? The man who wore that ring had punched her out four years ago. She had to stop thinking of Tyberius as the harmless, if irresponsible, decadent she'd thought him to be.

"Believe me, he had it coming," Tyberius muttered. "Seren and I have House Moralis matters to discuss," he added more loudly. "Excuse us, Centurio."

His words seemed to amuse Joren. "You're excused, Secundo. But I think it's the mistressa's choice if she stays or goes." Joren inclined his head to her, waiting for her answer.

Tyberius looked like he'd get into it with Joren if she didn't leave with him. A brawl on Pledging Night between House Moralis and House Takkakus with their new, secretive alliance would not be the sort of attention Uncle Tarquin desired. And Tyberius owed her answers.

*What would Valera say?*

"I thank you for your, ah, kind offer, Centurio Takkakus, but House Moralis matters take precedence."

Joren bowed to her, painstakingly polite. "Then I won't keep you any longer, Mistressa. But, Attica?" Joren's dark eyes hardened. "We must soon meet again."

A glimmer of sweat shone on Tyberius's forehead. "If you wish to continue where we left off, Takkakus."

Joren's thin lips pulled back in a twisted grin, and Seren stifled a gasp at the gap in his teeth. From the fight?

"That's as good a place as any, Tyberius." With that, Joren turned on his heel and vanished into the crowd.

The master of ceremonies seized that moment to bellow for House Moralis pledges. She took a step toward the dais, then hesitated. Tyberius had stalked over to a stone bench in a nearby alcove and was retrieving a flask from inside his jacket, his desire to talk to her seemingly forgotten. After disposing of her glass on a serv's tray, Seren ducked into the alcove after him. Whether she pledged first or last didn't matter. Right now she needed answers.

While he took a long swig, she let her gaze wander over him. There wasn't a mark on his lean face that would lead her to believe he'd been in a fight, yet Joren had a good fifty pounds on him.

"How, in the name of the republic, did you get the advantage on someone the size of him?"

*You know how, Seren*. He had his friends ambush Joren, their identities masked by hooded robes. Many against one was never a fair fight. Only she'd never seen Tyberius with other friends. And Joren had known full well who had attacked him. But why had they fought?

"Every opponent has his vulnerability, Tabby." He tucked the flask away. "You just have to be ruthless enough to take advantage of it. Now, do me a favour. Stay away from that pig."

The warning, and the irony of it coming from *him*, unsettled her. "Why?"

His eyes darkened. "Joren's dangerous."

The absurdity of it made her laugh. It was that or scream. "*He's* dangerous?" Her stomach lurched. "Does Quinton know what you did four years ago? What you did to me?"

*Please, don't let that be true.*

The blood drained from his face; then his lips pressed together, but he didn't deny it.

"Don't pretend," she bit out, raking him with a glare, "you don't know what I'm talking about." Three cracked ribs. Her left arm broken. Bruises everywhere. She'd been unconscious for days. "My first month at the Lyceum, someone wearing your ring knocked me out with a punch to the jaw, nearly broke that, too."

"It's not what you think, Seren." He motioned her to sit next to him, but she refused. "Four years ago, I did . . . nothing." He raised his head and looked her in the eye.

Then why did he have the ring? Why did he look so guilt-ridden?

"Let me guess. The ring isn't yours."

He sighed. "Would you believe me if I said it wasn't?"

*No.*

And yet, Seren found herself desperate to believe him. Besides Valera, he was the only other nob who had ever treated her like her heritage didn't matter to him. It made little sense that he would hurt her so terribly.

If it had been Tyberius who attacked her, then why hadn't he gone after her again? He'd had ample opportunities. Every full moon, she came home from the Lyceum to attend the ball, and both Tyberius and Quinton had lived at the House Moralis villa since their return from the Legion's engagements on the continent last year. Agrippa wasn't wrong that the Legion ate up a large portion of the treasury, but they also contributed to their upkeep by selling their services abroad.

But if Tyberius wasn't her attacker, who was?

Rarely did she try to remember that night, but now she did.

*The crescent moon painted the cobblestones silver. The crisp air licked at her heated skin after her soak in the pools. She pulled her cloak tight against the chill. Then a figure in a hooded cloak stepped out from the shadows.*

"Seren?"

She blinked away the memory. Her palms, laced with sweat, tingled. It wasn't fear. She clenched them tight to her sides. Could she trust Tyberius?

"If the ring's not yours, who does it belong to?"

"I can't tell you here, not like this." He slid closer to her on the bench and met her stare. Just like she needed. "Tomorrow, meet me for breakfast in the main hall."

If he wanted to lure her somewhere private, the dining hall at House Moralis wasn't it.

"If you're lying to me, Tyberius, I'll break every one of your bones—twice."

"Fair enough. I know how it feels not knowing who to trust."

*Just so.* The edge of her knife slipped quietly under the hem of his jacket and now grazed a spot below his ribs, ready to puncture a lung with a jab. He stilled.

"I'm not the little girl you once knew," she breathed. "I will end you if you've betrayed me, Tyberius Attica."

"None of us are the same, are we?" he whispered. "Every day we wake slightly different from who we were before."

Seren snorted. A convenient excuse for avoiding entanglements from the night before. She supposed he'd told many a lover that line as he walked out. And yet, the haunted look in his eyes belied it.

"Are you a philosopher, Tyberius?"

With a strange intensity, he leaned forward, pressing himself against her blade and bringing his talented mouth so close to hers. "Just a simple secundo."

With a death wish, it seemed. She pulled back her knife to avoid cutting his flesh. "Now that's a lie." She didn't know how she knew, but she did. "There isn't anything simple about you, is there?"

Something wild flashed in his green eyes.

"Mistressa Seren?"

A young page in House Moralis's colours gawked at their embrace. Seren couldn't untangle herself without revealing her knife. Except for the House swords of each patrius, weapons were taboo on this sacred night, so she sat there with her hand up Tyberius's jacket, like a fool.

She scowled. "Yes?"

Tyberius put his arm around her shoulder, and his lips brushed her ear. "A distraction."

She stiffened, and he nibbled her ear twice before she realized what he meant. Quickly, she slipped the knife out from under the back of his jacket, his arm and head blocking the action from the page. But now where to put it? Her wrap had no pockets, and she couldn't get in back under her arm without the page noticing.

His other hand, the one not currently rubbing her shoulder, gently closed over hers. "Give it to me," he murmured.

Without thinking, she let him take it, and Tyberius slipped it into his jacket—all while pressing a soft kiss at her temple, which she supposed would make the rounds of gossip tonight by the way the page watched.

Finally, Tyberius slid away from her. Vindicta's absence, however, jolted the fear of discovery out of her head. Like a first-year cadet, she'd given up her weapon—possibly to her enemy.

Focussing on the eagle emblem on the page's uniform, she straightened. "Speak."

"Sol steal your tongue?" Tyberius asked the open-mouthed youth.

The page snapped to attention. "Mistressa Seren, Patrius Moralis commands your presence."

It was then she looked past the boy, to the line of pledges to be accepted into House Moralis.

*Solfire*. They were gone.

## 6

The page led Seren toward the Pledging platform where Uncle Tarquin, Quinton, Silvestri, and a few advisers still clustered. While the other men conversed, Uncle Tarquin met her questioning stare without displeasure, and her thumping heart slowed. While she had pledged her loyalty in private, she was surprised how deeply she yearned to be accepted into House Moralis in front of the nobilis. It would be a formality, but one that would carry much weight among the Houses.

As she neared, Quinton downed the rest of his flute. Embarrassment prickled over her skin, and she scowled. Why had Lumina seen fit to have him be the one to catch her kissing Tyberius? Swiftly, her gaze skimmed over Quinton and off to the side of the stage where a group of new Moralis pledges clustered with their sigils. Seren was about to dismiss them when flowing blonde tresses that she'd know anywhere snagged her attention.

*What is Valla doing with Moralis pledges?*

The answer perched on the shoulder straps of Valera's

wrap: instead of the coiled cobra of House Takkakus, double silver eagles raised their wings.

Seren stumbled, catching herself before landing on her face.

"The girl should've been prepped," Silvestri muttered to the coterie around Uncle Tarquin.

Seren smoothed her face. Years of practice kept her lip from curling at Silvestri's stings. Yet the insinuation that she would disgrace the House made her throw her shoulders back.

"The outside shell is of little consequence," Uncle Tarquin replied coolly. *How badly did Tyberius dishevel her?* "Her blood will run true. I've had confirmation of it."

Silvestri's mouth thinned as he adjusted the cuffs of his overly-embroidered jacket. "As imperator, the nobilis and the servilis will expect a certain elegance from House Moralis."

Elegance in a spy? Seren held in a snort. Her stepfather must not have been privy to Uncle Tarquin's plans for her. Since his marriage to her mother ten years ago, he had tried to sweep Seren's existence aside in favour of her younger half-brother and half-sister. He would boast of his connection to her, though, when she brought victory to the republic.

The conversation ended as she closed the distance and sank to one knee before her uncle. "Patrius."

"I thought you understood to stay close, Niece."

The chastisement brought her up short. "I was never far, Uncle."

For several heartbeats, he said nothing. Then he extended his hand. "Walk with me."

Arm in arm, they left the others behind and circled the platform to the stairs at the back. Seren could discern no alteration in his usual demeanour as if his newly granted office didn't warrant any outward acknowledgement. At the steps, he halted.

"Niece, do you trust me to do what's best for you and House Moralis? For Luminaria?"

Her stomach fluttered in anticipation of receiving orders for her mission. "You have my complete trust and faith, Uncle."

A dark eyebrow rose. "As I should."

Seren bowed her head in acknowledgement, and together they mounted the steps. As they advanced onto the stage, their audience of new pledges and the city's nobilis pressed in. The coloured trim on their clothing sorted them into the Thirteen Houses of Luminaria, while the myriad of faces and shades of skin colour spoke to the former vastness of Primordia.

Uncle Tarquin's hand on the small of her back guided her to the centre. But he didn't unsheathe Magnanimous for her to kneel and kiss again. Instead, a broad figure in Moralis colours approached from the left. *Quinton.* A horn blared to draw attention to them, but it needn't have; the drums had stilled and the entire Amphitheatron watched with bated breath.

And why not? Uncle Tarquin was an influential man in Luminaria, even if few knew his new title. Quinton was once again the darling of the nobilis, many of whom wanted to ally with House Moralis by offering their daughters in marriage. And herself? If not loved by the masses, she was notorious. The Felinae Prince's bastard daughter—the babe who had sparked a war.

Her instincts screamed at her to run, but Uncle Tarquin held her right arm securely in his, and Quinton flanked her left, caging her.

"A House is as strong as the oaths of its pledges," Uncle Tarquin said, his voice booming; the acoustics ensured his words were heard throughout the Amphitheatron. "Tonight, each pledge will strengthen and build upon the foundation of their House. But a House is more than words of loyalty and fidelity. The actions we take to ensure our House's honour ultimately define Primordians."

He kissed her hand before letting go of her arm, which nearly vibrated with anticipation. Yet it was all wrong. Uncle Tarquin wouldn't announce her mission to infiltrate the Felinae so publicly.

"What better foundation—what stronger foundation—for House Moralis," he continued, "than to unite my heir and son, Quinton, to my sister's daughter, Seren."

*There's been a mistake.* On the other side of her, Quinton bowed to her, and her gut clenched while the crowd reacted. She wanted to scream, but a high-pitched buzzing filled her head. It was deafening, and she was drowning in sound—the clapping, the whispering, the laughing. She hadn't lost control of her senses like this in a long time.

*As the bee cannot visit every spring flower, you must choose where to focus.*

Another of Master Kai's maxims that he had scrawled in the sand for her. It helped, but not enough.

The faces in the private boxes and on the arena floor blurred before her. All except for one. Tyberius. He stood not far from the alcove. He wasn't clapping or whistling. He simply stared at her, and his flat expression steadied her so she could concentrate her ears on her uncle.

"—blood is strong in both of them, and their union will begin a new era for our republic, a time when Luminaria's enemies will bow before us. For we are Primordians, and united we shall end this war." Uncle Tarquin raised his hand in the V salute, and another round of applause rang throughout the arena.

Seren desperately tried to gather her thoughts. Why a betrothal? And why now, before her mission? Quinton despised her. He couldn't be in favour of this . . . and yet he stood beside her, smiling at the crowd.

The words of her nursemaid echoed inside her head with dizzying possibilities. *Whoever stands by her side will shape the course of our isle and decide the future for all the children of the moon.*

But it was nonsense. Because the old magic of the Felinae didn't exist except in children's stories.

A callused hand gripped her clammy one, and her heart constricted. It had been more than a decade since she'd held Quinton's hand, yet the memory came back to her. It had been the middle of the night, and he'd been whimpering in the dark —a fear she couldn't understand having never experiencing true darkness. At that age, she often snuck out to the garden when their nursemaid left them, but she'd invited him that night. Hand in hand, she'd dragged him through her make-believe legionnaire encampments of shrubs and fig trees to the overgrown grapevine that skirted the stone wall and covered the archway.

He hadn't climbed up to join her, and she'd assumed it was because he considered himself too old to be playing legionnaires with her. So she'd pelted overripe grapes at him until he was covered in the sweet, sticky juice. For reasons unknown, he hadn't run away, taking each hit so stoically that it had enraged her further.

The next day, on his ninth birthday, his belongings were moved out of the nursery. Nothing had been the same between them since.

Hand in hand with her once more, Quinton pressed dry lips to her brow, and the resounding applause, along with the tingling sensation on her back, shattered her stupor.

"Q, what's going on?" It wasn't completely unheard of for a House to consolidate power within by marrying two branches together, but the two of them?

"Our destiny, it would seem," he replied through a strained smile for their audience.

"Speak for yourself."

He winced, and she realized she was digging her blunt nails

into the back of his hand. "Isn't destiny but another word for duty? And we must serve House Moralis in whatever way we can."

Yes, she would serve House Moralis—as a spy in the Felinae lands. He should know that since he was at the Consul meeting.

Uncle Tarquin raised his hands to indicate he had more to say. "On the day after tomorrow, when we are all feeling more like ourselves"—the audience chuckled with him—"I invite you, the best of Luminaria, to join us on the High Temple steps at twilight to celebrate the nuptials of my son and his bride."

The world spun wildly around her until every sound and smell and sight made her numb. The rest of the evening became a blur of Ambrosia and dancing while one thought repeated, over and over again, like the wind chimes in a temple.

She was a weapon.

*A weapon.*

**7**

———————

With a groan, Seren nestled deeper into the softness around her. Drums pounded in her head, and her mouth tasted like she'd licked every stone from the Lyceum to the market. The light from her window was bright. She squinted at it—a westerly light so she wasn't in her room at the Lyceum. With that thought, she came fully awake.

*She was home.*

And she needed to go. Seren threw back the covers and raced in her shift to the water chamber attached to her room, a luxury she'd sorely missed at the Lyceum. That taken care of, she splashed her face with water from the bowl and poured herself a glass from the pitcher. The platter of fruit she ignored.

It was good to be home. Her room was as she had left it after her visit during the last full moon. The stark space was awash in stone and wood. In the corner, by the narrow windows, stood a heavy wardrobe, its doors flung open, revealing an assortment of leather, linen, wool, and silk. Next to it was her favourite dark indigo brocade chair, now covered in splashes of white.

*Two Pledging wraps.*

"Does this mean I must wake up, too?" asked a raspy voice. From under the coverlet emerged a pouf of blonde curls.

"Valera?" Seren jumped onto the mattress and threw her arms around her friend's round shoulders. She, too, wore a sleeveless shift that must have come from Seren's wardrobe. "It wasn't a dream then. You're pledged to House Moralis?"

A radiant hope poured out from Seren's chest. If her heart belonged to anyone, it was the friend who hadn't abandoned her.

At the Lyceum, the most influential young nobs had made it known that anyone seen with Seren would be shunned. No one except Valera Calissi, the daughter of a mid-rank country landowner, had braved the censure to befriend Seren. When Valera's patrius, Calvus Takkakus, ordered her to break all ties or face disownment from House Takkakus, she had reluctantly distanced herself.

But in the dead of night, Valera would open her window so Seren could sneak in. By candlelight, Valera had corrected the logic in Seren's arguments, and Seren had helped Valera improve her close combat skills so both of them could pass their yearly exams.

In her arms, Valera made a muffled gasp for breath, and Seren let go, but only to whack her friend over the head with a pillow. "Why didn't you tell me you planned to pledge to House Moralis?"

"I wasn't certain my pledge would be accepted, and you disappeared. Once your betrothal was announced, you were busy drowning yourself in Ambrosia." Valera's tone was light, but there was a wariness around her grass-green eyes. This morning the colour was an unwanted reminder of someone else. But Valera's words meant the betrothal wasn't a dream.

"Was I nauseous?" By the taste in her mouth, she must have been.

Valera winced. "Twice in an alcove. You succumbed soon after."

Dread coiled in her belly. She could imagine what Uncle Tarquin would have to say about her decadent behaviour. Such a public disgrace would be the talk of the nobilis.

A memory or a dream of someone holding her tugged at her. "And Tyberius—Secundo Attica—was he there?" she asked, striving to be casual. It dawned on her that she had long since missed meeting him for breakfast.

It rushed back to her then. The tunnels. The meeting. The kiss. The ring. The page. But she remembered nothing after Uncle Tarquin's announcement.

Valla wrinkled her pert nose. "He followed you into the alcove after you ran off during your dance with Centurio Takkakus. When I arrived, he was holding your hair as you vomited. Then he insisted on carrying you to the carpentum and Centurio Moralis."

Seren pressed the palms of her hands against her eyes. That was humiliating. The extravagant horse-drawn conveyance was reserved for aging relatives, as Uncle Tarquin preferred to ride with the House guards. And she'd been carried to it. Unconscious.

"Then what?"

"Centurio Moralis and I brought you home. He carried you to bed," Valera reported evenly, as if the servs wouldn't be gossiping about this in the kitchens today. "The House physician came to look you over. She said to give you water if you woke and keep you sleeping on your side. I volunteered to stay with you. The centurio agreed." She paused. "He seemed most concerned."

Seren snorted. "Relieved to make me your problem more like."

The betrothal made no sense. As the bastard daughter of a dishonoured prince, she'd had no ambition of marrying. And as the imperator's son—even as Consular Moralis's son—Quinton had his pick of the eligible nobilis. Why would her uncle betroth her to his son when she was already pledged to House Moralis?

"You didn't mention you were to marry." Valera studied her hands as she picked at the coverlet's stitching.

"Because no one thought to inform me I was." Did Valera truly think Seren had kept this from her? "I found out the same time you and the rest of Luminaria did."

*Solfire.* Quinton's charming words before the Consul meeting. He had been informed—and been about to tell her. Or warn her.

Valera's cheeks reddened and her shoulders pulled back as if she were preparing herself for an attack. "I don't blame you if you're angry at me for not telling you about my change in pledges."

Last night, Seren hadn't had time to contemplate Valera's sudden defection from House Takkakus. It was a considerable sacrifice on Valera's behalf since her family and her former House would consider her dead to them. A sacrifice that Seren, had their positions been reversed, couldn't have reciprocated. House Moralis was everything to her. It made Valera's decision seem twice as momentous.

"You're here with me for the rest of our lives." That Valera had kept a secret from her did sting, but then Seren's happiness smothered it. "How can I be mad?"

Valera let out a weak chuckle and ran a hand through her curls in an attempt to tame them. "Ser, someone looks at you the wrong way, and you hold a death grudge. I should've told you, but"—she hedged—"I didn't want to disappoint you if I couldn't go through with it."

Seren's jaw dropped at the admission. "Valera Calissi, impulsive?"

"Yes, well," Valera said, with a shrug. "Impulsivity seems to be a House Moralis trait."

Seren sobered. "Uncle Tarquin does nothing without purpose."

Which meant the betrothal was anything but a whim. But it still made little sense. She pushed herself off the bed and snatched up her Pledging wrap. Her fingers poked into the secret pocket. Empty.

Solfire, Tyberius still had Vindicta.

"We should dress," Valera said, getting up from the bed. "The day's half gone, and you're getting married tomorrow."

Seren uttered a low growl of frustration and pitched the wrap at the bed. "This marriage is absurd."

Why would Uncle Tarquin inform the Consul she was his weapon against the Felinae, then marry her off to his son? For moon's sake, Quinton was the boy with whom she had once shared a nursery.

Seren yanked the top drawer of her bureau open, already cursing that another knife would have to do for the time being. But there, amongst her assortment of holsters and a few daggers, lay the bone-white hilt of Vindicta in its leather sheath.

The intricately engraved M gleamed at her as she slid out the blade. Unlike the standard straight-edged knife used by legionnaires and guards, Vindicta had an elongated spine that arched downward two-thirds of the way toward the tip. On the edged side, the belly of the blade grew wider before tapering inwards again toward the handle, like a gentle wave.

A scrap of paper poked out of the empty sheath. She put Vindicta down on the top of the chest to unfold it.

*THOUGHT YOU MIGHT NEED THIS.*

*—TY*

Seren stared at the cramped writing. Ty must have come by when she didn't show up at breakfast. While both she and Valla were sleeping. If he was her attacker, wouldn't he have taken advantage of such a situation?

"Valla, did anyone come by while I was asleep?"

"Just the physician and Centurio Moralis before I retired last night."

Seren put the note in her drawer and closed it with a roll of her eyes. "For the love of Lumina, call him Quinton."

Spinning on her heel, Seren raised Vindicta by her ear, the blade pointed back. Twenty paces away, on the wall next to the window, was her splintered target board. She straightened her spine, exhaled, and let Vindicta fly. The knife rotated through the air and hit the target in the centre with a satisfying thud.

Forget Tyberius and the ring for now. She had more immediate problems.

"Marrying Quinton isn't what the stars have in mind for me, Valla." She pulled her knife from the target. "I'm meant for *something* else."

Something that would prove she was just as worthy as the next nob. Seren set up for the next throw.

"Something to make them all sit up and take notice?" Valera asked, calmly making the bed. Her friend was quite familiar with Seren's way of thinking her problems through.

She let Vindicta fly. *Thud.*

"Exactly."

"You can't do that by running one of the most influential Houses in the republic?" Valera fluffed the pillows—loudly—as if she didn't quite approve. "House Matronas are accorded a seat in the Senate."

"I've no desire to spend my days listening to senators bicker amongst themselves." Seren yanked her knife from the centre of the target and inspected the edge with the pad of her thumb. Blood welled in a thin line. Sharp. Unlike most steel, the knife rarely needed sharpening, and on those occasions, Master Kai performed the task for her.

"At some point, I'll be expected to oversee the running of House Moralis, host balls, and . . . then there's the matter of heirs."

Just the thought of what *that* would entail with Quinton made her shudder as she lined herself up with the target board.

"What does Quinton think of the betrothal?"

"It's our destiny or duty." The hilt became slippery in her sweaty palm. It was *not* her destiny. The thought flitted through her mind as she released the knife. *Thud.*

*Sol's hells.* The tip had embedded in the far-left corner.

"You missed," Valera said, surprised.

Seren strode over and yanked the wayward knife out of the wooden board with more force than necessary. "You were alone with him in the carpentum. He must have said something to you on the drive back."

"He said little." Perched on the tidy bed, Valera shrugged. "He admitted the two of you had grown apart, and he asked about your future ambitions. Whether you had your heart set on another."

Seren's throat thickened as she tapped the blade against her leg in a staccato beat. "And you said?"

"I told him about your plans for the Legion. That, as far as I knew, there wasn't anyone special." Her brilliant green eyes narrowed. "You disappeared before the Pledging."

Seren's blade stilled against her leg. "I did."

As the silence stretched between them, Valera came up to her. She had to reach up to tuck Seren's loose hair behind her ear. "Does your disappearance have anything to do with your neck?"

Seren rushed to the mirror over her desk and craned her head to the side. She had to set Vindicta down to get all of her hair out of the way. Over her jugular, two red splotches marked the soft skin. *Lumina have mercy*. Had the marks been noticeable last night?

"Quinton also disappeared before the Pledging." Valera's tone was neutral, yet Seren didn't know if it was better or worse if everyone thought he was responsible for the state of her neck.

Seren let her hair fall back down and met Valera's gaze in the mirror. "I was with Tyberius."

She had the satisfaction of breaking Valera's calm composure.

"You're involved with Tyberius Attica? Why, Ser?"

Irritation pricked along her skin at Valera's censure, and she paced back toward the bed. "It was one kiss. I didn't know about the betrothal, and we needed a reason for being in the catacombs." Her heart skipped a beat at the remembered heat of his mouth, and she collapsed backward onto the bed. "Oh, Goddess," she groaned, pulling a pillow over her head. "Quinton saw us. He found us in the tunnels."

The mattress sank as Valera climbed onto the bed next to her. "But why did you need a reason to be in the catacombs?"

Seren pulled the pillow down over her chest. Someone needed to help her figure out this mess. "There was a secret Consul meeting."

Quickly, she filled Valera in on the events of the evening— though she left out her waking nightmare. When she got to the part about the kiss, Valera fell back on the bed to lie beside her.

"And there's more." Seren's stomach twisted into a knot her prefect would be proud of. "Valla. I saw Tyberius wearing the ring."

That made Valera sit up. "*The* ring?"

Seren nodded. Valla was the only one she'd confided in about that night.

"Lumina, I'm amazed you let him walk away, let alone kissed him."

"It wasn't like that. I didn't notice the ring until after we kissed. Then he swore to me he had nothing to do with the attack. I—I don't think it was his ring back then."

"You believe him?"

"I want to," she admitted, staring up at the wooden beams in the ceiling.

"Then who did he get the ring from?"

Seren sighed. "I was to meet him for breakfast today to discuss it."

Valera thought about that for a moment. "You saw Joren Takkakus's face? Of course, you did. You danced with him. Well, I heard Tyberius did that to him over"—she lowered her voice—"a lovers' quarrel."

Tyberius and Joren? A rush of cold swept through her. There'd been something between them. Deep loathing on Tyberius's part. Hatred like that could spring from a deep betrayal of someone close to one's heart. A person who could inflict such injuries on someone he'd once loved? Well, it stood to reason that person could inflict worse on someone he'd only tolerated as his sword brother's younger cousin.

*Easy come, easy go.*

Careless words, yet there'd been no animosity for her in his gaze. Certainly, none while they kissed. There'd been that unguarded look after she'd given him a hard time for wanting to return to the celebration. But what she'd glimpsed was nothing less than a tormented soul.

But tormented over what?

"Please, stay away from him," Valera asked, turning over on her side to face Seren. "He's reckless and dangerous."

"That's what Tyberius said," she murmured.

Valera's curls shook as she clasped Seren's hand tightly. "Joren's a worm. But if what I heard is right, Tyberius Attica is the dangerous one."

Unable to contain her rising unease, Seren rolled out of the bed. "I'll deal with Tyberius later. I need your sharp mind, Valla. How does marrying my cousin figure into being Uncle Tarquin's secret weapon to bring down the Felinae?"

"Let me brush your hair, and I'll think on it." Valera motioned for her to sit in the chair. Before attending the Lyceum, Valera had braided her younger sister's hair every day —a task she claimed to sorely miss. Soon she had taken Seren's long brown hair in hand, and the brushing had become something of a ritual while Seren worked on her assignments in her friend's room.

As the brush smoothed the tangles, Seren let herself relax into the soothing routine. She'd nearly fallen asleep in the plush chair when the strokes stopped.

"When will the Felinae launch a full-out attack on Luminaria?" Valera asked.

"You're assuming they have the strength to do that."

"How do you know they don't?" There was no heat behind the question, just curiosity. "No one has seen them since the war began. They attack like the wind, then vanish —as the population of their settlements did all those years ago. Who knows what weapons or numbers they have since acquired."

"Well, I pray they do have enough warriors," Seren snapped, "because our legionnaires will obliterate them."

"Insufficient proof. We have no information on their offensive capabilities, do we?"

Done brushing, Valera divided Seren's hair into sections, then quickly threaded the strands in and out in a side-crown braid, the style Valera's sister had favoured. A sister Valera had given up for Seren and House Moralis.

"Doesn't matter, Valla. The Felinae fight as cowards. I doubt they'll come out of hiding long enough to launch a full attack on the city."

"Then it is to their advantage to remain hidden. We can't

defeat an enemy that can't be found. So we must go to them or lure them out."

The tugging on her scalp ceased, and Seren caught Valera's cool gaze in the mirror. Her shorter friend leaned her head against Seren's shoulder. "It's clear what Patrius Moralis was thinking, Ser. Brilliant."

"Marrying me to his son? That's brilliant?"

"You said he told the Consul he was sending you to spy—"

Seren hesitated. "He referred to me as a secret weapon, but never by name."

Valera didn't seem to hear her. "Any Felinae who is clever enough to sabotage us and route our legionnaires will realize who you are. You're the babe that started the war. So why would they trust a young woman raised by their enemies to hate them?"

"Because I am their late prince's daughter?"

"Maybe." Valera's smile sharpened. "But if there's a reason for you not to be loyal to your uncle anymore . . ."

*Sol's hells.* She hadn't thought that far ahead, but Uncle Tarquin had.

"Persecuted niece flees forced marriage and her tyrannical uncle." Valera's voice was full of admiration as she finished braiding Seren's hair. "You can run straight into the Felinae's arms with this story torn from tragedy, and Patrius Moralis's succession to imperator paints him as a vainglorious scoundrel."

"That does sound rather shrewd." The weight of Valera's reasoning coalesced into one possible action, and Seren's palms tingled in response. "Then I must leave tonight before the wedding takes place tomorrow."

Once she returned from her mission, Uncle Tarquin would explain to everyone that the betrothal was a ruse.

"That's what I said, wasn't it?"

Seren scowled at her friend's smug grin in the mirror. "Then why didn't my uncle simply explain all this?"

"Patriuses." Valera rolled her eyes, then with a twist of her wrist, she produced a red apple from out of Seren's hair and shined it on the hem of her shift. "They're so accustomed to power, they assume everyone knows as much as they do."

That Uncle Tarquin thought her clever enough to unravel his thoughts caused no small amount of pride, never mind she had needed Valera's help. She flung her arms around Valera and squeezed. "Well, I'm glad you pledged to House Moralis. Would have taken me days to make sense of it."

"Weeks," Valera chuckled around a mouthful. "Months, maybe."

Seren poked her smirking friend in the side and made a grab for the apple.

With a laugh, Valera twisted away before lobbing the pale pink fruit full force at Seren's head. "You'd have been married by then."

Seren's quick reflexes allowed her to catch it in time. She grinned unrepentant and took a bite, the taste as sweet as her current mood. Uncle Tarquin's advisers and servs would have their hands full with their new pledge. "Welcome to House Moralis, sister."

Valera's smile faltered before it brightened. "You can welcome me properly after you return in triumph." Then she turned her discerning eye over Seren's open wardrobe, a clear signal that she didn't wish to discuss her change of allegiance any further. "Now," she said, tapping her lips, "I'm thinking you'll need a lot of leather and a hint of steel."

## 8

The black coarse hairs of Bay's mane whipped Seren's wind-bitten face as her horse hurtled down the slick stone path along the top of the ravine. Below them, the churning waters of the Aegis River crashed against the rocky embankment like an untamed courser bearing down from the dark mountains in the distance. The sight of those snow-covered peaks had consumed her since they'd come into view. The North Pass was her destination. If she could get through, she'd reach the late Felinae queen's castle after a week's hard ride—according to Valera's calculations.

The Legion had never reached the castle. Frequent washouts and rockslides, suspected to be set off by the enemy, had made the path unpassable for horses and supply wagons. Not to mention the legionnaires who became buried under the rock. But it was the only way through the Selinens. For a few years, the Consul had tried sending ships to the northern tip of the isle, but few had returned and none with glimpsing more than a shadow of the Felinae's fabled fortress. It was said to have been called forth from the earth by arcane sorcery and protected by monstrous serpents and mists so thick, ships were doomed to wander lost until they wrecked on the dangerous shoals.

*Follow the Aegis*, Valera had advised. Seren snorted. Easy for Valera. She didn't have to ride through the scorched settlements or avoid the rebuilt logging camps for Uncle Tarquin's shipyard. However, the river was the swiftest route north. It split the isle in half, running up from the southern bay of Luminaria to where the North Pass became a gateway to the barren Felinae lands on the other side of the Selinens.

From the northernmost point of the isle, the Felinae queen and her husband had ruled—before they and their children were slain in their beds. Instructor Soronius had been rather vague in his lectures about who had done the grisly deed, but it was commonly believed an elite unit of legionnaires had been handpicked for the task. Though some whispered that the Consul had hired Marked assassins. Yet the youngest prince had supposedly survived. It was the only information Junius's scouts had gathered before the Felinae all up and disappeared.

There was a theory that the Felinae were holed up in the Veiled Isles from whence they had come to settle the southern reaches of the isle. Valera had pointed out, however, that the Felinae had originally left those isles for the larger isle of Luminaria because nothing grew in the mists. But who knew if that was still true? That information had come from travel accounts over a hundred years old.

Farther up the trail, a dark figure appeared on the side of the ravine. A thrill of excitement shot through her, and she squeezed Bay with her knees to spur the mare onward. Her thighs burned with the long days of riding. Everything else ached or had gone numb, like her bottom. She hoped the Felinae had warm baths wherever they were hiding.

As she and Bay came around the next bend, the light penetrated through the clouds, and the form up ahead became nothing more than shadows on an outcropping of rock.

"For moon's sake."

The disappointment of not sighting a single person for the last six days came crashing back, and Seren sagged in the saddle, soaked through her cloak to the bone and miserable. Since she'd left Luminaria under the cover of darkness, it had rained more than not. Today the spray from the river combined with the drizzle of the last hour had numbed her fingers through her gloves and chapped her lips. She pressed her chest close against Bay's neck for warmth and comfort.

The Felinae must have scouts stationed around the Pass. Once they saw her, all she had to do was act like she had switched her allegiance. Despite her drenched state, her mouth went dry. Pretending to be a traitor went against every bone in her body. Meanwhile, back home, her name would be dragged through the mud. Valera had warned her that Uncle Tarquin might need to publicly disown her. By running away from the betrothal and into the arms of the Felinae, it would appear as if Seren had broken her sworn pledge to House Moralis.

*If your uncle doesn't disown you,* Valera had reasoned, *the Felinae will suspect him and you of duplicity.*

"We might be disowned already, Bay." Seren murmured the distasteful words into the horse's mane, the implications hitting hard as each iron-clad hoof struck rock. To become one of the detritus was a fate worse than death. Without a House to swear her sword and loyalty to, she was nothing. No one. There was but one other status more abhorred by Prims—traitor.

And in the eyes of Luminaria, she would be branded that, too. And Quinton? He would be cast as the jilted lover and a hero if he returned with the ones responsible for the burning of Gull Harbour. The city would adore him even more.

It wasn't fair.

A tingle on her forehead made her hands tighten on the reins and the hairs on the back of her neck stand up. There had been no strange tingling since the night of her Pledging, and she tensed expecting another waking nightmare from her past. Now was not a good time to end up incapacitated by pain.

When no nightmare came, she recalled how she'd also felt it in the presence of Tyberius and Quinton. Both of them should be in Gull Harbour with the Legion by now. Still, the feeling of being watched lingered.

Seren twisted in the saddle to check behind her as Bay skidded on the wet rock. It sent her lurching forward in the saddle and the horse scrambling for solid footing. Quickly, she righted herself and tried to steer Bay away from the cliff's edge. "C'mon, girl."

Thunder cracked above the misty mountains, and the already skittish mare reared with a squeal. It was all Seren could do to brace herself against Bay for the icy plunge into the surging waters below.

*Lumina, this can't be the destiny you wrote in the stars for me. Dead at the bottom of the river without a soul to witness it.*

By some will of the Goddess, Bay found her footing on the path without throwing Seren. The sky, however, chose that moment to open up in a deluge, soaking her again and obscuring the way forward. It was too risky to ride, but neither could they stay put in the brewing storm. She'd have to dismount and hope there was a spot along the trail that might offer more protection.

Before Seren could get her foot out of the stirrup, a second rumble echoed through the ravine and up through Bay's haunches. She frowned, searching the skies. "That's not thunder, Bay."

From the crags above, a torrent of brown muck shot over them. *Rockslide.*

She dug her heels into the horse's flanks to get them out of the way. But it was futile. Under a surge of muddy loose rock washed down from the mountains, the ground seemed to crumble away and took them with it

Suddenly, she was gagging. Something was yanking her back—her cloak. It must have snagged. The clasp dug into her throat, while the torrent pushed her in the opposite direction from Bay, ripping the reins out of her hands. The mahogany bay horse disappeared into the muck. She gasped for air and mud filled her mouth and sight. Choking, she closed her eyes against the onslaught and fought against whatever rock or branch held her. She had to save Bay. Or go with her, together to the Vale.

Then the pressure on her throat disappeared and became a tight squeeze around her waist.

"Stop fighting me," someone roared in her ear.

But she couldn't. *Must. Save. Bay.* She tried to say this, but her mouth was full of mud and she was growing light-headed.

Then darkness, or another torrent of mud, swept her away.

---

Seren first became aware of a crackling fire and the savoury smell of roasting meat. She had to rub a gritty substance out of her eyelashes so she could see that above where she lay was grey rock. Light beckoned from the left, and she managed to turn her head toward it. The mouth of the cave opened into a clearing surrounded by tall pines. Between their prickly branches poked patches of clear blue sky. The storm was over.

Sitting up produced a spasm of aches through her body. So she supposed she hadn't died and gone to the Vale. Nothing, however, seemed broken or badly injured. And if her travelling outfit of a cloak, tunic, brown leather vest, and pants were caked in dried mud, it was still in one piece and dry.

*The rockslide.*

Bay's reins had slipped through her fingers as someone pulled her from the saddle. Her heart squeezed tight with hope, but no horse could've survived that, not even one accustomed to swimming in Luminaria's bay.

As she swallowed back any hint of tears and rose, her muddled head finally recognized she wasn't alone. At the fire, a broad figure sat hunched on a log as he roasted the flesh of some animal over the flame.

His long braids were streaked with dirt and full of leaves and twigs, making the colour impossible to tell. The scruff on his face, however, appeared dark blond. More dirt clung to the seams of his leather tunic and dark trousers, though the worst of it had been washed away. Braces encircled each enormous forearm, and what skin showed between elbow and bicep was bronzed and marked by faded scars. Finally, her gaze landed on his hands as they turned the skewer. They looked neither young, nor old; the knuckles, however, were cracked, either from fighting or the elements.

She didn't know what she expected a Felinae to look like. But her gut told her he was one of them. Coming face-to-face with her enemy, after the past week, made her blood quicken. Under her dirty cloak, the familiar hilt of Vindicta warmed her hand. Either he hadn't searched her, or he hadn't relieved her of the weapon. One made him thick-headed, the other foolish. Or worse, arrogant.

His weapons lay about him within reach. Yet at this distance, she could hit him with Vindicta before he had time to retaliate. But she'd have to kill him with that one hit because he'd be on her with that long sword otherwise. Next to it lay a sleek bow and a quiver propped up against the log. None of them were Primordian made. Seren frowned as she itched the tingle between her brows. She had a strong hunch there were others hidden upon him.

"You know who I am?" Her voice came out hoarse, her throat dry and gritty.

An unimpressed grunt.

Well, that made everything easier. It had been long suspected the Felinae had spies in the city. "And you are?"

Another grunt. Fine. Not important. Her gaze darted about the clearing with small hope that he'd miraculously plucked Bay out of the rockslide, too. "My horse? What happened to her?"

He turned the meat, not looking at her. "Alive."

Seren's knees buckled in relief as she stumbled closer. "How?"

"The current pushed her downriver. She kept her head and got herself out." His voice was dry and clipped, but his last words stung like a rebuke.

It was a moon-blessed miracle the horse hadn't broken her legs or drowned.

"I would've got us both out if you hadn't pulled me from the saddle." That was perhaps a stretch, but when he didn't call her on it, she lifted her chin. "Why did you endanger yourself for me?"

His jaw tightened, and his attention flicked to her before it returned to the fire as if he didn't understand why either. "Orders."

Then her assumption of spies was correct.

"You had orders from the Felinae prince to find me?" Her fingers twitched near her knife. If the two of them fought, she didn't know if she could win. "Or to capture me?

The prince or his advisers might believe she'd be useful as a hostage or prisoner, not that Uncle Tarquin would make sentimental decisions. But he would raze this man to the ground if he insulted House Moralis by daring to harm her.

Another thought chilled her. Did the prince already suspect her secret mission?

Valera's voice gently chided her. *Wouldn't you be suspicious if some half-Prim, half-Felinae had ridden into the city declaring a sudden change in loyalty?*

"I was sent to meet you," he replied. "I wasn't warned it would be necessary to rescue you."

Ah, an escort. She supposed he expected gratitude then for saving her. Irritation, however, came more naturally. "Before you escort me to the crown prince—my cousin," she added on the chance that wasn't clear to him, "we'll have to go back for my horse."

"Your Prim trackers grabbed her. They would have overtaken you yesterday if not for the rockslide." He turned his attention back to the skewer and shrugged. "And where we're headed, no horse can follow."

"Trackers?" She hadn't noticed a tail, but perhaps Uncle Tarquin had instructed them to make sure she reached the Felinae. Still, she didn't relish the thought of having to fight her House brothers or sisters on the off chance they hadn't been informed of her mission. "If I'm being tracked, we should be on our way."

"Soon. It's unlikely the stuffed-noses can pick up your trail after that storm." Unsheathing a small blade, he sliced off a chunk of meat.

Seren settled on the other side of the fire. After discreetly tucking her knife into her thigh-holster, she fanned her hands in front of the flames while the unnamed Felinae ate. Juices from the roasted meat ran down his scruffy chin, and as he tipped his head back, she noticed a long, white claw hanging around his neck. Her stomach rumbled. She'd eaten sparsely of the bread, goat cheese, and dried figs Valera had packed her, but her provisions hadn't lasted more than five days.

Finally, she couldn't stand it any longer. "I won't be alive long enough to present before your prince if you don't feed me."

"Why should I?"

"Because it's rude and cruel to starve someone?"

He wiped his mouth with the back of his hand. "Why should I let you within arm's reach of the prince?"

Seren licked her lips, imagining the savoury taste of roasted rabbit. "I'm Prince Morningstar's daughter and your prince's cousin. Isn't that reason enough?"

A twinge of doubt and embarrassment ran through her. In her eighteen years of life, no Felinae had ever tried to claim her.

He set his stick upright against the wood in the fire and wiped his hands on the ends of his tunic. "Prince Devan of the Morningstars brought war and death upon the clans. Why should the Throne shelter you when the fury of your republic will follow you?"

Some of that was true. But there were reasons why he should bring her to his prince. Reasons his prince, if not this warrior, was all too aware of. The lies waited in her throat for her to speak, mingling with the truth.

She shrugged. "Primordians care nothing for me. But the Legion will come for you whether or not you harbour me." There was more truth in that than she liked to admit. "My uncle will see the Felinae Dominion become his first conquered state under the Republic of Luminaria."

It was only a hunch, but she suspected Uncle Tarquin had further-reaching plans of a continent once again united under Primordian rule.

"Then why shouldn't I get rid of you now?" Hardened eyes conveyed his thoughts: no matter if he had rescued her from death, he wouldn't lose sleep over sending her back to meet it.

"Because"—she straightened her shoulders—"I'm here to atone for my father's mistakes." It wasn't entirely false. She would atone for her father's mistakes, but not in the way this Felinae might imagine.

"And your mother's mistakes?" he demanded.

Seren's temper lashed out. "I've been atoning for hers since I was born."

"So dedicate yourself to the life of a priestess," he said, shrugging those massive shoulders, "and leave the Felinae prince out of it."

Desperately, she searched for the words Valera would use to persuade him. *Make yourself indispensable.* "You can't win this war without me. I think like a Primordian, like my uncle. You need me, and your prince knows it." Her eyes narrowed. "It's why he sent you here for me, isn't it?"

It was a gamble.

Over the crackling fire, the Felinae considered her. While her heart thudded in her chest, she imagined all sorts of ways she could break his hawkish nose if he needed further encouragement.

Finally, he extended the half-eaten skewer to her. "Eat. You'll need your strength if you wish to find out."

**9**

———————

The nameless Felinae struck out in a north-easterly direction, away from the Aegis River and the North Pass. There was no path to follow, just him. At first, Seren tried to slip as quietly through the forest as he did, but her thighs ached from days of riding and she was nowhere near as light on her feet in the forest. A point that irritated her since someone so tall and broad had no right to be so stealthy. She soon settled for keeping up with his relentless pace so that he didn't lose her in the trees, which was perhaps his intent. A few times, he paused to get his bearings—or that was what she assumed he was doing—then they'd be off again.

After what felt like an age, the thick pines thinned into a gulch of pebbles and creeks, and she found him waiting for her at the base of a path leading up the rugged hillside. Beyond it rose the snow-dusted Selinens in their majestic glory— sentinels to the gods. Chest heaving from the last sprint, Seren slowed to catch her breath but found herself holding it instead.

The peaks were impossibly high, rebelliously piercing the white clouds at the gates of the domain of the Goddess Lumina and the divine warriors.

"Is this where you've been hiding?" She stretched her arms over her head to relieve the stitch in her side, pretending to be only mildly curious.

Without a word, he started up the craggy path.

"Will your vow of silence end once we arrive at your prince's camp? Or will I be ignored there as well?" His silence—no, his entire demeanour—rubbed against her like an ill-fitting breastplate.

"At least speak your name." She scowled at his back. She hadn't travelled all this way to be snubbed by a glorified messenger. "Then I'll call you 'the Felinae.' But won't that be confusing once there's more than one? Assuming you're not leading me off the steep side of a cliff—"

Abruptly, he swung around to face her, his braids whipping about him. Despite her height, he towered above her with the Selinens.

"In the ancient language, the clans referred to themselves as Keepers of the Elusive Mysteries. It's only after your Primordian ancestors arrived on the isle that we were called Felinae."

He meant in Low Prim. It had been the common tongue of Primordia, spoken by all its conquered subjects by law as the standard throughout the continent, and it fulfilled the same role on the isle after the Accord had established settlement and trade agreements along the Aegis between the Felinae Dominion and the burgeoning Republic of Luminaria.

"I am no keeper of those ancient truths," he added, as if to forestall any more questions or nicknames, before continuing up the path.

"Your mother gave you a name, didn't she?"

Abruptly, he stopped in the middle of the path. "Lion."

Whipping her head up, she searched the craggy ridge above them for the threat while drawing her blade. Predatory cats were rarely seen anymore, but their fur and heads were prized amongst legionnaires as adornments for their helms and cloaks.

Meanwhile, the Felinae had scratched something in the dirt.

*L-l-i-o-n.*

"My mother called me Llion." As he rose, he brushed his mane of braids to the side so the full weight of his brown-gold eyes rested on her. It was appropriate.

"My mother called me Seren."

He nodded—of course, he knew her name. "Star."

"Excuse me?"

"Seren means 'star' in the ancient tongue." A flush crept up his neck, and he cleared his throat. "I remember a few words."

"I didn't know that." She'd always thought it a shortened form of Serenia. It made her wonder if her mother had known the meaning. "Thank you."

Over the next few hours, the silence was, if not amiable, less tense. The sparse grass of winter gave way to grey rock, the path narrowing until Seren found herself hugging the protruding side of the mountain, her toes precariously balanced on a fine edge and her forearms straining to maintain her grip on the ledge above.

She scanned the dark rock for another foothold. Llion had long since crossed the overhang before her. The man was as fast at climbing over rocks as he was at running through forests. Yet he didn't have the lithe body of a climber or a runner. Plus, he was weighed down with weapons and gear. All she had left was her cloak and Vindicta. It would be rather embarrassing if she fell off the mountainside.

Gritting her teeth, she swung a leg up to hook her toe into a crevice while her bloody palms protested the bite of the jagged ledge. Surely the North Pass would have been easier—if he wanted her to survive this journey.

As she climbed, doubts crept into her thoughts about the

secretive Llion. Who was to say the trackers weren't legionnaires after him for some act of sabotage? A sickening feeling took hold of her. Under his musky scent lay a subtle hint of smoke and ash. Was it from the earlier fire, or had Llion come from the burning of Gull Harbour?

*There.* A small pocket for her right hand. She half flung herself upward to reach it. Then stretched for another foothold. After a slow ascent around the overhang, she caught sight of Llion's billowing cloak high above her against the grey rock.

Her anger ignited anew at the loss of innocent life in the coastal port. If Llion was guilty, she'd do more than break his nose. She'd drag him back to Luminaria and see him hang for his crimes. At the moment, however, she couldn't afford to dwell on the trackers or Llion's possible wrongs against Primordians.

First, she had a mountain to climb. *Up it is.*

It was close to another hour of climbing before powerful hands from above clamped onto her rubbery forearms and pulled her over the next precipice to a craggy plateau. Llion released her, and she lay on her stomach, catching her breath on the thin mountain air.

Lumina, she never wanted to move again.

When she lifted her head, he offered her his waterskin. She could barely raise her hand to accept it.

"Do you see that?"

"It's hard to miss," she said before swallowing another sip. The Amphitheatron paled when in proximity to the unending peaks of the Selinens.

Llion held out a hand for the waterskin, which she surrendered reluctantly, and then he gestured with it toward a ledge above their heads. "Take another look."

On her second pass, she saw it. High above them, on a lip of stone, was a narrow fissure, barely wide enough for the broad head of a war hammer.

"That's your way into our camp."

"You're joking."

There was no humour in his face. Even if moving her exhausted arms and legs was an option, entering the mountain alone unsettled her. But the crevice was far too narrow for Llion's build. And he'd said *your way*. Not *our way*.

The sheer rock would require her to jump her full height. In her mind, she ran through the combinations Master Kai had taught her.

In the distance, a hawk cried. Llion's gaze jumped to the black speck soaring down over the trees below. "Give me your cloak."

"Looking to replace yours?"

"One of your trackers has followed us this far." He held out a hand without looking at her, still tracking the bird. "I'll lead him away with your scent. They're decent at tracking for Prims."

If Llion could hear these trackers, his senses were sharper than hers. But then she was only half-Felinae. She fumbled to untie the knot to remove her cloak.

"This is your chance to go home. I'll make certain the tracker finds you." Now he looked at her. "You're not the first to run away at thought of marriage and then change your mind."

Seren didn't have to fake the spark of indignation in her voice. "I have no interest in marriage or in going back."

Not without her mission completed.

"If that's true, and you can find your way through the mountain to our den, the *sealgair*, Prince Alban's legatus"—*so that was her cousin's name*—"will offer you protection until the Throne summons you to present yourself." He scowled as if he disagreed with the sealgair's orders. "Until such time, you will train under the sealgair's command and be bound by the same oaths of loyalty as any other recruit."

Train with her enemies? Her fingers dug into the thick wool

of her cloak in disgust at the idea. The fact that the prince wasn't in this cavern didn't escape her notice either. Llion had misled her. Then the rest of his conditions hit her like a splash of frigid ocean water, and her mouth went dry.

"I am to swear an oath?"

"Do not, and we part ways here." It didn't seem like Llion wouldn't mind that.

A wave of unease washed over her. House Moralis already had her pledge of loyalty. But if she didn't swear the oath, Llion would abandon her, and it was doubtful she'd get anywhere near the prince, who had to be the ultimate prize for her uncle. If Prince Alban was captured by the Legion, then the Felinae would surrender to save the life of their last royal.

"You're asking me to stake my honour on an oath to someone I've never met?" She hesitated. Breaking an oath she never intended to keep wouldn't be the same as betraying her oath to Uncle Tarquin and her House, would it?

"You're asking us to do the same," he pointed out. "But as you've mentioned, the prince is your kin. The ties of blood bind you together."

Her eyes narrowed. "Then why does he need me to swear this oath?"

"His sealgair insists. For his protection." Llion glanced up at the circling hawk, and she suspected he was at the end of his patience. "What's it to be, daughter of the Morningstar?"

At her father's illustrious name, Seren scowled and tossed her cloak at him. She hadn't come this far to turn back empty-handed.

---

STREAKS OF DAYLIGHT from the fissure tempered the grey darkness inside the mountain. Not that Seren needed the light, but it would prolong her ability to use her night-sight without a headache. Her nose sifted through the metallic notes as she shuffled along the narrow corridor. Pebbles, dislodged by her boots, skittered down crevices, their *clinks* and *clanks* echoing back to her. Far below, water dripped, steady and constant. Otherwise, the mountain was a tomb.

Soon the crack widened enough that she could walk forward instead of sideways. Veins of white crystal wove through the black, glass-like walls, a sharp contrast to the mountain's dull exterior. If the bladesmiths of Luminaria came to know of this rich deposit of serendium, a gemstone found only on this isle, and only in small quantities, they'd be tripping over themselves to get their hands on it.

The air became colder as the passage led her deeper into the mountain until all natural light was gone. It finally opened into a small chamber with two tunnels, but there was nothing to indicate which one might lead her to the Felinae den. Seren listened at the one to her left. Dripping water. She scowled and went to the other. No sound came from it, but a tingle arose in her palms.

She tensed, but no pain followed as it had on Pledging Night. Dragging her tingling palm along the glass-like rock, she took another step into the tunnel. The intensity of the feeling lowered but persisted. Could the tingling sensation be more than lingering damage to her nerves? Absurd. However, she had the unmistakable feeling it was a sign of some sort.

*Tingle tunnel it is.*

Soon, the passage became so low she had to crawl on her belly. Jagged rock scraped against her arms and legs, her reinforced vest and leathers meagre protection as the tunnel became tighter. Sweat broke out on her face and under her arms, and soon her tunic was soaking wet as the ceiling continued to narrow. Maybe it hadn't been a good idea to listen to the tingling.

Then her shoulders snagged on the unmovable rock

around her. *Solfire.* Again and again, she tried to squeeze through, but it was no use. She would need to return to the cavern and choose the other tunnel. A solid plan—except when she tried to back up, she couldn't. Something—her holster?—was caught, and there was no way she could reach it to unbuckle it. She couldn't move forward or backward.

She was stuck.

Sharp laughter erupted from her, echoing down the crevice. Was this some sort of Felinae revenge, to make her die lost and alone, encased in rock along with the skeletons of others who hadn't passed this cruel initiation trial? It was too wretched of an end. Llion should have pushed her off the cliff.

Helplessness swelled within her until she wanted to scream, but she wouldn't give her enemies the pleasure of her frustration. Oh, why did she think a bundle of damaged nerves in her hands could lead her true? The tunnel with the water was the obvious choice now. Any camp of Felinae down here would need water to survive.

Her dire situation pressed against her as hard and demanding as the mountain. If she died, no one in Luminaria —not Valla, not Tyberius or Quinton—would ever know.

The republic would forever believe she was a traitor. Worse, Uncle Tarquin would come to believe she had switched allegiances when she never returned from her mission. Her name would be struck from the annals of House Moralis. The Goddess would leave her soul for Sol to collect, and she would burn with him for all eternity. No one would shed tears for an oathbreaker.

Somehow it was worse than dying at the bottom of the river.

*Goddess, if your light can reach me under this rock, I need you. Again.*

Expelling all her breath, Seren scraped herself forward, her nose brushing the black rock beneath her. One arm stretched forward with her head, the other hitting the protruding jag in the rock. Tears streaked her cheeks as she pushed with her feet to wrench her shoulder through. She had to fit. There was no going back.

With her other arm, she found a handhold, and she braced her boots against the rock. *Pull*, she commanded her arm muscles. *Push*, she ordered her legs.

Below her, loose rocks shifted.

With a sudden pop, her shoulder went through, and a wave of euphoria flooded her. Wiggling and pulling, she crawled on her belly the rest of the way into a passageway with a high ceiling. Then she collapsed, her heart thumping so loud it was all she could focus on.

She had done it.

When her heartbeat finally slowed, she heard a faint murmur. Not water this time.

*Voices.*

**10**

Seren crept forward on her hands and knees. Scraping sounds and thuds of metal hitting wood interrupted the voices intermittently. The ceiling rose, and if she crouched, she could now walk. She untied her boots and tucked them under her left arm to keep her knife hand free. A dull light penetrated the darkness, signalling the end of the tunnel was nearing, and she settled behind a boulder to listen.

"Seems like a waste of time to come all the way out here to wait around for some useless nob to show up," said an arrogant voice. "What's so special about her?"

"Her father was Prince of the Morningstars," said a softer voice, again using that same odd phrasing that Llion had for her father's title.

Goosebumps broke out over Seren's arms. Llion and these recruits had been expecting her. It meant there were spies in the city, but any spy in Luminaria would've had to race her back here—and they wouldn't have heard of her defection until the next morning at the earliest, though she suspected Uncle Tarquin would've kept her disappearance a secret as long as possible.

But Ty would've known something was up. She sucked in a breath. And he hadn't explained why he'd been spying on the Consul meeting. He'd sworn he hadn't been involved in her attack, but what legitimate reason could he have for spying on the consulars? Whatever the reason, he had rather let Quinton believe he'd been in the tunnels with her than come clean.

"Prince Devan died a traitor," the arrogant one huffed.

Seren's gut clenched. *Could Ty be a traitor?*

"No matter if her father was a prince or a traitor, she was raised by Prims," a third voice, filled with sharp edges, pointed out.

"She understands more than we could ever hope to about Primordians," said the soft voice. "She could help us win. Help Prince Alban."

*Help him surrender, more like.*

"No one asked you, Whisper." The arrogant one.

"It's Vesper." The soft voice was firm.

"Leave her be," ordered a voice that sounded like the singing of a crystal glass—clear and true and mesmerizing.

There was a shuffling sound. "You going to put down your book long enough to make me, Reul?"

"Seren Moralis is the enemy, Thane," interrupted the sharp voice. "And may I remind all of you, she was raised to hate us."

"If you had been raised by scorpions, would you not sting like a scorpion?" Reul asked, his voice so pleasing to her ears that she almost missed the fact he seemed to be making excuses for her. But he was right: her knife would sting.

"What in Sol's hells does that mean?" Thane demanded.

A soft bell tinkled.

"She's coming," snapped the sharp voice. The thuds and pings began in earnest again. Seren strained to hear what they heard: the lightest boot steps.

"Idleness and bickering will win you no wars, hatchlings."

The alto voice pronounced the Low Prim words with an

accent, reminding Seren of a trade delegation from the continent that had visited her uncle. But which one? Over the next quarter of an hour, metal clanged against rock more often than not. The foreigner eviscerated weak wrists and sloppy postures, sometimes in an unfamiliar language.

Soon Seren's aching muscles and empty stomach protested. There was no point in putting off her entrance any longer. If this was an ambush Llion had set up, waiting wouldn't improve her odds. This sort of situation, however, was the reason she'd worked so hard with Master Kai on her dancing. After lacing up her boots, she headed down the passage, not bothering to muffle her footsteps in the echoing tunnel. If they thought she was good at sneaking around, they'd be more on guard. Better to let them underestimate her abilities. By the time she reached the entrance, the recruits had stopped their drill and were staring at her, their throwing stars idly in hand.

A low luminescence from bundles of driftwood that lay on the ground and hung on the shimmering black walls allowed her to perceive colour. A quick scan of the cavern revealed the ceiling was high and, near the top, a ledge jutted out from a passageway. Below the ledge was another tunnel. One must be the way Llion would enter the cavern since it was impossible for him to have squeezed through the tight passages on her route here.

She spared a glance at the battered target—some logs tied together with rope and painted with white circles. The stars that had hit the target were clustered around the outer ring and more lay scattered on the grey clay ground. It hardly seemed possible that these were recruits for the Felinae forces currently plaguing Luminaria. None of them looked like much of a threat, except their instructor.

The short, fierce-looking warrior took Seren's measure from under a fringe of straight jet-black hair that fell to her chin. A wide leather belt, with three tightening straps, protected her torso while a sleeveless silver-mesh undershirt revealed well-defined arms. Her thumbs were slung into a low holster that strapped two curved swords at her hips. The outfit was completed with black leathers and knee-high boots. The workmanship was of high quality but nothing like the styles in Luminaria.

Despite the menace rolling off the petite warrior, Seren doubted the Felinae prince would trust a foreigner to lead his forces. And while mercenaries weren't plentiful in Luminaria, the games at the Amphitheatron did attract that sort. So it wasn't inconceivable the prince had hired her to train recruits.

Three such recruits flanked the warrior. Two young men, clad in brown leathers and sleeveless cream undershirts, and a young woman in a dark green tunic and black leathers. The tallest had unruly dark hair and a harsh set to his jaw. A glower sullied what might have otherwise been an appealing face. For that reason alone, Seren surmised he was the one called Thane.

"Well, look what the lion dragged in," he mocked in the familiar arrogant voice.

Seren lifted her chin. "No one dragged me here."

"Certainly looks like it." Thane's scornful gaze swept over her dusty attire.

She couldn't help stiffening. After four years at the Lyceum, she was done taking insults. "I found my way in by myself. At least, I have a reason for looking like shit. What's yours?"

"Where is Llion?" the warrior interrupted.

As to Llion's whereabouts—how in Sol's hells should she know? Annoyed, Seren opened her mouth to say that when a leather-clad figure the size of a boulder dropped from the ledge above, startling her into taking a step back before catching herself.

Llion landed in a crouch, then straightened to his full height, a sack of some kind in his hand. His bow and quiver, she noted, were missing. "Our Princess of the Morningstars made her own way in through the mountain."

"Princess?" she echoed. Was he mocking her? Her father had been a prince, but who gave titles to bastards?

The warrior lost some of her pinched expression. As she made her way to Llion, a tinkling followed her. On tip-toes, she reached up a half-gloved hand to remove a twig from his long, matted braids. It was a testament to their length that she could reach it. "Shade?"

It was a question of some sort.

"Morningstar is here to train with us like the others," Llion answered, expression inscrutable. "Not be waited on as royalty."

"I wasn't aware I had been given a choice in the matter," Seren muttered.

The warrior hesitated but then glided away to lean against a nearby boulder. The angle revealed a tattoo near the corner of her right eye—a triangle with a dagger inset.

*It couldn't be.*

It was the brand of the Marked, the most ruthless and notorious assassins' guild. While members were said to be handpicked from all over the continent and isles, the guild was headquartered in the resurrected Duchy of Rokkemar. Before the Republic of Primordia fell, the Grand Consul was said to have wielded control over the Marked, using them to silence many of their adversaries. Now, their guild master accepted contracts from the highest bidder.

The tiny bell in the assassin's left ear confirmed it. Those who heard the approach of the Marked had nothing to fear; it was the silence one had to be wary of, for that was when the Marked would strike.

Seren's heart pounded at the implications. Assassins training or working with the Felinae was worrisome. But another fear stole her breath—that Prince Alban had hired the

Marked to assassinate his enemies. As imperator, Uncle Tarquin would be a prime target.

"Do our accommodations meet with your approval, Seren of the Morningstars?"

It was the sharp voice from earlier, and it came from the young woman at the elbow of the other young man, who must be Reul. During their practice, the Marked had called her Kanta. Frizzy chestnut hair was piled high on top of her head, accentuating the sharp angles of the young woman's freckled cheeks and nose. A long, forest green tunic hit below her rounded hips, which flared out from a trim waist encircled by a leather belt with a silver bear head for a buckle.

In response to the question, Seren made a show of inspecting the cavern as her prefect would inspect their dormitories. Against the far wall, carved into the rock, was a series of wide step-like ledges. From the look of the blankets, they acted as beds. Packs lay scattered here and there, reminding Seren of the loss of her own down the river. She was distracted from that mournful thought by a savoury smell coming from an alcove where a cooking pit had been set up along with a wooden table and benches.

A cauldron hung over the fire, and a twig of a youth in a grain sack of a yellow tunic stirred it. *This must be Vesper.* From behind tawny hair, the young girl caught her gaze and smiled. The warmth of the greeting startled Seren, and she returned it without thinking.

Behind her, Kanta made an impatient noise.

"A little disappointing for a base of operations," Seren lied in the tone many nobs had taken with her when her uncle wasn't present. She ran her fingertips along the rough-hewn table, past crude trenchers and tin cups. Truthfully, the underground tunnels and caverns made an ingenious hideaway. How many might be positioned here? A hundred? Five hundred? "Where are the others?" *Not to mention the missing sealgair.* "The six of you won't stand a chance against the Legion."

Kanta let loose a harsh laugh as she nudged a stiff Reul with her elbow. "Mists of Time, she must think we've beetles for brains if she believes we'd reveal the location of our forces to a Primordian."

"I am half-Felinae," Seren muttered. It was the first time she'd ever said it out loud, and it grated against her teeth. At the Lyceum, everyone had been all too eager to remind her of that fact.

"Then welcome to the Elusives, Seren." Reul of the crystal-singing voice offered her a smile all the warmer for the surrounding glares. "I think *we*"—he glanced at Kanta—"forgot to say that."

"Elusives, as in Keepers of the Elusive Mysteries?" She was still half-mesmerized by his voice. And his hair, now that he had stepped more into the soft glowing light. It defied the simple definition of auburn or wine-coloured. A hundred distinct hues streaked through it as it fell across his prominent forehead. Mahogany, she settled on, like the rich colour of her horse.

Reul darted a questioning look at Llion as he lounged against the boulder with Silver, but he answered easily enough. "In part. The Keepers are long dead, but we strive to protect what knowledge they passed into our keeping. We may not be many or even Elusives yet," he added with a wry smile, "but that doesn't mean you aren't safe with us."

Seren swallowed a snort. Safe with them? None of them were safe with *her*. But she supposed letting them think she was afraid of the Legion might help gain their trust. So would letting them underestimate her.

"Am I safe?" She forced the words out past the lump of pride in her throat. "You have me at a disadvantage: I am but one, and you are many."

Of them all, Llion and the Marked assassin were the only ones who would pose a challenge in a fight—but Llion claimed the sealgair would protect her.

Thane snorted. "Get used to it, *Princess*."

His tone turned the title into an insult, and her skin heated. She refused to be their princess—no matter if her father was a prince. A cutting remark about how Primordian society had long ago discarded the tyranny of monarchy lay on the tip of her tongue. Instead, she retorted, "You must have lived your whole life under this rock if you believe I'm not well acquainted with being the outcast."

Confusion flashed in his eyes, then it was gone.

"I meant," Thane said, his voice low as he stepped in close, "you being at a disadvantage."

With a burst of speed, she kicked her legs out low in a drop sweep and toppled him into the dirt. In the next breath, she straddled his chest and pressed Vindicta to the underside of his clean-shaven jaw. A bead of dark blood welled on the tip. It wasn't much, but the coppery tang tainted the air.

"Hold!" Llion thundered from somewhere on her left flank. His order seemed to freeze everyone else in place, their stares burning into her back while Thane glared up at her.

"Is this what disadvantage looks like?" she snarled.

Thane's jaw tightened, the glint in his eyes promising retribution, but his body relaxed until he lay completely still beneath her. How vexing. She wanted him to resist—to give her a reason to do more. Then the corner of his mouth curved upward as if he read the dark desires in her soul.

Fury roared in her veins; her knife pressed hard enough that a thin line of red trickled down his throat. How *dare* he see her so clearly. But she pushed down her yearning for revenge. It would be all the sweeter when Uncle Tarquin won the war because of her information.

On the edge of her vision, she noted Llion's quiet approach. "You've proven your point, Morningstar. Release him."

In a graceful spring, Seren jumped up from Thane, keeping her focus on him the entire time. Once she was clear, he pushed off the ground with his hands beside his head, arching his back to spring up onto his feet in one fluid movement that didn't fail to impress.

"You didn't take her weapon?" he demanded of Llion. "For Lleufer's sake, she could slit our throats in our sleep."

She untucked her tunic to wipe Vindicta clean. "Then stop giving me a reason to."

From behind Thane, pale fingers reached for the blood on his throat. He jerked his head out of the way and stepped back from Kanta's touch.

"I can clean it for you," she offered, watching avidly as he wiped at the blood, then rubbed his hand on his pants.

"I'm good, thanks."

Llion cleared his throat, which sounded more like an irritated growl. "Morningstar, you made it here over dangerous terrain and through a mountain. Challenges that demonstrate strength of body and mind. But an Elusive recruit must also hone her ability to observe." He paused. "Did you learn their names before revealing your presence?"

Her temper flared at another insinuation of her unworthiness and yet another test to complete before meeting this sealgair. If she pretended ignorance, then she'd look a fool. A glance at Thane's smug look decided her.

She pointed to each of them as she rattled off their names. "Thane. Kanta. Reul. Vesper. No one called the Marked anything, except Thane, and"—Seren flashed her teeth—"I don't think you want to hear what he said."

From the boulder, the assassin's flat stare raked over Seren, and she fought not to flinch. "The names of the Marked are drawn in blood and may only be spoken amongst ourselves. But to the outside world, I am known as Silver."

An innocuous name for an assassin, though maybe that's what she requested for payment. Turning around, Seren made a show of looking high and low. "I guess that's everyone except your sealgair. Or is your warlord too craven to meet me?"

It was amusing the way Reul's throat bobbed like he'd swallowed a frog. "Ah, I'd say the most analogous term is legatus."

In the strained silence, Seren followed everyone's gaze to where Llion stood, thick arms crossed against the attention.

*He was the sealgair?* Seren failed to keep her jaw from dropping. The bastard had let her think he was nothing more than a messenger.

"You?" she choked out. If he felt a twinge of guilt at his duplicity earlier, he didn't show it. He stared at her long and hard without blinking.

"Do you remember what I said outside the mountain, Morningstar?" His low voice filled the entire cavern, a coil of menace that wound itself around her soul as he approached, one measured step at a time. Like Death itself was stalking her.

Her jaw tightened. "I am bound to train here under the sealgair's—*your*—command."

"Swear on your weapon that your loyalty is to the Felinae, that you agree to train as an Elusive and be bound by our laws until the Throne decides your fate." He stopped a few paces before her.

"And what happens to those who break their oaths?"

"Only oathbreakers need to be concerned with that."

Right. The M of her knife pressed deep into her sweaty flesh, the discomfort focusing her thoughts. She'd known this moment was coming. As she raised Vindicta in front of her, she felt a jagged wrench deep inside her as if her previous oath to House Moralis was being cut away. "I so swear."

"All the words," Llion demanded, as if he knew she didn't truly mean it.

Through gritted teeth, she forced each word out. Each one was a hangman's stone around her neck. *It doesn't count*, she told herself. House Moralis alone had her heart, her loyalty.

With practised ease, Llion drew his sword, and then with both hands raised the hilt upward, the tip of the blade pointed at the ground. "As Sealgair, I, Llion Llewyn, swear by the authority bestowed upon me by the Throne that Seren Morningstar, daughter of Devan Morningstar, is under my protection. All wrongs against her will be treated as offences against the Throne and will warrant the severest punishments."

By *severest* there was no doubt he meant death.

"Offences?" Thane asked.

"It means her life belongs to the Throne," Reul said. "Harm her, and the Throne will exact its punishment on you."

Seren raised a brow at the choice of wording, but she didn't argue. She supposed a prince would see everyone and everything under his rule as belonging to it.

Thane threw his hands wide in outrage. "*She* attacked *me*. Why is she allowed to keep a weapon?"

"Care to take it from me, Thane?" Seren asked in her sweetest voice. She flipped Vindicta in the air and caught the handle, earning her a scowl from both Thane and Kanta.

"All recruits are required to surrender their arms until I deem you fit to wield them, Morningstar. It will be returned."

For half a breath, she thought about challenging Llion to take it if he wanted it so badly, but Valera's warnings flitted back to her. *Play nice. You need to win their trust or they'll never let you near the prince.*

The tension amongst the recruits broke as she handed Vindicta and her holster over to Silver, whose solemn nod eased Seren's reluctance to part with it.

Besides, she still had a dagger in her boot.

"If you break your oath," Llion added, "the Throne may exact its severest punishment on you as well. Do you understand, Morningstar?"

"Understood, but why are you keeping me here?"

Llion didn't appear thrilled at the prospect of training her either. "We await the Throne's pleasure."

So Prince Alban was making her wait on purpose—putting her in her place or testing her mettle? Well, she'd waited eighteen years. She could cool her heels here and use the time to gather information.

While Llion issued tasks to the recruits for the preparation of supper, Vesper poked her tawny head out of the shadows and stared at Seren, her manner more curious than hostile. The girl's earlier words, however, rang in Seren's head.

*She understands more than we could ever hope to about Primordians. She could help us win. Help Prince Alban.*

Was that Llion's plan? Would he interrogate her about Uncle Tarquin and the military might of the Legion? Goddess, what had she done?

Hands clenched at her sides, she watched him as he gathered the sack by the far wall. "Oath, or no oath," she said, "I won't tell you anything about my uncle or House Moralis that will compromise their safety."

All activity in the cavern ceased.

"I won't raise weapons against my family," she continued. The blood in her veins turned to ice as Silver nonchalantly unsheathed Vindicta to inspect the edge. "Have your assassin interrogate me all you like."

The tales of what the Marked did to some of their targets were enough to make the noose look merciful.

Llion straightened, the bag falling from his shoulder. "What do you know of interrogation, Seren Morningstar?"

She flinched at her father's name. "All my life I've had to answer for the crime of my existence."

From the periphery of her vision, Reul sauntered over from where he'd been scooping water out of a barrel, breaking her sightline to Llion as he set his pot on the table. "It's Ellus —not Reul—at least to my friends. What do your friends call you?"

"Er, Seren," she sputtered at the non sequitur. Lumina, in proper daylight his smile was probably dazzling.

"Torture," Ellus declared solemnly, "is for our enemies, Seren. Let them darken their souls with it." Then, as if an afterthought, he ducked his head toward Llion. "Right, Sealgair?"

"They already have," Thane spat, dropping his load of strange, glowing white wood by the cooking pit.

"We cannot earn her trust with threats, Sionnach," Ellus argued, though his comment seemed directed at Llion.

Ignoring them both, Llion unrolled not a sack but her cloak on the cavern floor. Dun-coloured lumps of fur lay before them, unmoving. Mountain hares. Caught in snares, Seren guessed.

"And she must earn ours." Llion lifted one by the ears to examine it. "However, as the Throne's representative, I do not require that Morningstar tell us her uncle's secrets. At this time."

The other recruits returned to their tasks, and some of the tension in Seren's shoulders eased. But she didn't think Llion was finished with her. From his hip, he drew a claw-like knife made of the same shimmering glass-like substance as the black cavern walls.

With a few quick slashes, Llion cut the hare along its belly and hindquarters, then pulled off the fur, laying bare the dark meat as if the hare had simply shed its outer coat. With the skinned hare in hand, Llion stalked toward her.

When he tossed it at her, she caught it without thinking. Cool and clammy, the dead animal squelched in her hands. But that wasn't why she shivered. While Llion shielded her from the view, she imagined what his knife could do—*had done*—to the flesh of his enemies.

In a flash, he sank his black blade into the hare, and she flinched, her hands clenching into the soft meat, but she didn't drop it. Nor did she look away from his golden-brown eyes. She'd never been hunted by a predator before, but she supposed this was what it might feel like.

"Make no mistake, Seren of the Morningstars," he whispered, withdrawing his bloodied knife. "When the time comes—when the Throne desires your secrets—you will bare them to me."

No one attacked her in the night.

She'd half-hoped Thane or Kanta might give her an excuse to put them in their place, but evidently the sealgair's warning was enough. That, or Thane didn't have the nerve after she had put him in the dirt yesterday.

With a yawn, Seren stretched her legs out. While the hollowed-out sleeping ledge in the wall was more comfortable than it appeared, it was no bed.

Like a gust of northerly wind, a tingling sensation swept over her forehead, and she had the unsettling feeling of being watched. She glanced up at the jutting ledge where Llion had jumped from yesterday. *Empty*.

Still, she had to assume the Felinae were watching her and suspicious of her defection. If a half-Prim, half-Felinae appeared at the Lyceum claiming a change of loyalty, she would doubt the defector, too. But as long as Llion and his recruits suspected her of duplicity, they wouldn't reveal anything useful.

Seren groaned and pulled the wool blanket up to her chin. *Valla would know what to say or do to gain their trust.*

The absence of her friend weighed heavily on Seren, and her mind drifted to House Moralis. Valera would be waking up in her newly assigned quarters. Perhaps she would spend her day preparing for Uncle Tarquin's first act as imperator, if Uncle Tarquin had appointed her as a junior political aide as she desired. A condemnation of Gull Harbour, perhaps. Or—her gut clenched—would Imperator Tarquin Moralis's first act be to declare Seren a traitor?

Only four people in the world knew her true purpose with the Felinae: her uncle, Valera, Quinton, and Tyberius. Quinton had heard his father's plan for her to be a weapon at the Consul meeting. So had Ty. Though they hadn't discussed the specifics of the meeting before she'd kissed him. The tightness in her stomach became one huge, fluttery knot, and her palms tingled as if they once again slid through his hair. Instead, they wound through her own.

*Solfire*. She couldn't afford to think about such distractions. He had made it very clear in the catacombs that's all she was to him—a distraction. And all Ty was to her was a thread to lead her to answers. After she returned to Luminaria with information on the Felinae, she'd get the full story of the ring's origins and sort out her confusing feelings.

An ear-splitting clanging had Seren sitting straight up. Silver approached the ledges, dressed in her silver-mesh undershirt and black leathers without her swords and banging a pot with a bent ladle. "Up, up, up!"

Groans came from the ledges above. From below, Vesper stretched her arms over her mussed hair and yawned. "Already?"

Silver banged the pot again for good measure. "Last one down the Gauntlet and back is on cooking duty!"

Before Seren could wipe the sleep from her eyes, Vesper flew out of her blankets like a loosed arrow seeking Silver's vanishing form. Then two forms sailed over Seren's head—

Ellus and Thane. Neck and neck, they raced toward the tunnel while Kanta hopped behind them on one foot, trying to get her other boot on.

At the mouth of the tunnel, Ellus turned around and jogged backwards. Thane blew by him, and Kanta was gaining momentum. Time to go.

"How well do you cook, Seren?" Ellus called out, as she jumped from her ledge. He had waited for her.

She landed in a crouch, one brow lifted. "I could ask you the same question, Reul."

With a warm chuckle, he took off into the tunnel. "One day, you'll find out," he called out, bounding away from her and Kanta. "But not today."

She rolled her eyes and ran. Her first day as an Elusive recruit had begun.

———

AFTER A BREAKFAST OF BURNT PORRIDGE—COURTESY of Kanta— Llion opened a satchel on the table and drew out a set of knives carved entirely from wood. The one he handed Seren was slim and sanded smooth, with lines etched on the handle for grip. She tested the weight and feel of it in her hand. *Too light.*

Thane flipped his wooden knife in the air and caught it. "How are we supposed to gut nobs with these splinters?"

Llion didn't bother to answer. He and Silver walked over to the middle of the cavern, where a large circle had been drawn in the dirt. All eyes turned to them as they squared off. By size alone, it wasn't an equal match. The muscle in Llion's upper arms flexed freely in a sleeveless cream undershirt much like the ones Reul and Thane wore for fighting. In his left hand, he gripped his serendium knife; such weapons were said to be the sharpest edge around, and the claw-like blade glinted in the dull light from the strange glowing wood that lit the cavern —*moonwood*, Vesper had called it.

Silver crouched and raised her leather-wrapped hands. After the run, she'd donned her thick black belt. It would act as some protection, but Llion's reach was nearly twice as long as the assassin's. The top of Silver's head was a few fingers shorter than his shoulders. On the other hand, that left him scant area to strike.

"To be an Elusive," Llion said, his gaze not leaving Silver, "you must be able to defend yourself and your fellow warriors. Sometimes you'll have a weapon. Sometimes you won't."

On some unseen signal, the two began to circle, and, to Seren's surprise, Vesper beckoned her over to sit on the ledges with the others. Making friends wasn't something she had much experience with, but proximity seemed key. She settled in next to Vesper as Llion's knife swiped in a blur of speed at Silver's midsection. In a display of Marked skill, Silver spun toward the strike, knocking Llion's arm—and the knife—off its path.

"Parry one!" Silver called out. Her words were barely out before Llion struck again.

For every one of Llion's strikes, Silver parried, dodged, or blocked, each one faster than the last. Seren couldn't help but admire Silver's fluid manoeuvres and the way Llion struck with complete commitment. Either he trusted Silver's skill to protect herself, implicitly—or did not care if he mortally wounded her. Silver, for her part, crackled with vitality as she spun and fended off the attacks of her larger opponent. But then, she was one of the Marked, a living legend of terror and death.

After several stalemates, in which both parties failed to get the upper hand, the duo repeated the defensive manoeuvres, more slowly so Llion could describe the techniques. Each strike was aimed at a vulnerable part of the body, starting with the throat and going lower to the armpits, lungs, lower abdomen, and upper legs. Seren paid little attention. After attending the Lyceum, none of this was new.

Compared to the dance Master Kai had taught her, the drills were without the whole-body harmony that connected each one in a larger story. Seren didn't know the proper name of the martial art or where it had originated. From Master Kai's odd mannerisms and his shelf of books in languages she couldn't read, she imagined the dance came from the continent. It would be to her advantage in a fight if the Felinae knew nothing of it.

The demonstration finally concluded with Llion and Silver staring at each other, their expressions unreadable, their chests heaving, and sweat glistening on their skin. It appeared as if they were caught in a dance of their own.

One Llion ended by sheathing his knife. "Pair up," he ordered.

"Do you want to practise with me?" Vesper asked, hesitantly. Her eyes had grown wider and wider during the match. It wouldn't be a fair fight, and at the moment, Seren wanted to see what the others could do.

"I'll sit this one out."

On the other side of Vesper, Ellus's smile lost none of its brilliance, yet she had the feeling she had disappointed him. He made a sweeping gesture to the circle as if it were a ballroom. "Shall we then, Vesper?"

As Thane and Kanta paired up, Seren settled back into the stone ledge, eager to see what Elusive recruits were made of. Llion and Silver circled the pairs, shifting body parts into the correct positions. It was a joke. Second-year cadets could perform similar drills in their sleep. The issue, however, had never been Prim military strength or expertise; it was the lack of knowledge of the locations of their warriors and clans.

Despite Llion's brusque manner, his comments were aimed at improvement, and his patience with Ellus's and Vesper's mistakes was galling after his threats to her yesterday. Watching Silver lash Thane and Kanta for their poor performances proved far more entertaining.

After a while, a figure blocked her view.

"I don't have a partner," she said before Llion could reprimand her for not participating.

Llion pointed to himself, a glimmer of challenge in his eyes, and her blood quickened as she rose. She shouldn't reveal what she could do, but she could pretend to be worse than she was. She was well-practiced at that. Another of Master Kai's maxims she'd committed to memory sprung to mind: *An enemy who sees your knife but not your teeth is an enemy already beaten.* Or was it bitten?

"Seren can work with us," Ellus called out from where he had been half-heartedly practising with Vesper.

Seren bit her tongue. *Those two couldn't block a breeze.*

"You consider yourself better than your fellow recruits, Morningstar?" Llion asked. All practice ceased with his question.

She did, in more ways than one, but admitting as much wouldn't gain her any friends. Solfire, but she wished Valera was here with her to speak with her charmed tongue.

"I think . . . they haven't had the same training opportunities as I have." Too late she realized she'd insulted Llion's instruction. "I mean they must have some potential, but it's not for whatever they can do with a blade. Not yet. " She clamped her mouth shut before she made it worse.

From behind Llion, Thane tapped his wooden knife against his cheek. "Shall I show you what I can do with a blade, *Princess*?"

She snorted. "What? Fall on it?"

Vesper giggled, then clapped her hand over her mouth, and Seren shared a grin with her.

"Morningstar, in the circle," Llion barked. "No knife. You'll be defending. Everyone else, line up."

Thane came first to try his luck. Seren spotted his feints and blocked his strikes, though his reflexes, unlike the Lyceum cadets, were as nearly as fast as her own and his reach a tad longer. He had to be as tall as Ty, but he was sloppy and impatient. On the fifth strike, she used his momentum to propel him behind her into the ground.

"Out!" Silver declared.

Next came Kanta, as slow as Thane was fast. Her body tensed and her eyes announced each intended target. After Seren sidestepped a few of these strikes, she dropped to the ground and swept Kanta's legs out from under her.

Spitting dirt from her mouth, Kanta pushed herself to her feet. "That move wasn't one of the manoeuvres."

"You think legionnaires will care which manoeuvre you use?" Seren asked.

When Llion declared her out, Kanta stormed off down the tunnel, Thane close on her heels.

Ellus noticed them leave, too, but he got into position with his knife, so Seren wasted no more time on Kanta's tantrum. While Ellus put some effort into his manoeuvres, he lacked speed and commitment. She let him take a few swipes before she twisted his knife arm behind his back. He froze. The knife fell from his captured hand, and she tightened the hold so his back pressed against her chest and his silky hair brushed her lips.

"I surrender," he murmured, "my *banrigh làidir.*"

Before she could ask him what that meant, Silver called him out. Seren released him, and he bowed to her as if she were a true princess. Unable to hide her eye roll at his theatrics, she gave him a light push out of the ring but softened it with a grin.

On the sidelines, Llion stood by table with Silver, his arms crossed and his mouth a stern line. In response, Ellus shrugged, as if to say, *I tried.*

Then Vesper dropped her knife before Seren's feet. Good, the girl knew she was outmatched—but then the wooden blade was whistling by Seren's ear. Caught off guard, Seren jumped backwards to land on her hands. Vesper came in fast, her fists swinging, and it was all Seren could do to dodge. When Vesper went for a low strike, Seren caught hold of her arm and flipped the young girl onto her back. The impact dazed Vesper, and she lay there, gasping for breath.

"Out!" Silver called.

Seren offered her hand up. "You're fast. And a smaller opponent than I'm used to fighting. Are you hurt?"

"Not much," Vesper wheezed, taking her hand. "Can you show me how to do that?"

"Sure." Seren needed something to do to pass the time before Llion took her to the Throne.

Once Vesper was on her feet, Seren glanced over at Llion to see how he was taking her victories. He'd clearly been trying to humble her by pitting her against the other recruits. His expression was not altogether displeased, despite his recruits' dismal results. She supposed he'd provided a reason for the others to respect her. Or a reason to hate her, she thought, noting the sullen return of Kanta and Thane.

Llion noticed them, too, and he nodded at Silver. "Run everyone through the windmill drill."

From the ensuing groans, Seren understood this was a punishment for their failures—and her victories—today.

———

SEREN DIDN'T DARE HOPE this was the last drill. The stale cavern air was laced with the sourness of sweat from their exertions. Over the past hours—time had little meaning in the dark cavern—she had pushed herself to outshine the others in a series of climbing, strength-building, and running drills. Still, Ellus had surpassed her in climbing; Thane had outstripped her in lifting boulders; and young Vesper had outrun them all.

For what felt like the hundredth time, Seren resisted the urge to wipe her brow. Sweat coated it, her back, and her tunic. But whenever she stopped, Silver insulted her ancestors, so she kept her head down as she pushed her body up from the dirt floor, again and again, welcoming the burn in her arms and her core.

But after Llion's boots passed by her, she surrendered to the urge to rest on her forearms and watch him. The recruits referred to him as *the sealgair* as if he were the sole one, which, if true, meant their numbers were indeed small. The Legion's legatus was far too occupied with other matters to oversee the training of first-year legionnaires, let alone Lyceum cadets. Llion, on the other hand, apparently had time to train a handful of young recruits. Though, the Throne had also ordered him to watch over her, or so he had said. But why? He should be planning their next attack, their next Gull Harbour.

Whatever the reason, it sent a message even she could understand: the prince valued her safety highly enough to send his best warrior to watch over her. It should've made her feel honoured. Instead, it made her feel *caught*.

Scuffed black boots—smaller than Llion's—stopped before her face. "Loafing around already, Morningstar? That's how empires fall."

Seren glared at the ground as she raised her aching body for another push-up. "Primordia was a republic."

That was true. Once. The fallen republic might have lain in ruins across the sea, a darkness sweeping its way across the broken domains of the once-unified continent, but Uncle Tarquin would restore the glory of the Republic of Primordia here on the isle. And his first step would be to conquer the Felinae and restore peace.

"Republics, empires, city-states, and 'doms of all kinds," Silver drawled, "none survive without people to believe in them."

Before Seren could make a retort, Llion whistled for a break, and he and Silver disappeared down the tunnel. There were a few passageways off the main one, which Seren had discovered on the morning run. In their absence, she rolled onto her back to rest her arms.

Next to her, Vesper did the same, offering an encouraging smile between panting breaths. "It's not like this every day. I think you ruffled his feathers."

Seren was too sore to shrug. She'd only done what Llion asked her to do—defend herself.

On the other side of Vesper, Ellus rolled onto his elbow to face them. Moon above, that face must have slain a few hearts back in his clan. A grin that was becoming familiar lit up his crystal blue eyes. "Sometimes, it's worse. Never mind making the cut as an Elusive, I don't think I'll make it another day if Silver works us that hard again."

No nob would've dared confess the possibility of not graduating from the Lyceum or legionnaire training. Those who squeaked through were allowed a token position within their House. Those who failed became detritus.

Still, she couldn't stop from grinning. "Goddess, preserve us from Silver then, for Ellus' sake."

"My sake? It is not myself I worry for," he said in a mock-serious tone. "Instead, think how dreary your existence will be without me."

Vesper's giggle faded as a shadow fell over them.

Seren sprang to her feet. It had been a while since she'd brawled, and her blood pulsed in anticipation.

"Wishing you stayed home in your fancy bed, Princess?"

Thane crossed his bare arms over his undershirt where the dark V of his sweat ended. Was he out of sorts for losing against her again? That often happened at the Lyceum. But the other recruits had their asses handed to them, too.

"My bed here is fine," she said, flatly. She tried to step around him—Valera would be proud—but he stepped in her way.

"You must have thought you'd be treated like royalty." His nostrils flared while his dark eyes burned. "Isn't that why you're here? To wear a crown?"

"Burn your crowns and thrones," she hissed, her fists clenching at her sides. "I care not for them."

Thane's dark eyes narrowed. "Then why are you here, Seren Moralis?"

# 12

One by one, Seren made her fingers unclench. Thane wasn't much different from the nobs at the Lyceum. While there was nothing she could say that would satisfy him, she also knew he wouldn't leave her alone until the matter had been settled in his eyes. And maybe some blood was spilled.

Before she could respond to his taunt, however, Ellus wedged his lean shoulder between them. "Her reasons are not your concern, Sionnach."

True. But she could tell Thane that herself. With her fist, if he preferred. "Move aside, Ellus," she snapped. "This isn't your fight."

For a moment, she didn't think Ellus heard her, which was impossible; then he shifted so they stood shoulder-to-shoulder against Thane. On her other side, there was a flash of yellow. Vesper hung farther back but close enough to show her support. It was both vexing and touching to have these two stand up for her on such short acquaintance. But she didn't need their help.

"It's a reasonable question, Reul," Thane said, his glower switching to the new target. "One the sealgair didn't ask."

"Perhaps it has been asked. Perhaps you're not privy to the answer." Ellus's tone had gone from jovial to as frigid as winter's kiss goodnight.

"Oh, I'm not *privy to* it? Does the princess already have you and the sealgair wrapped around her finger, lordling?"

She should have put it together: Ellus's manners, his speech, the aura he exuded—all spoke to a privileged upbringing.

"If you're invoking titles, Sionnach"—the lean muscle in Ellus's upper arms flexed as he crossed them over his chest in a mirror of Thane—"you should have the courtesy to bow."

Both of them seemed to have forgotten her in this stand-off.

Disdain rolled off Thane in hot waves as he stretched his jaw. "Why should I lower myself to those who never had to fight for scraps?"

"All clans lived through lean years," Ellus conceded, his tone shifting to something close to conciliatory. "I imagine my belly was fuller than yours. Clan Stagona, are you?"

And hers fuller than all of them. Guilt pricked at Seren, but she pushed the sensation away. What did she have to be guilty of? It was the Felinae who had brought this upon themselves.

Kanta, who had been watching silently, joined Thane. "As lady of Clan Urso, my mother made it so our family ate last. And I can tell you, there are scant pickings in winter in the north. While the southern clans are better off, none of the clans should've had to do without. None of us should have had to eke out an existence in hiding, while others enjoyed the bounty of this isle."

"Seren's not responsible for that either, Kanta. Neither are we." Impatience crept into Ellus's voice with the high colour in his cheeks. "She was but a baby, with us not much older."

Maybe bringing it upon themselves was too harsh, Seren

amended. Her father was responsible for this mess, but they weren't innocent either. *Remember Gull Harbour.* Yet these deluded Felinae refused to admit they had broken the Accord as much as the Primordians had.

"She's not a baby anymore, and neither are we," Thane pointed out. "So which clan is your mother lady of, Reul?"

The question seemed to knock Ellus back. "None. She's dead."

Thane's mouth compressed into a thin, cruel line. "So is mine. But she didn't live and die a lady with her every whim waited upon."

The air crackled between them.

"Be careful what you say next, Sionnach," Ellus warned.

Kanta glanced warily between them. "I think we've made our point, Thane."

But Thane wasn't backing down. "And I think we all deserve to know why she left House Moralis."

This time Ellus didn't argue.

Seren pushed her shoulders back. It wasn't like she hadn't known this question would be coming. "Would you stay where everyone despises you because of your heritage?"

"With a name like Moralis, that's hard to believe, Princess."

She shrugged off her bitterness. "My uncle's name opened doors for me. But it never made them despise me less."

*Prince's bastard. Traitor's spawn. Felinae filth.* All the insults over all the years rang in her ears.

Kanta glared at her as if she didn't want to believe it. "Why leave now?"

Seren's throat dried up. She'd rather have their disdain than their pity. "My uncle betrothed me to his son without my consent. If I refused, I'd be disowned. One of the detritus."

"Typical spoiled princess doesn't want to marry a prince." Thane's upper lip curled. "Though, I hear Quinton Moralis doesn't pride himself on virtue, princely or otherwise."

There was a gasp from Vesper. Maybe Quinton had earned that, but her cousin's private life was his affair. Not Thane's.

"How far did Devan Morningstar's 'princely virtue' take him in life?" Her brow lifted. "Oh, right. Straight to the executioner's block."

It was Kanta who came back at her, spitting like a tightly wound cobra. "You don't feel a drop of remorse for the injustices Tarquin Moralis committed against your own flesh and blood. Or how many Felinae he sentenced to death, do you?"

With the ferocity of a wild stallion, Seren's temper dragged her toward a precipice. But she didn't care anymore if they hated or suspected her. "Should we talk about your sealgair's atrocities? All the dead burned at Gull Harbour?"

The toes of Thane's boots bumped hers, and he stared down at her from his couple of fingers' worth of extra height. "Oh, don't hold back, Princess. Tell us how you truly feel."

Distantly, she heard Ellus telling Thane to back off, but it was too late. Her mouth was already forming the words she'd buried for so long. "Your Prince of the Morningstars broke the Accord, dishonoured my mother, and then denied his responsibility for it and me. Like the craven bastard he was."

"That's not the way I heard it," Thane murmured, so close his breath fell on her cheeks. "I heard your mother spurned her husband and ran after Prince Devan's attentions. When Morningstar tired of her, she got her revenge." He grinned, and she imagined knocking out every single one of his teeth. "Maybe that's why you left? You needed a Felinae to satisfy you, Princess?"

One of her legs spun out at his knees, but he shot straight up, faster than any Prim she'd fought. Before she could marshal another strike, Ellus swung at Thane as he landed on his feet.

The punch glanced off Thane's shoulder, and Thane used it to grab onto Ellus and hold him close. Two powerful punches were delivered into Ellus's exposed stomach before anyone could react.

"Vesper, get the sealgair!" Kanta shrieked as Ellus doubled over in a coughing fit.

But Ellus brought his fists up again, and while she had to give him his due for not surrendering, this wasn't his fight.

"Take a seat, Reul." She eyed a smirking Thane who stood ready for round two. Good. She would enjoy putting him on his ass again.

Instead, Ellus rushed Thane with an inarticulate roar.

Thane easily dodged the wild swings and seized Ellus's upper arms in a grappling hold. While the two struggled, Seren considered stepping in, but that would make it two against one. And Ellus hadn't asked for her help. *You didn't ask for his either, but he gave it.*

It was just as well Kanta came up behind Thane then with a large pot and hit him square between the shoulders. "Let go of him, pheasant brain!"

With a startled cry, Thane let go. Freed, Ellus swayed back a step, but not far enough away. Staggering forward, Thane executed an uppercut to the jaw that dropped Ellus to the ground with a loud *thump*.

With a curse, Kanta dropped the pan and rushed to Ellus's side. Seren turned away from them to focus on the threat. Thane stood, shaking his hand, his face scrunched in pain. It looked like his wrist and forearm hadn't lined up for the last hit. Served him right. The fight had been over.

Seren settled into her stance. "Want to try your luck with me, Sionnach?"

"Any time, *Princess*," he spat, trying to flex his hand, and when that failed, raised his left.

Someone should teach him when to quit. She'd knock him to the ground and call it even for Ellus. Her foot swept round at his face—then came to a jarring stop.

Silver stood between them, holding Seren's leg immobile. The Marked had appeared out of nowhere—without the tinkling of her bell to announce her.

"Save it for the ring," she warned, her voice a quelling bucket of ice water. With a heave, Silver twisted Seren's leg, which spun Seren around to land chest-first in the dirt in time to see Llion stride in.

Thane didn't even attempt to defend himself as Llion shoved him back against the cavern wall, pinning him with a forearm across his throat. Maybe recruits couldn't fight outside the ring, but the sealgair didn't have the same qualms.

"If you want a fight, I can give you that," he rumbled in Thane's ear.

Gasping for a breath, Thane rallied with a weak sneer over Llion's shoulder at Silver. "So generous. More like whatever the sealgair wants, he takes."

Silver's bark of laughter was possibly more frightening than Llion's temper. It was doubtful anyone could take anything from the Marked she didn't wish to give. For a long moment, it looked like Llion was deciding whether to bash Thane's head against the rock or strangle him. Or both.

"You're more fool than I thought, Sionnach," he finally said, releasing him. "Few get what they want in this life."

———

SEREN SCOWLED into the pot and stirred the thin soup. Without a hare or pheasant, it wouldn't be much more than bone broth, and she had the feeling Llion wouldn't return soon. From Kanta and Vesper's muted conversation at the table, Seren deduced it was customary for Llion and Silver to leave the cavern together in the evening to check snares or hunt.

Tonight, Silver had been left behind to oversee them.

The heat from the open cooking pit licked at Seren's legs. It was a decent fire she'd built from her wilderness exercises, not that anyone had noticed. While she stirred the soup—the only task Silver trusted her with—Vesper and Kanta cleaned and cut an early spring crop of sweet peas and shallots at the table. It made her wonder if the Felinae sowed their own crops topside or if these were raided from Prim farmlands.

Supply procurement gave her something else to think about than the brooding mahogany-haired Felinae behind her. Sitting as stiffly as frost upon glass, Ellus pressed a wet cloth to his swollen lower jaw. He refused to meet anyone's gaze. Out of anger or embarrassment, she wasn't certain.

"*Davikking edred.*" The longer Llion was gone, the louder the Marked muttered in Rokkish, circling the cavern. Puffs of grey dust bloomed with each of her steps. After circling the table yet again, Silver halted and glared at them. "No brawling while I check on the sealgair, or you'll all be running the windmill until you're mewling for your mothers."

Satisfied by whatever she saw upon their faces, Silver tore down the passageway with her swords at her hips and her earring tinkling, and Seren returned to her pot.

After a while, the crackle of the fire and the muted sounds of the domestic chores were broken by the *thwick* of a pea husk. Then another hit the side of Ellus's head and fell to the table.

"What was that for?" he grumbled, rubbing his temple.

"For starting a fight you couldn't win," Kanta said, abandoning her task to sit beside him. With a critical eye and firm hands, Kanta examined his black eye and swollen jawline. His perfect nose was intact. Nothing that wouldn't feel better in a few days, though by then it would look worse.

After her examination, Kanta flicked Ellus on the ear, eliciting a yelp from him. "What got into you?"

Seren found herself watching them intently; she hadn't realized the two were so familiar with each other.

He shifted away, putting the wet cloth back under his jaw. "I don't know." At Kanta's annoyed look, he added, "You have my thanks for your aid. I hope I can always count on Clan Urso."

That seemed to mollify Kanta. "Of course. However, I'm not taking back what I said earlier." She shot a sideways glance at Seren. "Many in the clans will agree with Thane's opinions. But he's a notched arrow eager to fly at the closest target. Don't give him one."

It was sound advice, but Ellus didn't seem keen to take it.

"Sooner or later, I will be one anyway," he muttered.

Unable to listen to any more whining, Seren pointed the ladle at him. The fire hissed as the broth slopped over the side of the pot. "You made yourself a target when you left yourself wide open. And you as plain as day warned him of your strikes before you moved."

"What about, 'I appreciate your assistance, Ellus'? Or 'That looked like it hurt, Ellus'?"

Seren flicked a wide-eyed glance at Kanta. "I guess he's used to being coddled?"

Twin spots of red blossomed on Ellus's cheeks while Kanta's freckles scrunched up in a snort that made her face less severe. "She has you there, El."

Vesper, who had been quietly cutting shallots, stood abruptly. "We should collect more water."

It was sweet of Vesper to try to rescue Ellus from his embarrassment. But Thane was at the pools, soaking his hand, though his head probably needed some cold water, too. And he might be looking for another target for his foul mood. Seren stopped her stirring. "I'll—"

"Accompany Vesper, would you, Kanta?" Ellus asked with a lopsided smile of puffy lips that elicited a sigh of acquiescence from his friend. Seren frowned, more than willing to accompany the girl, but Vesper tucked her hair behind her ear and stood taller.

"I can hold my own with Sionnach, Ellus." The quiet

confidence in this statement made Seren reconsider the mettle of the girl.

"No doubt better than me," he replied wryly.

"I'm a lot harder to catch," Vesper rushed to add, though she had the grace to wince at her unintended insult. She nodded at Kanta, who had already gathered the buckets. "But if two of us go, we won't need to fetch more water after supper."

Kanta handed one to Vesper. "And someone should check on Thane. Probably best it's us."

Their footsteps and amiable conversation faded away down the tunnel until Seren was left alone with Ellus. In the silence, his open stare became more and more awkward.

"What?"

"You didn't step in," he said quietly. "You let Thane destroy this." He waved a hand around his swollen face. There was genuine hurt in his tone, though he was trying to laugh it off, as well as a thread of curiosity.

However much her unit had trained to work together to take down a threat in preparation for joining the House guards, City Patrol, or the Legion, they'd never worked cohesively—with her. Eventually, she just tried not to get in the way. True, she could've taken Thane unawares from behind, like Kanta with her pot. Even just tripped him.

But she hadn't. Such tactics went against her code of honour. And perhaps, if she were honest, there hadn't been anyone she'd ever wanted to step in and save before.

"One"—she held up a finger, stirring with the other hand—"your good looks aren't destroyed. Two, unless someone can't fight back, I don't interfere in a fair fight. It was one against one."

Ellus gave her a tight nod, so she continued, her tone turning defensive. "Three, I didn't ask you to fight for me. I could've thrown Thane on his ass by myself. And if you hadn't gotten in my way, you'd be none the worse." She raised the ladle at him again. "And don't blame Thane either—you attacked him first."

Ellus had the grace to look sheepish as he gazed up at her through long, dark lashes. The truth was hard to swallow sometimes.

"I chose to fight, and I lost," he admitted at last. His lips twitched. "And you would've won. Lessoned learned. You've had a great deal of practice winning, haven't you?"

"Not really." A mahogany eyebrow rose in disbelief, and she couldn't help how it warmed her cheeks. "It wasn't until the end of my second year that I was capable enough to win matches. When I had a winning streak in third year, it became a problem."

When she won, she was criticized for the brutality of her Felinae blood. When her classmates won, they were congratulated on the prowess of their Primordian heritage.

"So I went back to losing to the top fighters," she finished. It wasn't an easy decision. "Led to fewer fights outside the ring." And less chance of being kicked out by the Prefect and declared detritus by her uncle.

"You didn't let any of us win earlier," he pointed out. "I find it difficult to believe you let anyone beat you."

The ladle slipped in her hands and sank to the bottom of the pot.

*Never again.*

"I don't let anyone beat me, Reul. For every hit my opponents land, I make them hurt," she said, pushing steel into her voice and spine. "They might win the match, but they don't beat me." She held his gaze until she was certain he understood the difference.

"And you won matches only once in a while?" Ellus asked, his voice skeptical. Like he didn't believe her but in a way that made her flush with pride.

"Might have been more than that." She ducked her head

over the soup to buy more time to gather her thoughts. "Come to think of it," she said once the fluttering inside her had mostly settled, "I didn't make many friends."

*Except for Valera.* The thought of Valla came with a dull ache in her chest that squeezed tight.

Soft footfalls alerted her to Ellus's approach. She tensed as his arm hovered around her shoulders, giving her ample time to move if she wanted to. She didn't. The weight felt solid, and she let him lean on her. Let him pull her into a half embrace. Warmth from his body spread throughout her, settling oddly in the middle of her forehead.

"Well, if you plan to lose fights, do it soon. According to my count, it's five wins for you and zero for everyone else. We're all looking inept and rather worse for wear."

"I can't help it if you don't protect your face." A face that was very close to hers.

His swollen lips pulled back in a painful grin. "That's two comments about my face now. I'm beginning to think you like it."

Maybe she did, but he didn't need to know that. She jabbed him in the side without mercy. "You leave your abdomen open, too."

"Hey!" he gasped. "Watch it. Invalid here." His arms gently tightened around her so she couldn't jab at him again, which tilted his head against hers. Warmth spread throughout her chest. It felt . . . right.

"And for future reference," he murmured, "this Felinae has no reservations about you fighting your own battles or with you saving me."

A laugh burst from her, and Seren gave him a light bump with her hip, breaking his hold on her. "Understood. But you must learn how to win your own battles."

"I suppose I already excel at losing," he admitted ruefully.

"But if you will tutor me, then I am confident I can win my battles. I may also need lessons on when to cut my losses."

"If you wish." Agreeing to help Ellus an easy decision after Thane had pummelled him.

With one last squeeze, Ellus returned to the table, his good mood restored. He lifted the dull paring knife—the only blade they were trusted with—to attack the pile of pea pods and froze, a strange glint in his blue eyes. "You know, with you at my side, I feel like I could topple mountains."

She arched a brow. "Mountains? Let's worry about Thane first."

"I am yours to command," he said, contently, before returning to his task.

Without the ladle, she could only grin into the bubbling broth. Maybe she didn't need to win everyone over.

## 13

Some spy she was turning out to be.

Despite spending much of her time working with Ellus and Vesper on their fighting skills over the next weeks, Seren didn't learn anything more about his noble family or the prince. Since the fight between Thane and Ellus, opportunities to question them were scarce. She and the recruits were rarely left unsupervised; either Llion or Silver stayed within sight or earshot at all times. And if their attention happened to be elsewhere, all Ellus had to do was smile at her, and it became impossible to ask about his late mother and see that smile slip away. It surprised her how much she liked having him smile at her.

But after half a moon cycle without seeing the sky, Seren suspected she was more prisoner than recruit. The others, at least, were invited by the sealgair to join him topside to hunt or gather. But not her. The exclusion, and the feeling of being trapped under a mountain, grated on her until what little patience she possessed was scraped raw.

The constant scrutiny didn't help, either. Silver and Llion

were bad enough, but the morning after Ellus's fight with Thane, an older woman in a frayed garment of thick grey wool had appeared up on the high ledge. The same spot Seren's tingling had warned her about. The woman's steel-grey hair was shorn close to her scalp, and she was unremarkable in every way, being of both middling height and weight. Despite her drab appearance, she held herself confidently, with her pine-green cowl, pinned with a metal brooch, resting around her mule-like shoulders like a mantle of distinction.

The Felinae respectfully called her *Taibhseir*, and since her arrival, she'd been observing their fighting skills and disappearing each afternoon with one of them in tow. First Thane, then Vesper, and finally Kanta. Never Ellus. Never Seren. Then the rotation would start again. Sometimes the older woman disappeared with Llion, and Seren assumed it was to discuss the recruits' progress out of earshot for the woman barely spoke in Seren's hearing except to tell stories around the fire.

This afternoon, the taibhseir hadn't disappeared. Instead, she stood up on the ledge, her weathered, brown hands wrapped around her walking staff, while she watched Vesper, Kanta, and Thane perform strikes and blocks with Silver and Llion. At the top of the wooden staff rested a glittering black shard of serendium, and the same eerie feeling from her first morning swept over Seren.

Tearing her gaze from the gemstone's vitreous lustre, Seren raised her forearm to parry the swing coming her way. But Ellus slipped inside her guard—as she'd taught him—and grabbed ahold of her shoulder while snaking a foot inside of her leg to trip her. It was graceless but an improvement.

And she could've evaded him. Instead, as she fell, she took hold of his shoulders and twisted them both in the air. He landed underneath her, breaking their fall on the hard dirt with a loud grunt. This wasn't the first time she'd knocked him to the ground in the practice and drills that consumed their days. The physical exertion, however, was a welcome distraction from her failing mission.

And so was Ellus, if she was honest with herself. She pushed herself up to a sitting position, admiring the elegant planes of his face and smooth skin, a shade darker than hers. The puffy lip she'd accidentally given him yesterday only invited more attention to his mouth. Sometimes, it was difficult to remember he was her enemy, especially when he didn't try to defend himself.

"Focus," she said, including herself in the reprimand. "How will you get out of this?"

His mouth slanted upwards as he blew a dark mahogany lock out of his blue eyes. "Who. . ." She shifted lower to remove her weight from his lungs, and he hissed. "Who says I want to get out of this?"

She flushed, aware of the ridges of his hip bones digging into her inner thighs. Despite the flirting, he seemed to want nothing from her except camaraderie. That was surprisingly easy to give since only he and Vesper spoke to her outside of training.

"How will you make Thane regret picking a fight with you if you don't try to win?" she asked.

From under long lashes, he studied her, then winked. "Who says I'm not winning?"

Seren scowled and rolled off, trying to make sense of him. The flippant words were said so earnestly, she almost believed him. As she offered him a hand up, her skin prickled. Someone was watching them, and she bet it was the taibhseir. "You know I could have pulverized that exquisite nose of yours, right?"

Ellus put his hand in hers and accepted the help—a small thing—but Seren could count on one hand the cadets at the Lyceum who would have accepted such a gesture from her.

"Then I am in your debt, Princess. Ask any favour."

He uttered the title with such sincerity she could almost believe she deserved it. As she pulled, he sprang up from the ground, and their chests bumped together, those startling sapphire blues so close. The priestesses taught that the eyes were the keyhole into one's soul, and if one could open the lock, one would see the moonlight Lumina placed there to ignite their mortal bodies.

Seren wasn't certain that was true, but looking this closely into Ellus's eyes felt as if he—like the Goddess—could see everything inside of her soul. And she could, too. But instead of Lumina's light, a cold darkness coiled there.

Startled, she took a step back, and Ellus let go of her hand. The connection broke, and the image vanished. Ellus stood there, one brow lifted. He hadn't seen what she had then. It took another moment to remember his offer of a favour. What she wanted was information on the crown prince—but again, everyone could hear them.

"Who is this taibhseir? What's she doing with the other recruits?"

For the last few days, it had been on the tip of her tongue to ask. Llion hadn't explained the woman's presence beyond saying she was part of their training to be an Elusive. From Vesper, Seren had learned that *taibhseir* meant something close to High Seer. Of course, Seren knew a seer was like an oracle, in that she could divine the future. But there were no oracles left —if there ever had been any.

Ellus brushed the dirt off his leathers and chuckled. "You didn't have to beat me into the ground to ask that."

With a tilt of his head in invitation, he crossed the cavern to the water barrel near the table. While he scooped a cupful, she took a seat on the bench. He was careful not to slosh the water as he handed her the cup to drink first. It was a gruelling hike down to the underground pools to collect more.

"I don't know why the secrecy, since you'll find out eventually." He straddled the bench, facing her as she tipped the cool liquid down her throat. "As the taibhseir of all the clans, Gwenna Drakori advises the regent using her visions, but she is here to help those with Inheritances master them." He must have read the confusion on her face because he added, "Inheritances come forth during the transition between child and adult."

Inheritances—the Felinae nursemaid in her nightmare-come-true had used that word, too. "You're not talking about anything to do with the family jewels."

Over the rim of the cup, she watched his mouth twitch upward. "Nothing so mundane."

When she handed it back, his fingers briefly brushed against hers. There was no reason for her stomach to flip-flop since touch was unavoidable during their practices. Then the spot between her brows tingled, and she rubbed it to dissipate the sensation. If Ellus noticed anything amiss, he didn't show it.

"Have you noticed your senses and reflexes are far better than your Primordian peers?"

"You're saying the Felinae inherited heightened senses? From the Goddess?"

"Those are traits all Felinae possess to varying extents." Ellus stretched back to dip the cup into the water barrel, and her gaze was drawn to the flex of lean muscle. "But few Felinae in the last two centuries have manifested an Inheritance."

The date was seared into her mind. Her history lecturer had declared it the moment the Republic of Primordia on the continent had begun to decline, both economically and morally. Soon after, the ships of Luminaria's nine Founding Houses had landed on the isle. "Since the Prims and Felinae signed the Accord?"

He nodded, pleased. She hadn't pegged Ellus for a scholar, but he spoke with the passion of one who read dusty tomes by choice. "Inheritances were never common, though, occurring in about one out of every five hundred births. Until the last two decades."

"Since the war began, Inheritances have been increasing," she guessed. Like the Goddess knew the Felinae were in need of an advantage over the Primordians.

"So it appears. Of course, some lineages produce more Inheritances than others." He looked down at the cup in his hands before meeting her gaze again. "I haven't manifested one, though several strands run through my bloodlines." He lifted a shoulder like it didn't matter, yet by his strained expression she doubted it. Inheritances—whatever they were—seemed to be highly prized by the Felinae.

"How do you know you don't have one?"

And could she have one? Had her father had one? At the thought, her palms began to sweat, and she rubbed them against her thighs.

Ellus took a lingering sip, and then set the cup aside. "Most Inheritances manifest around Vesper's age, at the onset of maturity. If I had one, I would've shown signs by now."

That was a relief. She was well past that. *Thank the Goddess.*

Unless . . . "What would these signs be like?"

"Like you can suddenly do something no mortal should be able to." His eyes narrowed, piercing her. "But so little of our knowledge about Inheritances remains. Anything out of the ordinary could be a nascent sign."

She swallowed. "Like tingling on your forehead?"

He didn't laugh like she hoped he would, but he leaned forward. "Did it begin when you were between ten and eighteen?"

"I was fifteen." Months after the attack, the Lyceum physician had explained the tingling as a lasting effect of her injuries. "But nothing out of the ordinary has happened."

That was a lie. She knew it as soon as she said it. The

strange nightmare of Uncle Tarquin smothering her as a baby had been nothing short of extraordinary. The tingling had also led her out of the mountain and perhaps had tried to warn her of the rockslide and the taibhseir's arrival. But sometimes it seemed to happen for no reason, except in the presence of certain people. A coincidence, surely.

He peered at her. "Are you certain of that?"

"And Drakori's Inheritance allows her to see the future?" she guessed, changing the topic. "Have any of her visions come true?" It wasn't until the skeptical words were out that Seren realized Drakori could overhear them from the ledge.

Ellus stilled as if considering the same. "The taibhseir saw you would come looking for us here, and you did. She convinced the Throne's regent to send the sealgair to find you because she foresaw that you would be vital to achieving"—he faltered—"our survival."

Goosebumps broke out along Seren's arms. "Impossible."

Ellus merely shrugged. "Not all put stock in the seer's visions."

"Are Vesper, Kanta, and Thane seers, too, then?" The idea of Thane as someone with wisdom of the future was laughable. But the thought that she was surrounded by seers was alarming.

Ellus shook his head, and his rich mahogany hair fell across his eyes, shielding them. Her fingers itched to tuck the fallen strands behind his ear. "No, seers appear once every few generations, if we're lucky. Drakori will help them tap into their Inheritances. While much of our ancient knowledge has been lost, she carefully traverses the past to see how our ancestors nurtured their Inheritances."

There was no point arguing about the impossibility of traversing the past, so she changed tactics. "There's a regent? Why doesn't the crown prince rule?"

"He was a babe when Queen Ellowyne and King Lynus and

their daughters were murdered," he answered flatly. They would be her father's sister-in-law and brother. "Before your father was charged and executed, whispers of unrest in Luminaria sent Lady Istra Boreal to Caisteal Dìomhair to warn the royal family. On her way, she found the youngest prince abandoned in the forest. Lady Boreal was too late to save anyone else." He paused, and his meaning was clear. "Next to the infant prince, Lady Boreal had at the time, the closest claim to the Throne. She promised to safeguard our people as *riaghladair* until Prince Alban came of age."

Before she could ask another question, Ellus drew her attention to where the others had been practising. "It's starting."

In the dirt floor of the cavern, a circle had been drawn. Inside it stood Thane, who seemed to add muscle to his frame every day, and lithe little Vesper. While Llion had so far kept them to drills, he had promised they would begin testing their new skills against each other today.

Her short fingernails dug into the wood beneath her. If Vesper needed help, she'd break her code and intercede. Because this wasn't fair. No matter that pairings like this happened all the time at the Lyceum. "Thane will flatten her."

Ellus climbed on top of the table for a better view, his knee bumping her shoulder lightly. "We'll see."

"Rules," Silver announced, coming to stand between the opponents. "No weapons. You must stay inside the ring or be disqualified. Winner must put his or her opponent on the floor for a count of three. No injuries that prevent training tomorrow." The assassin scowled before reluctantly adding, "Inheritances allowed."

Thane scoffed at that but took his position. Even with her fists raised, Vesper looked like a blade of grass that a strong wind could knock over. Though, she looked lithe and agile in a cream sleeveless undershirt instead of her usual oversized yellow tunic.

Once Silver stepped out of the ring, the two began circling each other, Vesper in a crouch that made Thane a tower of muscle in comparison. He flexed his fingers, as if he were deciding where he could land a strike that wouldn't put her out of training. Vesper, for her part, stayed out of reach.

Then Thane rushed forward. His right fist came up under her guard to knock the air out of her—but Vesper wasn't there.

Seren blinked, certain she hadn't missed Vesper moving, but the girl was already behind Thane, her foot striking low and hard at the back of his knee. His leg buckled, but he didn't go down. He whirled, recklessly swinging a fist, but Vesper had already darted out of range in a blur. In another blink, she was in his dead angle again, striking his knee in the same spot. Before he could react, she was standing out of reach by the edge of the circle.

*By the Goddess, how?*

Seren's arms prickled with a chill as Vesper flashed in and out around the ring, her swiftness unnatural. Thane desperately tried to avoid her kicks, but his reflexes were no defence against her speed. Strike after strike, the attack took its toll, and soon Thane panted heavily.

Vesper paused long enough for Seren to glimpse a tremble of a smile.

"An advantageous Inheritance, the Swiftfoot," Ellus murmured.

Advantageous, indeed. "And Thane's?"

So far, he hadn't retaliated with anything other than what she'd come to expect from a Felinae.

"His is more unique," Ellus replied.

Their attention was drawn back to the match. Thane feinted a blow to Vesper's head, or where her head had been, then rushed her to bring her to the ground. But his arms swept through empty air. Abruptly, his knees buckled, and he pitched forward onto his front with a grunt. Over his motionless form stood a triumphant Vesper, her chest heaving from exertion.

Thane hadn't landed a single blow.

"Match to Vesper!" Silver called out.

Grinning, Seren stomped her feet in the tradition of the Lyceum and Amphitheatron. With more training and a blade, the girl would be deadly. Seren's grin faded. *What would a strike force of Swiftfoots look like?*

Like phantom attacks. It explained why the Legion had failed so far to capture the saboteurs.

Ellus's whistling pierced Seren's dire thoughts about the number of Swiftfoots under Llion's command. He bounded over to Vesper and raised her arm in the air in a show of victory.

She blushed and ducked her head, mumbling her thanks while Ellus clapped her on the back before releasing her.

Back in the circle, Thane had managed to sit up, and Silver crouched beside him, checking his vision. When she was done, Thane gave Vesper a grudging nod.

"Good match, Swiftfoot. I could've used your Inheritance a time or two back home."

"It's gotten me out of trouble more than once." Vesper grinned. "But I honestly can't say I'd wish to have yours, Lockpick."

Was his Inheritance thieving?

"Few would," he conceded with a grimace as he tried to stand. He looked paler than usual, his mouth set in a firm line. The leather around his knee bulged outward.

Vesper offered him a hand up, and Thane stared at it for a long breath before wrapping his larger one around hers. Between Silver and Vesper, they got him over to the table, and Seren shifted down the bench to make room.

"Was it not clear he was to train tomorrow?" Llion muttered, kneeling to unlace the sides of Thane's pant leg.

"He wouldn't fall." Vesper wrung her hands at the sight of the swollen flesh exposed. "I didn't think I was striking hard enough."

Pain laced Thane's features at Llion's inspection of the flexibility of the joint. "My sister always said," he gasped, voice rising as his knee tried to bend, "that I was too knuckle-headed for my own good. Besides, against the enemy, you don't want to show mercy."

Silver came over with bandages and hovered over Llion's shoulder as he wrapped the knee. "He'll need to soak in the pools," she observed, expression bland, "if he's to be of any use tomorrow."

Tomorrow was overly optimistic, but Seren kept such thoughts to herself.

Llion hauled Thane up by the arm, eliciting a hiss of pain before Thane clamped his mouth shut. "Don't faint on me," Llion ordered, before shouldering most of the younger man's weight to help him down the long tunnel to the underground pools.

Silver didn't spare them another look, already organizing the next match between Ellus and Kanta. It proved to be as ordinary as any at the Lyceum; whatever Kanta's Inheritance was, it wasn't useful in a fight because Ellus, as Seren was pleased to see, was holding more than his own.

After a clean hit to Kanta's midsection, Seren returned her attention to Vesper, who had joined her at the table to slake her thirst. As much as Seren was relieved and happy for Vesper's win, the strangeness of the girl's speed made her uneasy. More tales her nursemaid had whispered to the servs in the kitchen while Seren eavesdropped came flooding back. How, before the war, the nursemaid had seen fire dance along a man's fingers in the market. How the Felinae had simply vanished, leaving bowls of porridge for the Legion to find in their abandoned villages.

"How do you move that fast?" Seren blurted, eyeing the girl's small frame. It shouldn't be possible.

Vesper wiped the water running down from her wide mouth and grinned impishly. "It's my Inheritance like Ellus told you." She bit her lip, and Seren took it as contriteness for listening to their conversation. "I've always been quick, but after the taibhseir helped me find my connection to the Moon Goddess through my mark, I've been able to move faster than ever. I've been wanting to show you," she admitted, "but the sealgair ordered that we not say anything about it."

Mark? There didn't seem to be any marks or scars on Vesper. The girl seemed to be waiting for a response, so Seren stuck with the truth. "I've never seen anyone move as fast as you."

While Vesper blushed, Seren's gut clenched tight, the water she'd shared with Ellus souring in her stomach. Who knew how many Swiftfoots Drakori and Llion had already trained? What other Inheritances might the Felinae be hiding?

Here, the taibhseir had gathered a Swiftfoot and a Lockpick. And what about Kanta's? And Ellus said he didn't have one, but then why else would he be here? There must be a reason Llion had chosen these unlikely four to train with her.

Then there was Uncle Tarquin's knowledge to consider. She would need to warn him. All her life, the otherworldliness of the Felinae had been scoffed at—put down as fanciful stories and trickery. But Vesper's Inheritance was real, so the taibhseir's could be real, too. And if Drakori could scry the future, how could Seren possibly hope to get near the prince, let alone sneak information of his whereabouts out to her uncle?

The precariousness of her situation hit her in a wave of nausea.

Vesper peered at her as she bent over clutching her abdomen. "Are you unwell?"

"Cramp," she lied. She snuck a glance upward at the taibhseir whose attention appeared focused on the match. Drakori must not have foreseen Seren's true purpose here, though, or she wouldn't have sent Llion to save Seren from that rockslide. The thought soothed her roiling stomach, but it was a small relief. For how long did she have before Drakori's visions revealed the truth?

# 14

As the day dwindled into what passed as night in the cavern, Seren rubbed her temples, trying to relieve the pressure. The eerie light from the smokeless moonwood fire and the bundles around the cavern eased the strain of using her night-sight day after day, but it didn't prevent her headaches. Almost worse was the fact that she alone seemed afflicted. Her desire for a moonwood torch or two had been vetoed by Llion. The unnatural wood it seemed was in limited supply, and the smoke from natural fires would spoil their noses for hunting—though she suspected he meant tracking any Prims who might come nosing around. Not that she was allowed to outside to hunt, which only served to strengthen her irritation.

Next to her, Ellus shifted his legs, trying to find a comfortable position on the ground while Taibhseir Drakori finished another tale around the white-flamed fire. Was this the one about how Queen Raina united the warring clans of the Felinae Dominion again? The first tale tonight had been about a clan princess who imprisoned her true love in a tree because

143

anyone the lover touched fell in love with her. It was too absurd to be true, no matter if Inheritances like Vesper's existed.

After her win today, the girl was nearly asleep sitting up on the other side of Seren. Her tawny head resting on her arms that were crossed over her drawn up knees. She was in far better shape, however, than Thane. He lay in his sleeping ledge with his injured leg propped up on a bundle of moonwood. It looked preferable to sitting in the dirt, but she was loathed to be near him and his unknown Inheritance. Lockpick didn't sound terrifying, but neither did Swiftfoot until seen in action.

Her temple throbbed again. If only she had her vial of lavender-mint oil, the one Valera had surprised her with on her last moon day. Unfortunately, it had been lost with her saddlebags in the rockslide with Bay. Of course, the vial would be emptied by now. After every day of training, her head ached more than her muscles.

Drakori cleared her throat, and Seren hoped it was to dismiss them for bed. Llion and Silver had long ago retreated to wherever they spent the night.

Regrettably, the taibhseir remained seated on a wooden crate of supplies. "Once, long ago, two sister moons shone together over our isle—Lumina and Seline."

The absurdness of two moons, on top of everything else, jerked Seren upright from her slump. Everyone knew there was but one moon in the sky, and one Goddess of it—Lumina. Though, if she recalled correctly, the Felinae nursemaid in her waking nightmare had mentioned a Seline.

"This was before Sol escaped his cage in the bowels of the earth to fly his fiery chariot during the day." Hazel eyes twinkled at Seren over the flames as if sensing her rising objections to the story.

Flying the chariot was Sol's punishment for trying to steal the celestial fire from the Goddess. Was Taibhseir Drakori purposefully telling it wrong?

"Night after perpetual night, Moon Goddess Seline would listen to the mortals of our realm, while her sister ignored them. Lumina, jealous of her sister's attentions to the world below the Mists, listened when the Sun God Sol whispered of a way to keep her sister with her forever."

Drakori's attention became lost in the white flames as if she could see the betrayal unfurling there. "Some Keepers maintain he struck a bargain with Lumina—his freedom for the pomegranate seed he gave her. The next night, before Seline disappeared down to the earth, Lumina asked her to break bread with her. Hidden inside the loaf was the seed. The seed of betrayal."

From above came a snort, breaking the spell of the story.

"You doubt that the one closest to you would betray you, young Sionnach?" Drakori asked.

Thane didn't deign to open his eyes. "That's the only part I do believe."

"Maybe Lumina thought she was acting for her sister's own good," Ellus suggested. He sat spine straight as if the matter they discussed was of great theological import, and maybe it was to him. "The writings of the Light Keepers call the Sun God a trickster. Maybe she didn't realize the seed would destroy her sister's godhead."

"That's what they all say," Thane muttered.

She had to stop this nonsense. "The Goddess never had a sister."

"Well, she doesn't now," Kanta grumbled into her mug of nettle tea from the other side of Ellus.

Since the fistfight between Thane and Ellus, Kanta had kept a cool distance from her, which she didn't mind in the least. However, the underlying note of accusation in Kanta's tone compounded with the nonsense about a sister moon had Seren's hackles rising. She didn't want to examine too closely why their version of Lumina bothered her so. "Is that also my fault, Urso?"

Kanta's eyes flashed hotly, and Seren's blood quickened at the promise of a fight even as Ellus raised his hands on either side of him in a placating manner.

There was a commanding thump from Drakori's staff hitting the ground, and the sound prompted Seren to compose herself as if Master Kai were the one admonishing her. With the attention of the recruits back on her, Drakori continued, "The Goddess Seline was not destroyed, merely made unable to walk among mortals. It is said when the second moon shattered, the shards were flung into the sky to illuminate the night. There, amongst pieces of her sister, Lumina the Betrayer reigns, unable to set foot on solid earth until her sister is restored. Meanwhile, Sol's ball of fire rises to remind both sisters of their mistakes."

"The Betrayer?" Seren tore her attention from staff's black, multifaceted gemstone as it glinted in the fire's glow. "How do you know there was a second moon? Have you seen it?"

Silence met her question until Vesper lifted her head from her arms with a yawn. "We can see the stars—and they're pieces of Seline. She's all around us." She threw her skinny arms wide, pointing inexplicably around the cavern.

The infuriating argument drove Seren to her feet. "The constellations are the writings of the Goddess Lumina, our history and future laid out for all to see." Well, for the priests and priestesses to interpret. "And there's one Moon Goddess, Lumina the Light, Bestower of Wisdom, and her consort, Prince Lleufer, Warrior of Justice."

Drakori peered placidly at her over the glowing moonwood. "How do you know Prince Lleufer existed? Have you met him?"

Seren gritted her teeth. It was true no one had seen Prince Lleufer or any of the goddesses for thousands of years. "His sons from Lumina were the first Primordians. The stories tell us—"

"Ah," Drakori interrupted, with a mischievous tilt to her mouth. "The stories of the past can teach us much if we're willing to listen."

Blood pounding in her head at Drakori's insufferable reasoning, Seren stalked back to her ledge. With her face pressed into the cold rock and her back to everyone, she willed sleep to come. What did she have to learn from these stories? Nothing. The betrayals of gods and goddesses long ago didn't concern her. Just the betrayal of her father.

It was a story she had listened to many a time. A story that lulled her cracked heart to sleep with sweet promises of retribution for all she had lost.

---

A HAND on her shoulder startled her awake. *Solfire.* She'd become complacent. In the slumbering quiet of the cavern, one of her hands sought her knife, which wasn't there. The other she clamped onto the oddly gentle hand at her shoulder while her heart thumped against her chest. All this happened before she discerned the familiar scent of sweet oak in the air and the face before her came into focus.

*Ellus.*

She released him, and he held a slender finger to his finely drawn lips before he jumped to the cavern floor. In a fluid movement, he popped back up to his feet. Then his head tilted toward the tunnels.

Common sense told her she shouldn't go off alone in the middle of the night with her enemy. But this was Ellus. Besides, she needed more information on these Inheritances and how the sealgair planned to use them. And it wasn't as though she couldn't handle Ellus if he tried anything.

When she threw the blanket off to follow, a grin flashed across his face, and he took off into the grey darkness.

So he wanted to play chase.

Careful not to wake the others, she jumped down, grateful that Silver's early morning run meant she always slept in her clothes and boots. Soon her footsteps echoed in the tunnel's silence, and her nerves had her checking over her shoulder. Sneaking around at night was hardly a treasonous offence that Llion could hang her for, yet her heart fluttered at the thought of being caught alone with Ellus by the sealgair. She didn't think Llion would be happy about any of his recruits spending time alone with her, but doubly so for Ellus.

Fifty paces into the tunnel, she caught up easily, and Ellus broke into a dead run. He wasn't a Swiftfoot, yet he bounded along like a roebuck and didn't slow until they came to another cavern of serendium. The ceiling here was high-pitched with stalactites the size of legionnaires hanging down from the centre like an enormous dark chandelier. Crisp, fresh air flowed down over her face through an open crevice above, which let in a beam of starlight that lit up the spikes of violet crystal-encrusted stalagmites rising out of the ground. Gemstones covered the cavern walls, she realized, but only the ones in the light shone their true colours for her night-sight. Some were the dark purple of the ink of sea snails, others the lighter shade of crocuses.

Was this what he had brought her to see? She couldn't voice the question—it seemed profane to speak in the presence of such an awe-inspiring creation of the Goddess. Her arm passed under the light. Until that moment, she hadn't known how much she craved to feel the night sky on her skin.

Ellus met her questioning stare with a confident look before springing up, nearly twice his height. Grabbing at the protruding crystals, he scaled the curving cavern walls toward the top. For someone so uncoordinated at fighting, he was exceptional at climbing. Seren scrambled to keep up, trying to find the same holds where he'd placed his hands and feet. When he leaped out into the open air toward the chandelier —*of all the foolish things*—she expected to see him impaled on the rocky spears below. Somehow he latched onto a dangling stalactite with all four of his limbs, and in a blink, he had disappeared into the night above.

The sky—it was so close.

Seren redoubled her efforts on the slippery rock until she could see a patch of stars winking between dangling stalactites. She hesitated, eyeing the jagged rock below, but if Ellus could do it, so could she. Heart in her throat, she leaped toward the spear, and her arms and legs wrapped around the jagged structure to keep her from sliding off. Ignoring the prick of crystals digging into her palms, she slowly pulled herself up through the crack and onto a narrow precipice jutting out from the mountainside.

Thousands of stars lit up the boundless expanse, as though a child had thrown handfuls of white sand into the black depths of the sea. Tears pricked at her eyes. The magnificence was overpowering, and her breath caught in her chest on the cold, thin air.

At the edge of the precipice, Ellus stood with his back to her, his arms out wide, and his head tilted back in awe; the night sky wrapped around him, like a glittering star-dusted crown.

"It rather obliterates the soul, doesn't it? Makes me wonder if anything we mortals do endures against the stars."

It took a moment for her to realize Ellus had spoken. Then another to make sense of his words. *Obliterate.* Yes. Her perception—her entire being—seemed off balance as she stepped toward him, trying to gather her thoughts. "Our destinies are written in the stars, placed there by Lumina. So everything we do will endure."

From over his shoulder, Ellus looked at her with an intensity that pulled her the last few steps toward him. He sat down on the edge and leaned back on his hands, leaving little room for her except beside him. The jutting ledge seemed sturdy enough to hold them both, though a glance over the edge left her with no desire to dangle her legs. Climbing up here was one thing. Looking down, an entirely different matter. But if Ellus could sit at the edge of the world, so would she. Cross-legged, though.

"You can't believe that completely," he replied, as if the priests and priestesses hadn't taught that for centuries. "It implies everything that has happened—to me, to you—was preordained. According to that logic, you can't blame your father for what he did. He—we—would have no culpability."

Anger, hot and roiling, flared through her, and her gaze flicked to the sliver of the moon. "Maybe Lumina simply knows our nature—our choices—before we do. That doesn't mean we can't be held responsible for them."

"Or maybe we're put here to write our own destiny, not adhere to any fate that may or may not be reflected in the stars above."

To avoid the brilliance of his blue eyes—which might make her believe anything he said—she focused on the triangular dip at the base of his neck and collarbone, where his soft brown tunic opened at the throat. Such a delicate, vulnerable spot. A blade could easily find its way to a body's heart through there.

A shiver ran up her spine. The cold. She should have thrown her tunic over the silver-mesh undershirt Silver had given her. "Ellus, why did you bring me here?"

He gestured upward. "Isn't this reason enough?"

It was . . . and it wasn't.

At her pointed look, he sighed in defeat. "I thought you might have some questions you'd like answered without being overheard by everyone. You're rather uncurious about us—about your heritage."

"I suppose I wasn't encouraged to ask about it." That was putting it mildly. She did have questions, however, and they all clamoured to be heard—the loudest being about what she witnessed today. "Can you explain more about Inheritances? How did you get them?"

The more she knew, the more she could help Uncle Tarquin fight them.

"It's said that the Felinae are descended from the union of the Moon Goddess Seline and a rather amorous *lugh*, which is a grey wildcat if you can believe it. That is why we are supposedly endowed with keen feline senses and some of us doubly so with god-like abilities."

The suggestive waggle of his eyebrows did interesting things to his face, but Seren couldn't laugh.

"Or if you go by the tomes of the Light Keepers," he continued, warming to the subject, "the Goddess Seline put moonlight in all her children's souls so we could prosper in the long night before Sol brought forth the sun. Such light seeps out of our eyes, lighting the world for us so we never know true darkness. If we're blessed, some of that light also gives us our Inheritances." He shrugged, making the mannerism elegant. "A bit of the godhead, flowing into us, if you were."

"Our priestesses say something of the same—about the light and our eyes, not the, ah, flowing godhead. Who are these Light Keepers?"

He blinked as if surprised at her ignorance. "A group of scholars over the millennia who recorded our history and ancient knowledge before we left the Veiled Isles. Because of their wisdom, they are known as the Light Keepers and their seminal writings delve into the Elusive Mysteries. I've spent much of the last few years studying what was left of their writings. After the Night of the Broken, most of it was lost, burned as our castles and keeps were plundered."

Seren fought to not grind her teeth. The Night of the Broken could've been avoided if her father and the queen had bowed to the demands of the Consul. But that was history. Right now she needed practical information about Inheritances that would aid her uncle's efforts.

"You didn't explain Kanta's and Thane's Inheritances."

One perfect eyebrow rose at the topic change. "Why didn't you ask them?"

"Let's see." She tapped her chin. "Kanta would only give me a knife if I asked her to stab me with it, and Thane would sooner spit in my eye."

Maybe that was unfair. Last week, Kanta had begrudgingly given her an old tunic so she could make monthly flow cloths. Still, she suspected Ellus had somehow interceded on her behalf.

"I think Sionnach would sooner spit in everyone's eye, and Kanta isn't accustomed to trusting outsiders. She'll come around."

"I couldn't care less what they think of me, but I don't like not knowing if they have an Inheritance that could be used against me."

"They wouldn't dare with Llion sworn to protect you, but fair." Ellus settled back farther on his elbows, so he was almost supine, and looked up at her through a long fringe of eyelashes. His rolled-up sleeves revealed sinewy arms—arms that had wrapped themselves around her countless times during their practices.

"Kanta understands the mysteries of blood. A Bloodkin can reveal your family bloodline or if you carry illness, among other things." His lips twisted. "Her Inheritance I've experienced firsthand. After the Night of the Broken"—his voice grew thick—"after the queen and king were slain, along with the princesses, the new settlements along the river burned to the ground. Families were torn apart." He paused. "Once Kanta came into her Inheritance, she restored some of the lost lineages by identifying their orphaned descendants, some too young to know who they were at the time."

The hairs on the back of Seren's neck stood up. "How?"

"By ingesting a drop of blood," Ellus said, watching her closely.

She recalled how Kanta had tried to wipe the blood from Thane's neck like it was something precious. "And the Lockpick?" she asked to quickly move past the need for an Inheritance to sort lineages of orphans.

"His *is* an odd Inheritance. There's been but two recorded Lockpicks in our histories."

"So Thane can pick locks?" That didn't seem so terrible. A long time ago a pickpocket had tried his hand at her pocket in the market, and she'd chased him all the way back to the Detritus Quarter.

Ellus shook his head. "A Lockpick doesn't unlock physical objects. He unlocks the secrets of your heart. Ones you might not even be aware you keep."

The stars swirled before her. Her secrets. Could he have already stolen them from her?

"How?" she gasped.

"By touch. Skin to skin."

She swallowed hard, the fear tight in her throat. To think everything could be undone by a touch. That's all it would take. If Taibhseir Drakori didn't see the truth of why Seren was here in a vision, the Lockpick could steal it from her.

And to think Thane had been so close to her bare flesh while she held her blade to his throat that first day. Her hands tightened into fists in her lap. How long did the contact between skin need to be? A tap? Or would he need to hold onto her for some length of time?

Slowly, her fingers uncurled, but not of her own accord. Long tan fingers laced between her hard-callused ones, and his touch soothed the chaotic tumble inside her.

"A touch like this?" she breathed out, marvelling at their entwined hands. If Ellus were Thane, all her secrets would now be uncovered. Thank Lumina Ellus didn't have an Inheritance. Her hand had never fit so perfectly in another's.

"I haven't seen him use it," Ellus confessed. "I'm told he's learned to control it."

His thumb grazed over the inside of her palm, drawing soothing circles on the sensitive flesh that set her forehead to tingling; she felt him shiver, but it must have been in response to the horror of Thane's Inheritance. It couldn't possibly mean anything else.

The Lockpick, however, she would need to keep at arm's length, though she was half-surprised he hadn't tried to rip her secrets from her yet to satisfy his suspicions. Perhaps that fell under Llion's orders not to harm her. A thought occurred to her.

"Is that why you fought Thane for me? So he couldn't use his Inheritance on me?"

A pretty flush crept up Ellus's throat. "No, I, uh, wasn't thinking of that. It would be seen as a grave trespass if he used his Inheritance on you without your consent. Has anyone told you about your father's family—the Morningstars? How Devan received his royal title?"

Seren stiffened. "He's dead. And nothing you say will change my opinion of him." Truthfully, she didn't care about a past that had no future for her. "Does Prince Alban take after his dishonourable uncle?"

"I—I don't know." His hand, once pliant, tightened around hers. But he didn't pull away, so she didn't either. Almost as if it were a dare to be this close to her enemy.

Still, the awkward silence drew out between them, and

Seren didn't want to ruin it further with more questions about her royal cousin when it was clear Ellus was too polite to confirm her suspicions as to the moral character of Alban.

"Do you want to go back?" he asked politely.

"To House Moralis? Or to the cavern?" Something inside her balked at retreating.

"Um, either? Is it time to cut my losses?"

A strand of her brown hair blew across her face, and he tucked it back behind her ear, his fingertips spreading warmth as they softly brushed her cheek. To slow her racing heartbeat, which his ears could definitely hear, she turned her attention back to Lumina's beauty because the tenderness in his eyes was too much.

"Not . . . yet."

Ellus didn't comment, didn't speak again, and truth be told, it was difficult to think of anything to say under the moon's watchful eye. They sat beside each other, their hands entwined, as if the rest of the world didn't exist.

No House Moralis. No clans. No Throne. No war. No prince.

Just her. Just him. And the stars.

Her heartbeat fell into rhythm with his until they were one steady pulse of life. For what seemed an eon, the rhythm kept her tethered to the mountain. Without it, she was certain she would've floated off into the endless night.

# 15

Playing Elusive recruit had become tedious.

Seren drummed her fingers on her sleeping ledge where she had sat for the last hour, watching the others spar. Since waking to the banging of Silver's pot, a frenzy had consumed the cavern. Maybe the desire to top Vesper's spectacular performance from a few days ago urged them on. Or maybe the silent scrutiny of Llion and Drakori made them desperate to outshine each other in today's matches.

For Seren, an indescribable restlessness surged in her veins, a behemoth of an ice serpent, rippling under the surface. Being under the open sky with Ellus had awakened something inside her—a hunger to go beyond the cavern's walls. To get closer to her goal. For the last few days, Seren had tried to come up with a way to motivate Llion to take her to the Throne and failed.

"You came close that time, Reul." Thane sauntered out of the ring, forehead sweaty and his undershirt streaked with grey dirt from their match. His knee was mostly healed, but Silver had bound it for stability and declared it off-limits as a strike point. At the water barrel, he splashed water on his sweaty face. "Close to losing with some self-respect."

Ellus rolled his eyes at the remark. With the end of his untucked tunic, he wiped his face, then grinned at her. "If I'm getting better, it's all thanks to you."

She inclined her head as Master Kai had been wont to do after she'd learned a new movement to his satisfaction. Ellus had held his own fairly well, but the match was over when Thane incapacitated him in an arm-hold similar to the ones she had seen in matches at the Amphitheatron. Though not as well executed, certainly. Despite the loss, she was proud of how Ellus had made Thane work for every hit. Then because she knew Ellus was used to more than Master Kai's standard acknowledgement, she said, "You weren't awful."

His mouth twitched upwards in one corner, before his attention slid to the sealgair, who stood in the centre of the drawn circle, expression unreadable. "High praise, indeed. If only our sealgair agreed."

Seren stared at Llion as well, willing him to choose her next. Kanta and Vesper had sparred first, the Swiftfoot emerging as the victor after Kanta's temper had gotten the better of her. A fight was exactly what Seren needed to get rid of her doldrums, and she was the only one who hadn't fought yet today—or any day. Since the debacle on the first day with the training knives, Llion hadn't matched her against anyone. Oh, she helped Ellus and Vesper with their technique, but she hadn't truly fought against them.

"Vesper," Llion called, "you're up!"

*Perfect.* The competitive part of Seren's soul ached to see if Master Kai's teachings would be enough to beat a Swiftfoot, and she was inside the ring even before Vesper.

The young girl smiled at her tentatively, but Llion's gaze flitted over her as if she wasn't there. "Ellus, get back in the ring."

"He just fought." Seren's fists curled at her sides. "It should be my turn."

Now Llion looked at her. "Are you questioning me, Morningstar?"

She shifted her weight to the balls of her feet, ready to move should the sealgair make any sudden movements. Though there hadn't been any more violent displays of anger by him, she hadn't forgotten how Llion had pinned Thane to the wall.

"If I'm to train as an Elusive," she said, lifting her chin, "I should have a chance to show what I can do for the Throne."

She nodded at the taibhseir, whose face remained expressionless. The seer had convinced the regent to send Llion and the recruits here to intercept her. Maybe if Seren could impress Drakori, the seer would decide the Throne must witness Seren's abilities straightaway. That, and Seren couldn't sit still for a moment longer.

Llion's nostrils flared, but before he could respond, Ellus had jogged over to her side, and his friendly squeeze on her shoulder mollified some of her irritation. "Seren should be treated the same as any of us, Sealgair. What can it hurt to let her fight?"

At Llion's scowl, Ellus's hand melted away. "The Throne put Morningstar under my protection, recruit Reul. And I intend to follow my orders. If you have a problem with that, you can take it up with the riaghladair when we see her."

How Llion must hate that he'd been forced to play glorified nursemaid while the Throne dithered about what to do with her.

For a moment, Seren thought Ellus would argue further. Instead, twin spots of pink coloured his cheeks. To escape the platitudes she could already see forming in his eyes, she walked away from both of them.

Llion wouldn't risk her in a match? Fine. But she wouldn't be pushed off and forgotten about. Eyes closed, she breathed in deeply to centre herself to the rhythm of her heart. *Da-dum. Da-dum. Da-dum.* Instinctively, her body swayed back and forth to the primal beat. From beginning to end, she would stay in constant motion, like the moon's path through the sky.

"Morningstar, sit down," Llion growled.

Someone chuckled, but she didn't see who because the dance had begun. One after another, her legs executed the wide sweeping kicks of the Full Moon Rising, drawing arcs high over her head with a symmetry all their own.

The martial art was like nothing else Seren had ever experienced. Not the shock of frigid water sluicing over her skin as she swam in the Aegis, her against the elements. Not the power of a galloping horse beneath her and the wind in her face. Not the exhilaration of finding an opponent's weakness and using it against them. It was none of these things, and yet all of them combined, and more. It was tranquility and strength in a fluid harmony of mind, body, and soul. And she revelled in it.

Without Master Kai's drumming to keep time, she relied on the pounding of her heart as she flew through a series of flips and half-twists, rolls and handsprings, meant to evade an imaginary attacker in the Waning Moon portion. And slowly, a song of her own took shape in her soul to a driving cadence only she could hear.

As she pushed herself faster and harder, the muscles of her legs and abdomen burned. It had been nearly a full moon cycle since she'd practised, and her muscles were making her pay for it. She embraced the sensation, using it to push herself further. In the absence of an opponent, she fell into a routine of feints, kicks, and evades that Master Kai had drilled her with as a beginner.

As the music inside her slowed, she executed the finale, Moon Over Sunrise. Her right hand slammed to the ground, while her heel kicked up in a rotation that set her spinning with her legs scissored outward. With a twist, she landed in a perfect crouch and righted herself. Each and every nerve in her body thrummed with life. With unapologetic pride of who she was.

As her eyes blinked open, her gaze settled on Ellus. Her triumph faded as she waited for him to whistle and clap as he had for Vesper's victory over Thane. Instead, his face was carefully blank.

Not Vesper's. In a burst of speed, she rushed over to Seren, eyes large as full moons. "Can you teach me how to do that, Seren?"

A bang of wood upon rock forestalled any reply. From the ledge above, Taibhseir Drakori peered down, her eyes as dark as the serendium in her staff. "Child, who taught you our sacred art of the moondance?"

Seren's jaw went slack as she looked from Drakori to Ellus. "Your moondance?"

"I told you she was keeping secrets," Kanta hissed at Ellus's elbow.

"Were you taught it at the Lyceum?" he asked.

Seren snorted at the thought of her former classmates performing the flowing dance, so unlike the stiff and controlled strikes of Prim fighting style with their short swords and war hammers. "Lumina, no. Master—" She bit her tongue. "A master from the continent tutored me. Uncle Tarquin arranged it after . . ."

After she had healed from her attack, a note had been left by her bedside with Master Kai's name and the address of his schola. Although the note hadn't been signed, her knife—with an M for Moralis—had been tucked inside of it. A gift from her uncle.

"But the moondancers are all gone!" Kanta glared at Seren as if she was responsible for both their disappearance and finding one.

"Apparently not," Drakori mused. "We need to locate this master, Sealgair."

Llion looked relieved to be told what to do. "I'll send a bird to the city."

"Why do you want him?" How could she have been so foolish as to reveal Master Kai?

"To speak to him," Drakori assured her. "If he knows the way of our lost moondance, we'll need his help to recover it—and yours. Kanta is correct in that we thought the knowledge of our ancient art lost to us. It would aid the Throne greatly if you would give us a name and location for this man."

"Your ancient art?" Seren echoed, slowly catching up. Master Kai must have studied from a Felinae moondancer in his youth. No matter, she doubted her reclusive tutor could be found by anyone—even a seer—if he didn't wish it. Since he had taught her and not the Felinae, his allegiance was clear. And so was hers. Her lip curled. "Find him yourself. Isn't that your specialty, Taibhseir?"

Drakori pursed her lips. With her staff, she beckoned for Llion to join her. He exchanged a look with Silver, then scaled the rock with a series of leaps to Drakori's side before disappearing into the tunnels with her, presumably to send the message.

Seren kicked the grey dirt with her boot. Her gambit had drawn Drakori's notice, but not the results she desired. From across the cavern, she felt Thane staring at her, along with everyone else, until Silver assigned them all star-throwing practice. Ellus didn't move, however, and Seren shifted under his curiously wounded expression. Like she'd been purposefully withholding this from him, which was uncomfortably close to the truth.

Let him and the others think whatever they liked. She had nothing more to say.

She strode past him to get a drink and splash water over her face. Maybe the coolness would wash away her warring feelings of triumph and guilt. The ladle slipped out of her hands, however, at the heat of another body suddenly behind her. A long, tan arm reached around her to fish it out of the barrel.

"Did you know—" Ellus's voice caught in his throat, and his hand touched her shoulder for balance. A tingle ran up her neck, settling again in her forehead, but then he pulled away. Had he felt the tingling, too? Was this a form of Felinae Inheritance, or was it something else? "Did you know your father's soulshielder, Kynden Startaker, was a moondancer? The last fully trained one, we thought."

She turned around to look at him. "What's a soulshielder?"

Ellus ignored her question. "Your tutor never told you the name or origin of what he was teaching you?"

His tone was neutral, giving her the benefit of the doubt, yet her temper blazed to life. "He's an ascetic, Ellus. One who took a vow of silence. And believe what you want, but he didn't tell me anything about what he taught me. You think I would have—"

Lumina, she'd almost said she would never have agreed to learn such an art if she knew it was Felinae in origin.

"Seren—"

She held up a hand. "My whole life has been one big, long test to see if I'm Primordian enough." The words soured on her tongue, and she rushed on, not eager to examine why. "And for the past weeks, you've all been testing me." Her hands went wide, her voice rising. "To see if I'm Felinae enough."

Ellus hung his head in chagrin. When he looked up, his expression had softened. "Seren, you don't need to prove anything to me. You astonish me at every turn."

Her heart flipped—why did it flip?—just as a thud on the floor signalled Llion's return. The cavern quieted, and Seren found herself in the unlikely position of being grateful to the sealgair for the interruption. The feeling of being watched returned, and sure enough, Drakori was staring at her as if she could peel back Seren's flesh to see straight into her soul.

In silence, Llion climbed on top of the table, and she forgot about getting a drink. Dark blond braids rained down around him like a waterfall, but they couldn't hide the scowl on his face. With his arms held out from his sides, he pivoted in a circle. His long leather tunic had been discarded for his sleeveless undershirt that pulled taut over his chest. Two belts hung low around his waist with a pair of knives, and his sword was slung over his back in a baldric. He wasn't wearing his serendium knife or his bow, however. "What weapons do I have?"

Seren didn't think this test was Llion's idea. He was clearly irritated to be the centre of attention. Feet shuffled closer, but no one answered him.

"When a Prim comes after you with a sword, intent on ramming it through your heart, what do you need to know?" he demanded.

Kanta sauntered closer. "How to defend yourself."

"And while you're busy dodging his sword or striking back, what's your opponent doing?" Llion countered.

At the other end of the table, Thane snorted. "What nobs do best—shoving a dagger in your back."

"Knobs, like on drawers?" Vesper's nose scrunched in confusion.

"The nobilis are the upper class of the Primordians." Thane fiddled absently with his throwing star. "Vultures, all of them, feeding on the blood and sweat of the servs and detritus." He glared at Seren. "You and the lordling have that in common."

Her brow furrowed. For a Felinae, Thane knew a lot about Primordian society. Though he was incorrect about how the classes functioned. Each one supported the other to build a strong and stable House, except for the detritus. There were simply those who could not function properly within society's rules—as her uncle would say. Though she supposed it wasn't fair that some were born to riches and others to serve. But that was the will of Lumina, wasn't it?

From the top ledge, Taibhseir Drakori banged her staff on the rock. "We can debate inequalities in societal structures after you've both gained a wider perspective—if you live long enough to do so. Please continue, Sealgair."

"When you encounter the enemy, you need to determine all the ways they could attack you. Surprises will get you killed." Llion raised his thick arms like the great wings of a predatory bird. "Locate and name one of my weapons and you'll earn a trip outside the mountain. Fail to do so and you're on cooking duty all week."

Kanta was the first to pipe up. "The long sword on your back."

Seren couldn't help but roll her eyes at the obvious choice, though there were sighs of relief that dinner wouldn't be burned. Llion drew the sword—a utilitarian piece but well-crafted for beating on armoured legionnaires—and laid it at his dusty boots. "What else?"

"The knife on your belt, left side," Thane said in a bored tone before she could.

Llion withdrew the knife and flicked it into the wooden table a handspan from where Thane stood. He jumped backwards, then straightened.

She smirked. That left—

"Don't forget the one on your right thigh, Sealgair," Thane added.

In a blink, the other knife joined its mate in the wood. *Sol's hells.* There were no obvious weapons left, and she couldn't be wrong. If she hoped to get word to her uncle about the Inheritances, she had to leave this cavern.

After years at the Lyceum, Seren very well knew the likely spots to hide a weapon—along the back in a spine holster, under the armpits in a holster, around the torso in a band, on the thighs, calves, or boots. There might even be a garrote wound around one of his braids. She concentrated on each spot, looking for a telltale sign.

"A stiletto in each boot," Ellus called out with a cocky grin, and two skinny daggers joined the pile.

A good guess or prior knowledge?

She could imagine Valera's response. *Four blades and a sword? Compensating, much?*

Llion did another full turn, and Seren raked her gaze over him. Was there anything left? His arms were bare except for his bracers.

"The claw around your neck!" Vesper shouted with a clap of triumph. "What? You could poke someone's eye out with that."

With a grimace, Llion pulled out the strip of leather around his neck for all to see. The bone-white claw was filed to a dangerous point. How could she have forgotten about it?

Everyone turned to Seren, including Llion. For a while, she could only stare back at his piercing eyes. Should she try a garrote in his hair? Or maybe the claw-like knife was hidden somewhere? Her forehead tingled, and she scratched it absently.

"Are you to be our cook then, Morningstar?" Llion rumbled, crossing his arms over his wide chest.

"Along—" She gritted her teeth as the tingle on her forehead intensified into a stinging burn. What was happening to her?

Then, it didn't matter, because she *knew*. "In the small of your back, tucked under your belt. Something narrow and sharp—smaller than a dagger. A needle?"

A choking sound came from Thane's direction. He was *laughing*. "Where I come from if someone claims you have a needle in your trousers, that's a grave insult."

The fool truly desired for Llion to crack his head open on the rocks. But Llion didn't react, except for the flaring of his nostrils. "I suppose you're an expert on that, Sionnach." To her, he said, "Why a needle there?"

"If your hands are manacled behind your back, you could use it to pick the lock." The answer rolled off her tongue without a thought. She frowned. Where had it come from?

"So"—Thane leaned on the table in a show of disinterest—"is the princess right?"

"No."

Seren's jaw dropped. Llion had to be lying to deny her a trip outside or make her look the fool. Every part of her being insisted it was there. "It's there."

If Llion was insulted by her all but calling him a liar, he didn't show it. He leapt off the table before presenting his back to her. "See for yourself."

To refuse would imply cowardice. Her forehead tingled again. She refused to itch it. The silence grew awkward, and she avoided meeting Ellus's eyes. Once her face was schooled into a mask of coolness, she tentatively slipped her fingers below Llion's belt at the back.

Nothing. Not a thing, except his warm flesh. The blood rushed to her cheeks as she stepped back. When Llion turned around, his eyes were hard slits. "Do not accuse me of lying again, Seren Morningstar."

Behind her, someone made a noise in their throat, and Llion whipped around. "Do you have something to say, Reul?"

"Only that many live behind a lie—or two. The Keeper Iolair wrote, 'We lie so skillfully to ourselves, it becomes our truth.'"

The air crackled with tension. This didn't seem to be about whether Llion had lied about the needle anymore. However, if Llion went after Ellus, she'd intervene this time. Instead, strangely enough, Llion looked more wounded than displeased.

"Speaking from experience, lordling?" Thane scoffed.

"I would think," Ellus said mildly, "the Lockpick would be more understanding. For where secrets lurk, lies abound. And we all have secrets, don't we?"

With one thick arm, Llion blocked Thane from reaching Ellus. "Sit down, Sionnach."

Thane ignored the sealgair, his chest pushing back against the arm that held him. "Are you accusing me of something, Reul?"

"Just stating the obvious, Lockpick."

For a tense moment, she thought Thane wouldn't let it drop; then Vesper cleared her throat. "Seren, why do you think the sealgair has a needle?"

Goddess bless her, Vesper was trying to save Ellus—and maybe Thane, too—from bodily harm. But what could she say? That her forehead itched? They'd think her a fool.

"I *saw* it," she repeated, jaw tight.

It was enough to break the tension. Once Thane had taken a few steps back, Llion exchanged a weighty look with Drakori, who had watched the entire scene in silence. "Is this what you wanted, Taibhseir?"

"It will do." On that cryptic note, Drakori disappeared into the passage again.

Seren sighed. The seer's exits were becoming tiresome, and now Seren wouldn't taste fresh air unless she snuck out again with Ellus. The last couple of nights, when she'd awoken, he'd been gone—without her, perhaps. And that was . . . disappointing. She hadn't risked going back by herself on the chance he was there and didn't desire her company.

The almost noiseless sound of Llion swinging his sword home into its scabbard drew her notice, and she found him staring at her as if trying to see into her soul. "Best follow the seer if you want answers, Morningstar."

**16**

Dismal sunlight penetrated the grey clouds and stung Seren's eyes as she exited the mountain, not far behind Drakori. She blinked in the glare, unaccustomed to its shine from living in shadows. Like a starving person, she stretched her arms over her head, into the fresh air, and breathed in a lungful, savouring its tang of pine and mineral.

They were in a gully, protected on all sides by walls of sheer grey rock. A glance around told her she'd need claws to climb out of it. From one cliff, a trickle of water fell into a small pool beside a few boulders smoothed by time and water. The splash of a pebble reminded Seren that she was not alone. Never alone anymore. Another cage within a prison.

"Did you make the needle disappear?" she demanded.

Drakori ignored the question as she settled cross-legged on one of the flat boulders near the water's edge. Her staff rested nearby on the surrounding grey pebbles. In her equally grey knitted garment and silver hair, the older woman blended in with the barren oasis. One worn boot came off, then the other, along with her stockings, to reveal the callused feet of a woman who walked, not rode.

Seren tried again. "I know the needle was there. I saw it."

"You did see it." With a roughened hand, Drakori indicated the boulder across from hers.

Seren sat, though she wouldn't be placated like a petulant child. "How? It wasn't there when I checked. Is that Llion's Inheritance? Making objects disappear?"

Fear clawed up her throat. How could you fight an enemy that made weapons disappear?

"Hardly." A silhouette of a hawk crossed over them, and Drakori's gaze drifted upward to the bird with a faint scowl. "Meddling mother hen," she muttered, inexplicably.

When she spoke again, it was with more weight. "The Felinae forces may appear ragtag, but we aren't charlatans performing magic tricks. The sealgair has inherited many fine qualities from his parents. Such as loyalty, a sense of duty, and fierce protectiveness."

"Those are natural qualities."

"To be sure," Drakori continued, "though in this broken realm, where betrayal is expected, loyalty and fidelity are all the more astonishing."

Seren bristled at the insinuation she'd betrayed her Prim family. Or was the seer referring to her father's betrayal of both her and the Felinae?

"Dear child," Drakori sighed, folding her hands into her lap and straightening her spine, "if every Felinae had an Inheritance, I assure you, we would not still be living in caves."

Seren's eyes narrowed. That wasn't a denial that the sealgair had one. "But Vesper, Thane, and Kanta will help change that?"

Drakori waved away that topic. "I didn't summon you here to discuss them. You asked me how Llion made the needle disappear. He didn't."

So much for gleaning insight into the Elusives' plans. Then

it hit her. "Are you saying I made it disappear? That I have an Inheritance?"

"I already explained—no one made it disappear," Drakori huffed. "Where in the realm would it go? Now, tell me, did you feel a burning sensation here?" She tapped the middle of her forehead. "Or tingling anywhere else?"

The persistent itch and tingling in Seren's forehead and her palms—did it have to do with an Inheritance? Drakori caught her looking at her hands. "Eye on hand? Hmm."

"What does it mean?" Seren hid her hands under her, but without saying anything, Drakori already seemed to know.

"It's your Eyes opening. You have inherited future sight. Possibly present as well."

*It can't be.*

Seren scrambled to stand on the boulder, her chest tightening as she shook her head. "I'm not like you."

Unperturbed, Drakori broke out in song. "Eye on head, future read. Eye behind, past in mind. Eye on hand, sifts the sand." She tapped her forehead, then her back with one hand over her shoulder, and finally splayed open her palms in conjunction with the lyrics. "A children's rhyme, but it gets the point across."

The first two were clear enough. "What does 'sifts the sand' mean?"

Drakori crossed her palm with her finger. "An Eye on your palm means you can sift through the present to find what you are looking for. A Finder is a seer with that ability alone. They can locate objects or people in the present by a sense of where they might be or, if strong enough, through vision-walking. Often, those with Seersight will have present along with future or past sight. Rarely, however, is a seer thrice-marked."

"But you have all three," Seren guessed.

Drakori inclined her head, and Uncle Tarquin's words came

back to Seren, hard and cold. *Another path was revealed for you. A different path for House Moralis.* Was this part of it?

"Did my father have this Inheritance?"

"It's not the plague, child," Drakori scolded, but she hesitated in answering. "And no, he didn't. The Morningstar line is not known for clairvoyance. But if you wish to harness your Eyes, we must get on with it. I feel we will not be here much longer."

Seren didn't budge. "You weren't in a hurry to tell me before, and so far, I'm not convinced I am a Seersight."

"So you were wrong about the weapon you saw in the sealgair's waistband?"

"No, I—I just don't know how to explain it." Somehow Llion must have fooled her. Seren gritted her teeth. "Even if I am a seer, why should I learn to tap into my Eyes?"

Drakori didn't flinch at her scowl. This woman could call herself *taibhseir* all she wanted. It didn't mean that she was a seer, or that Seren herself was one either. But . . . if what Drakori said was true, Seren would be able to see where the Felinae prince was hiding.

*That* would be useful.

"You already have your reasons, child."

"Could I see my future? Or past?" she asked.

"Those with the Eye on their back can see their past, though it can be a dangerous temptation for Seersights to live in their memories until they are unable to return to their corporeal bodies."

Something akin to regret or sadness flickered across the woman's lined mouth. "But a Seersight cannot divine her own future. A few powerful ones manipulate Time's Flow to show them what they wish to know by seeing the futures of those around them, but the Flow does not always bring forth what is desired. It is up to the Goddess to decree what we see.

"Others never learn to use their Inheritance and are drawn

into wild, violent visions when their unused Eye latches onto an eddy in Time. Then their soul is forced into the temporal and into the body of another until that eddy plays out." The older woman peered at her. "You must take care. Such a situation can end badly for a trained seer; for the untrained, she may become trapped in the past or future, unable to return to her corporeal body. And without a soul, the body will wither away."

In a chilling rush, the memory of being inside her uncle's body and standing over her cradle swept over Seren. "Are all past visions dangerous?"

"Only the ones the Seersight does not initiate herself. The more a seer suppresses her Eyes, the more violent her visions will become." The pinched expression on Drakori's face softened. "That's why it is urgent we train you now that your Inheritance has shown itself."

"What of the future? Is it the same?"

"The future is usually too"—Drakori waved her hand in the air like a butterfly—"weak and changeable. The past, however, demands to be heard."

Seren's scepticism reared. "The future is written in the stars by Lumina."

The woman's mule-like shoulders sagged. "If so, it is not one we can read. A future foretelling is never absolute. There is, you might say, a path for us." That word again. *Path.* Seren was coming to hate it. "But every path has many side trails. Some lead to the same destination, while others lead elsewhere. A vision is but one possible path. Our actions or lack of action can change it."

Seren felt like screaming. *What good is Seersight then? Why bother with it?*

"Because sometimes, your visions will be true. Sometimes, our action means a better outcome for all."

Panic seized Seren at the uncanny answer to her unvoiced question.

Drakori held up a hand. "And no, I didn't read your mind—only your expressions, and that does not take any special talent. Are you ready to test your future sight, Seren Morningstar?"

Strangely, she was. Since Prince Alban had a seer, it was an advantage she needed to harness—for Uncle Tarquin, of course. "I suppose you saw this happening, anyway."

Drakori's mouth twisted upward a touch. Acknowledgement enough.

The taibhseir, for all her prowess, must still not have seen a glimmer of Seren's true purpose among the Felinae. If Drakori had, Seren reminded herself, then she wouldn't have sent Llion to save Seren. Or he'd have her in chains by now. Strangely, it was knowing how Llion would react to the truth that comforted Seren in the presence of the taibhseir's Inheritance.

But how long would it be before Drakori saw something damning in Seren's future?

"For your first exercise," Drakori said, cutting through Seren's misgivings, "I want you to expand on your vision of the needle. We might learn why the sealgair may need it one day."

More than a little disconcerted, Seren settled herself into a similar pose, palms on her knees, back straight, eyes closed.

"Breathe deeply, in and out like the ebb of a wave."

Within a few breaths, Seren fell into the rhythm Master Kai had drilled into her.

"Imagine a river. In this river flows all time: yesterday's, today's, and tomorrow's. For those without Seersight, it flows around them, embracing them along the journey from childhood to old age. The future flows down from a waterfall, coming closer, until it reaches them for a moment, becoming the present. Then it, too, passes by into the warm pools of the past."

A gentle buzz warmed Seren's hands, forehead, and back,

and she almost felt as if she were floating in such a pool on a warm, hazy summer day. She had never thought of time that way before, but the clarity of the analogy struck her.

"Those with Seersight, however, may use their Inheritance to move through the water, to follow the currents of the future or the past. Now hold the image of the needle in your mind."

It was bone-white and sharp. Too large for sewing fine clothes.

A finger tapped her on her forehead, and the tingling began in earnest. "Now, open your inner eye."

Seren cracked an eye open. Drakori sat on her boulder, eyes closed, face serene, but upon her forehead was a black circle with a diagonal slash through it.

Just like Ty's ring.

"What is that?" Seren scrambled backward off the boulder. Fear pressed in, taking away her air, and she braced herself for the white light and the impact of the ringed fist.

"It's the Eye of the Goddess," Drakori said, peering at her. "Those who have an Inheritance are marked so."

"It wasn't on your forehead earlier." And she'd never seen it on her own.

"One must channel their Inheritance for it to appear."

Was Drakori lying? Were the Felinae involved in her attack?

"Vesper doesn't have one," she continued stubbornly.

Drakori threw her hands up in the air. "I suspect if she slowed down long enough for us to see, she would."

It was Drakori's exasperation, more than her words, that helped Seren slow her racing pulse.

"Does it mean anything else? I've seen it before," she hedged, "on a ring."

Drakori looked at her strangely. "Where did you see this ring?"

"In a book," Seren lied.

Drakori pursed her lips, but she didn't question her further.

"The circle is a symbol of the moon and the shape of the divine soul. But on the ring, the circle also symbolizes a shield, and the diagonal line represents how the Goddess Seline cleaved the soul into two for two mortals to possess. All of us given mortal life are destined to search for the other piece or pieces of our soul. For some of us, that other soul is romantic love. For others, it is platonic or familial. But it is the most sacred of bonds in our culture. Few find the missing pieces to their soul in this life. Those that do undergo a ritual binding with a ring."

A sacred bond? For Seren, the symbol meant nothing but fear, pain, and shame.

"Those who are soul-bonded," Drakori continued, "are bound to protect one another from harm, not only from physical wounds but from that which would tarnish one's soul. In the tongue of our ancestors, *unamkhara* means—"

"Soulshielder." The meaning had slipped into Seren's mind. "Ellus said my father had one." Speaking of Devan Morningstar was like pouring a bucket of cold water over her head.

"Aye, Prince Devan and Lord Startaker were soulshielders to one another."

"So where was this Startaker when my father decided to pursue a married nobilis woman?" Some soulshielder to let her father tarnish his soul.

Shadows of guilt flickered in Drakori's eyes as her gaze drifted away. "Devan always let Kynden get away with too much, and Kynden—that boy rarely could give advice. Sparkers have fire in their souls and tempers to match. But he was loyal to his soulshielder. If I had but seen all the currents in Time's Flow . . . "

Drakori paused, lost it seemed in the past. When she spoke again, her voice was sharper. "Suffice it to say, we might all make different choices if we knew precisely how our actions would affect ourselves and others."

*Choices.* The pebble Seren tossed into the stream sunk to

the bottom. She would not feel sympathy for the man who had flaunted the Accord and abandoned his unborn child out of shame. "A conscience would have done the same. Pity Devan Morningstar didn't have one."

The older woman bristled. "You know nothing of the prince, or you'd know how absurd that accusation is. Do you want to see if you're right about the sealgair's needle or not?"

Seren straightened, knowing full well the woman was manipulating her. "To be clear, I want to know if you're wrong about me being a seer."

Drakori harrumphed. "I am never wrong about Inheritances. If you require more proof, you must open your inner eye, and then the Goddess mark will appear on your forehead."

*Proof.*

For all to see. Dread squeezed her chest tight, but Seren met the challenge in the old woman's swirling hazel eyes. Then she closed her eyes and took a deep breath.

"Go back to your river, the Flow of Time, and enter it," directed Drakori.

In her mind, Seren pictured a river much like the Aegis looked outside the city on a placid, sunny day. She took a step into the current, the pebbles digging into the soles of her bare feet, the icy water cutting against her ankles.

"Pick up a stone." The seer's voice sounded small, as if far away.

Seren reached down into the water and pulled out a flat, round stone. Everything was overly bright and hazy, like in a dream.

"Your Eyes are like smooth skipping stones. Send them out, up the river to the time that hasn't come to you yet. To the future."

The stone was heavy in her hand, her forehead burning.

"Look in the water, Seren, with your Eye."

The sound of rushing water filled in her ears as the river surged toward her. "For the needle?"

Drakori's voice became stronger, more insistent. "What into yourself, Seren Moralis. What do you see?"

Seren looked into the waist-high water, into her distorted reflection. Long, thick brown hair. A proud nose in an angular face. Dark brown brows and eyes. And in the middle of her forehead, the mark. Proof. Seren reached out toward it, but her reflection sank into the murky depths. Panic seized her. *Come back!*

She plunged her hand in, desperate to catch it. Pain radiated up her arm from a hundred little stings, and she gasped. Something had a hold of her, and it wouldn't let go. The water surged, rising all around her until it washed over her head. She struggled to get a breath, to free herself by kicking and thrashing against the downward pull of whatever had her by the hand.

*Goddess help!* As the dark water closed over her, she looked up toward the surface for Taibhseir Drakori, certain she'd see the old woman's face. But no one was there.

---

With a dull ache in her head, Seren awoke. She lay in the quiet light for a while before realizing she was in her bed—her enormous featherbed in House Moralis. She should probably wake up. Uncle Tarquin would be looking for her at breakfast, and she wanted to speak with Valera first. On her desk sat a silver tray with a pot of hot chocolate and a folded note. She snatched it up, her eyes flickering over the unfamiliar hand.

*I missed you.*

Strong arms slipped around her shoulders from behind, and she was swept up in an embrace. The arms let her go, and she turned, not knowing whom she'd find. Her nose seemed to be all snuffed up.

"You're back!" Quinton grinned at her, dimple and all. One dark lock hung over his brow. The sight of him smiling buoyed her spirits, and she rubbed her hands up and down the sleeves of his white silk shirt—just to be sure he was real. It was so good to be home. Though where she'd been, she couldn't quite remember.

His hands came to rest on her shoulders, his face suddenly grim. "The city is laughing at me, cousin, because of you. Why did you run away?"

She had run away. That's right. How could he not know that she was sent to spy on the Felinae? Why hadn't Uncle Tarquin told his son about her role in his plan? "You must know, Q."

Quinton's gaze shifted behind her, his face clouding with anger, and she twisted her head to see another man in her room, this one wearing black and looking out the open window with his back to her.

"Tyberius?" she called. When he looked over his shoulder at her, his wry grin sent a rush of warmth through her veins.

Quinton's hold on her disappeared. She reached for him, but her fingers snatched at nothing. Where did he go? Maybe Ty knew?

"You ran away, Tabby." He said it lightly, but Seren could hear his sorrow.

In a few steps, he crossed the room to her. He didn't touch her, but she was now close enough that she had to tilt her head upward. Immediately, she wished she hadn't. Those wild green eyes of his were heated.

"Didn't I deserve a farewell, Seren?" The words were both a caress and a scrape along her skin.

Had he deserved one? She didn't think so.

"After Pledging Night, you knew what I had to do." He'd been at the Consul meeting. At the betrothal.

"But leave without me? We never got to talk."

"I thought you had already forgotten about me. *Easy come, easy go.* Remember?" Why was she telling him this? Everything seemed so foggy.

"How could I forget about you?" His lips barely parted, yet the memory of the hot, hurried kiss washed over Seren's mouth.

"You walked away like it didn't matter."

"You were promised to my sword brother. Is it him you want, Seren?" Ty cupped her chin with his hand and ran his thumb over her lips.

A rush of heat spiked through her. "No."

"Do you want me?"

*Yes. Maybe. I don't know.* She closed her eyes, saw Ellus's face, and the touch stopped. Ty had vanished.

A flash of gold drew her to the open window. In the courtyard below, Quinton, dressed in his legionnaire armour, was marching a manacled man in a grimy cloak out of the cell tower.

Did this mean Quinton and Tyberius would be successful in capturing the Burner of Gull Harbour? His physique didn't resemble Llion's, however.

The prisoner struggled, the skin on his arms red and raw looking, but Quinton's hold didn't waver.

A thick mist swept over the courtyard. Something wasn't right. The sound of roaring water assailed her ears, and she covered them, cringing in pain.

*I am stone. I am stone. I am stone.*

"Don't come home, Seren," said a girlish, spiteful voice. "No one wants you here."

She flinched as if she'd been struck.

"Who is that?" Taibhseir Drakori's stern voice echoed in the rising mist. "What are you doing in my dreamscape?" There was no reply, but Seren had the impression of a girl in braids sticking out her tongue before the mist enveloped everything.

———

WHEN SEREN OPENED HER EYES, she was still sitting on the boulder by the pool. Her head felt thick, like it was wrapped in a pile of wool blankets. Had she had a vision of the future? But Drakori had said a seer couldn't foresee her own. Truthfully, it had felt more like a dream, though she could remember little about it. Quinton had been there. Ty as well. And she had returned to House Moralis, so maybe it was a future after her mission here had been completed.

Across from her, Taibhseir Drakori remained seated, her eyes closed and twitching back and forth underneath her eyelids.

Cautiously, Seren leaned over a small pool of water trapped between the boulder and smaller rocks. Her reflection revealed the fading remains of the circular mark with a slash through it on her forehead. She swallowed down her uncertainty. It was only visible when she was using her gift, she reminded herself. No one back home need ever see it.

"Resorting to eavesdropping?" Drakori scolded.

Seren's heart leapt into her throat, but Ellus stepped away from the mountainside. Her gaze narrowed in on him. How long had he been watching?

"Apologies, Taibhseir. It was rude of me." He flashed Seren a tentative smile, head so low that he peeked out at her through his mahogany strands. "How did the session go with our new seer?"

Using her staff, Drakori struggled to stand, as if she too were off balance, and Ellus rushed to her side to help her off the boulder. She waved him off. "We have more pressing matters, my lord. Inform the sealgair one of his informants will be captured by Tarquin Moralis. We leave at once."

**17**

———

In their haste to leave the mountain, Seren didn't have time to sort out her vision in Time's Flow. Dangling off a mountainside seemed the worst time to let her thoughts stray, but the question of who Llion's informant might be would not rest. Somehow Drakori must have entered her vision and recognized him.

Distracted by that new thought, Seren's foot slipped, sending a few loose stones the size of her fist tumbling down. "Heads up!"

The stones narrowly missed Ellus, who was directly below her. Below him, Vesper swung lightning-fast out of the way. The girl shot her a reassuring smile, hanging one-handed longer than necessary in a show of strength while Seren scrambled to keep from dislodging more or losing her borrowed pack of meagre possessions.

"If Morningstar falls, I'm not catching her," Kanta called from farther down, where she and Thane were two tiny spots against the cliff.

"If she falls, she'll take us all with her," Thane muttered darkly.

A charming thought, which almost made the situation better. Seren ignored the inclination to brush the sweat collecting on her brow. Going up hadn't been this difficult. Even Drakori, who had to be three decades older, was climbing at a respectable pace over the rock.

"There's a better hold to your left, over and down an arm's length," Ellus offered. While the others continued downward, he waited and stared up at her with full confidence.

"Morningstar!" Llion bellowed from so far down he was the size of her thumb. "Eyes on the mountain."

*Eyes.* Seren turned back and found the crevice Ellus had pointed out to her. Slowly, she began her descent again. How many Eyes did she have? One? Two? Knowing the future would be helpful—if it could be pinned down. Present sight, however, would be the most useful.

Then maybe she could learn who it was that Quinton had put in manacles. She hadn't been able to see the man clearly, and now her memory of the vision was blurry. The question of who had betrayed the republic to be an informant for their enemies vexed her.

One familiar face from her vision reluctantly came to mind. Even if Ty wasn't the one in manacles in her vision, he had been spying on the Consul meeting, and it begged the question, for whom?

The muscles in her arms and legs protested the unending strain, pushing the unsettling idea of Ty as a traitor out of her mind. It took all her concentration to follow Ellus's whispered directions or risk proving Thane correct. And soon his voice lulled her into a smooth rhythm, hand, foot, hand, foot.

Once they reached the ground—after descending what Seren figured was triple the height of the thirty-tiered Amphitheatron—Llion allowed them a brief rest before plowing into the pine-covered hillside on a path only he could see.

Eventually, Drakori drew Ellus into conversation about his reading of some ancient scrolls, which suited Seren as she had no desire to talk after the gruelling climb. But it wasn't long before Vesper fell in step with her.

"Do you think the sealgair will need us? For his rescue mission?" A mixture of excitement and wariness churned in her large eyes.

That particular idea had not yet worked its way into Seren's worries.

"Since he barely lets us practise with weapons, I can't see him putting untried recruits into action."

Despite arguing with Llion that she and the other recruits should be given weapons to protect themselves on the journey, he had refused. And she was beginning to think it was more about keeping her unarmed.

Vesper's thin shoulders slumped, but she rallied quickly. "Well, if we're to be stuck at the Wolvair den during the mission, we'd best savour the fresh air."

Seren perked up at this tidbit of information. She'd have to take careful note of natural landmarks so she could inform her uncle. To cover her interest, she sighed. "I had hoped we'd head to the Throne first, so I could make my appeal to my cousin."

In the middle of inhaling the scents of the forest, Vesper stopped and stared. "Stars, I forgot! Prince Alban is the nephew of Prince Devan of the Morningstars. They were all your cousins, your aunt and uncle."

Seren looked away, so she wouldn't have to explain her dry cheeks. They weren't her family. But her curiosity did itch about one matter. "Why do you all call my father 'Prince Devan of the Morningstars'?"

Vesper brightened. "Oh, that's the title Queen Ellowyne of the Fallenstars conferred on him when she married his older brother. It's not uncommon tradition amongst the Felinae, to raise the sibling of your consort since the royal family is so small. But my mother also said Queen Ellowyne wished Prince Devan to be her representative in Luminaria. It was thought that your Consul would respect a prince more than an ambassador."

At Vesper's wince, Seren shrugged. They both knew how that had turned out.

"And now, I guess you are Princess Seren of the Morningstars."

*Heir to a legacy of war.* Some title. "I don't think being a princess fits me, to be honest."

They resumed walking, and after a while Vesper spoke again, her voice subdued. "You may not be the only royal to think so. A few years ago, there was a rumour that Prince Alban's older brother was found alive."

Seren's heart skipped a beat. "A rumour?"

"As far as I know." Vesper shrugged sheepishly. "I shouldn't raise your hopes for nothing. But I guess it would be a comfort if he had lived, wouldn't it? More family for you." In the silence, Vesper kicked a pine cone, sending it skittering over the gnarled roots, crisscrossing the path. "Anyways, to go back to your wish to see the Throne . . . Prince Alban isn't 'the Throne.' At least, not yet. Riaghladair Boreal—our regent—sits the Throne until he marries, and then his wife will sit the Throne with him."

Seren had to concentrate on the words Vesper's mouth was forming. "Is the crown prince to marry?"

Uncle Tarquin would not want another heir to the Felinae kingdom born.

Vesper looked surprised at the question. "Before his coronation. It's tradition. A queen must always sit the Throne."

"Why?" While gender didn't keep a nobilis Prim from becoming a matrona, a senator, or a consular, there were notably few women in such roles.

"Because the Goddess gave her mortal reign to Raina, the

first queen of the Felinae, and she, in turn, chose the ladies of the clans. It's the best way to ensure proper succession." Vesper gave her an amused look. "A babe's mother is never in doubt."

True. Seren stooped low to avoid a low branch. "So why are we headed to the Wolvair den? Is that the sealgair's clan?"

"Lady no, it's the closest den to Luminaria from the east." Vesper covered her mouth, like maybe she shouldn't have said that.

"Are the Wolvair also underground?"

"All the clans are underground. It's where we went after the war began. Taibhseir Drakori had a vision and led us to the dens. She says the Keepers created them long ago from the serendium." Vesper glanced sideways at her, and Seren remembered their argument about the rock's origins.

Still, this was information Uncle Tarquin would do anything to possess. "Are there many clans?"

"Well, there's six. My clan, the Llewyn in the southwest. Clan Stagona isn't far from where we were in the Selinens. The Urso and Ermine dens are farther west, on either side of the mountains. Clan Talúin—"

Thane shouldered past her, his pack knocking into hers, and Vesper stumbled forward. "Why don't you draw her a map, Llews? Better yet, deliver it straight to her uncle."

Before Seren could think of a retort, Vesper righted herself and rolled her eyes. "Oh, drink piss water, Sionnach."

He scowled at them both for good measure but stomped away. However, Seren didn't dare ask more questions, too preoccupied with the thought of what the Lockpick might do if he came to possess her secrets.

For the next three nights, they slept under the stars. The rocky ravines gave way to hillsides of towering pines that led into meadows of yellow grasses and dull pink heather. The needles on the trees broadened into leaves as they made their way south, toward Luminaria. Seren soaked up the light of the sun and the moon and enjoyed Vesper's aimless chatter and Ellus's quieter company. He didn't outright avoid her, but he didn't seek her out. Before bed, she tried using her Eyes under Drakori's instruction, but the river of Time—past, present, or future—evaded her.

On the third night, when Lumina was high in the sky, Seren returned to her blanket after failing yet again to access Time's Flow and found Ellus missing. The rest of the group was fast asleep from the gruelling march—except Drakori, who sat staring into the fire, and Llion, who had climbed a large oak for the first watch.

Seren nudged Vesper with the toe of her boot and indicated Ellus's empty blanket. The sleepy-eyed girl pointed toward a cluster of crags at the top of a nearby hill before curling up under her blanket.

Maybe it was the stars reminding Seren of that night on the mountain alone with Ellus that had her feet making another climb. Maybe it was that he'd been closed off to her since the discovery of her Inheritance and the capture of the informant.

From the trees, she spied him sitting on the rough white stone that jutted out from the hillside, his slim, straight back toward her. Moonlight glinted off the deep reds in his hair while stars blanketed him on either side. The sight made her hesitate in the shadows.

"Can't sleep either?"

Of course, he knew she was there. "You're angry at me, aren't you?"

She planted her feet solidly behind his rock and braced herself for his response. She couldn't bear to ask if he hated her now. Usually, she knew when she was unwanted. Her enemies insulted her. Fought her. Or snubbed her.

Ellus had done none of those things.

"Why do you think that?" he asked, but he didn't turn around.

*Because you've stopped talking to me?* That sounded so much like the pathetic nobs that chased Quinton that she couldn't say it.

Her cheeks burned as she came around the rock to face him. "Is it because of my Inheritance? Or because I can moondance?"

Or because he'd finally recognized that Kanta and Thane were right to distrust her?

"When I was little, I dreamed of having Seersight," he admitted up to the sky, lacing his fingers behind his head. "It might've made certain aspects of my life easier. But the burden of seeing the future, or possible futures, is heavy on the shoulders of a mortal—maybe heavier than any other cross to bear." He met her gaze. "I'm not angry with you, Seren. Maybe I'm angry with myself. And maybe a little resentful of the life Seline chose for me."

She frowned, even though she was relieved. "Careful, or I might think you do believe in fate."

That earned her a wry grin. "Fate, no. Destiny, yes? If one can believe there is a purpose to one's life but that the end is not yet written. I confess part of me is envious of your training. I've never seen anyone moondance. It was a sore reminder of what else I lack from my Felinae heritage. I've been away for so many years, some will argue I'm not Felinae enough for my responsibilities. But that's not your fault."

His voice grew grave as he looked out at the silhouette of the treetops darkening the skyline. "From those who have the greatest gifts bestowed upon them, Seline asks for the greatest sacrifices. So perhaps it's for the best that I am not bestowed with the greatest gifts."

"Sacrifice?" she echoed, horrifying tales from her nursemaid coming back.

"Personal sacrifice, like a life of servitude or putting others before yourself." He rolled his eyes, and suddenly all felt right again. "You do have some strange ideas about us."

As if to take the sting out of his words, he held out his hand to her in silent invitation. Before she knew it, she had slid her fingers through his and settled down beside him, shoulder to shoulder. The warmth of him tingled through her palm and up into her forehead. After its absence the past few days, the familiarity of it comforted her, and she welcomed it.

"Enough about burdens and sacrifices. Let's play a game." A grin lit up his eyes. "I'll tell you a truth about me, and then you return the favour."

Seren shrugged to hide her eagerness to learn more about Ellus and her trepidation that she might let too much of the truth slip. She'd always preferred the challenge version of this game when she and Valera played.

"I'm nearly twenty," he began.

He must know how old she was—almost as old as the war. "I'm nearly nineteen."

"See, that didn't hurt," he teased, squeezing her hand. "I was born at Caisteal Dìomhair. You?"

"You must know I was born in Luminaria."

"Consider it a warm-up." He winked. "I lived once in a city, though I saw little of it."

There were no other cities than Luminaria on the isle, and of course, he didn't grow up there. "You've lived on the continent?"

Ellus nodded. "Soon after my parents died. My aunt didn't think it safe for me here. She took me to Andaavia, where we lived with a relative of hers."

Andaavia was said to be a cursed land of ice. There were tales of colourless beasts with fearsome wings who lived under its frozen seas. Not even at the height of its power had the Republic of Primordia sought to conquer the Ice Court.

"Why wasn't it safe for you in the dens?"

"My family was dead, and my aunt didn't want anyone finishing off my lineage while I was young and weak." He sighed. "I guess not much has changed."

"You shouldn't think of yourself as weak. I don't." That drew a small smile of disbelief. It was true, though. "Your character doesn't lack strength. You've stood up to Thane and the sealgair for me. I appreciate that."

"You *do*?"

She laughed and gave him a gentle shove, her fingers sliding over the supple leather of his jacket. "Maybe I didn't then, but I do now." She cleared her throat. "Not to wish you ill, but couldn't your aunt continue the lineage?"

"Oh, she's my foster aunt. I'm fortunate she found me outside my parents' home the night they died, or I might've grown up an orphan, unwise to who I am. Or died from the elements."

The image of her uncle standing over her cradle burned in Seren's mind. Yes, they both were fortunate to survive their infant years. How was it she had so much in common with this Felinae?

"My mother washed her hands of me and remarried." Something akin to sympathy was building in his eyes, so she lifted her chin. "But my uncle is—was all I needed. He taught me to be proud of who I am—a Moralis. He—" She faltered. "He shaped me into who I am."

"Until he handed you off to his son?"

She scowled. She hadn't been handed to anyone. But there were questions in Ellus's raised eyebrows that she didn't want to go into. "What was Andaavia like?"

"Cold," he said with an easy laugh and exaggerated shiver.

Seren rolled her eyes, but a streak of jealousy wound itself around her heart. She'd never been off the isle, though Quinton and Ty had spent a year with the Legion on the continent. She still had the one letter they had sent her, ostensibly from them both but it hadn't been in her cousin's handwriting.

"I returned recently," Ellus continued, "to become acquainted with the scions of the Felinae court. It was . . . lonely in Andaavia."

"I was raised with my cousin," she offered. "There were children around, but none we were permitted to play with." Seren paused. "After Quinton turned nine, I didn't see him much."

"Until you went to the Lyceum?"

Seren snorted. "He avoided me like the plague there, like everyone else except my friend Valera."

"But you are his own kin."

The familiar ache squeezed her heart. "Yes."

"And if he wouldn't tolerate you, no one else would," Ellus surmised to her shame. "Despite this, your uncle betrothed you to him? And Quinton agreed?"

"He did, they both did," she whispered. The betrothal, she reminded herself, was a sham to have the Felinae trust her. Yet Quinton hadn't given her any indication that he understood his father's plans for her. She felt a stab of annoyance at her uncle for the secrecy.

"Your turn. Any marriage proposals at court?" She smiled in jest, but Ellus paled.

"A few." His fingers found a small pebble, and he threw it into the stars as if in protest to his destiny. "My aunt's been pressing me about choosing a suitable wife, by which she means accepting her choice."

"And you don't like your aunt's chosen one?"

"I haven't met her," he admitted. "Her father kept her with their clan instead of sending her to Caisteal Dìomhair with the other noble heirs."

"I can't imagine being married." Her pledge to House Moralis was the sole commitment she desired. "Do most

Felinae marry young? Vesper said the crown prince is also set to marry."

Her words left Ellus speechless, and she wondered how she'd blundered. But he cleared his throat. "Ah, yes. I mean, no. We don't all marry young." His smile returned, though it seemed strained. "But there's my family's legacy to be considered. Just as I suppose, the prince is concerned about his own."

Before she could ask more about Prince Alban, he said, "I'm surprised your uncle betrothed you to his son. My aunt won't consider anyone who does not bring an advantage to the union."

She bristled, but he hurried on. "I meant no slight on your person. You"—he lifted their entwined hands—"were already a member of House Moralis. What further gain would Tarquin Moralis achieve by the marriage?"

Seren's brow furrowed. She couldn't say that the betrothal was made up to give her a reason to run away.

"All I've got is me," she confessed to the stars, desperately hoping, suddenly, that it wasn't true. And it wasn't. She had Valera. Uncle Tarquin. Maybe Tyberius, too—if he truly was innocent in her attack—but they seemed so much farther away than these stars. Than Ellus and his acceptance of her.

"There's more power in you than you know, Seren."

The wonder in his voice resounded through her. She turned to him, and their eyes locked, drawing her closer. Something warm bloomed in her chest. He moved a hair's breadth toward her until his lips ghosted gently over hers.

Another kiss flooded her mind, but, no, Ty had walked away from her. She was free to kiss anyone she liked. Even her enemy. Was Ellus her enemy though? It was so difficult to remember who he was.

His lips slanted over hers, but she wrenched herself backward. "What is this, Ellus?"

"I think I'm falling in"—he raked a hand through his hair rather sheepishly at her glare—"er, on my face? I'm drawn to you, Seren. Don't you feel it, too?"

A new flush filled her as she stood and backed away from him. She did feel something—or the spark of something. But Ellus couldn't be the one Lumina had chosen for her. Could he?

Then a dark thought speared her. "Did the sealgair or the taibhseir put you up to this? To kiss me and gain my trust? Find out if I'm telling the truth?"

He rose slowly, face solemn. "I swear on the honour of my parents no one has put me up to kissing you." He ran another hand through his mop of hair. "Llion would sooner string me up by the teeth."

Was it the truth or a pretty lie? Seren couldn't tell. The heat in her body chilled to cold determination. Maybe it was best to clear the air. "Well? Ask me, so we can get it over with. You want to know if my uncle sent me to spy, don't you?"

A question she had no idea how to answer.

Ellus took a step toward her, palms up. His eyes burned with a dark intensity she'd never seen in him before. "You don't have to justify yourself, Seren. Not your existence, not your decisions. Not to me."

Her knees buckled, and a choked cry burst out of her. His words unlocked a tidal wave of emotions, and they engulfed her.

*Resentment* that she'd always had to justify her existence— to the nobilis and the city, Quinton, her mother even, but most of all, to herself. Why had Lumina seen fit to bring her into this world if no one wanted her?

*Resoluteness* to prove her worth by finding the Felinae and their prince. *Fear* that there was nothing she could do to atone for her existence and never would be.

And now her enemy was telling her she didn't have to explain herself to him? It was . . . unfathomable.

"I'm lousing this up," Ellus muttered. He knelt before her in the grass like she was a goddess. "You can't possibly be expected to act on any feelings when you've left everyone you knew and loved behind."

She swallowed, unable to manage more than that.

He sucked in his lower lip, considering. "Seren, I understand what it's like to be on your own. I'm not all by myself, but I felt that way when I was in Andaavia. And sometimes I still feel very alone here."

It was her turn to face the stars. "You must hate me for the loss of your family. Why pretend to be my friend?"

Soft fingers touched the back of her hand as it hung at her side. "Whatever you may think of me, now or later, I'm not pretending to be your friend, Seren. I respect you. You've more resolve than I fear I will ever have. If you embraced your power, you'd be unstoppable."

Did he know her secret? And not care? No, he couldn't know, or he wouldn't have tried to kiss her.

"When Thane picked a fight with you, I meant what I said. You aren't to blame for what the Prims did, what your parents did, or your uncle." Seren stiffened, yet he didn't stop. "Just as I'm not to blame, none of us are to blame for the choices and actions of our parents. We can't settle the debt for the dead—not with more death."

His incredulous words slowly sunk in. "You want peace?"

"Why not?"

Seren grappled for a response to the impossible. "Because we're enemies? And you've been recruited by the Elusives to terrorize Primordians."

An enigmatic look flitted through Ellus's sapphire eyes as he stood. "Maybe we have no choice. Our options are to starve underground or fight those who will slaughter us if we reappear. What would you have us do?"

Surrender. It was on the tip of her tongue. "I suppose you have a point," she said tightly.

"But whether I want peace or not," he said, bitterness creeping into his tone, "we all bow before the will of the Throne."

And how could the young prince want peace after the death of *his* family? Seren sucked in a breath. This was her chance. "You've met my cousin, Prince Alban?"

"Oh, yes. And his brother."

"His brother is alive?"

The colour leached from Ellus's face. "I wasn't supposed to tell you that. Few Felinae are aware the elder son of Ellowyne and Lynus survived."

"I don't have anyone to tell, do I?" Not yet. "But isn't it hard to hide a prince?"

A muscle twitched in his cheek. "You'd be surprised. He refused the crown. Royal life isn't for everyone."

Crowned or not, her mission had suddenly become twice as hard. If one prince was captured, that left the other to lead. She doubted the Felinae would surrender to her uncle unless both heirs to the Throne could be thwarted. "What are they like? I mean, if I'm to petition them, I'd like to know what to expect."

Some of the tension drained out of his mien. "Well, the older one likes to give orders. The younger one thinks himself clever, though that's up for debate." His lips twisted ruefully. "Alban's truly trying his best, in my opinion. Both are."

He spoke as if he knew them well. "Are they friends of yours? Do you think they'll grant me asylum?"

Ellus shoved his hands in his pant pockets, as though to keep from touching her. He still stood so close warm puffs of his breath grazed her chin. "Is anyone ever a friend to a prince? As long as Prince Alban is unwed, Regent Boreal will have the final say. But if asylum is truly what you desire in your heart, I see no reason she would turn you away."

A companionable silence fell around them, but Ellus didn't return his attention to the night sky. After a while, he sat again, and his shoulders slumped as though each star were a burden pressing down on him. "I've often wondered why Lumina spared me. All those who died, my parents, my sisters. Why did I get to live?"

"Vengeance?" It was why she was here. And it was disconcerting to realize that Ellus had as much or maybe even more right to it than her.

"Revenge won't bring my family back. It will only deprive other children of their families and families of their loved ones. Those left alive will demand their own revenge." He waved at the stars. "Is that our cyclic fate? To chase revenge as the moon chases the sun?"

Who would she be without her vengeance? Her determination came from that burning need to right the wrongs done to her and her House.

She looked to the stars for an answer. It was, after all, where the temple priests looked. But the stars only glittered back at her in silence. Finally, Seren sat back down beside him. "I was taught to believe the Goddess Lumina had our futures mapped out for us in the stars. But if there is more than one path for us" —absently, she rubbed the spot of her Future Eye, then realized what she was doing and dropped her hand—"if nothing is predetermined for certain, then our actions must matter to the Goddess. Our actions must have consequences here. Otherwise, your parents died for nothing. My father, too."

The innocent children in Gull Harbour, their deaths would mean nothing. And yet, Llion would free a man who was complicit if he could. "These types of actions can't mean nothing, Ellus."

"You sound like my aunt."

"If she's at court maybe you can introduce us?"

"That you'll meet her, I have no doubt. I feel that is written in the stars," he added solemnly, echoing their previous conversation under the night sky. Then, in a blink, playful Ellus was back, and he gave her shoulder a light bump. "Maybe we are, too. I feel we were destined to meet, Seren Morningstar."

*Maybe.* Yawns soon overtook her, however, and they made their way back to camp through the trees. Before they broke cover, Ellus halted.

"You do believe me?" he asked abruptly. "About being your friend? There are things I am forbidden to say, but if I could, I hope you know I would tell you. If that makes any sense."

It did. But then, she wasn't being completely honest, either. So it was only fair he kept a secret or two.

She took his hand in hers and squeezed. "I believe you."

And it surprised her to find that she did. But while Ellus maintained she didn't need to justify herself and her choices, would he feel the same once she betrayed him and his princes?

No, he wouldn't cling to his dream of peace then. When the time came, she only hoped he would believe she hadn't meant to hurt him with her lies.

**18**

---

Near the end of the fourth day of their trek, the retreating sun gilded the blooming meadow before Seren in warm golden tones, the tall grasses swaying around her in a quiet greeting. It was easier to let her mind wander to the tiny yellow and purple flowers than dwell on how Clan Wolvair would welcome her. So the snap of a twig startled her.

Up ahead, Kanta picked up the bent stick from under her boot, signalling the end of the tedious game of stealth that had occupied the recruits since that morning. Seren had lasted half the day but lost when a stone she'd stepped on had wobbled and dislodged a few pebbles. For the past hour, the last two remaining had been Vesper and Kanta. That Vesper, the youngest, had bested them made Seren smile.

"You cheated." Kanta tossed the twig away. "You put it there before I could see it."

A few steps ahead, the younger girl chewed on her lower lip. "The rules didn't say we couldn't use our Inheritances."

Unappeased, Kanta crossed the distance to poke Vesper in the chest. "It doesn't count. You cheated."

In less than a heartbeat, Seren had dropped her pack to pull Kanta back from Vesper. "Let it go, Urso. So she threw it there. It was a game."

"You don't intimidate me, Moralis." Kanta swiped her wayward curls out of her eyes to glare up at Seren. "But I'm not surprised you'd condone underhanded tactics."

Seren clenched her fists. It would be so easy to wipe that glower off Kanta's freckled face—too easy. Instead, she took a deep breath. "Well, I am surprised you lose with such little grace, seeing as you have so much practice at it."

"You—"

Before Kanta could finish, Ellus was beside her, a consoling yet firm hand on her shoulder. An absence Seren felt on her own. "Kanta, I understand you feel it was unfair because you couldn't react in time to prevent yourself from stepping on the twig. Maybe we should have specified whether participants can foil their opponents. But Vesper is a Swiftfoot. We can't blame her for using her talents to win. We all use the advantages we have at our disposal."

"Do we?" Kanta demanded, shrugging off his hand. "At what cost?"

"The Prims surely will," Thane muttered darkly as he strode by them in the knee-high grass.

"As do the Felinae," Seren retorted. She ran after him, her blood crying for a fight after Kanta's accusations. And Ellus hadn't spoken out about Kanta's assumption that Seren was a cheater. Not that she needed Ellus to defend her honour. She could defend it just fine. Though, was spying cheating or all fair in war? It was clear that Llion had spies of his own. So it was only fair that Uncle Tarquin had her to spy for him.

"Don't tell me," she said when she caught up to him, "that the Elusives haven't been using their Inheritances to their advantage in their attacks, Sionnach. Gull Harbour was a massacre."

Thane stopped to glare at her, but any further argument was forestalled by the approach of Llion and Drakori from behind and Silver's return from scouting the brush ahead.

"All clear," Silver called.

As if on cue, the twang of bowstrings filled the air, and Seren's head snapped up to sight the arrows, coming from their left flank. Her pack—and her sole means of shielding herself— was back where she dropped it. Llion's bow sprang to his hand and, within a heartbeat, he was firing back while Silver ran in the threat's direction, twin swords in each hand as if to slice the arrows from the sky. The air whistled as her blades swung upward.

Then Seren was falling to the ground, a heavy weight forcing the air from her lungs. Someone had tackled her. Panic sank its sharp claws into her chest—she couldn't breathe. Her arms and legs didn't seem to work. Immobile, she waited for the punches and kicks of her nightmares to start.

*Thud. Thud. Thud.*

Three arrows, fletched in black and red, quivered in the tall grass a hand's span from her head. Several curses from Luminaria's docks blasted her ears, each one filthier than the last. The weight rolled off her, and Thane was on his feet, pulling her up by the arm. The Lockpick. Bile rose in her throat as he released her sleeve-covered arm.

*They hadn't touched skin to skin.*

"To the treeline!" Llion bellowed as more twangs filled the air.

"Move it, Princess," Thane grunted as he fled in the wrong direction, his cloak billowing behind him like a dark cloud and a black and red feathered arrow sticking out of his pack.

It snapped Seren out of her daze. *Fool.* What was he doing?

Whoever was shooting wasn't waiting to see if their aim struck true. More red and black feathers dotted the grass on her left flank. Close. Too close. She turned and ran toward the trees.

When the air twanged again, Seren had nearly reached cover, and she dove into the brush. Reedy branches whipped her in the face and arms until she slid into a tree of substantial girth. When she righted herself, she strained her eyes and ears for signs of pursuit but could find none besides Thane. He came barrelling into the forest with his pack in front of him. Behind her, at the edge of the forest, Llion stood with his back to a tree, an arrow nocked and ready to draw as he scanned the trees on the far side of the meadow.

Sol's hells, she'd left her pack out there—not that she had much besides a few borrowed clothes.

"Looking for this, Princess?" Thane pushed her pack into her arms, none too gently. His, she could see now, was still on his back and sporting another arrow.

"Yeah," she murmured, uncertain what to make of his behaviour. His mouth twisted in a sneer as he strode off, deeper into the forest to where the others gathered.

Following, Seren scanned the wooded area until she found dark mahogany locks. Unscathed, Ellus hovered near a wide-eyed and shivering Vesper. Over the top of Vesper's unruly head, their eyes met, and the tightness in her chest loosened. *Safe.*

They should get moving. Yet Llion wasn't budging from the tree he leaned against. And Drakori sat on a moss-covered log, eyes closed, lips moving indistinctly. On the seer's forehead, the black slashed circle flickered in and out. Was she trying to see the archers?

After a quick check on each of the recruits, Silver came up on Llion's left flank, fingers splayed against the twin short swords at her hips. "I'll circle around and catch the cowards from behind."

"No." Llion didn't take his eyes from the empty field. When

no more arrows flew at them, Llion lowered his bow but not his gaze from the horizon. "We need to get the recruits and Taibhseir Drakori to the den. And I need you here." A pause. "You take the lead. I'll cover our rear."

"Could it be legionnaires?" Thane asked, pulling the arrows out of his pack. It was as if he hoped to find his enemies close.

When Llion didn't answer him, Seren's gut tightened. "Give me my knife—I should have it if we're attacked."

"A knife won't protect you against an arrow, Morningstar. If they were going to rush us, they would've done it by now. Follow the taibhseir and Silver to the den, all of you."

No one argued, though Seren thought about it as she bent, pretending to tie her boot. Carefully, she removed her dagger from the slot and tucked it into the back of her leathers under her vest, already feeling better to have it closer. Not that she had anything to worry about if their attackers were legionnaires.

*If.*

As she straightened, Ellus was upon her. He looked her over from head to toe, and she wondered if he'd seen the dagger. Then his hand reached out, and she thought he might brush those long fingers against her cheek. Instead, he plucked a leaf from her hair.

"That was quite the dive you took." His eyes darkened at a point over her shoulder. "He didn't try anything, did he?"

"What?" Then she realized Ellus was staring at Thane as he followed Silver through moss-covered trunks and young saplings. "No, he didn't," she admitted, not quite believing the Lockpick hadn't stolen her secrets either.

Still, she was glad Ellus stuck close as they trudged onward. Having unknown foes and Llion at her back made her cast frequent glances over her shoulder.

It wasn't long before the sealgair fell behind. As he

staggered to a broad elm, a flash of red and black caught her eye. The shaft of an arrow stuck out of his upper thigh.

"Llion's hit," she called to the others. As he leaned against the trunk for support, pain rippled across his face. He snapped the shaft in half and stuffed the fletching in a pocket on his pack.

"Keep going," Llion growled at them, limping onward. Seren exchanged a look with Ellus—but Silver hesitated but a moment before continuing to lead them on some unmarked path. When they reached the foot of a small green copse, a rail-thin Felinae waited with a longbow. Unlike Llion's leathers, his vest was made of grey fur. Wolf, if she wasn't mistaken. His gaze jumped like a jackrabbit over each of them, and he blanched at Llion's thundering countenance—or maybe it was the line of blood dripping from the broken arrow shaft below his hip. Or maybe Silver's glare from under her black hooded cowl.

It was lucky for him that the arrows in his quiver didn't match the one stuck in Llion.

"Sealgair, Taibhseir," the stranger began, bowing.

"Greetings can wait. We were followed," Drakori huffed, out of breath and leaning on her staff. "Open the door."

Confused, Seren glanced sideways at Ellus, and he grinned.

The Wolvair clansman led them to a mound of black soil with twisted roots sticking out of it—the bottom of a massive tree that had fallen and taken the earth with it. He pulled on a large, gnarled root, unfamiliar words tripping off his tongue like a prayer.

Ellus's lips brushed her ear. "Only a clan member can call the door to their clan's den. A gift from the Goddess Seline."

The roots parted to reveal a slab of polished serendium, as though it had always been there. Interlocking swirls gilded in silver rose to the surface, but there were no iron hinges or door handles. The lines slowly converged to shape the moon in all her phases—from crescents, spanning inward toward the full moon in the centre, slashed in half on a diagonal. One side was silver, and one side was black.

Seren's jaw slackened.

The unamkhara symbol. The Eye of the Goddess.

"Open it," Drakori ordered impatiently. The Wolvair put his hand on the centre, and the door swung inward to reveal a dank, earthy tunnel. He entered, disappearing, with Drakori on his heels.

Was this what Silver didn't want her to see? Even if she told her uncle where this entrance was, no Prim could open it.

"So this is how you've stayed hidden," Seren murmured as Vesper, Thane, and Silver slipped through. Not just secret tunnels in the mountains. *Magic.*

No wonder the Legion had failed to flush out the enemy. But if she could pinpoint the entrances, traps could be set for warriors like this one who would pass through the door before launching their attacks on Luminaria.

At the door, Ellus paused and traced the slash of the unamkhara with a finger. "The Goddess Seline sent Drakori visions of the dens and their doors in our hour of need. The rock here is said to have fallen from the sky when the second moon shattered." At her raised eyebrow, he shrugged. "Seline, in her infinite wisdom, foresaw the day would come when her children would need a safe place."

"And in her infinite wisdom," Llion interrupted, bow still loose in his hands. "Seline kept her mouth shut about it."

Ellus's shoulders stiffened. Then his warm hand slipped into hers. She was too startled to resist. "Seren chose us. Trust must start somewhere. I trust her to keep our secrets and our people safe."

She forced herself not to wince at the both brave and foolish sentiment. He'd never forgive her when she inevitably betrayed his misplaced trust.

Llion didn't fail to notice their linked hands, and his eyes narrowed. "As much as you trust Riaghladair Boreal and me to do the same, recruit?"

Ellus's hand turned clammy in her grip, but he didn't let go. "To do otherwise would be treason, Sealgair."

Llion's mouth tightened, but he didn't respond as Ellus strode through the enchanted door, sweeping her along with him.

Without a sound, the door closed, casting the tunnel into near darkness until the grey hues of her night-sight took over. As she followed Ellus, Seren's heart hammered with excitement —she was inside an actual Felinae den. Instead of the wood of the tree trunk, the walls were packed tight with mud and round stones of all sizes. Here and there, between the cracks of stone and earth, tiny clusters of mushrooms broke up the darkness with their eerie glow, similar to the moonwood from the cavern.

After a descent of a hundred paces, the tunnel widened into an enormous cavern of gleaming serendium, with large, zig-zagging veins of quartz and amethyst shooting through the walls. It was fifty times larger than their training cavern—large enough for a village. Moonwood torches and candle lanterns hung from posts, creating false daylight over cloth huts. With her heightened vision, it was almost as bright as an overcast day when the fog stole into the harbour. The octagonal huts spanned out in an orderly manner, much like a military camp, with a wide corridor cutting the cavern in two.

On the edge of the huts stood a silver-haired man and a much younger auburn-haired woman, both clothed in layers of fur and embroidered grey silk. While the silver in the man's moustache and short beard was more prominent than the streaks of black, his body was broad and imposing, even if a wide ornate belt hid a middling paunch.

"You're later than expected, Sealgair." Neither the man's craggy face nor his gravelly voice held any warmth of welcome.

"Someone else expected our arrival as well, Lord Wolvair,"

Llion replied coolly. A trail of blood stained his trousers. Despite the broken shaft still sticking out of his leg, he stood straight, almost a hand's span taller than their host.

The auburn-haired woman next to the lord gave a small gasp. "You're hurt, my lord."

"See to the Sealgair, Lady Fawn," Drakori directed, "and have food and huts set aside for the rest of us. We travelled as quickly as possible, and these old bones need a hot pot of tea before I consult Time's Flow." Drakori tapped her staff impatiently as if that was the worst of their worries. "We're tired and hungry, Linney."

"The words have not been said," Lord Wolvair said stiffly.

"We formally request the hospitality of Lord Wolvair and Clan Wolvair in the name of the Throne. Does that suffice, my lord?" The words, polite enough, were uttered in an acerbic tone that matched the severe look Drakori levelled on the lord. Seren had to swallow a snort. The Taibhseir was clearly not asking.

"Granted, esteemed Taibhseir," Wolvair replied with a slight bow of his head, though he looked as if he wished he could have said otherwise.

The exchange seemed to release Lady Fawn, who rushed to Llion's side to place a gloved hand on his arm. The finger sleeves were cut off, and Seren noticed the woman's callused fingers looked accustomed to work despite her finery. When the lady caught Seren looking, she curled her light-skinned hand tighter around Llion's forearm. "Come with me, my lord."

"Lord Wolvair," Llion said, without glancing at the comely young woman, "I must send messages."

"You'll bleed all over the paper," Silver muttered under her breath from where she hung back near the tunnel, with her hood up over her head and the cowl shielding her lower face. In her black leathers, she nearly vanished into the quartz-veined serendium of the cavern. Still, with Felinae hearing, she was easily overheard.

Lord Wolvair's head jerked sharply. "Since when are outsiders permitted into our sanctuaries?"

Seren half expected Silver to skewer Wolvair or Lady Fawn with her swords, but the Marked didn't move from her relaxed lean against the rock. "I do not come for your head if that is what worries you."

A *yet* seemed to linger in the air, and Drakori banged her staff on the ground as if to dispel it. "Training Elusives, that's what she's doing, Linney. Come, we've no time to waste, my lord." To Llion, she added, "Have your injury tended to, Sealgair, then join us. We must discuss the matter of Tarquin Moralis's prisoner." Drakori paused, tilting her head upwards. "I feel an eddy in motion, and I will need to consult Time's Flow and confer with Belden. Messages can wait until then."

"Prisoner? We do have much to discuss then, Gwenna," Wolvair replied, his tone more conciliatory. "And I'd like to hear about your altercation so close to my territory, Sealgair." His gaze raked over Seren and then the others. "Most disturbing considering your illustrious companions."

Llion threw off Lady Fawn's supporting hand, eyes ablaze. "Disturbing is one word for it, Wolvair. Treason is another. You alone were sent word of our arrival, yet we were greeted with an ambush."

Seren's gaze flickered between the two men. If clan division existed, it was a weakness Uncle Tarquin could exploit. Drakori opened her mouth to intercede, but Lord Wolvair held his hand up to silence her, his affront plain in the rigidity of his mien.

"Taibhseir, I understand Sealgair Llewyn has lost a great quantity of blood. Otherwise, I am certain he wouldn't question the loyalty of the Wolf, ere the beast turns on him." Without a glance in Llion's direction, he held his arm out to indicate

Drakori should precede him. "For the respect I hold for his mother and father, I will overlook such an insult. Once."

Although it looked like Llion wanted to challenge the lord's loyalty again, his face had taken on a sickly pallor. She wasn't the only one who had noticed. Before Silver could reach him, however, Lady Fawn spoke. "Let me tend to your wound, Sealgair. If the rumours of the Legion ships returning are true, our young prince—all of us—will need you at your strongest."

This time, when Lady Fawn took him gently by the arm, he didn't resist.

# 19

Underground pools were a decided benefit of den dwelling—one she could become accustomed to indulging in.

To her delight, after a cold supper had been rustled up, a clan member had escorted them down several sets of stairs to a set of underground pools, each within its own cavern. Ellus and Thane had ducked into one, leaving Seren, Vesper, Kanta, and Silver to enjoy the other in privacy. Neither Kanta nor Silver had been inclined to immerse themselves longer than necessary for a cleanse before departing, and Vesper had disappeared without bathing. Perhaps, to explore the new tunnels.

As Seren leisurely swam another lap to stretch her muscles, the cool spring water soothed her aches from the long journey. It didn't take her long to cross the length of the circular pool, but the water was so dark from the surrounding serendium, she couldn't tell how deep it might go. *One way to find out.*

With a gulp of air, she kicked her way down into a blackness she'd never experienced before. Far from feeling trapped, it was freeing. No one could see her here. No one could reach her here. This far down, there was a feeling of weightlessness, like she was floating free of the constraints of her body, rocked in a gentle embrace of a watery mother. And her worries drifted away.

All too soon, her lungs burned for air, but she kicked farther still, letting small breaths out as she did. Still, the bottom didn't come. Finally, dizziness and her survival instinct shot her toward the surface and into the dim light. As she surfaced, she gasped for breath, her heart thundering in her chest from the exertion. She let herself float on her back while she recovered.

The whimsical splendour of the spikes of rock and crystal above the pool was so different from the carefully designed mosaic murals in the Lyceum's bathhouse. When she had frequented the bathhouse, she had marvelled at the artists' skill in depicting the Moon Goddess Lumina and her mortal consort. Her mind circled back to one time in particular. The steam of the air had swirled around her, along with the whispers and laughter of her classmates. She'd fled into the night. It was the last time she remembered running from a fight.

They were probably still laughing and whispering about her in the bathhouse. It galled her to imagine the smug expressions her former classmates must have worn ever since she had left Luminaria. By her apparent betrayal of Quinton, she had proven their former distrust of her as justified. But they'd eat every insult thrown at her when she completed her mission and handed the Felinae Dominion over to her uncle.

A cough and flicker of movement had Seren righting herself in the water. The biting smell of the lye was tempered with sweet notes of lavender. Over by the water's edge, Vesper applied soap flakes to Seren's linen shirt. Her own mustard-yellow tunic lay drying on the rocks, and she wore her sleeveless undershirt. The girl must have returned while Seren was under water.

Seren swam over to the edge. "You don't have to do that." Though the undershirt *was* in desperate need of a wash.

"Thought I might as well do yours while you swam." Vesper bit her lip and looked down as she rubbed the fabric together to suds the soap. "I hope you don't mind."

"Not in the least. It needs a good scrubbing."

Vesper returned Seren's smile. "Back home, I helped my mother in the laundry. There's something satisfying about washing away the dirt. Giving a garment new life."

"I can't remember helping my mother with anything." House Moralis servs did the cleaning around House Moralis. Just the idea of doing something with Adalyn was absurd. Yet, Seren envied Vesper's happy memory.

"Do you miss your family?" As Vesper scrubbed the linen, she watched Seren but not with suspicion. More like with sympathy.

Could one miss something one never truly had? She hadn't missed Adalyn in a long time, though with a pang she remembered wishing her mother had attended Pledging Night to see her become a member of House Moralis. But even Valera had been on her mind less of late. The mission, of course, took precedence.

"Missing them will achieve little. To them, I'm a traitor. Do you miss yours?" Seren was suddenly curious about Vesper's life in her clan.

The girl's slender hands slowed their methodical movements. "I want to see my mother and my clan, but this has been a change of air, you know? Something new. And using my Inheritance, learning under Taibhseir Drakori and Sealgair Llewyn, well, I want to *do* something more. Help my clan, all Felinae. It isn't right we're forced to hide underground to avoid a war." She swallowed. "This isle is our home."

That was true. The Felinae had inhabited the isle before the first Primordian ships arrived.

"You're right. This isle is your home. Your people welcomed us here. And you shouldn't have to live in hiding because my parents broke the Accord." Seren's anger at her father rose to the surface. It wasn't fair that because of Devan Morningstar and her mother's mistakes, the rest of the dominion had to suffer.

Not seeing the moon for weeks on end had given Seren a new appreciation of the Felinae's lot. But it wasn't like her uncle would force the clans to leave after going through so much trouble to find them. Rule under republic law would bring peace to both their peoples. But she understood perfectly Vesper's feelings of being trapped.

"I wanted—want—to do something, too," she began hesitantly. "Something great to bring honour to my House." She flushed at the grandiose words. "That's impossible now, of course," she lied.

Vesper considered her, her hands stilling. "Maybe it's not. Maybe Ellus's dream of peace is possible—with you and Prince Alban to bridge our peoples."

Seren stared, slack-jawed at what the girl was hinting at, until Vesper chuckled. "Well, you were going to marry one cousin. Why not another?"

Seren swallowed down her rising panic at the thought, suppressing a shudder. "I've no desire to marry anyone, and"—considering Ellus's words to her—"I doubt very much Prince Alban would consider a bastard princess with a traitor for a father as an advantageous match."

Desperate to change the topic, Seren gestured to her tunic, thick with a layer of soapy froth. "I think it's clean."

Biting her lip, Vesper looked down at it, too. "I'll give it a rinse."

On her knees, she dunked the cloth into the pool beside

Seren. White bubbles frothed to the surface in foamy whorls. For a while, they both stared at them until the silence grew strained.

"Just say it, Vesper."

"Oh, I was thinking about a story my mother told me." She sat back on her heels, the garment forgotten in her hands. "She danced with your father once, at the Frost Moon Ball at our embassy in Luminaria." A pink blush dusted her cheeks. "She worked as a lady's maid there for a time before the . . . war."

"I see." Of course, her father had danced with a maid—probably all the maids. Seren's tone or expression must have betrayed her thoughts for Vesper nearly dropped the shirt in the water.

"It wasn't like that. My mother told me Prince Devan had a good heart, through and through. It was her first moon ball, and no one had asked her to dance."

Seren refrained from pointing out that being kind to one woman hardly absolved her father of his ill-treatment of another. "The Felinae allow their servs—er, maids—to dance at balls?"

"In the clans, everyone works and celebrates together. Maybe at court it's different, but at the embassy, my mother said if you weren't needed for duties, then you were welcome to attend." Vesper rushed on, eager it seemed to get back to her story. "It was actually Lord Startaker who made my father envious by dancing with my mother for several processions in a row. The next morning, my father asked my mother to join him for a picnic, and that was that."

Startaker was clearly not the man to be advising his soulshielder on morality.

"Your parents, what do they think of you being an Elusive?"

Vesper froze, then focused all her attention on wringing out the shirt. "I never met my father. My mother left him and the city after she learned she was with child. She didn't think it would be safe for us any longer in Luminaria, so she returned to her clan."

"Your father was Primordian?" Seren couldn't believe it. Vesper was four years younger than her, born after the Felinae had already disappeared.

As the water dripped into a puddle on the rock, a wistful look entered Vesper's eyes. "My father begged her to stay after the Accord was broken, after the Felinae were banished from the city, and the war began. He promised to protect her. Or that's what she says. And she did stay, for a few years, despite the danger."

"So we're the same." Seren's anger fizzled. Vesper was half-Felinae, half-Prim, just like her. She wasn't alone.

"While there are few of us moonlight children with a foot in both worlds, we do exist. I'd like to say differently, but many Felinae have no great love for us either. Because of my father, some in our clan shunned my mother and me. But that's no longer tolerated under Lady Lenore's rule."

A surge of compassion and self-righteous anger engulfed Seren. She knew that pain in Vesper's eyes. "They treated you like an outcast."

"A few. But others stood up for us." Head down, Vesper busied herself laying Seren's tunic to dry on the rocks. Her shoulder-length hair hid her face. "The sealgair knows about my father. But the others don't."

Seren crossed one arm over her chest for modesty and pushed her torso up out of the water so that the red crescent-shaped scar on her ribcage was visible. She didn't want to feel protective of the young girl, but how could she not? Their stories weren't so different.

"This scar? I got it my first month at the Lyceum. I was fourteen—your age. They broke some ribs and my arm, along with my collarbone." She traced the jagged line on the underside of her jaw. "And this was courtesy of the ring one of them wore."

The ring Ty still needed to explain.

"Because of who your father was?"

Seren shrugged and sank back into the water. "And because I'm like you. Half in this world, half in the other."

"Not exactly like me, I bet." Vesper took a deep breath. "I was assumed to be a boy when I was born, but that's not who I am. I feel happiest as a girl because I am one, even though it can be awkward with those who don't understand or don't want to. I wasn't sure how you might react if I swam with you."

Seren wasn't sure what to say. Anatomy wasn't a mystery to her. But she understood about being shunned.

"You define who you are, not your anatomy. It doesn't change how I feel about you. You're still Vesper. But I can leave if you want the pools to yourself."

A genuine smile broke out on Vesper's face. "No, stay. I was right to trust you. It's a feeling I've had since you came. Kanta and Thane, even the sealgair, they'll see they were wrong."

*Trust.* It was as though Vesper had given her a living piece of her heart to treasure and protect. "I am honoured then by your trust."

Or, maybe Vesper was right, and Seren could restore peace between the Felinae and the Primordians—their shared peoples—by helping her uncle forge a new Accord with Prince Alban.

"Does everyone else know, or is this a secret like your father?"

Seren didn't know how accepting the Felinae were. It was the one thing the Exiler Houses had brought with them to Luminaria that she agreed with—a wider knowledge and acceptance. In the more progressive Houses, as long as you brought honour to your House, it didn't matter how you dressed or who you loved. Heirs, like Quinton, were the one exception. They were still expected to produce more heirs, one way or another. Though an heir could step down in favour of a younger sibling or relative.

"To me, it isn't something to be ashamed of, nor is it anyone else's business. Everyone in my clan knows, as do the other recruits. Most are accepting of those who are like me." Vesper blushed. "I'm one of the two-souled or many-souled. There's quite a few of us in Clan Llewyn."

"But you don't think they'll accept you as half-Prim? A moonlight child?"

"It's hard when no one"—Vesper swallowed, cheeks flushed —"has anything good to say about Prims."

Seren couldn't blame Vesper for feeling that way, since she felt the same about being Felinae. "I understand. My classmates at the Lyceum never let me forget my Felinae heritage." She pushed off from the ledge. "You know, someday, you'll wish you swam in an underground pool with the infamous Seren Moralis," she teased, "if only so you can regale your clan with the tale as you age into your golden years."

Vesper's laughter bubbled up freely, warming Seren in the same way Valera's smile did. "More like the tale of how I beat the Princess of the Morningstars to the bottom."

Without further warning, Vesper dove off the ledge, and Seren quickly followed her down. As she descended into the inky depths, a strange new possibility simmered within her: a place where all children could live freely and safely, unashamed.

**20**

———————

White light scorched Seren's eyelids, heralding the familiar explosion of pain in her temples. A distant part of her understood she was asleep on the floor of the tent between Vesper and Ellus. It had been nearly a full pass of the moon since her slumber had been disturbed by the familiar nightmare; the last one had occurred a few days before Pledging Night. After four years of fitful sleeps, however, the sequence was seared into her soul, and as the fragmented images of that night punched through her mind, she was helpless to hold them back.

First, the cloaked figures, with hoods drawn over their faces, came out of the night and surrounded her in the narrow alley. Her arms, heavy as stone, refused to rise to block the first blow from the widest of the figures. Agony blazed through her abdomen, and her breath rushed from her in one large whoosh. Hard hands grabbed at her from every direction.

*Thump.*

The back of her head connected with cobblestones as those hands pinned her down. Her vision blurred; the dull pounding in her head became a welcome distraction.

217

*Crack.*

A backhand rattled her teeth, cutting the tender flesh of her mouth. The tang of blood flooded her tongue. She tried to spit it at the ugly face above her, but her mouth felt full of wool.

A boot to her side, then another. Sharp pain spasmed in her stomach. Her body tried to fold in on itself, but the hands wouldn't let her.

The snap of bone. A piercing agony that nearly sent her under. It stole her breath away, and her insides writhed in torment while the pounding in her head made her heave.

Then, as usual, a fist with a gleam of a black gemstone came toward her face—that slashed circle glinting mockingly at her. She braced herself, grateful in her dream at least that it heralded the end.

But this time, she didn't succumb to the darkness after the blow.

Footsteps sounded in the distance. A faint *Halt, there!* Through half-closed eyelids, she watched two shadowy figures run toward her while her assailants fled. Except for one. The leader. She desperately tried to focus her blurry vision as his face hovered over her, so she would know who to exact her revenge on. The tears didn't help, but she couldn't stop them.

A thumb grazed her swollen lips as tenderly as a lover. "I'll come for you," he promised, his voice low and familiar. His thumb came away red—that much she could see—before he fled into the night.

She shivered. It was over, and indeed the darkness was creeping in. Her body became weightless, growing lighter and lighter. Distantly, as if floating far above herself, she observed the back of her rescuers' heads as they knelt over her body. One dark. One like a flame.

Their murky forms tugged on her memory of that night before they shattered into a thousand jagged shards of black glass, and her along with them.

———

"You're wanted at Wolvair's tent."

Seren woke abruptly from her night terror, covered in a cold sweat and with Silver's sharp face hovering over her. By habit, she reached for her absent knife before registering the words. Why was she wanted?

By the time she'd sat up, Silver was settled cross-legged in the corner, where she promptly resumed sharpening one of her short swords over a smooth stone in the glow of moonwood. "You won't be alone."

Seren glanced at the sleeping form of Ellus next to her.

"Drakori and Shade are still there. And Wolvair's not stupid enough to try anything while we're in his den."

Some of the tension in Seren's chest loosened, though she half-hoped Ellus would wake up and offer to come with her. But maybe she'd learn something useful, and truthfully, she wouldn't sleep the rest of the night.

Once her vest was laced up over her slightly damp undershirt, Seren slipped out of the tent. In the grey darkness, a tired-looking woman, in a long woollen garment like Drakori's, waited. When she saw Seren, she wordlessly turned on her heel and began walking toward a clearing at the back of the den. Along the edge of the path, moonwood glowed weakly as though it, too, knew the hour was far too late for polite conversation. Although space must be coveted in the den, there were no tents closer than a hundred paces to the grand domicile composed of tanned hides and cloth that must belong to Wolvair. The better to protect the lord's privacy, she supposed.

The woman left her at a set of wide steps hewn from the serendium rock and continued back down the road. Murmuring voices and scents drifted in the night air. As she approached, Seren decided there were five, not three, Felinae waiting for her.

"Bah, get rid of her now. If she's a spy, then you're a hero, Sealgair. If she's not, well, one less Prim is nothing to regret."

Wolvair—his nasal tone was as distinctive as the dank mushroom smell that clung to him.

"She is necessary to the future of our people—and the continuation of the Felinae Dominion," Drakori countered.

"Necessary or not," Llion cut in, "Seren Morningstar is under my protection until I deliver her to the Throne. Unless she breaks her oath to us, I cannot break my oath to her."

There was a pause.

"What about the princeling?" Wolvair demanded. "Has he become more of a warrior under your tutelage, Sealgair?"

"The crown prince is all he needs to be," Drakori retorted. "Have faith."

Wolvair made a disdainful noise in his throat. "So say your visions. You and I have both known Time's Flow to lie, Gwendolythe."

"It is not that the divinations lie, Linneas." It was said as if this were a long-held argument between them. "The future is an ever-changing destination, and many possible paths will present themselves. Our freedom is not a lost cause."

"Are you certain the fault lies not in the seer?" Lady Fawn asked, far too sweetly to be meant as anything but an insult.

"All of us are but flawed shards of Seline's own soul, Lady Fawn," Drakori replied. "We must all examine our thoughts to uncover how prejudices or biases may obscure the truth before us."

"And you don't suffer from these prejudices, Taibhseir?" Wolvair demanded.

"My eyes have been clouded in the past, yes. At present, however, I see clearly that our preconceptions are limiting our paths to a better future."

Lady Fawn sighed. "But no clear visions about our future outside these dens or why the Moralis girl seeks sanctuary? Or if Riaghladair Boreal's plan is successful?"

*A viper in silks, that one.* But there were all questions Seren wanted to know more about.

"Like Belden, I have seen nothing tangible, my lady," Drakori bit out, clearly out of patience. "Time's Flow isn't an enchanted mirror that reflects your desires on command. Those with Seersight are granted but a sliver of the Goddess's vision of the future—when She wills it." Drakori frowned. "But I believe an unknown seer is blocking my Eyes where Seren is concerned."

"An undiscovered youngster from one of the clans?" asked a mild voice.

"I am not certain. She's untutored and capable of drawing on copious amounts of divine power. Enough to force me out of my dreamscape while I was exploring Seren's unam."

The vision had been a trick? The vileness of such an intimate trespass and fear at that kind of power clamoured inside Seren until her blood burned to defend herself. Yet she couldn't help her sigh of relief at Drakori's continued ignorance of her mission.

The voices inside ceased. Had she given herself away?

Seren barely had time to compose her face before the flap of the tent opened. Still, the scrawny youth on the other side seemed to know what she was about by his cool demeanour. He led her into a large chamber of braided tapestries over heavy black brocade for walls. The gaping maw of a wolf's head hung across a rafter behind her audience, who sat in high-backed chairs in a semicircle around a low table with a silver platter of candles.

The attention of the room shifted to her. Seren met Drakori's mild stare, but she wouldn't underestimate the woman again. Drakori had invaded her mind back at the mountain without permission and watched her dream—perhaps even orchestrated it through Time's Flow.

Wolvair made a guttural noise in his throat, and Seren dragged her attention over to him. He gave her a dismissive flick of his ringed fingers. "The sealgair failed to introduce us earlier."

Llion pushed himself out of his chair, mouth twitching. "Your Highness, may I introduce Lord Linneas Wolvair and his daughter, Lady Fawn Wolvair. Lord and Lady, you sit before Princess Seren of the Morningstars."

Both Wolvair and Fawn looked like they had swallowed a wriggling frog. Could that truly be her status among the Felinae? She'd thought Llion had been mocking her when he first called her a princess.

Despite his injury, Llion bowed to her, which caused further stir and Wolvair's face turned a mottled red as he sputtered at the outrage. Seren didn't care that he didn't bow like the others. She suspected Llion was only paying her such homage to goad the lord for his earlier remarks, not out of any sense of fealty. The ostentatiousness of the title, however, sat uneasily on her shoulders until she had to tear it off.

"Moralis," she snapped, giving them her scowl. "I am Seren Moralis."

She thought Lady Fawn might spill her wine on her plunging furred neckline or grey silk bodice, adorned with the tiniest embroidery. A pattern of arrows and feathers. The bottom skirt flared in panels, revealing doeskin breeches over lithe legs. Seren was suddenly cognizant of her dishevelled state. At least her leathers were clean, and she'd had the forethought to braid her wet hair before bed.

"I never suspected," Wolvair said, rallying, "that I would drink with"—he paused obviously groping for a polite word—"a Moralis."

Seren almost laughed. "Just think of me as a sheep in wolf's clothing. It should be easy for you."

Wolvair's brow furrowed at the barb, and a braying laugh from the portly man in brown robes next to Drakori broke the tension. He slapped his ample stomach in appreciation. "Oh ho, I think you have that first part backward, Your Highness. Allow me to introduce my humble self. I am Belden Buhair, seer of Clan Wolvair, and while I do not possess the talent nor the skill of our illustrious Taibhseir, I had troubling visions around you." He wagged a finger at her, then smiled kindly. "However, I am pleased to see you arrive unscathed, Princess."

"You foresaw our arrival and attack?" Seren frowned. How many others had been aware of their journey to the den?

"The attack only—and not your location or the attackers. By the sacred waters, if I had realized you'd be set upon outside our door, Clan Wolvair would have come to your aid."

"But you're certain, Belden?" Drakori cut in sharply. "The arrows were meant for her, not another member of our group?" She had to be worried that the sealgair of the Felinae was being targeted.

"I believe so, Taibhseir. You know how fickle the waters can be. In my vision, however, the arrows were stakes—my visions aren't as precise as our Taibhseir's—and they pinned our lost princess in four spots. One in each hand, one between the shoulder blades, and one here." Buhair tapped the spot between his bushy grey eyebrows.

All four locations on Seren tingled in phantom sympathy. It was a gruesome, ridiculous story meant to scare her, though she might have expected factions of the Felinae to prefer her gone, or those like Lord Wolvair who wouldn't shed a tear at her death.

"The real arrows were fletched in black and red," Lady Fawn added. At Llion's startled look at her knowledge, she shrugged. "The feathers were sticking out of your pack, my lord."

Wolvair sat forward so quickly his wine sloshed. "Mountain Clan colours."

The air thickened in the warm tented room. The arms of Llion's chair squeaked in protest as his large hands clenched tight, and Seren half-expected to see claws scrape against the wood.

"Either the Mountain Clan is responsible," Buhair said, "or someone wants us to think they are."

"Sealgair, you know those reclusive beasts better than anyone." Wolvair's gaze narrowed, his wine cup forgotten. "You were raised by them."

Seren held her breath, the threat of violence hanging in the air. Was Wolvair too soused to sense the danger? Or had he baited Llion on purpose?

"If the Mountain Clan sent archers to kill us, the arrows would have hit their target," Llion replied coolly.

"Would they have?" Lady Fawn snapped, but then her forehead smoothed as she laid long fingers on Llion's bracer. "Maybe Seer Buhair is wrong. Maybe *you* were their target, Sealgair. You *were* hit." She glanced up at him through her eyelashes in a way that made Seren roll hers—not that Llion paid any notice to her attentions. "A sad day today would have been if that arrow had felled our prince's staunchest ally."

"Sad, indeed." Buhair cleared his throat, so much so that Seren worried the man might choke on his phlegm. Then he raised his goblet. "We can all give thanks to Goddess Seline that the archers weren't as skilled as they thought themselves to be. And that our Lady Fawn inherited her dear departed mother's healing touch."

Wolvair swiftly raised his silver goblet in agreement. "To my daughter, a lady with no equal in all the clans."

Since Seren had no goblet to raise, she watched the

responses. Lady Fawn humbly bowed her head, but her shoulders remained stiff as if the toast had insulted her in some manner. Drakori barely sipped hers while Llion drained his to the bottom. It was more a sign of his irritation with his host than in agreement, she suspected. And Buhair watched her so intently, her skin prickled.

Drakori rapped her staff on the table. "Belden's vision is not directly why we summoned Seren here at such an hour. Sealgair?"

Would they be sending her on to Prince Alban?

"Word has reached us that your absence in Luminaria has been declared an act of treason by the new imperator, who we've learned is none other than your uncle." Llion shifted in his too-small chair, either uncomfortable from the pain in his hip or from having to deliver this news. "Tarquin Moralis has disowned you and offered a reward for your capture."

*Detritus.*

But it was a ruse—not true. Still, her knees went weak as she clenched her fists. "I expected as much."

"A substantial reward," Wolvair murmured, strumming his lower lip and looking at her as if he saw the bags of coin before him. "There are rumours inside the city as well."

Heat crept into Llion's voice. "We did not bring her here to discuss rumours, Lord Wolvair."

"Then get on with it, Sealgair," Wolvair said, waving a hand in the air. "I grow tired of company."

"You saw in Time's Flow that one of my informants has been taken prisoner," Llion said to her, tone utterly bland. "On our journey, I received confirmed reports that he is being held at House Moralis."

"And?" she asked, thinking quickly. She had never seen a messenger or scout approach their group, though she supposed Llion could've snuck away at times to meet his spies. Whoever this captured informant was, though, he was important to

Llion, or he wouldn't be telling her this information. And the informant would also be highly prized by her uncle, or he wouldn't be holding the spy under his roof instead of in the city cells.

In the silence of the room, Llion held her gaze. "The Throne would look favourably upon your assistance in this matter."

Her mouth went dry. Here it was. "And what exactly does the Throne want from me?"

"The layout of House Moralis."

It was a slap in the face, and it shocked her into numbness. "You promised I wouldn't be asked to betray my family."

A muscle twitched in Llion's recently shaved cheek. While the loss of his scruffy beard made him look younger, his eyes hadn't lost the heaviness of a man with many burdens. "What I said was that the Throne did not require you to divulge information—at the time."

Her nostrils flared at the reminder of the threat Llion had delivered with the skinned hare: a promise to wring every last secret from her, if he desired them. "And now times have changed?"

His lack of a response was answer enough.

"The layout of the villa, that's all?" It was still too much. Too intimate of a betrayal.

"The layout of the villa and grounds. The guards' routes, schedules . . ." As Llion droned on, Quinton's face swam before her. *Traitor*, his visage snarled, and she flinched. "And where Tarquin Moralis might sequester a valuable prisoner." When Llion finished, he leaned forward so the candlelight flickered over the harsh planes of his face. "It's crucial our informant's knowledge does not fall into Tarquin Moralis' hands. Hundreds of clan lives will be put at risk. Would you sentence so many to death?"

Here it was. A test of her loyalty. Her fists clenched at her sides before she could draw her dagger and stab another hole in Llion for putting her in the position of executioner. None of the others said a word while they waited for her response.

There was only one. She drew herself up, tiny fissures cracking in her heart along with her oath. "When you put it like that, I can't very well refuse."

**21**

———

The quill sat idle in her hand.

Seren rolled it between her fingers. Her tutors had tried to make a calligrapher of her, but she'd never cared to improve her penmanship beyond legible. After a morning of scribbling in Llion's tent, the layout of House Moralis blurred before her with her quill poised to mark the guard posts and the paths of their patrols.

Lumina, how could she do this? She had promised herself she'd never betray House Moralis, but refusing would raise suspicions of her allegiance.

At first, she'd thought to draw it falsely, but Llion would realize her duplicity once he arrived at her uncle's villa. Might even construe it as breaking her oath to him. So she crumpled up that map and drew the layout accurately enough, if badly. And perhaps if no one could read the maps . . . No, Llion was determined. The prisoner had valuable information Llion didn't want in the hands of Uncle Tarquin.

As she stared at the rough paper, an idea took form. If she could persuade Llion to take her along instead of leaving her here, then she could leave a note and map for Uncle Tarquin, to warn him of the unnatural and powerful Inheritances of the Felinae and tell him about the underground dens.

It would not be without risk of discovery. If she was spotted and captured by House Moralis guards, who thought her a traitor, Llion might leave her behind, and any chance of learning more about the Throne and Prince Alban would be gone.

Her ears twitched. Light footsteps approached. Quickly, she folded a blank sheet into a small square and tucked it inside her bandeau. The tent bells jingled, and the scent she associated with Ellus filled her nose as she bent her head over her scribblings.

When he saw her, he froze, as if surprised to see her in the sealgair's tent, but he quickly recovered. "Here you are! I thought you'd been abducted by wolves."

For the first time that day, a smile broke out on her face. "Just a lion. The sealgair has work for me." She put down the offending quill, and her smile slipped away. "But he's not here," she added, catching Ellus's darting glance to the privacy flap to the sleeping quarters.

That seemed to be all the permission Ellus needed to come around the desk and lean over her shoulder, close enough she could taste the cloying scent of honeyed pears, bergamot, and oak. A finer soap than the kind she had been given to use. While she basked in his warm presence, a tingle began on her forehead. This wasn't the first time she'd felt tingling in the location of her Future Eye with Ellus nearby . . . but no vision ever came. She tried to concentrate on the sensation, but the roaring water of Time's Flow was silent.

"You've been drawing maps all morning?" he asked, staring at her work.

Her pulse quickened. Each page illustrated a floor in the House Moralis villa and its surroundings. But did it matter if Ellus saw? The chances of him setting foot in her uncle's villa were slim. Elusives must be on their way to meet Llion to infiltrate House Moralis—the irony was not lost on her.

"The Sealgair asked me to provide the layout and details of the guard patrols for House Moralis," she said flatly, trying not to let it show how difficult this task was. Peeling off her fingernails might hurt less.

"And you're conflicted."

"It's one thing—" A lump swelled in her throat, preventing her from speaking the words.

"It's one thing to leave. It's another to act against him," he finished quietly.

Close enough. It was one thing to pretend to be a traitor; it was another thing to *be* a traitor. How did this Felinae understand her so well? It wasn't fair.

"Don't report me to the Throne for treasonous thoughts," she joked, fiddling with the quill to cover her fluster. "I'm already wanted by one regime on that account."

Ellus's face darkened as he knelt before her and clasped her ink-smeared hands in his. She held still to prevent the ink from rubbing on the white sleeves of his shirt. "Sol-damn the Throne. You don't have to do this, Seren. It's not a condition of your protection. If Llion said so—" He bit off his last words, mouth compressing into a thin line.

The truth threatened to spill out of her. *Listen, I'm here to atone for what my father and mother did. To end this war, they started. I started. You must convince your prince to surrender.*

And he would look at her with those sapphire blue eyes . . . and condemn her.

Ellus might sympathize, but he was a Felinae lord, sworn to Prince Alban. He wouldn't let her blithely continue gathering information for Uncle Tarquin to overthrow his prince.

So instead of the truth, she gave him a lie folded into a smile.

"My petition hasn't been decided, Ellus. I make the wrong

move and"—she made a slashing movement with an ink-spattered hand—"Regent Boreal and the prince could deny me. I'd have nowhere to go."

*Lumina.* It was all lies, and they rolled right off her tongue. She had somewhere to go. Back to House Moralis—as long as she was victorious in her mission. So why was her chest constricting?

If she failed, if she went home with mere scraps of information about the dens and nothing about the crown prince and his mysterious brother, how would Uncle Tarquin convince the Consul and the city she wasn't a traitor?

Worse, would he try? She'd be worthless to him—a failure. To be successful, she had to earn Llion's trust.

She removed her hands from his to pick the quill back up. "I have to do it, Ellus."

It was a means to an end. One little betrayal of her oath to House Moralis to uphold the larger stratagem at play. Her uncle would surely understand.

The tent's flap flew open, startling them both with a harsh jangle of bells. Llion appeared, fully armed with his sword and knives at his hips and a cloak around his shoulders. His mane of braids was tied back, and he barely favoured his uninjured leg. In his wake, Silver followed like a shadow, likewise cloaked, armed, and in her full assassin getup, minus her cowl so they could perceive her scowl. But it wasn't directed at them.

From his kneeling position at her side, Ellus stood in his fine boots, shoulders back, as if daring the sealgair to say something.

A vein bulged in Llion's neck, but he ignored them in favour of the parchment on the table. "Are the maps done, Morningstar?"

She barely restrained herself from throwing her body across the table. Instead, she hunched over the last map, scribbling the guard posts on the perimeter. "Almost."

"Seren shouldn't be forced to do this, Sealgair." Ellus's voice rang with the sort of clarity of those accustomed to voicing their opinions—and being heeded. He seemed to have no fear of challenging Llion, which she admired, though it was foolish. It struck her that Valera must have felt the same watching Seren respond to her enemies' taunts.

"Do I need to explain simple tactics to you again, Reul?" Llion asked, and it was enough of a rebuke to bring a pink flush to the tips of Ellus's ears. "At this moment, Tarquin Moralis is doing everything he can to wring every last drop of information about us from Dobhran. We'll need every advantage we can use."

*Dobhran.* The lingering fear that Tyberius was the informant dissolved, but the bald fact remained that if she did this for Llion *she* would be a traitor.

"Be that as it may," Seren said stiffly, "my uncle cared for me for many years. I have no wish for him or the members of my House to come to harm."

"An oath?" Ellus suggested.

She tried not to flinch at the word.

Silver plopped into the empty chair across from Seren. "Felinae and their oaths." She reached for the carafe of cider beside a basket of stale bread. "Prims are no better."

Llion put his palms flat on the table and leaned into her space. "Like the Marked of Rokkemar are any different?"

Silver glowered up at him as she poured herself a generous cup. "We have contracts—not oaths. And that is what Morningstar should have. A legal document that specifies the parameters around ending or reneging on the contract."

"Aye, so much better to be paid for your loyalty," Llion shot back. "How is that working out for you?"

The slight didn't stop Silver from quenching her thirst. When she was done, she wiped her mouth with the inside of her wrist. "Once, you thought so, Shade. At least when a contract ends, you have something to show for it. When an oath ends, all you have is betrayal and revenge."

With an inarticulate sound, Llion pushed away from the table but had scant elsewhere to go in the small tent. Idly, Seren danced her fingers over Vindicta's empty spot on her thigh, considering him as he prowled like a caged animal over to the tapestry of a silver wolf howling at the moon. Temper aside, she believed Llion was a man of his word, and it was clear Ellus trusted him.

"Swear to me, Sealgair, that this information on House Moralis is for your eyes alone. Not to share with Wolvair or"— her eyes flicked to Silver—"anyone else."

"Agreed." The swiftness of his response told her Llion hadn't been about to share it with Wolvair.

"And promise me that this is a rescue mission." She gave him a hard look, then glanced at Silver's earring. "Not an assassination attempt on my family, including Imperator Moralis, or anyone pledged to my uncle. Nor will you order or conduct one after the rescue, at any point in time, with this knowledge of House Moralis."

"Swear it on your sword, Sealgair," Ellus suggested, though it sounded oddly like a command. Blocking Llion's view by angling his body, he brushed his hand over her fingers nervously tapping on her thigh where Vindicta should be, and a kernel of warmth flared within her.

Llion raised a recalcitrant eyebrow but drew out his sword and wrapped both hands around the hilt. "I, Llion Llewyn, swear to avoid death where possible. My objective is solely to rescue my informant, and I will not use the opportunity to target your family using this knowledge of their home, now . . . or"—he grimaced—"hereafter. I will, however, protect myself and mine with deadly force. Anything else, *Your Highness*?"

It would have to do.

"And the maps are to be destroyed once you and your band of Elusives are done with them."

"I so swear." Llion said it so gravely, it should've made her feel better, but her betrayal of House Moralis, however small, still stung. There was no getting around the fact that Llion and the Felinae would possess intimate knowledge of her home after this.

Silver snorted and propped her dainty feet up on the table, crossing her boots at the ankle. "There's no 'band' of Elusives going with him, and my skills are apparently better suited to guarding hatchlings, while this one"—she jerked a thumb in Llion's direction—"thinks he can slip in with a wounded leg and drag Dobhran out the city gates by himself."

"Is attempting this alone wise, Sealgair?" Ellus interjected, letting go of Seren's hand. "The Throne cannot afford to lose you."

"I'll go with you." Seren stood, certain they could all hear her heart pounding. "I know the layout and the guards. And I'm your best fighter, next to Silver." And this was her chance to leave word to her uncle and earn Llion's unwavering trust.

"Sit down, Morningstar," Silver snapped, standing up herself with a scrape of the chair. "You'll be staying here with the other recruits. I'll make sure the sealgair doesn't get himself killed. And he can't very well order me not to."

No one said anything. Llion closed his eyes, gathering patience or listening for eavesdroppers. When he opened them, he spoke in a measured tone. "The recruits can't stay here. Those arrows were made to falsely accuse the Mountain Clan. And were possibly meant to kill one or more of us. I don't dare trust their safety to anyone but myself. But from what I've seen of Morningstar's maps, I can't pull this off alone."

"You can't mean to take them." Silver's hands punched into fists when Llion didn't assure her differently. "If they're captured, they'll be interrogated until broken. Shade, they aren't ready—"

"War doesn't call us when we're ready," Llion interrupted. "And what do you care? As you say, you have no contract with us—no payment for your loyalty."

"That's unfair of you, and you know it," Silver lashed back, unsheathing one sword to point it at him.

Seren's gaze darted between the two warriors. Tempers were running high, and neither seemed to care they had an audience. Silver's lack of a contract was a surprise since it was the sole reason Seren could think of for the Marked assassin to stay on their little isle, training *hatchlings*.

Llion advanced, not caring, it seemed, that Silver widened her stance. "I need someone to head west and warn the others that Dobhran may have compromised their locations." He halted when the blade was a finger span below his sternum. "Someone I trust. The fate of the Elusive network can't be left to Wolvair's caprices or my birds."

"Send the recruits west then," Silver argued. "Ellus knows the hideouts. Tell him—"

"Ellus stays with me," Llion broke in harshly.

Seren frowned at Llion's possessive tone. He almost spoke about Ellus as if he were his father, but at most there was a decade between them. For his part, Ellus held himself rigid, avoiding her questioning glances.

"I won't abandon him—or the others." Llion didn't try to disarm Silver. Instead, he crossed his arms as if to keep from touching his knives or her. "Drakori scried this morning and does not foresee any of them being captured or killed if they come with me. I wouldn't risk them unnecessarily."

"Do you hear yourself?" Silver scoffed, her sword not wavering. "The Shade I knew and fought beside on the continent wouldn't trust our lives to portents and dreams."

"The Shade you knew is *gone*," Llion growled, leaning down

into her face. The short sword pressed at his leather tunic. "I am no longer a mercenary without a home, without responsibilities."

"No longer without a master," she said, her frosted tone as bleak as a long winter's night. She lowered her sword. "Pity. It was much easier to talk sense into him."

Llion made a guttural noise and spun away, his predatory gaze shifting to Seren. There was that look of hard glass again—the one that had dismissed her life as expendable as a hare in one of his snares.

"Before I take you on this mission, Morningstar, answer me this: why would you betray your House and put your life in Tarquin Moralis's hands for a Prim traitor?"

Seren took a deep breath to marshal her thoughts. She must persuade him. "I am detritus to my family. Despite not wishing them harm . . . I no longer have a House or a family or a home in Luminaria." She swallowed. "If I risk my life to save your informant from my uncle, you, Prince Alban, and Regent Boreal will have little reason to question my loyalty."

Llion considered her. "Pack. We leave within the hour."

Relief filled her, but Silver wasn't about to let the matter or the sealgair go. The assassin slipped in front of Llion, blocking his retreat to his sleeping quarters.

"Doesn't the fact that she's a Felinae princess grant her protection? Why must she forsake her family to prove her loyalty to you?"

Behind her chair, Ellus shifted uneasily, embarrassed perhaps for his prince or from the emotional display before them, and Seren pretended to work on the maps.

"You advised me not to trust her!" Llion roared, throwing his hands wide.

"I don't trust anyone." Silver didn't budge—they were toe-to-toe—her hands on her hips, near her swords again. "Tried it once. Didn't work out."

Llion had over a foot on Silver, yet he flinched as if struck. Seren braced herself on the chance they couldn't contain their fight to verbal volleys.

"Please, Silvanysilatha'na," Llion pleaded softly. "Go west. For me."

All the fight drained from Silver. "You're a *davikking edred*."

"So I've been told." He unclasped the claw necklace from around his neck and fastened it around Silver's. "To show you speak for me." Then he withdrew a folded piece of parchment sealed with wax from a pouch on his belt. "Instructions for the leaders to send their fastest to alert the dens. We'll meet again at Caisteal Dìomhair."

Silver palmed the note. "And if I had refused?"

He shrugged, and she shook her head in irritation before stopping in front of Seren on her way out of the tent. All her fierceness returned. "If he dies"—she jabbed a thumb in Llion's direction—"by Moralis hands, your uncle's days will be Marked." Her eyes flicked to Ellus. "May your enemies never see your blade, Reul."

"May the Goddess light your path, Silver," Ellus replied solemnly.

With that the Marked assassin disappeared under the flap. Seren didn't have time to further consider the threat. Silver's empty chair creaked under Llion's weight; he extended his hand, palm up, across the table to her.

"Now, let's see what we're up against, Morningstar."

## 22

It wasn't the homecoming Seren had imagined.

No parades. No crowds. No laurels thrown at her feet. Only Lumina near her fullness and the familiar constellations above to witness her procession through the city and into an Elusive safe house. The existence of which made her head hurt. First informants, now collaborators—how deep into the republic did Llion's network run?

From the second-floor window, Seren breathed in the welcoming aroma of grilled fish and lemon from the neighbour's kitchen and the sweet mellow notes of the violet-blue evening flowers blooming in window boxes. She had missed the city more than she realized. Absently, she redid her braid while acquainting herself with the sleepy quarter. The safe house was a sand-coloured dwelling composed of crumbling diamond-shaped tufa blocks and mortar. It was one in a long line of cramped domiciles in a servilis quarter on the western side of the Aegis. House Oceala's quarter, she noted, from the simple mark of the fish sigil above the doorways. Hanging lanterns lit the street, though a young boy ran about dousing them for the night. A handful of men and women hurried home over the uneven cobblestones, returning from a night shift at the docks or private homes of House Oceala's nobilis.

Her scrutiny of these servs sharpened into mistrust. Any of them might be the traitors who had given up these living quarters to Llion, and perhaps they were now staying with a neighbour. The home had been empty when they arrived, and maybe that was for the best since the occupants might have recognized her. Unfortunately, it meant she couldn't supply their names to Uncle Tarquin in her report.

Thinking about what was to come had kept her nerves on edge during the journey. Passing through the northern gates as farmhands on a night off had been easier than she liked with the identity medallions from House Oceala that Llion had produced—which gave her reason to believe the informant was from that House as well.

It struck her then that *Dobhran* might be an alias. It wasn't a Prim name.

*Please don't let the traitor be Tyberius.*

Her eyes travelled toward the bay, where shadowed rooftops merged until the heart of Luminaria rose into domes and granite columns of the temples and civic buildings. From there, it was a short ride to Accord Bridge, the tops of its arches barely visible from here. Memory traced the grand arcs stretching over the Aegis in two tiers, each stone cut precisely to hold each other up.

On the other side of it rose the walls of House Moralis.

*Home.*

So close.

Throwing caution into the night air, Seren leaned out as far as she could, the billowy sleeves of Ellus's borrowed shirt rippling in the salty breeze. She stared as hard as she could in the direction of House Moralis—waiting for some sign of what was to come.

"Did he not want to come with you?"

The question startled her. Vesper sat on one of the three small beds in the room, drying her tawny hair with a threadbare towel. In her shift, she looked even younger.

"Who?"

Vesper put down the towel and bit her lip. "I thought maybe you didn't wish to marry your cousin because there was someone else who had your heart?"

A handsome face with familiar coppery hair and a knowing smirk rose in Seren's mind, but the thought of Ty conjured too many conflicting feelings to sort into words. Did he have her heart?

No, but she couldn't honestly say he hadn't caught her eye. Long ago, if she were honest with herself.

"There was someone—maybe." She sighed. "I do love Quinton." The spot between her shoulder blades tingled, then dispersed. The past? Was the tingling trying to tell her Quinton was in her past? "But not as a wife should. And there's so much I want to do before I'd consider marriage. To anyone."

Vesper smiled rather sheepishly. "My mother says I'm a hopeless romantic."

"She must be one, too," Seren mused, remembering the ballads Valera enjoyed reading, "since she ran off to the city and fell in love with a Prim."

That drew forth a chuckle. "Eglantine Llews doesn't care to have that pointed out." Vesper abandoned the towel and joined Seren at the window. "She left him. Not the other way around."

It struck Seren that Eglantine Llews could've been executed for loving a Prim, for staying in the city after the war began. The Consul, at her uncle's urging had hunted the Felinae over the years, effectively breaking Vesper's family in half.

"Why don't you hate me for what my parents did all those years ago? For what my uncle's doing now?"

Vesper scrunched up her nose. "Seren, what your uncle

does has nothing to do with you. Same with your parents." She bumped Seren playfully with her hip. "Besides, I could never hate you. You keep Thane the Pain in his place, and Kanta's too busy being sour with you to order me about."

Seren sighed. "Not everyone sees it that way. They blame me." Prims blamed her for what her mother and father did or didn't do. Felinae would blame her for her uncle's victory.

"Well, I'll tell them where to stick their noses if they do. Us half-moons got each other's back."

That sounded good. For so long, she'd been the only one—one against hundreds. "You know, Vesper, your mother has something very special that your father doesn't—you."

The girl turned her wistful face up to the stars. "She told me she was afraid to ask him to come with her. Afraid he'd leave the city, his family and friends, and one day hate her for it. Afraid her clan wouldn't accept him—or worse. But my mother gave him the choice."

And it was clear he'd said no.

Seren found herself settling a sympathetic arm around Vesper's shoulder, the pain of a father's scorn all too familiar to her. The girl stiffened but relaxed into the embrace, the top of her head settling against Seren's shoulder. It felt good to offer this small comfort. Maybe this was what it felt like to have a younger sister, which reminded her how much Valera had given up by joining House Moralis.

"Part of me accepted the sealgair's offer because I knew I might get the chance to come here," Vesper confessed. "Might see him. And now I'm here, and all I want to do is leave. I don't want to hurt anyone, Seren. That isn't why I became an Elusive." Vesper twisted away. "I don't know my father's name, or where he lived, or if he's still a guard. My mother wouldn't tell me. All I have is this."

From her pack on the bed, Vesper withdrew a plain silver locket. Inside sat a miniature painting of a man with light brown hair and a stern countenance. There was a slight likeness to Vesper in the thin nose and lips.

It was strangely comforting to know they were both haunted by who they might meet in the city. At once, the selfish thought brought heat to Seren's cheeks. Unlike her, Vesper wanted to meet her father. Maybe one day, Seren could help her find him.

The locket clicked closed with a sniffle. "I'm pathetic, huh?"

Gently, Seren put a hand on her shoulder. "No, you're not. If there was the possibility of running into my father, I'd be a mess, too."

Devan Morningstar was dead, but she might very well run into Quinton or Tyberius during the rescue. Her stomach flipped over. Those two she would have to avoid at all costs. Either might try to stop her, and she couldn't afford for the dream or vision Drakori had orchestrated to come true. It was crucial she leave a note to warn Uncle Tarquin about Taibhseir Drakori and the Inheritances. Or maybe she'd get the chance to slip away and tell Uncle Tarquin in private.

A loud knock below at the front door startled them both, and they raced to the window. At the sight of two figures in black City Patrol uniforms, Seren broke out in a cold sweat. One had a bag slung over his shoulder. Had someone recognized her on the streets? She stepped back from view, bringing a wide-eyed Vesper by the hand. They'd have to make a run for it—out the window once the CPs entered the house. Then run along the roofs—

"City Patrol," the woman announced.

At the same time, the door to their sleeping chamber flew open. In the doorway stood Ellus in his undershirt and leathers, his hair damp from washing. Silently, he raised a finger to his lips. Relief buzzed through Seren as she greedily soaked up the sight of him, committing every garnet strand to memory. If they were arrested, this might be the last time they were together.

"Open up on the authority of the Imperator, Tarquin Moralis of the First Founders of Luminaria!" the man outside demanded. Ellus quietly closed the door, as if two closed doors could keep the CPs out.

It didn't matter. They were discovered, just as Silver had predicted. Maybe Ellus would flee with her. She crossed to him and placed a hand on his firm shoulder. His nostrils flared as his sapphire eyes darkened. She was about to whisper her plan to escape over the rooftops when the bolt on the front door scraped against the lock.

"Does the imperator know what time I wake up to load his blasted ships?"

Seren couldn't stop her brows from rising at Llion's gruff dockside accent.

There was a pause and then a throaty chuckle. "Aren't you a tall drink of honey. Bet you go down smooth and sweet, too."

Beside her, Ellus made a choking noise, and she clapped a hand over his mouth, his soft lips pressed to her hand. After a moment, he nodded, and she removed her hand. Thank the moon and stars Prims didn't have Felinae hearing.

"Save it for later, Mercia," the other CP said wearily, as if it wasn't the first time. "We still have two blocks to cover, and I'd like to see my bunk before I need to wake up for the hanging."

"Hanging?" Llion asked.

"Good news for you, honey," Mercia said. "You can sleep in tomorrow. Imperator's declared it a holiday."

"All are invited to see the traitor hang at the eighth hour after midnight, to be followed by Centurio Moralis's duel," added Mercia's partner, clearly by rote.

It was nearly midnight by Seren's calculation, which left them eight hours to prepare and pull off a jail break. Then the last part of the announcement hit home. Who was Quinton duelling? The Legion's annual competition wasn't until autumn, but perhaps Uncle Tarquin had arranged something similar.

"What about my pay?" Llion demanded in a lazy drawl. "Is the imperator docking me a day?"

Boots retreated on the cobblestones. "You'll have to ask your dock master about that, honey. But if you want some company tomorrow afterwards, you ask for Mercia at Glory's."

"Might just do that, Mercia," Llion said in a low tone so suggestive, Seren's cheeks flamed red as she caught Ellus's glance.

From the window, Vesper whispered, "They're moving on."

As soon as she heard the front door close, Seren bolted down the stairs with Ellus on her heels. It would take an hour to move across the city to House Moralis—longer if they didn't wish to be noticed. With her mind sorting through the best routes to take, she didn't see the danger until she collided with a wall of carved muscle. It was like hitting an unmovable rock, and she bounced backward. Llion's hand shot out, lightning fast, and he caught her elbow before she fell.

Her face burned. No wonder Mercia had been interested. But it wasn't the expanse of muscle—well, not entirely—that made her eyes widen. It was the criss-crossing of old scars that covered him. In the shadow of the doorway, they must not have been as visible.

*What do you know of interrogation, Seren Morningstar?*

Llion let go of her. He tugged his undershirt free from where it hung on his belt and pulled it over his head. His leather armour, visible weapons, and holsters were still stowed away since farmhands entering the city rarely had more than a knife on them.

"That was close," Ellus said from behind her, and she stepped aside to let him and Vesper down the stairs. *Too close.*

Kanta and Thane appeared from the kitchen doorway, the

latter with a look of contempt. "That a trick you learned on the continent, plying the old mercenary trade, Sealgair?"

A rumble started in Llion's chest, and Seren tensed before she realized he was laughing. "One I learned at a young age, Sionnach. If you give people what they want to see, they don't look any further."

"But how did you know it was what Mercia wanted to see?" Seren blurted.

Abruptly, Llion looked down at a rolled paper the City Patrollers must have handed him, his braids falling down to hide his face.

Kanta sighed, long and hard. "Come on, Morningstar. Have you not noticed the scent animals give off before they mate?"

Heat suffused her cheeks for a second time. A full Felinae's nose must be far more sensitive than hers.

"Fauna lectures aside, are we too late to rescue Dobhran?" Ellus chose a spot against the wall in between her and Kanta, as if to keep the peace, and Seren silently thanked him for taking the attention off her.

In response, Llion unrolled the poster. There were two, actually—one inside the other. Whatever he saw in the first one made his mouth tighten, and he quickly tucked the offending paper into a leather pouch on his belt. The other he barely glanced at before he held it out for them to see.

The words *Burner of Gull Harbour* blurred in front of Seren as she considered the sketched likeness of the man she was to rescue. His face was long, his cheeks gaunt, and his eyes large and brooding under a prominent forehead. A corpse of a man. Three hundred and fifty deaths stained his soul in the Gull Harbour burning alone. The poster also listed multiple raids of the city's armouries over the past three years and *other acts of aiding and abetting the enemy.*

The name emblazoned across the poster, however, was Alphonius Luther—a Prim name. So Dobhran was a Felinae alias. But he wasn't Tyberius. Yet she wasn't truly relieved. The growing tightness in her chest made her gulp for air, except there didn't seem to be any in the cramped atrium. By all that was just in the world, Dobhran—Luther—deserved to die for his crimes.

"You brought this Prim over yourself?" Her voice held a reckless edge, one she probably shouldn't take with Llion. She tried to appear uncaring as she followed Llion and the others into the humble kitchen. Two pots and a pan hung on the walls over a chipped yellow-and-blue ceramic tile counter that her fingers danced along. In the middle of the rectangular room was a rough wooden table and two stools where they had eaten a cold repast of dried dates, goat's cheese, and bread earlier. The opposite wall boasted an unlit stone oven, and the kitchen's hearth was likewise cold. No one had cooked here for a while.

Llion leaned back on the oven and crossed his arms. He was the one in charge of the Elusives. Ultimately, her anger rested with him, Regent Boreal, and Prince Alban. But what had tempted Alphonius Luther to turn? To betray his House? His family? His people? What had tempted the people who supposedly lived in this house?

"Three years ago, he found his own way to me. I owe him a life debt. I won't abandon him." Llion's gaze became hazy, like he wasn't seeing them all at all.

"What about his knowledge of the Elusives and the clans, Sealgair? Have we been compromised?" Kanta plopped down on one of the stools, her foot tapping out an irregular rhythm.

"How badly compromised you mean." Thane joined Kanta at the table, leaving Vesper to sidle up close to Seren at the counter. "Dobhran's been in Tarquin Moralis's tender care for almost a week now."

He was right. Uncle Tarquin and his interrogators had probably wrung every Felinae hidey hole out of Dobhran or he wouldn't be hanging tomorrow. Llion must know that. But it made her wonder if Dobhran knew where Regent Boreal and Prince Alban kept their hidden court. If Uncle Tarquin had all the information he needed from Dobhran, then he wouldn't need her to spy. And her opportunity to prove to all of Luminaria how loyal she was, how Primordian she was, would be gone.

What would she do then?

"What do we do?" Ellus asked from the doorway, echoing her thoughts so closely she thought he was speaking to her alone. "We're not ready. We haven't slept. The plan was to—"

But, of course, Ellus was talking about the rescue mission. A sheen of sweat covered his forehead, but it was the change in scent she noticed. The briny smell of fear. And it wasn't just him.

"Plans change." Llion tossed the paper into the unlit hearth. "We go tonight."

## 23

High in the branches of old lemon trees, songbirds trilled in the warm night air. The evening, however, was quickly winding toward dawn, and for the twentieth time since Llion had entered the guard tower alone, Seren shifted from one knee to the other, grinding the same amaryllis petal into the cobblestones beneath her. The blood-red blossoms were everywhere. Even in the three-tiered marble fountain. Someone's idea of decor, she supposed. Someone with a more artistic touch than the patrius of the House.

*What other changes have happened at House Moralis while I've been gone?*

In her position behind the hedgerow, Seren especially didn't appreciate whoever had strung red blown-glass lanterns overhead from the third-floor balconies to the villa's ramparts. A few still burned, bathing patches of the manicured gardens and marble statues in a soft, candlelit glow. It had forced Seren and Thane to take a more circuitous route through the garden to set up their position around the tower. If she blinked hard enough, she could almost believe she was hiding in the gardens of some decadent Exiler, not those of her childhood.

Part of that was because it had been so long since Uncle Tarquin had hosted a ball. He despised them for their extravagance. It wasn't a moon ball either. The full moon wouldn't rise until tomorrow night. Yet the nobilis had been here—and some remained—celebrating the night before the execution of the traitor. This disturbing thought unsettled Seren more than being alone with the Lockpick. And in a couple of hours, if Llion failed, the rest of Luminaria would celebrate the traitor's death at the Amphitheatron.

Seren didn't know why such a thing should upset her. Dobhran deserved his fate for breaking his oath of loyalty to his House. *But what if it had been Tyberius?* The question seemed to come out of her mind, yet the sly voice niggled at her.

*Tyberius isn't the traitor.*

*No, but you are*, the voice taunted. *Maybe the imperator will hang you in front of the entire city.*

Seren refused to dwell on such a nonsensical idea. But it did make her wonder what loved ones Dobhran was leaving behind, and how they might feel tomorrow during the spectacle of his death.

An arm's length away, Thane peered through the leaves at the four guards posted at the main villa's front entrance with an intensity that impressed her. Under a black leather jacket and cuirass, his body was tense, ready to spring at the slightest sign of their discovery. She hadn't expected Thane to care about the success of Llion's mission given their taut relationship. But Thane shared no love for the Primordians—the nobilis in particular—so she supposed she shouldn't be surprised at his eagerness to fight.

To that end, a long knife hung at his side. Before they left the safe house, Llion had handed out an assortment of serendium knives and daggers with holsters to the rest of the recruits and returned Vindicta to her. Seren wasn't sure how much damage they could inflict with their weapons, but it was something to defend themselves with. She tried not to think about who Ellus, Vesper, Thane, and Kanta would be defending themselves against.

However, with Llion busy searching the cells in the guard tower, the time was ripe to ditch Thane and slip inside to leave her note for Uncle Tarquin or speak to him alone in his rooms. But she had to do it unseen by any Prims or Felinae. The thought crossed her mind that Llion had stuck Thane with her to keep her from such an attempt. Who better to remind her that her secrets weren't safe?

"So, Princess," Thane whispered, keeping his attention on the bored sentries, "is Dobhran rotting in that tower?"

She scowled to hide the quickening of her blood. "It's where oathbreakers are locked up."

It was true, and it was possible Dobhran was there along with those being disciplined for various infractions against House Moralis. Some would be accepted back into the House after serving their punishment; others would be sent to the Detritus Quarter or worse. But by the time Llion searched half the cells, the House guards would be alerted to his presence and the mission would be over. They'd escape, and Dobhran would meet his justly deserved death at the Amphitheatron. And in one fell swoop, she would've helped the sealgair and won the favour of the Throne without betraying her uncle —much.

Thane made a noncommittal noise, but under his usual cowl of apathy buzzed something close to excitement. "I bet you drew those maps poorly on purpose. No nob's penmanship could be that poor."

She huffed. "Like you could do better?"

"Once a nob, always a nob."

*Once a Moralis, always a Moralis.*

"The sealgair won't give up if he doesn't find his man in there." Thane jerked his thumb at the tower behind them. "And the guards are bound to notice a Felinae the size of a small mountain with the temper of a pissed-off hornet."

This was the most he had said to her since her first day. He was, however, obliquely accusing her of lying to Llion. Had the sealgair ordered him to use his Inheritance if he thought she was withholding information? It was a chilling thought.

He spared her a glance. "All I'm saying is our likelihood of walking out of here increases if we find Dobhran without alerting every guard."

She shifted to her other knee. Capture at this point in her mission would mean failure.

"And maybe you've another idea of where a valuable prisoner might be held. Never hurts to have someone like the sealgair owe you."

As much as she didn't want Dobhran freed, having Llion's trust and gratitude would go a long way to securing her an audience with the crown prince—maybe even a private one. Once her uncle negotiated the Felinae Dominion's surrender, Dobhran would be at the mercy of Prim law once again.

She hadn't consciously thought about the black room in ages, though she supposed there was a reason she didn't include it on her maps. Llion had asked where Tarquin kept prisoners, not where she thought Dobhran was held. And deep down she knew that was exactly where they'd find the traitor. It would be risky to enter the fourth floor, where security would be the tightest, but it would serve her purpose since her uncle wouldn't discover her note in the hedges.

"You're being awfully amiable all of a sudden, Sionnach. Thought you despised me."

He shrugged without looking at her. "Maybe I want to earn some of the sealgair's gratitude as well by rescuing his informant. Doesn't mean we have to braid each other's hair, Princess."

But how could she pretend to suddenly know where Dobhran was without admitting her deception to Thane? Without giving him the means to tattle to Llion?

Her palms tingled. *Of course.*

She scowled at Thane for good measure. "I don't know where—"

Without warning, she slumped toward him with a soft groan, her eyelids fluttering as she pretended to fight to stay awake. Thane cursed but caught her in his arms, the leather of his jacket a welcomed protection from his touch. If she wanted him to believe it, she'd have to commit to it. So she let her head to loll against his shoulder.

"Seren?"

The scent of dry leaves and a hint of something sweeter became stronger the longer she lay there. She moaned again for effect. How long did a vision usually take? Her palms throbbed as if crying for attention. Could she truly use her Eye to find Dobhran? Or had Drakori's talk of an Inheritance all been a ruse to get inside her mind?

Thane's arms tightened around her as a slew of muffled curses blistered the air. That was probably long enough. Besides, she didn't need a Third Eye to tell her where Dobhran was being kept. She opened her eyes to find Thane staring into hers.

Relief flashed over his pale face. "I thought you passed on to the Vale, Princess."

His hands fell away, and she sat up, brushing non-existent leaves from her sleeves to cover the sudden awkwardness. "In your dreams, Lockpick."

He didn't smirk like she thought he would. If anything, he became paler.

"Llion threatened me with a fate ten times worse if I let

anything happen to you, " he admitted. "So don't die or anything."

For moon's sake, Llion couldn't care less if she died, whether at the Lockpick's hands or the hands of her House. It must be his oath or his orders he was worried about. "Relax, Sionnach. If I wanted you dead, I'd do it myself."

She tapped her palms. They tingled in response, the Eyes rising to the surface of her skin. Making the marks rise was the only part of her Inheritance she'd mastered so far. But Thane didn't need to know that.

"You had a vision?"

In answer, she directed her gaze at the fourth-floor balcony overhanging the white marble steps of the grand entrance to House Moralis. "I know where Dobhran is."

She didn't suppress her shiver. Uncle Tarquin would want to punish Alphonius Luther for daring to betray the republic. For that, he would put the man in the black room.

---

ANOTHER LOW CURSE filled her ears as her stolen bronze boot stomped on Thane's hunched shoulders and her leather pteruges hit him in the face. Honestly, he had given her this idea so he shouldn't complain. Once she was standing on top of his shoulder guards, he slowly straightened. Now her hands could get a hold on the edge of the second-floor balcony that ran the length of the south wall—out of sight of the sentries. From there, she and Thane would climb up to the fourth floor before the eastern patrol returned.

The patrol had recently passed through the gardens on their route to the back of the villa's grounds, where the docks were situated. There, Ellus waited with their packs, guarding the tapered skiffs that they had used to approach the property unnoticed. She suspected Llion had given Ellus that duty to keep him out of the fight should one break out. Although his fighting skills were much improved, Ellus had lost all his matches—both with weapons and without. While he had been clearly disappointed at being left behind, he hadn't argued. She prayed a patrol didn't find him.

After hauling herself over the balustrade, Seren reached down for Thane's hand as light footsteps approached from the garden path. She froze. A guard? A guest? Vesper and Kanta should've immobilized the other patrols by now.

Her fingers found the pommel of her sword, pilfered along with the bronze armour from the two guards who had wandered into the shadows of the hedges to relieve themselves. Down below, Thane also drew his sword, though it didn't look like he had much experience with one.

"Care to explain what you two are up to?"

Thane lowered his newly acquired sword. "Are you trying to scare the souls out of us, Reul? Why aren't you guarding the skiffs?"

Stepping out from the maze of hedges, Ellus gazed up at her with an apprehensive frown. "I had a feeling something was"—he pursed his lips—"wrong."

"Ellus." Even though her ears were telling her she was safe, it took seeing the sculpted lines of his face bathed in moonlight for her heart to believe it.

"Is everything all right, Seren?" He glanced between her and Thane.

Relief and the realization she had almost voluntarily touched the Lockpick's bare skin rippled through her. At that moment, a gust of wind blew in a slight figure in tight black leather with windswept tawny hair.

"Why is everyone out of position?" Vesper's eyes widened as she took in the bronzed breastplates, pomegranate tunics, and leather pteruges that Seren and Thane wore. She grinned. "Are we joining the festivities in disguise?"

"A man's hanging is not cause for merriment," Ellus snapped with uncharacteristic impatience, and Vesper shrunk in on herself. Seren knew Vesper had no desire to see anyone dead, but before she could defend her friend, Thane spoke.

"For Tarquin Moralis, it is." He sheathed his sword with a nod at Vesper. "Seren had a vision. Dobhran's imprisoned inside the villa. We're going to rescue him."

At this, Ellus shot her a worried look. "This changes the plan. We should alert Llion. Where's Kanta?"

"Guarding the skiffs," Vesper answered, her quiet confidence restored. "When we returned to the dock and you weren't there, we thought you'd been captured. I volunteered to find you or Llion as I'd be faster. And someone had to stay behind to guard our escape plan."

Ellus had the decency to look chagrined. "I didn't think of that."

"No time to inform either of them," Seren cut in. Llion might insist on a solo mission. That wouldn't work for her plans. "The eastern patrol?" she asked Vesper.

"Sleeping soundly. And the southern and western patrol. They'll have splitting headaches in the morning, courtesy of that move of yours." Vesper mimicked the strike Seren had taught her with a proud grin, and she had the right to be pleased with herself.

It had taken Seren weeks to learn Nightfall from Master Kai, whereas Vesper had performed an effective knockout strike —on Seren's neck—after a few stolen hours of training at night on the journey to the city. And now dozens of guards were incapacitated. Once fully trained in the moondance, the girl would be an unstoppable force.

Guilt tarnished her pride at the blow Vesper had dealt the House Moralis guards, but better a headache than a knife in the ribs.

"Well?" Thane prodded, his dark eyes meeting hers. "Are we

doing this, Princess?" He extended his hand up to her. A clear challenge.

*Dare she take it?*

Before she could, Ellus clamped a hand on Thane's armored shoulder. "We are. Give me a boost, Sionnach."

Thane frowned but made a foothold with his hands. Seren reached down to help Ellus, but he sprang upward into the air with a hearty heave from Thane. His hands found purchase with the top of the balcony, and he swung over it, as agile as when he had scaled the ceiling of the mountain to show her the stars.

Vesper stepped up to Thane for her turn. A tingle started in Seren's forehead, along with the feeling of icy fingers walking up her spine.

*Vesper shouldn't come into the villa.*

"We need a lookout." Seren pointed to the hedgerows near the fountain, from where Vesper could safely watch the front entrance.

"And someone to retrieve our clothes," Thane added, pointing toward the shrubs where they had hidden them.

Vesper's face fell at the dismissal, but she nodded and blurred away. With no one to give him a boost, Thane ran at the balcony, then sprang upward, his pomegranate cape billowing behind him as he sailed through the air. Dirt-lined fingernails grabbed at the bottom of the balcony. In response, her calves twitched. These Felinae were far too lithe for her liking.

"A little help?" Thane grumbled through clenched teeth.

Bending over the marble balustrade, Seren reached down as far as she could before she could think better of it. "Can you reach my hand?"

Muddy brown eyes stared up at her as Thane let go with one hand to grab at hers. Before he could, hands encircled her waist.

"I got you," Ellus murmured.

Lowering her down gave her the reach she needed to clasp onto each of Thane's bronze bracers, and his hands latched onto her bracers. With Ellus's support, she hauled him up until he could get his footing on the ledge. Then she distanced herself quickly as she could, despite savouring the feel of Ellus's hands around her. Something she absolutely should not be thinking about.

The next two balconies were easily scaled from jumping off the balustrade below, and then the three of them stood before the double-wide glass doors to Uncle Tarquin's private dining room. The door handle stuck in her hand. Locked. She withdrew her short sword to break the glass with the pommel. Before she could, Thane jostled the handle. Within a few twists, the door sprang open.

He glanced at her over his shoulder. "Your uncle should have that lock fixed."

Eyes narrowed, Seren swept past him, straight to the hall door to listen. She could hear at least two people from the direction of her uncle's personal wing. She peeked out. Every twenty paces a glass lamp along the wall cast a pool of light on the rich black and gold carpets of the empty corridor. At the end of this hallway, around the corner, were her uncle's private rooms, and next to them was the black room.

Doubt seized her. What if she was wrong and Dobhran wasn't there?

All the better. She could drop the note and leave.

She turned back to find one House Moralis guard and one Felinae staring at her.

"What now, Seren?" Ellus asked. The complete faith in his eyes nearly felled her.

A plan took shape as she moved to the heavy curtains. "You'll be our prisoner." Her knife made a quick rent in the rich red fabric, then she used her hands to tear it into two strips. "If we're stopped, we've orders to take you to . . . where

Dobhran is." She didn't know what Uncle Tarquin called the black room.

She held up the torn cloth to Ellus in apology. "I'll tie this around your mouth. Tighter around your hands, as if they're shackled behind your back. Act like you don't want to be here."

He attempted a grin. "Easy enough."

After she tied the cloth around his mouth and secured his hands, he glared straight ahead with such menace she didn't think he was pretending. No matter his talk of peace, rage stirred deep inside him over his dead family and his stolen life.

Well, what about her dead? Her fellow Prims had burned alive in the fires of Gull Harbour. Women, children, the elderly —all trapped while flames ate their flesh to the bone, then burned so hot, nothing was left but white ash. The Burner of Gull Harbour had those dead on his soul. And if she was right, he was down the hall, waiting to be punished.

"It's like you were born to wear shackles, Reul," Thane remarked, giving Ellus's restraints the once-over.

Ellus moved his constricted hands in a gesture she had seen Thane use more than once. Thane just smirked, looking more like a House guard in his uniform every minute.

"Don't give anyone a reason to question us," she reminded them. She took her own words to heart, coiling her signature brown braid into a knot at her neck.

"Won't you be recognized?" Ellus mumbled through the gag.

She hesitated. "Like Llion did, we give them what they want to see. No one will be expecting me to turn up inside House Moralis in a guard uniform. We bluff until we're caught. If need be, I'll use Nightfall." Her eyes narrowed on Thane, whose hand rested on the hilt of his sword. "Remember, no bloodshed."

Thane took his hand off his sword and gave Ellus a push toward the door. "If we play this right, all their attention will be focused on our prisoner. But better you walk behind us, Princess."

After she showed Thane how to hold Ellus's elbow to keep him secure, they slipped into the hallway. In the short distance to Uncle Tarquin's rooms, Seren's body fell into the familiar rhythm that had been drilled into her at the Lyceum. If she hadn't run away, Uncle Tarquin might have made her a House guard before sponsoring her for the Legion.

Or would she have been Quinton's bride? Uncertainty pricked at her like a thorn in her heel.

"Less swagger," she muttered to Thane, ahead of her. Cockiness radiated from him. But she had to admit it was a fair approximation of most nobs and some of the guard. As they padded down the hallway, both he and Ellus were enjoying their roles far too much for her liking. Every few steps, Ellus pulled hard away from him, forcing Thane to stumble and jerk him back. Perhaps they should've had Ellus pretend he was unconscious.

As they rounded the corner, two sentry guards stiffened to attention. Both had the black hair and bronzed skin of so many of House Moralis. While she supposed she'd seen them around the villa, neither were her uncle's usual sentries. Past them and the double mahogany doors of her uncle's rooms was a black marble door.

As a child, she'd once glimpsed inside the black room. Determined to find Uncle Tarquin and tell him of some childish achievement that day, she'd followed him to the fourth floor, quiet as a mouse, and seen him enter. While the guards had their attention on their patrius, they hadn't noticed her slip in behind him before the door closed. Adults, she had found, rarely looked down.

In the silence, Uncle Tarquin had taken off a pomegranate formal jacket, folded it, and laid it neatly on a marble table, where a horsewhip lay. He'd begun wrapping it around his hand. When he'd finished, he looked up, his grey eyes widening a fraction when he saw her standing in the doorway. Young as she was, she could tell he was displeased by the downward twitch of his lips.

"Run along, Niece," he'd told her calmly, gaze flicking to something behind the door, something she couldn't see.

*Niece.* He always called her that, never using her name.

But her stubby legs hadn't moved. She'd stood transfixed by the dark liquid pooled on the black tile, and the guards had squeezed her arms to drag her out, apologizing profusely before slamming the door.

"Halt and identify!" blurted the younger guard.

The other one, with a pointed chin beard in the style of conquered Espana, put his hand casually on the hilt of his sword. It took all of her self-discipline for Seren to ignore the threat and salute with her right hand, making a V over her heart. To her relief, Thane did the same.

"Who does it look like? Your mother, Novi?" Thane drawled in a passable nob accent. The familiar slang for the novitius rank was another surprise. Had Llion briefed him and the others without her knowledge?

The baby-faced guard scowled at the flippancy, but his bearded superior—a tertius— chuckled and gave Ellus an appreciative once over.

"Lumina's tits, but this one's prettier than your mother *or* sister, Pullo."

*Reglio.* That was the tertius's name. She'd caught him smirking at her more than once in a darkened hallway. The scowl on Pullo's face deepened, and Ellus cursed them both through the gag, which only made Reglio chuckle harder. Uncle Tarquin must not be inside his rooms for the guards to be so free. That meant they were here for Dobhran's security.

"But the novitius has the right of it," Reglio continued. "You and your novi aren't familiar, Quartus, and neither is your prisoner. Report."

She stared at the back of Thane's head, praying Reglio didn't recognize her. *Quartus Adrata*, she mouthed. It was a minor family in House Moralis. *He's Tertius Reglio*. And, unfortunately, one rank above a quartus.

"Quartus Thanatus Adrata. I arrived with the latest legionnaires from the continent. Served in Centurio Moralis's former centuria. He promised me a position with his guard when I returned home. And this one"—he jerked a sullen Ellus about—"hasn't been taught manners yet, but maybe the imperator will let you have him when he's learned his lessons." He took a confident step toward the black door, dragging an uncooperative Ellus with him.

Novitius Pullo stepped in their path, his barrel chest puffed out. "We've no orders about another prisoner, Quartus."

"That's because he was caught tonight trying to rescue the collaborator." Too close to the truth for comfort, yet Thane was damnably good at lying. "Now we have orders from Centurio Moralis," he continued amiably, "to deliver this prisoner to that room. So it's your heads, not ours if you insist on denying us. I'd rouse the centurio myself for your benefit"—he smirked—"if I knew where to find the man at this hour."

Reglio's questioning gaze rolled over Thane and then Seren, but he removed his hand from his sword with a sigh. "Let them pass, Pullo. I'll shake hands with Sol in hell before I send anyone into the Detritus Quarter to find the heir with the imperator and his guards away tonight."

That confirmed her guess. Seren bent her head to hide her face as she followed Thane and Ellus toward the door.

"Besides, it's about time we brought the slippery bastards to their knees." Reglio leered as they came abreast of him. "I'll enjoy my time with this one later."

In a flash, Ellus whipped his head up. "You're pith stainths on your mother's soulths—"

*Crack*. Thane backhanded him hard. Then she was stumbling back against the far wall under Ellus's weight. A bit of blood smeared the corner of his mouth, but he stayed limp against her as she steadied them both. Had the guards noticed Ellus's manacles were nothing but fabric?

Thane grabbed Ellus by his shirt and hoisted him off her, a move which blocked Reglio's and Pullo's view. Any private amusement she expected to see in Thane's features from the hit was supplanted by stark fear. Neither of the guards had protested, and the ease with which they accepted Thane's retaliation was troubling.

"Maybe that will shut you up," Thane muttered, taking hold of Ellus's elbow once again. Ellus head hung low, but otherwise he didn't react.

A silver key glinted in Reglio's hand as he inserted it into the lock. "Give him the ol' Primordian welcome for us, brother."

*A test*. Reglio had been testing their loyalties, and Thane had passed. So why was her stomach still churning at Reglio's insinuation?

"Oh, I've been looking forward to doing that—and more— for some time, Tertius." As soon as Reglio opened the door, Thane pushed Ellus over the threshold.

For the second time in her life, Seren entered the black room, uncertain of what she might find.

# 24

Fathomless darkness greeted her.

Seren took a moment to lean back against the double thick door and get her bearings. Remembering the black room and being inside it again were two different things. Moonlight filtered down to the black-tiled floor through a high slit window, or she might not have been able distinguish the floor from the walls. The stone on all surfaces was the same as in the cavern and the Wolvair den, only cut and polished. *Serendium*. It created a strange, disconcerting sensation.

Ahead of her, Thane froze in mid-step, his back blocking her view of the room while Ellus worked his hands free of his bonds. It was then the coppery tang and sour stench hit her full force.

The coldness of the stone door anchored her, the carved grooves digging into her palms. There was no bolt, however, to secure it from the inside. She supposed no one dared interrupt the work in here. Still, they should barricade it against Reglio and Pullo.

"Hit me again, Sionnach," Ellus said in measured tones

while wiping the blood from his mouth on his sleeve, "and your life will be forfeit."

The threat didn't seem to penetrate Thane's thick skull. His head stayed pointed to the left, where she didn't dare look yet. The shallow breathing in that corner and the quick inhale from Ellus told her enough. She strode by both of them to the other end of the room where a white marble table gleamed except for a rust-coloured smear down the middle. Iron manacles at both ends of the table indicated its intended use. Past it, along the outer wall, ran a steel counter, the tools upon it methodically arranged: metal instruments of all shapes and sizes, syringes, a glass bottle of clear liquid, and a coiled whip.

"Dobhran?" Ellus whispered. "We've come for you."

Finally, Seren could delay no longer.

When she turned, a naked man more dead than alive hung against the wall, his manacled wrists taking the brunt of his weight. His shaven head sagged forward, his face slack with unconsciousness. Thick manacles secured his feet at the ankles to the ground, preventing any comfortable position. Angry red lacerations and whorls had transformed his flesh into a bloody tapestry, and Seren's gorge rose even as she told herself he deserved it. He was a traitor.

At the rattle of breath, Ellus rushed to wrap his arms around Dobhran's wounded chest in an effort to ease the burden on the man's arms, taking as much care as though handling a baby bird with a broken wing. Still, a sharp cry of torment sprang from Dobhran's cracked lips.

"And they call the Felinae animals," Thane muttered. He crouched to examine the manacles. After checking all four, he looked up at her. "Four keys."

"Seren, did you see the keys in your vision?" Ellus's voice was heavy with the strain of holding the unconscious man.

"No. And they aren't back here." She swallowed, eyeing the

implements on the counter. Her voice sounded hollow even to her.

"No matter." Two thin pieces of iron appeared in Thane's fingers from behind his ear, and all her confidence in a failed mission vanished. He began tinkering with one of the locks around Dobhran's wrist.

"A lockpick in more ways than one," Ellus murmured.

*So it seemed.*

It wasn't Thane's fingers that held her attention, though. It was Dobhran's untouched face, propped against Ellus's shoulder. Nothing disfigured his features for the traitor's identity would need to be unquestioned by the throng in the Amphitheatron. In Tarquin Moralis's book, there was no point in executing someone if no one believed you had.

His features, however, didn't match the hooked nose, curled lip, and heavy brows in the poster. His was an ordinary face, behind which hid no ordinary man. Three hundred and fifty burned to death in Gull Harbour, she reminded herself. A squad from the City Patrol, slain defending an armoury. Shortages of food because of burned farmlands. He was a traitor to the republic.

What had made him do it?

Sweat shone on Ellus's forehead, and he adjusted his grip on Dobhran. "Might Reglio have the keys, Seren?"

"A tertius? No, my uncle will keep them on his person."

Ellus shifted Dobhran to the other shoulder so he could see her better. "I guess that was too much to hope for. Your vision didn't show you how we rescued Dobhran, did it?"

Words refused to move past her throat, past the lie she'd let him believe, so she shook her head and stopped to hover over Thane's shoulder.

"Güztenmeinier," he commented, as if she had asked. "These locks are worth twice their weight in gold. Each one would feed a family in the Detritus Quarter for a year." He paused, glancing up at them. "They seize up if anyone tampers with them—if they don't know what they're doing."

Seren raised an eyebrow, silently pleased at his progress was slow. "Did you expect this rescue to be simple? My uncle would only commission the best locksmiths."

The click of a tumbler moving punctuated the room, as did the flash of a cocky grin under black-brown fringe. "Simple? No. But challenges—*real challenges*—are few and far between, Princess."

The bottom of her stomach dropped away in dread. Could he do it? Could he unlock all four?

"Few locks to crack in Clan Stagona, I suspect," Ellus remarked.

Seren frowned. No, a pastime of picking locks didn't jibe with a sheltered life underground. One which, if anything like Clan Wolvair, lacked locked doors.

Ear back to the lock, Thane was nonchalant. "You'd be surprised. Taught myself. Easy if you know what to listen"—three more clicks came in rapid order—"for."

The lock sprang open, and Thane grinned like a satisfied cat as he slipped the cuff off Dobhran's bloody wrist. The half-conscious man barely twitched.

"Three more," Ellus reminded him tersely.

But in a matter of four twists of his picks, Thane had freed Dobhran's other wrist, and Ellus lowered the ravaged man to the floor.

*Unbelievable.*

A loud bang on the door cut short Thane's exultation.

"Adrata, is everything all right in there?"

"Just making our prisoner feel at home with the traitor," Thane yelled, moving on to the ankle manacles. His picks moved in and out, but Seren had no idea if he was close to unlocking them or not.

"Finish up and secure him," Reglio called, his voice muffled through the door, "but leave the traitor untouched. If he dies before he hangs, we'll all be strung up tomorrow instead."

Silence fell as Thane got back to work. The locks on the foot manacles proved more difficult. Time seeped by, the air in the room suffocating as Thane laboured on his knees, the frustrated hiss of his breath between clenched teeth and his picks the only sounds as she and Ellus watched uselessly.

Until another moan from the traitor interrupted it. Dobhran was speaking—or trying to. His voice was hoarse, and Ellus immediately went to the glass bottle on the back counter.

In half a breath, she crossed the distance to him. "That's not water."

He locked eyes with her over his shoulder. Endless blue engulfed her. It wasn't the first time they'd captured her, but tonight they were sharper, with new, uncharted depths.

"S-s-said too much," Dobhran gasped.

Gently, she took the bottle from Ellus, but it was he who moved away first to kneel on the other side of Dobhran. With tender care, Ellus eased the broken man up into a sitting position. "We're getting you out, Dobhran. Llion is coming."

The Burner of Gull Harbour licked cracked lips, his gaze flicking around his cell. "Tell him . . . the crescent . . . his weapon."

Uneasiness ran through Seren as Dobhran's gaze landed on her. The weapon was *her*. But what was this talk about a crescent?

Thane lifted his head from where he worked on the ankle manacle. "What about weapons?"

Ragged breath was the sole response. It wouldn't take the noose long to finish him off.

"Focus on the locks, Sionnach," Ellus ordered. "Does Moralis have some kind of weapon, Dobhran?"

Seren started at her name, then realized Ellus meant her uncle.

"Moonlight in the blood," Dobhran mumbled, eyes fluttering. "Beware. The girl sees too much."

Her hands tightened on the bottle. That was close to how Vesper had described herself and Seren. *Lumina,* did Dobhran know about her mission and her Inheritance? If he did, her days as an Elusive were over.

"Time's running out," she interrupted. Reglio's and Pullo's morning replacements would report soon, and the guards at the villa entrance would notice that the southern foot patrol was late in their sweep. Once someone was sent to investigate, the patrols rendered unconscious by Vesper and Kanta would be discovered. "We need an exit plan."

"Not without Dobhran." Ellus glanced back at the bottle. "If it's not water, what is it?"

Seren's gaze slid to the bloody whorls burned into Dobhran's chest and lower.

Ellus's jaw ticked. "Let's try it on the chains then." When she didn't move, he held out his hand, and she parted with the bottle. With a steady hand, he poured the liquid where the chain met the manacle on the opposite leg from Thane, careful not to let it drop on Dobhran's skin. The liquid bubbled and hissed, but the iron remained solid.

Thane twisted his head to look at Seren, his picks idle in his hands. He understood.

It was over.

"I thought you liked a challenge, Sionnach?" Ellus snapped, pouring more liquid onto the lock.

Even if they freed Dobhran, they'd have to haul him out of the House, fighting the guards in the hallway. Four against three. More would be called up.

Ice water pooled in her belly. "We can still walk out of here as guards without them suspecting why we came. Regroup, and try to free Dobhran when they transport him to the Amphitheatron."

"Taking the prisoner we said we were escorting here?" Thane snorted. "It's either using the rooftop or fighting our way out of the hallway. Can't you knock them out?"

"Only if I can get behind them." Which was doubtful in a narrow hallway.

"Wait, it's working!" Ellus glanced up at her, hope as wide as his grin.

Was the metal weakening? Seren came closer to check, and Thane twisted his head to see. The liquid had eaten into a thin layer of the chain. Seren swallowed a curse. If Dobhran was free, it would have to be the hallway. No way any of them could haul the man up through the narrow slit of a window.

"Drop what's left in the keyhole," Thane instructed. "It might destroy the mechanism."

A hissing sound rose as liquid met metal, then Thane inserted his picks back into the lock. Seren's eyes swept up Dobhran's ruined body and her breath hitched, imagining Ellus in his place. She had to convince him to leave Dobhran behind. "If we're captured, my uncle will hang us"—*you*—"or worse."

Muffled shouts and the clang of swords from the courtyard caught their attention. Llion had been discovered.

"We have to leave him, Ellus."

Another bang on the door. "Adrata! Recreation time is over!"

"Just finishing up, Tertius!" Thane's hands continued their work, but his face was grim.

"K-kill me," Dobhran begged.

Her vision went black as rage reverberated through her until she trembled with it. The bastard had killed innocents. The Burner of Gull Harbour wasn't dying here without being held responsible for his crimes.

"No."

The force of her certainty raised the boys' attention. Tension seeped out of Ellus's face, and the look he gave her? Gratitude. And something more. She didn't deserve it, and it made her want to slap it off his face. Moon above, he thought there was mercy in her cold Moralis heart.

She couldn't afford to feel that, not for Dobhran and not for the Felinae princes, who one day might occupy this same room, their own flesh ruined beyond salvation. She had to remind herself that the brothers would use their subjects' unnatural powers to avenge their slain family. Unless she could stop them before they accomplished anything worse than Gull Harbour.

Seren jumped up on the white table and broke the double-paned glass in the ceiling with her sword's pommel. It was the only other exit. Glass rained down around her, along with clear shouts of alarm, the slap of heavy boots against stone, and the ringing of steel.

At a distant growl and the frost-bitten reply from Quinton, her heart punched up against her chest, and she forgot all about Dobhran and the princes.

Could Quinton defeat Llion? Her cousin was one of the best swordsmen in Luminaria, but a mercenary who was on a first-name basis with one of the Marked assassins of Rokkemar was clearly no stranger to meting out death.

"Don't," Dobhran whispered, bloodshot eyes opened wide as he leaned his head against the black wall. One had burst vessels, and Seren doubted he could see out of it. "Don't . . . leave me here alive."

Broken. The man was completely broken. No threat to her mission.

"We have to go." She didn't know who she was saying it to—Dobhran or Ellus. But first, they needed to barricade the door. Since they would need the table to reach the window, she motioned Ellus over to the counter, and together they half lifted it, half dragged it over. Some of the tools slid off, clanging to the floor. It wouldn't hold the guards off forever, but it would buy them some time.

Anguish tore the beautiful planes of Ellus's face. "We can't leave him like this."

"We can't save him either," she said impatiently. "Right now, your sealgair is battling my cousin—the best swordsman in the city. Where Quinton goes"—*Tyberius follows*—"guards follow. Llion will be surrounded, and we're not there to back him" —*Quinton*—"up."

Outside, the melee continued, underscoring her words. There were faint grunts of pain, and she feared it was Quinton or Ty. Llion had sworn not to hurt her family unless they threatened him or his recruits. If she was the means to Ty's or Quinton's deaths, she'd never forgive herself. Or Llion.

Ellus looked torn. "Llion can take care of himself, and he has a Swiftfoot."

"Do you think Vesper can knock them all out?" Seren demanded, half afraid the Swiftfoot could and half afraid she couldn't. "She doesn't have the stomach for killing."

*And neither do you.* She tried to keep the judgement out of her eyes. "Remember when you asked me to help you decide which fights to win and which to lose?" she asked softly.

He blinked at her, then nodded once.

Lumina, she'd go to Sol's hells for this. But it was true. There was nothing else to be done. "You need to lose this one, Ellus."

Once more, Dobhran lifted his searing red eyes. A warrior looked at her now, fully cognizant of his situation. "I'm ready."

Despite the bile rising in her throat, it galled her to grant Dobhran's last wish, but from Ellus's steely expression, he wouldn't abandon Dobhran while a chance for rescue remained. While she hesitated, Thane startled them both by stepping forward, hand on his sword.

"Stand aside, Reul."

Ellus tensed, then his shoulders sagged. "First, I need to know what's been compromised. The sealgair will want to know."

Now it was Thane who hesitated. It wasn't until after he clamped his pale hand on Dobhran's ruined shoulder that Seren realized what Ellus had asked for.

*Dobhran's secrets.*

She didn't have time to examine her revulsion or fear at the intimate invasion of Dobhran's mind because the unlocked door banged against the counter. Once. Twice. Thrice. Each time the counter moved. Her hand went to Vindicta. Then Ellus lunged against the counter, shoving it back. She joined him, trying to dig her heels into the smooth floor. There had to be more than just two guards now pushing.

On the fifth shove, she and Ellus gave way, tumbling back into the black room. Backlit from the hallway, a furious Reglio stood in the open doorway, blinking at the darkness while Pullo and two more guards crowded behind him. First, he took in the unlocked manacles; then his eyes alighted on her face in the moonlight. "Mistressa Seren."

The eagles on their bronze breastplates made her hesitate, and for a moment, they stared at each other, unmoving.

With a groan, Thane broke contact with Dobhran, staggered forward, and promptly emptied the contents of his stomach on the polished serendium floor.

The moment shattered.

"Take the traitorous bitch alive!" Reglio yelled. He pushed the counter aside and rushed at them, his sword high. "Kill the others—"

Before Seren could draw her sword, Thane whipped one of Silver's stars at Reglio. It struck home, and he fell to his knees, clasping at his bleeding throat. More blood bubbled out of his mouth and down his beard as she stared in horror.

Behind the dying Reglio stood a terrified Pullo. He tried to turn and run, but the guards behind him pushed him back inside as they hollered for more of their brethren. Pullo stumbled backward over Reglio's dropped sword, and Ellus caught hold of the leather lappets hanging from Pullo's belt and yanked.

The novi crashed to the ground, and Ellus was on him. To Pullo's detriment, the House guard often didn't bother with helmets as they limited vision. Ellus smashed the handle of his dagger against Pullo's head several times, knocking him out cold.

Vaguely, Seren heard Thane snap at her to fight as he lunged, sword first, at the next guard through the door, but her attention had already turned to Dobhran's slumped form on the floor. With one hand, she grasped his hair and wrenched his head back to expose his throat to her knife's edge. His skin seared her hand, but she didn't let go.

A thunderous roar filled her head, blocking out the fight behind her, and she braced herself. The waters of Time's Flow surged at her, but it wasn't a vision. No, the waves were surging at Dobhran. Breaking against the man for whom Time was at an end.

Kneeling next to him, she brushed her lips against his ear. "A Moralis sees it to the end."

Dobhran stiffened in her grasp. There would be no Vale of peace awaiting one with so much blood staining his hands. Seren raised her knife, and the metal caught the reflection of his eyes—his yearning startled her.

"Please," Dobhran choked out. "Do it."

A frustrated sound ripped out of her throat as she hesitated. She shouldn't give him his last wish. She *shouldn't*. But spilling the blood of the traitor Dobhran was better than Llion spilling the blood of Quinton and Tyberius.

"Seren." Her head snapped up at Thane's voice, her knife

wavering. It was quiet in the black room again. He and Ellus slumped against the heavy white marble table, which had been pushed against the door in place of the counter to keep the guards out.

Time seemed to pause, as if a single moment was being stretched out before her. One that decided her future, maybe all their futures. Reglio was dead in a pool of his own blood. Pullo looked to be breathing if unconscious. Their replacements were slumped on the floor as well. Had they heard Reglio call her name and sounded the alarm?

Thane's mouth was moving. All she heard was "We need to go."

This time Ellus knelt beside Dobhran without arguing. "May we find one another again in the Mists."

"Tell my loves," Dobhran rasped, barely audible even to her ears, "I await them there, Lockpick."

Before Seren could move her knife hand away, Dobhran lurched forward against the blade, and the sharp edge tore into his throat. Someone swore. Blood flowed over her hand as Dobhran sagged against her, gasping for breath, his body's survival instinct taking over.

Thane stared at her, his eyes full of the secrets of the traitor.

Her jaw nearly dropped at the implications. Ellus had told her that Drakori had foreseen Seren coming to the mountains and sent Llion. Thane must have been handpicked to "train" with her in order to steal her secrets. Valera would have seen right through this trap. A Lockpick to steal her secrets. A Swiftfoot to catch her if she tried to escape. A Bloodkin to—what? Confirm her lineage?

That left Ellus—with no Inheritance. Why was he selected as part of her welcoming party? To befriend her as the prince's eyes and ears? Her heart sank. She'd hoped—

Best not to think about what she'd hoped right now.

"To the end," Thane said, interrupting her thoughts and echoing her words back to her. Was it a threat? A promise?

She didn't have time to contemplate it. Dobhran's end was here, and she had to see it through.

Without taking her eyes from Thane's, she ended the suffering of the Burner of Gull Harbour, whether he deserved it or not.

## 25

The cloudless night was not in Seren's favour.

Lumina lit the red clay tile for any Prims to see her as she ran lightly along the ridges and valleys of the roof toward the clash of steel in the middle courtyard. Her heart lurched as the sword fighters came into view down below. Without waiting for Ellus and Thane, she dropped into a crouch on a third-floor balcony. From the balustrade, she scanned the scene below: bodies of Moralis guards in their bronze armour lay prone on the stones. In the centre, Quinton and Llion circled each other, swords clanging as they tested each other's mettle.

As far as she could tell, neither had the upper hand, nor were they injured. Perhaps Quinton had finally met his equal. A fair fight. She couldn't—shouldn't—interfere. But unlike the guards, her cousin wore no helm or breastplate. The alarm had caught him out of uniform in a white silk shirt and black trousers—and not in the Detritus Quarter. He had a sword and picked up a discarded shield, which he used to hold off his opponent's barrage. While Llion had no shield or armour, he wore a battered leather cuirass with pauldrons and a pair of bracers for protection.

Absently, she registered Thane landing beside her while below to the left, on the edge of the gardens, Kanta and Vesper kept five legionnaires in unfamiliar gold sashes from interfering. Quinton's new personal guard, she supposed. These guards were dressed for battle. Quickly, she searched the faces under their golden helms. None were Ty. Her chest loosened, but there was also an echo of disappointment in her relief. The two of them were fated to meet again, if only because of the ring he wore.

A tingle on her forehead and the rushing of water between her ears brought her attention back to the sword fight. Lumina, not another nightmare. *Not now.* But she didn't have a say. Dark pools of red shimmered on the stones beneath Llion's and Quinton's boots, and her gut clenched. Yet neither man slipped. Before her eyes, the pools disappeared like a mirage in the Cartarchaan deserts.

Frantic laughter burbled out of her. The blood hadn't truly been there. Not yet. Drakori had said the future wasn't set in stone. It could change. Maybe she could change it.

But she'd have to break her own rules and interfere in a fair fight.

Abruptly, Llion leaped backward, farther than seemed possible. With the counterweight removed, Quinton stumbled forward, his head dipping low and unprotected.

"Quinton!" The scream tore from her throat.

Time itself slowed to an agonizing crawl as her cousin lifted his head. His shield was halfway up, and he faltered just as a different roar filled the courtyard and Llion's sword flashed in the moonlight.

Desperate, she reached out with her hand as if she could stay the blade. "Llion Llewyn, you gave your oath!"

Without acknowledging her, Llion altered the trajectory of

his sword in mid-strike, narrowly missing the back of Quinton's exposed neck. The scraping of steel on the cobblestones was an ungodly sound, but it was more welcome than the rolling of her cousin's head, and it spurred Quinton into action. As she leapt over the balustrade, uncertain how she would end the fight, her cousin pressed his attack. Without his armour, Quinton was more light-footed than usual, and he needed every bit of his dexterity against Llion's quick reflexes and powerful thrusts.

When she hit the stones, she rolled to a standing position. A ball of black leather with mahogany hair tumbled past her. From the corner of her eye, she saw a House guard with a gold sash rush toward him. Oblivious to the danger, Ellus came to a halt on his back, in front of the helmed guard, who was raising her sword above her.

Already running, Seren's heart lurched into her throat. *No.*

But the blow didn't fall.

A sword pushed down through the vulnerable neck opening of the guard's bronze breastplate toward the heart, and the young woman gasped her last breath. Seren looked up, shocked to see her own hands wrapped around the hilt. Thick blood welled at the blade's entry point and drops splattered on the cobblestones before the shorter guard fell to her knees.

What had she done? Another roar of water filled Seren's ears, and this time she trembled as it stole her strength.

From below, Ellus stared up at her, eyes wide and a smear of blood on his cheek.

*Unamkharaunamkharaunamkhara.* The indistinct murmur echoed through her mind, louder and louder until her whole body—her whole being—reverberated to its thundering call.

A murderous cry pierced through the cacophony inside her. Steel clanged. She looked over to find Quinton glaring at her from across the hedges, his sword locked against Llion's.

He had seen her kill a House sister to protect a Felinae. The connection between them lasted less than a blink; then Quinton needed all his attention to parry Llion's strikes.

The weight of the dead guard bowed Seren's arms. She pulled her sword free, and the guard's body collapsed to lie face-up next to Ellus. Strands of short, honey-blonde hair peaked out from her helm, framing a wide mouth and unseeing brown eyes—a familiar face. *Sila Utticor.*

She swallowed. Now was not the time to deal with it. She offered Ellus a hand up. When his skin touched hers, a shock ran through her body, straight to her core. The Eye on her forehead pulsed, and she nearly let go, but Ellus gripped her hand tightly.

"Seren, do you feel that?"

Her skin tingled all over, a rippling sensation that stirred her blood. *More.* Trembling, she wrenched her hand free before she heeded the silent demand. "It's battle fever, that's all. Come on. We need to stop them."

As they came down the steps, Llion took note of their arrival from where he and Quinton were still engaged around the fountain. Sol's hells, how could she keep Quinton safe?

Beyond the courtyard, an unnatural blur in the hedgerows drew her eye. While Thane and Kanta distracted the last of Quinton's guards, Vesper darted in and out, felling them one by one. Seren could barely see the girl, but since the guards slumped unbloodied to the ground, she assumed Vesper was using Nightfall. It was astonishing to watch. Vesper was tiring, though. Her chest rose and fell heavily when she paused long enough in one spot.

With a lunge, Llion drove Quinton back with a vicious slash and kick to the knee. It buckled, and Quinton fell; instead of pressing the advantage, however, Llion retreated to her and Ellus. A deep crease divided his brows, his bronzed skin glistening from exertion. "Where were you, and why did you abandon your posts?"

Before either of them could respond, Quinton's low chuckle filled the night air. His boots clicked against the stones. "My cousin has trouble keeping her promises."

*I am keeping my oath*, she wanted to shout. "I'm trying to save your life, Q," she snapped. "Look what's happened to your guard."

"Spare me your lies." Rancour twisted Quinton's face into a cruel sneer, accentuating injuries she hadn't noticed earlier. A faded bruise ringed his right eye and jawline. His left cheek was scabbed over as if something had scraped the skin raw. Llion hadn't given him these wounds.

His contempt stung. As much as she wanted to believe Quinton was acting along with her subterfuge, deep down she knew he wasn't. For unfathomable reasons, Uncle Tarquin must have kept him in the dark about her mission.

"They're not dead," Vesper piped up from the other side of the courtyard. She sagged heavily against Kanta, who supported her. All around them, bodies of House Moralis guards littered the cobblestones and garden paths.

"Not yet," Kanta threatened, a guard's stolen sword in her free hand.

Vesper, Thane, and Kanta closed the distance between them until her cousin finally seemed to realize the situation he was in. Surrounded by the enemy, his guards incapacitated, and without his sword brother. There was still no sign of Ty or the rest of the House guards—all could be indisposed, however, from the night's celebrations.

But time was on Quinton's side. All he had to do was wait for the rest of the garrison to muster, though she wondered what was taking them so long. And Uncle Tarquin might return any minute with his personal guard. Once the rest of the guards arrived, the fight would be bloody. Vesper could barely stand, Thane looked like he would vomit again, and Ellus appeared dazed from his brush with death. They needed to leave.

Quinton raised his sword at Llion, ignoring everyone else. "I challenge you to Aequitas for the corruption of my cousin. Fight me, if you have a shred of honour."

The fool. She swallowed, wondering how she could avert Quinton's death again when Llion lowered his sword.

"My oath to your cousin prevents me from accepting such a challenge. But should we meet again, I will gladly accept. For now, drop your sword and direct us to Alphonius Luther."

A sneer darkened Quinton's face. "And why would I do that?"

Again, the pool of blood on the cobblestones around Quinton flashed before her. Seren gritted her teeth. The current could change, but Llion wouldn't leave if there was a chance of rescuing Dobhran.

"Dobhran's dead." His blood, barely dry on her hands and stolen armour, now mixed with Sila's. "And Quinton's stalling for reinforcements."

If she was captured now without solid information on the whereabouts of the rest of the Felinae and the princes, it was tantamount to failure. And if Dobhran had already spilled that information to Uncle Tarquin, then she'd need something else to prove herself. Something better.

Llion kept his sights on Quinton. "How?"

She couldn't stop the guilty flush creeping up her neck.

"She slew him, too." By his tone, Quinton might as well have called her a bloodthirsty bitch. "Did you also empty the tower? Is this your revenge on us?"

Seren didn't have time to parse Quinton's last remark. Ignoring them both, she caught Vesper's eye and gestured, hoping the Swiftfoot would know what she meant.

"Seren had a vision," Ellus explained, though his eyes were still too wide. "We snuck inside to rescue Dobhran, but we couldn't free him, Leo. We had no choice."

A growl of pure rage erupted from Llion; it reverberated off the stones, no doubt waking the rest of the villa.

To forestall any retribution, Seren slipped in front of him, praying Llion remembered his oath. She faced Quinton's sword, likewise eager to distract her cousin from what Ellus had said.

"You seem to be missing someone tonight, Q. Is Tyberius not your faithful shadow anymore?"

The taunt worked. Quinton lunged at her, and she dodged the lightning strike. It was all Vesper needed. There was a blur to his left as the Swiftfoot struck at his neck, but he didn't go down. Staggering, he lashed out at his unseen attacker with a dagger in his left hand, only for Thane to bash him on the head with a discarded shield. Quinton's eyes rolled up in his head before he dropped like a sack of stones into her out-stretched arms.

*Several sacks of stones*, she amended, groaning under his weight. Quickly, she lowered him down on the cobblestones and then placed two fingers above his jugular. Despite all his faults, he was her family. His pulse was strong, thank Lumina, and his chest rose and fell steadily. Thane lingered, shield in hand, but made no move to get closer to her cousin, either to end his life or steal his secrets

"Morningstar," Llion barked. It was a question. Was she with them?

Quinton thought she was a traitor. So would Uncle Tarquin once he learned of her actions here tonight. She had to prove him, and all of Luminaria, wrong. In her boot, her foot tingled where her note had been. It waited now for her uncle in the hand of a dead man, her first act against her father's dominion.

She pushed a stray lock of dark hair off Quinton's forehead and then rose. "Until we meet again, cousin."

# PART III

## A PRINCE TO RECKON WITH

**26**

A moment had passed in Luminaria, one that had decided her future, maybe all their futures. Seren could feel the weight of it deep in her soul, and it became heavier with every step that led her farther away from House Moralis. Her enemies—*she must remember exactly who these Felinae were to her*—trudged in a line through the ankle-deep water of the city's dank sewers, wordlessly following Llion, whose silence in the aftermath of his failed mission thundered in the echoing tunnels.

They emerged in another servilis quarter, through the bottom of a bathhouse. Back under the rising sun, Seren adjusted the straps of her pack, concentrating on the cobblestones as Llion cut a path through side streets. She tried not to think about how once Quinton awoke, he would inform his father about how she killed a House sister to save a Felinae. Her body flushed hot, then cold as she imagined how the lines of disapproval would tighten around Uncle Tarquin's firm mouth. He'd believe she had betrayed them—and she had, in body if not in mind. Bile burned in her throat, and it was all she could do not to vomit on the dusty stones.

Her note, she hoped, would explain the situation to her uncle. He'd understand she was playing a long game—that she wasn't a traitor to her House. Once Uncle Tarquin read it, he would send the City Patrol or legionnaires to arrest the true inhabitants of the safe house for collaborating with the enemy. Perhaps they were on their way right now.

But what if Uncle Tarquin hadn't returned to House Moralis yet and, therefore, hadn't received the note? What if the guards didn't bring the note to Quinton's attention when he awoke? If so, the City Patrol may very well be rousing the awakening city in search of her and her companions. It was best that she and the others be long gone before the city gates were locked.

A lifetime later, despite her worries, they made it unchallenged to the forest outside the city's western wall. Whether by luck or by her uncle's design, she wasn't certain. It was in their favour though that the bulk of the Legion had marched north days ago and the legionnaires left behind were bitter enough to shirk their foot patrols along the ramparts.

Once the trees hid them from view, Llion halted at a creek for a brief respite. From his pack, he retrieved a round loaf of bread, which was passed around, with everyone breaking off a small chunk for a poor but welcome breakfast. Since she and Thane could no longer impersonate guards, it was time to ditch their stolen House armour. The extra weight would only slow them, and the pomegranate tunic and cape were too bright to hide amongst the deep greens and browns of the oaks, ashes, and chestnuts.

After changing back into her own leathers, Seren secured the House sword high on her right hip for same-hand draw; at the flash of the blade, her mouth went dry as her treacherous mind splashed the last few seconds of the Sila's life before her eyes. The murder of a House member was grounds for execution—and she could not claim self-defence. There was no clemency Uncle Tarquin could or would offer an oathbreaker such as she.

Everything she'd done had been to atone for her father's crimes—for his dishonour in breaking the Accord, for the dishonour to her mother and House Moralis. But how could she atone for her own dishonour? She'd stolen a life, arguably two, from House Moralis.

Her guilt plagued her like a swarm of buzzing insects as Llion led them onward into the forest. She was too exhausted and worried to care about where exactly they were headed or about anything. Until the shadow of a wood-hawk flitted across her path.

To be a bird without oaths or dishonour, loyalties or betrayals. Such freedom taunted her. Through the leafy canopy, she tracked its silhouette against the brightness of the midday sun; her eyes watered, and she stumbled over a root.

A gentle hand under her elbow steadied her. Ellus smiled tiredly, black circles under his eyes, and her chest squeezed tight against the image of Sila's steel poised over him. Why had she taken a life for him? Other ways to disable the guard sprang to mind, but in that heated moment, she'd reacted to the threat and chosen a killing strike with no room for mercy. She didn't know why—no, she didn't want to know why. She couldn't consider what Ellus Reul meant to her. That he could be anything other than a means to an end was preposterous.

His hand dropped away, and he readjusted his pack. "Least I can do is save you from a tree."

The words were light, but his eyes weren't. They churned with weightier emotions she didn't care to examine. He would've done the same for her, she told herself. Attacked any Prim to protect her, if their places had been reversed. And he had taken on Thane for her, but would he sacrifice the life of a Felinae if their positions were reversed?

*And for future reference, this Felinae has no reservations about you fighting your own battles or with you saving me.*

"Truth be told, I owe you a life debt, Seren of the Morningstars."

A life debt sounded useful, though it could never fill whatever she owed Sila. As she waited for him to say more, he bit his lip, looking around as if to gauge whether the others could hear—which, of course, they could. "You felt it, too, didn't you?" he asked under his breath.

Immediately, the feeling of her soul being struck like the ringing of a bell came back to her. And it was too much—too many of these out-of-body experiences. For Lumina's sake, she didn't want this, even if she was almost certain she knew what Ellus would say.

Down that path lay nothing but heartache.

Fortunately, further conversation was forestalled by Kanta rushing past them. "Sealgair, our tail draws closer." As Llion turned around, she stepped backward at his glower. "As I'm sure you're aware. What should we do?"

Dread curdled in Seren's veins. Try as she might, she couldn't hear anyone in the forest behind them. But Kanta was a full-blooded Felinae. "We've been followed?"

Could it be Quinton?

"I noticed the tail once we left the wall," Ellus admitted, and from the expressions on Vesper's and Thane's faces, they had, too.

"A legionnaire, you think, Sealgair?" Vesper leaned heavily on a sturdy branch Thane had cobbled into a walking staff for her. After being carried piggyback by Llion through the sewers, she had regained enough strength to walk on her own. "Or a Moralis guard?"

Or perhaps it was the same trackers who had pursued Seren into the mountains before? Llion had led them off her trail once. Surely, he could do so again. A chill worked its way up the backs of her legs. She couldn't be taken back to House Moralis without her honour restored. But neither could she harm another House sibling.

The wood-hawk's call echoed through the trees, and Llion tilted his head upward as if he could find the answer to Vesper's question in the forest canopy. Dirt streaked his quickly growing beard, and dry leaves and debris littered his long braids, such as it had when they first met.

"Unclear," he said finally. "It's one man, however, and he's closing in as I intended." When his gaze descended on them, it was scorching hot. Despite the fatigue around his golden-brown eyes, he looked downright eager for the confrontation. "If you're ready to follow orders this time, I have a plan."

———

Nettles caught in her braid as Seren lifted her head to peer over the bracken. She didn't know why she bothered since the others would hear him before she would see anything.

From the other side of Ellus, Kanta made an irritated noise. "Wait for the signal, Morningstar."

Seren settled back down on her stomach in the prickly scrub and tried not to fall asleep. Exhaustion from the last day and a half was setting in. Across from them, Vesper, Thane, and Llion also lay hidden in a cluster of brambles, and between them lay a muddy trail of boot prints and trodden plants to lure their tracker.

She jerked her head up, spitting dirt. Had she fallen asleep?

Next to her, Ellus and Kanta tensed, and a few breaths later she heard footsteps. He had an uneven gait and was breathing hard. As the shuffling grew closer, the insufferable wood-hawk swooped down over them—the signal—and her pulse quickened. Following Llion's orders, Seren leapt up and over the troublesome bracken, Vindicta in her hand to confront the Prim, praying it wasn't Quinton.

Sunlight shone through a gap in the trees, casting dappled shadows over the tall, lean figure. It was a weak excuse for not recognizing him. Then he stepped fully into the light. It rippled off the gold in his coppery hair as she took in his green eyes and vulpine face. Tyberius was the last person she had expected to see—and yet, she wasn't disappointed, especially when he looked at her like that. Like he had found exactly what he was looking for. It made her heart race.

"Miss me, Tabby?" His expression transformed into a more familiar grin; one she'd seen him flash numerous times at numerous moon balls. Just never at her.

From the trees, Llion quietly stepped out and slid his sword under Tyberius's scruffy chin. "Hands where I can see them."

Seren's blood ran cold. Tyberius hadn't been part of the plan. "Don't you dare hurt him," she warned, tightening her grip on her knife. If she threw Vindicta, however, the blade wouldn't reach Llion in time to save Tyberius.

"That's up to him," Llion replied coldly. "And whether he cooperates. Who are you and who sent you?"

All her former suspicions that Ty was a spy for the Felinae fled. Whatever he had been doing at the Consul meeting, it hadn't been at the behest of Llion.

"At the pointy end of a sword, I can be anyone you want me to be," Ty choked out, his throat bobbing against the blade. "Except your enemy. I prefer my head attached."

Now was not the time for flippancy with Llion's temper holding by a thread, his mission in tatters at his feet, and his informant dead. How much had Ellus told Llion about what exactly happened in the black room? If he knew she'd been the one to end Dobhran, he might decide to take out his anger on Tyberius.

A light touch on her arm startled her. Ellus. "You know this Prim, Seren?"

She couldn't very well deny it. "He's my House brother, Tyberius Attica. Secundo to my cousin, Centurio Moralis of the First Cohort of the Legion."

"A legionnaire!" Vesper squeaked.

"He looks more like an outlaw or a beggar," Kanta sniffed.

It was true. A dark cloak covered black leathers, all the worse for wear. From the smell, he hadn't bathed in days.

Ty raised an eyebrow at Seren's introduction. "That's one way of describing who I am. I'm not here on orders," he assured them. Right, best not to alarm everyone. "And who do I have the pleasure of being threatened by?"

"The man behind you is Llion Llewyn, Sealgair of the Felinae." Seren waved a hand around. "And these are some of his Elusive recruits."

"Charmed," Ty said tightly.

"Kanta, Vesper, take his weapons," Llion ordered.

From his belt, a dagger and a silver flask were extracted while a knife and short sword were removed from their holsters, all standard House Moralis issue. Except for the flask.

Llion released his hold on Tyberius but didn't sheath his sword. "Speak, Secundo. Why were you following us?"

Tyberius rubbed his throat, looking hesitant for the first time.

For a moment, Seren thought maybe he'd come because of her . . . She scoffed at herself. It was *one* kiss. Perhaps Uncle Tarquin had sent him with a reply to her note?

"Has Centurio Moralis sent you to negotiate for his cousin, Secundo Attica?" Llion prompted. The suggestion flummoxed her, but the question seemed to snap Ty out of his uncertainty.

"Truly, Quinton has not. Though if I were here for that purpose, I'd expect to negotiate directly with Seren—not you— since she is here of her own free will, correct?" His mouth quirked into a charming smile that he levelled at Kanta and Vesper, who had each tucked his weapons about themselves. "Please, keep them. I shouldn't have any need of them among friends."

"We're not friends, *nob*," Thane spat. His sword was still in his hand, and he looked like he was itching to use it.

"Neither are we enemies. Or perhaps I should say we share an enemy since the same man wants us dead." Ty looked around at their blank stares. "Tarquin Moralis? Imperator of the Republic of Luminaria? Ring a bell?"

"How can that be? Why would my uncle want your head?" *Was this a ruse to fool the Felinae?*

"Much has happened since you left, Seren," Ty murmured, his eyes heavy with meaning. "Sealgair, your spies must be piss poor if you haven't heard."

Llion, who had circled around his prisoner, stopped. "I have heard."

"Heard what?" Seren looked from one to the other. Llion pressed his lips together, but he had sheathed his sword. Instead of reassuring her, it had the opposite effect. Still, she sheathed Vindicta as Ty took a cautionary step toward her.

"We fought, Quinton and I."

Quinton's bruised face last night. Ty must have done that. The two often sparred aggressively in training. But, in all their years of friendship, Seren had never heard of any heated quarrels between them. Joren's mangled face, however, swam before her—a testament to Ty's high temper. "You weren't sparring then."

Ty shook his head.

"You lost?" Thane scoffed.

Seren couldn't detect much evidence of that, except for his limp and the tight way he held himself. But she had known Ty to come out of worse fights the victor.

"I threw the first punch, but it's difficult to defend yourself when guards are holding you down," Ty replied, flippantly. His eyes, however, stayed on her. "The matter of Quinton's honour was to be settled by Aequitas, and, as per the imperator's wishes, it was to be to the death. Of course, I am now several hours late to the Amphitheatron, as is Dobhran, may his soul be at rest."

The hairs on the nape of Seren's neck stood up. Quinton had never lost a sword fight—friendly or otherwise. Few crossed him. Yet it was difficult to believe that her cousin would demand Aequitas of his sword brother and closest friend, knowing it was little more than a death sentence.

Ty shook his head to the side like a *tsking* matrona. "No hanging, no duel? The imperator will have a tough crowd to placate." There'd be riots, she imagined. "My thanks to you, Sealgair, for unlocking the cells in the tower."

"A diversionary tactic to draw away the guards," Llion grunted, his shoulders stiff at the unwelcomed gratitude.

"You were locked in the cells?" she exclaimed.

"That is where you're sent if you refuse orders and assault your superior. It didn't help that my superior is—*was*—also the first centurio and the imperator's heir."

Heat warmed her cheeks at the reminder of House protocol. "What in the moon's name possessed you to hit Quinton on duty in the first place?"

"He said something unforgivable. But I'm not proud of it." With a shake of his coppery head, Tyberius pulled out a folded paper from his boot and passed it to her. The City Patrol had delivered two posters last night on the same such paper. One of Dobhran's hanging. The other Llion hadn't shown them. On this poster was a caricature of Quinton and Ty pulling on the arms of a woman between them. *Her.* At the bottom, the reasons for Aequitas were written.

She read it three times, and it still didn't make sense. According to the poster, she and Ty were accused of breaking their oaths to House Moralis and her betrothal oath to Quinton. Never mind she and Quinton had been betrothed but one night. Never mind it had been one kiss with Tyberius in the dark. Her stomach roiled.

"Not a flattering likeness," Ty commented on the crude drawing. "I've half a mind to complain to the artist." When she looked up, he shot her a pleading look.

This must be a ploy then, and she was to play along and pretend that they were lovers. But why had he fought with Quinton? Surely, Q knew there was nothing between them? Except he had seen them in the catacombs on Pledging Night. Tyberius could have easily cleared that up. Yet he hadn't, or Quinton hadn't believed him.

She didn't know how to feel about that. But she couldn't throw Ty on Llion's mercy. The sealgair had none. No matter this misunderstanding with Quinton, Tyberius was a legionnaire, pledged to House Moralis. And ultimately, he didn't deserve exile either. They hadn't betrayed Quinton, and besides that, the betrothal was a ruse. Like this jealousy on Quinton's part must be, too.

"How did you find us, Secundo Attica?" Ellus asked, his crystal-clear voice startling her. She'd forgotten he stood beside her, not protecting her but standing with her. "You weren't behind us in the sewers. We would've heard."

"Seren left me directions to your safe house so I could join her." Tyberius stated it so baldly that if she hadn't known better, she would've believed him. "When you didn't arrive there, however, I made for the nearest city gate. I nearly caught up with you at the wall, but a patrol delayed me. I followed your trail and your avian friend from there."

She frowned. Did he mean the wood-hawk?

"Funny, Seren didn't say anything about you." Kanta raised Ty's sword, taking a fighter's stance. "I told you she wasn't to be trusted, Ellus."

Quickly, Seren tucked the paper into her vest to free her hands for a fight and braced herself for his condemnation.

"Seren must have had a good reason," Vesper interjected, an all too hopeful light in her eyes. "Maybe she was protecting him."

"She didn't even know he was in the cells." Below severe brows, Kanta's gaze narrowed while Ellus remained awfully quiet. Had she broken his trust for good?

"Of course not," Vesper replied as she hobbled closer to Seren with her walking staff. "That happened after she left." Her chin lifted. "How many of us have shared our most fragile hopes and fears with Seren?" When no one responded, Vesper nodded to herself. "That's what I thought."

But Vesper had shared her fears. Ellus had. Of course, there had been nothing to confide in them about Tyberius back then. Seren shifted her weight, waiting to see how Llion reacted while she inwardly cursed Ty for both mentioning and finding the note. And then cursed herself for not deserving Vesper's trust. She had to say something, though she loathed to tell yet another lie.

"I had hoped to have matters settled with Prince Alban before seeing Ty again." Which was true, if misleading.

Though Llion's fingers twitched toward his sword, his hard eyes barely flickered. She and Ty were walking a fine line. If Llion decided she had broken her oath to the Elusives, he'd not hesitate to deliver retribution; yet he seemed to be waiting to cast judgement.

Finally, he asked, "Who else knows about the location of the safe house?"

"No one else. I destroyed the note to cover our tracks." Ty hesitated, then blew out a long breath. "Our plan was that I would join Seren later, once she sent word of where. In the meantime, I would settle some private matters in Luminaria before securing what coin I could." He winced, and she suspected he had escaped with not a single copper on him. Then he smiled tentatively at her. "I suppose it was Lumina's will that Seren was able to send word the night before my final hours and that by your actions last night, I was freed and able to follow her. Our fates must be written in the stars."

When he put it like that it did sound as if everything that had happened had been according to some grand plan. At the same time, all her hopes that the note would soften her uncle's reaction to Sila's death perished.

"Join her for what exactly?" Ellus's voice was distant, his expression reminding her of an architect surveying the building of a bridge he had designed when the labourers had deviated from his instructions.

In response, Ty took her hand in his, drawing her to his side. She noticed he wasn't wearing the ring anymore, and she sighed in relief. Her palms tingled as he pressed a kiss to the back of her hand. "Where Seren goes, I go."

Out of the corner of her eye, she saw Vesper nearly swoon. Without the walking staff to prop her up, she probably would've fallen. "You and her!" she squealed. "And you gave up everything for her, like Prince Lleufer in the stories."

Seren had the urge to rip her hand from Ty's and shake the romantic vision out of Vesper's head. Whatever had brought Ty here, it wasn't love. It couldn't be. Not after one kiss.

"That, and to be honest, I didn't desire the death that waited for me in the arena." Ty squeezed Seren's hand—a comforting gesture—but concern on Ty's behalf wasn't something she had to fake at the moment. She was desperately afraid Llion could see through their charade.

"Lovely as this is"—Ty gestured to the circle of armed Felinae around him with his free hand—"I'd like a moment with Seren in private. We have our future as exiles to consider."

*Exile.* Ty had fled Uncle Tarquin's cells, refused to duel Quinton in Aequitas. He couldn't return to Luminaria without being executed or forced to continue the duel. While Ty was a skilled brawler, his swordsmanship, though adequate for the Legion, was nowhere near the calibre of her cousin. She'd often suspected Quinton had chosen Ty as his sword brother to keep his friend safe. From the age of eight, Quinton had been taught by master sword fighters from all over the continent. He'd been declared Champion of the Legion during his brief service.

And she had murdered Sila Utticor in front of him to save Ellus. There might be no coming back from that betrayal. Her heart twisted. Both she and Ty were traitors now in the eyes of her uncle and her cousin.

"Future?" Thane snorted from their other side. He leaned against a wide tree with his arms crossed, barely awake. "Contemplate a future as our prisoner, Prim."

Ty remained unfazed. "Your sealgair has three options. One, he can kill me. Two, he can take me prisoner. Or number three."

Seren's heart thudded at options one and two. Three couldn't be much worse, yet she couldn't bear to ask. Llion continued to scrutinize Ty but said nothing.

"The first sounds fine to me," Kanta mused, brandishing her new sword.

"What's three?" Vesper whispered.

"Extend the same offer to me as you did to Seren." Ty let go of her hand to splay his palms outward, like a huckster showing he had nothing to hide before he swindled the crowd. "But I'll sweeten it. If your prince grants both of us asylum with all rights and privileges of free citizens, I'll divulge everything I know about Tarquin Moralis and his secret weapon."

## 27

Seren's body ran cold, then hot, then cold again. If Ty wanted Llion's attention, he certainly had it.

"Convince me why I should take the chance on welcoming an enemy amongst us for what may be nothing more than lies," Llion countered as he leaned like Thane against a wide trunk for support. Despite his bland expression, his leg wound must be paining him.

The charming facade of an entitled nob fell from Ty. "Tarquin Moralis manipulates and twists others for his own gain—and I'll no longer be party to it. Seren and I are wanted traitors to the republic, and should we return, we'll be executed for our crimes. So I have no compulsion or duty to spy on you for Tarquin Moralis or spread his lies." The words were uttered with a heavy rawness, and her breath hitched.

Ty's gaze cut sideways to her before he squeezed her hand again. "My loyalty is to Seren and her alone. But you should consider me a valuable asset, Sealgair. I've observed Tarquin Moralis and what goes on in Luminaria under the noses of the Consul. Tales to scare you all back to wherever you disappeared to nineteen years ago. I do not exaggerate when I say your prince will be interested in what I have to say."

The firm resolve in Ty set her pulse racing. What did he know that she did not? For he could not be loyal to her *and* divulge what he knew of the "secret weapon."

"Your information best be as valuable as your life, Secundo," Llion rumbled, stepping away from the tree. "For now, we'll keep your weapons."

It seemed Tyberius would be granted a reprieve. It was better than Seren dared hope.

Then Llion stared up into the tall oaks and chestnuts that surrounded the brambles and swayed on his feet. Or maybe that was her. "We need rest now. Find a spot in the trees, out of sight."

"Who's on watch?" Ellus asked, stifling a yawn. He looked about ready to fall down—everyone did. It had been nearly two days since they had slept. But this might be a chance for her to speak to Ty without the others overhearing.

"We're dead on our feet—those who've used their Inheritance, at least," Thane muttered, already walking around the worst of the bramble patches, eyeing the thickness of various branches.

Seren tried to look alert. "I'll take first." Maybe she could speak to Ty while the others slept.

Thane shrugged. "It's your neck if you fall out of a tree from exhaustion, Princess."

"We'll all sleep," Llion ordered, though it sounded more like a sigh. "Without rest none of us can put up much of a fight if Moralis sends the Legion after us. And the wrens are agreeable to keep watch." He whistled a few high notes, and a handful of brown-speckled birds twittered back in response. As if they understood him.

A black speck appeared on his earlobe, so small she

probably wouldn't have noticed if she wasn't looking for it. The mark of the Goddess.

Seren's mind reeled. The wood-hawk. It had circled them for so long. "Your Inheritance allows you to speak to birds?"

It explained how he had found her in the rockslide, how he had known there were trackers following her. That Bay had survived. That's how Llion had known where the wall was unguarded yesterday and again this morning so they could scale it unnoticed.

A bird would go unremarked in the windows of her uncle's villa—in any of the consulars' estates. It would be the perfect spy—depending on how much information it could actually relay.

When no one answered her, she glanced over at Ellus, who was somehow paler than before. He pressed a hand against a tree for support. "He's a Warbler."

A warbler. It struck her as hilarious, and she grinned at the absurdity of it. *The lion who talked to birds.* Ty must be wondering what was going on, but he didn't say anything. Probably a smart choice.

Thane didn't find Llion's Inheritance as funny. He had swung himself up onto the second branch of a tall elm. There he crouched like a pissed-off alley cat. "Why haven't you used birds to set watches before, Sealgair?"

"Seline, take you off our hands," Kanta snapped from halfway up her sprawling oak. "Did you not notice the owls that hovered around our camps each night?"

"But we still took watches!" Thane spluttered as Llion climbed the crackled bark of another elm like a squirrel.

"Discipline," Llion replied after stopping to sit halfway up his tree. "That's one area the Legion excels at where we could improve." His scowl discouraged any further complaints. "We mustn't rely solely on our Inheritances. It will weaken us in more ways than one, and the Legion will use any weakness against us."

While Ty gawked at the swift climbing skills of the Felinae, Seren searched out a sturdy tree with low branches for him to scale. She found an oak near Vesper's tree. Already hidden from view, the girl's soft snores indicated the depth of her exhaustion from using her Inheritance.

"I've never slept in a tree before, but it can't be worse than a cell." Ty gave her an unreadable look. "We still need to talk."

"Later," she promised, backing up for her run. After jumping to the first branch, she caught sight of Ellus gracefully swinging his legs up and over the third branch of Kanta's oak. He stood, balancing on it like he'd been born to it.

If Ellus felt her gaze on him, he ignored it in favour of the tree on the other side. "How can you trust their loyalty to you, Sealgair?" His usually amiable tone was as bitter as winter berries. "The birds, that is. Might not something catch their eye and cause them to forget their purpose?"

Seren's shoulders stiffened as she gave Ty a hand up after his running jump fell short.

A whistle pierced the air, and a wren flew by their heads to where Llion sat high in the branches of his elm. It landed on his outstretched fingers. With his other hand, he petted its feathered back. "No creature is completely faithful. Each has a heart driven by its own need to survive. You can trust that." With a flurry of wings, the little brown bird took flight, dipping and diving as it flew to the next tree. "These wrens nest here. They'll warn me of intruders because it's in their best interests, too. And that is all I can expect from them."

After she and Ty secured themselves to the tree with their belts, Ellus's response lingered in her overburdened heart. "Perhaps that's all any of us can expect from each other."

———

A LANGUID HEAT, heavy with the promise of summer, clung to the canopied forest when Seren awoke to her palms tingling. Something was wrong.

One look below revealed Ty's branch was empty. Panic gripped her. One hand went to her knife as she scanned the ground below for his prostrate form, spying nothing but the faintest disturbance of the leafy ferns at the base of the oak. For a moment, she wondered if his arrival had been nothing more than a dream, but his colourful scent from days locked in the tower lingered. Had Llion taken him for a more intimate interrogation while she slept?

But no, her ears counted five separate heartbeats in the trees around her. After making certain Llion and the others still dozed, she followed Ty's trail as quietly as she could—watching birds be damned. It wasn't difficult to track him. He'd taken no care to hide his direction, and his scent steered her through a copse of silver birch nestled among bushes of ripening purple berries. Afterward, she'd have to ask Vesper if they were edible.

Soon the sound of splashing greeted her ears. The trees gave way to a sandy shore on the lip of a wide lake, and she found his clothes drying on the low branches of a birch and his legionnaire boots abandoned in a clump of clover. By the Goddess, a dunk in the water to wash the last day away was exactly what she needed. With impatience, she dropped her pack and freed her own feet of the sweaty confines of leather and wool.

As she made her way to the water's edge, warm sand squished between her bare toes—an utterly divine feeling she decided. The afternoon sun dappled the rippling blue lake where powerful arms cut through the water. He dove under only to resurface closer to shore. Familiar green eyes took in her presence, and then he was walking toward her, more and more of him emerging. Ty's legionnaire days might be behind him, but he hadn't lost that layer of muscle such intense training afforded.

It was a challenge to keep her gaze from lingering over his sculpted chest as more of it appeared, especially as she took in the yellowing bruises that covered his sides. Her hands clenched at the sight, her brow furrowing. He'd been hurt more than he'd let on. Whether it was her scowl or the level of the water—now at his waist—he stopped.

"I knew you'd show up, Tabby." She jerked her gaze up to his grinning, unblemished face. "You always could find Quinton and me, no matter where we were hiding in House Moralis. What gave us away?"

"Your smell." She sniffed. It was true, but not in a bad sense. She had always kept a close watch on Quinton when he was home from the Lyceum—and Ty, too. But was that how Ty thought of her still? A childish nuisance?

He laughed without embarrassment. "An unfortunate downside to those exceptional senses of yours."

She crossed her arms over her chest, determined not to be distracted from getting answers this time. "Are you a traitor, Tyberius Attica?"

"Tyberius Valerian Attica," he corrected in mock earnestness.

"What?"

His mouth curved upward in a self-deprecating way. "If you must scold me, you'd best invoke all my names. My mother did so when she was alive."

She hadn't known his mother had passed, but then she knew very little about Ty's family in Quarton, the main mining settlement on the southwestern peninsula. "May her heart rest easy in the Vale." Her eyes narrowed. "Now answer the question."

His shoulders, glistening in the sun, rose and fell. "You didn't clarify whom you are accusing me of betraying. We've all betrayed someone. Sometimes," his voice hardened, and those shoulders squared, "there's no good choice. Your uncle declared me a traitor as he did you. Are you one?"

"No," she snapped. Certainty rang through her like a bell. She wasn't a traitor. But she had given Llion information on the guard patrols and the layout of House Moralis. She had ended Sila's life. While Ty had struck Quinton on duty. Refused orders. Spied on the Consul without permission. Now he had promised to reveal secrets about her uncle and his weapon to Prince Alban. All traitorous acts. But not nearly as treasonous as hers. What would he think of her when he learned about Sila? What did the Goddess think?

One of his hands dragged through his wet hair, and she crossed hers over her chest as if to quell her pounding heart. "It's not a simple question, and there's no simple answer," he said as though he'd heard her inner debate. "But we do need to talk. Will you join me? As I remember, you always loved a swim in the Aegis, and I promise to be on my best behaviour."

"Fine." She swallowed the sting of disappointment at his last words. Cleary everything he'd told the Felinae about them had been an act—which she knew. She ducked her head before he could see her blush and began unlacing her vest. After the punishment her muscles had taken, a chance to stretch them was just what she needed. That, and after trudging through the city sewers, she could use a bath. The vest came off and her fingers froze. Swimming nude meant he'd see the sign of her failure and shame—the red crescent-shaped scar. She could count everyone who had seen it on one hand, including Vesper. But it seemed wholly cowardly to wear the billowy shirt when he had not a stitch on him.

But she needn't have worried. As she reached for the hem of her shirt, Tyberius swiftly turned his back on her. The courtesy shouldn't have surprised her. He may have teased her as a child, but he had never been cruel. But the tattoo on his back was unexpected. He hadn't had it when he'd left for the continent with Quinton and the Legion.

Tall black letters in High Prim were inked across the top of his well-formed shoulders. Like all Lyceum cadets, she had entered reading and writing Low Prim and had been required to learn High Prim as part of her studies.

*He is stronger who conquers himself.*

If that wasn't a challenge in itself.

Her shirt hit the sand, along with her leathers, and as soon as the water was deep enough, she dove under. The cold sliced through her muddled mind, sharpening her wits. When she surfaced further out, she was ready to pry the truth from him.

"My note, how did you come across it?" she demanded as he swam over to her, the sword and moon of his legion tattoo rippling with the flex of his left bicep. The water hit her at her shoulders, him a bit a lower.

"Before I escaped, I went to do what I could for Alphonius Luther." He gave her an unreadable look. "Was the centurio dead when you found him?"

Startled by both his concern for the traitorous Prim and the guilt Dobhran's death summoned, she kicked and glided away on her back into deeper waters. "We couldn't free him. The guards were upon us. He asked for a quick death." A quiet death, away from the chanting of the masses. She'd given him that much. She pushed that unsettling memory away and faced him again. "Did you truly destroy the note?"

Ty followed, his serious expression deepening. "Seren, your uncle would've ordered the execution of the family who lives in that house."

"The members of that famliy are traitors to the republic, Tyberius. They deserve their punishment."

"So are we considered traitors," he said softly. "Do we deserve to die?"

She bit her lip to stop it from trembling. The water was

cold, that was all. It wasn't the same; she was trying to bring honour to her House.

As she put her feet on the sandy bottom, she scanned the surrounding treetops. Little birds twittered, but none seemed overly interested in her and Ty. At best, what could they report to Llion? That she was bathing in the lake with Ty? That didn't break her oath.

Still, she lowered her voice. "Didn't my note make it clear? I'm here on my uncle's orders to spy."

"Sol's hells, Seren." Ty ran a hand over his face, and the black circle and diagonal bar of the ring transfixed her. It was once again on his hand. "You truly believe that?"

"What do you mean? You were there at the Consul meeting. You heard him say I was his weapon to win the war." At the look on his face, something cracked inside her. "You're not here on his orders to help me, are you?"

He took a deep breath, as if gathering his courage or the last of his patience. "The secret weapon Tarquin alluded to is his Crescents," he said flatly, ignoring her question.

She pushed down the mounting dread in her chest. "What are you talking about?"

"You honestly don't know." He gaped at her, and it made her feel keenly each of the three years that separated them. "The Crescents are like you, Prims born with Felinae blood. But they have unnatural abilities like this sealgair of yours—though not the same kind I believe. One controls fire, I know that, and Tarquin Moralis has been exploiting some of them since they were children." He snorted distastefully. "And some are still too young to be trained at the Lyceum."

Her jaw went slack. Uncle Tarquin already had knowledge of the Inheritances of the Felinae. More than that, he was using them to his advantage in this war. Without her. The crack inside her heart—or was it her soul?—widened. Her information was worthless to him.

She was worthless.

The clouds, the sky, the water—it all spun around her in a wash of colour—the world no longer made sense. She might have floated in a sea of stars instead of a lake.

"All this time, my uncle knew about Inheritances?" *But he'd never told her.* No one had taught them about Inheritances at the Lyceum, either. But then Ellus had told her how rare they had been up until the last few decades.

Ripples of water lapped gently against her as Ty shifted restlessly in the water. "From what I've read and been told, these abilities, Inheritances, were rare even back at the time of the Accord. So rare, most Primordians believed them to be more myth than truth." His expression darkened. "But I've seen them be used before your sealgair today."

"Why haven't I heard of these Crescents? Why am I not—"

*Why am I not one of them?*

"I wondered that, too. When you went missing, I thought maybe you'd finally been recruited or worse, force into it." He cut her a sideways look. "Most of the families of these Crescents aren't in positions to say no to Tarquin Moralis, even less so now that he is imperator. When his lackeys collect the children, he either bribes or intimidates their families into silence."

She couldn't believe it. There were more moonlight children. Like her. Like Vesper. And her uncle had gathered them into an elite group to fight the war.

*Without her.*

A shiver wracked her, and she crossed her arms over her chest, holding herself tight and sinking lower into the water until only her head was above it. When she finally spoke, her voice was as small as she felt. "Why didn't he train me with them?"

Ty's gaze softened as he sunk down to her level. "I suspect it's because you don't have an Inheritance."

"But I do!" She surged upwards, then clamped her mouth

shut at his widening eyes. She hadn't meant to admit that. "Tell me first about the ring," she deflected. "You promised you weren't the one who attacked me with it, so how did you come by it?"

His eyes shuttered. "I won it in a fight."

The water closed in around her, and she fought to keep from trembling uncontrollably in its cold embrace. She had waited so long for this, and every nerve in her body vibrated with need. "A name, Tyberius."

"Joren Takkakus," he whispered, eyes opening. "He's the one."

The air rushed out of her as the name conjured the image of the broad, thick young man with the busted face and shaved head from Pledging Night. She refused to break again. But she must have made some sound of distress for warmth spread around her as Tyberius gently enveloped her in his arms. The tiny pieces of her, threatening to fly away, settled back inside her. And like sparks, they ignited a flame of rage. Soon she was smouldering with it.

"Are you certain, beyond any doubt, the ring was Joren's back then?" Thankfully, the words came out hard, not broken. Maybe her rage could reforge the splinters inside her.

Ty's hold tightened on her as if she were holding him together. "Yes."

"When did you take it from him?" she murmured into his neck. His skin here was so soft and warm.

"A few days before Pledging Night, the last night I"—his voice cracked—"met with him. I think he wore it as a warning to me. But it had the opposite effect, if that's what he desired. Once I saw that ring, I want to say I lost control, but I didn't." His chest trembled against her, and she pulled him tight to her. Maybe holding each other together they could remain whole. "I knew what I was doing. I hit him, Seren. Over and over and over until he didn't get up." His lips brushed the side of her forehead. "Then I took it. For you."

She forced herself pull back so she could see his face. "I don't understand. How did you know what the ring meant to me?"

His entire body went taut, and he looked away. "Joren bragged more than once to me of what he'd done that night to you." He paused, stricken. "I should have done it sooner. I should've made certain he never got up off that floor."

*Yes.*

That one word bubbled up from a dark part of her soul. But if Tyberius had killed him, then she would have lost her chance at revenge. And repay him, she would. With a broken arm, a fractured collarbone, two broken ribs—the rest bruised, a bloody nose, and a swollen jaw. Then there was the scarring. She still didn't know how he'd done it.

Ty's troubled gaze met hers. "I should've told you everything."

"Why didn't you?" Some of her doubt came nipping back.

"There never seemed to be a right time. But to be honest, I was afraid of Joren, and what he might do if he learned that you knew." Ty ran a hand through his mop of wet hair again, the gemstone winking in the sun, and she shivered. "You survived, Seren. And against evil, that's winning."

Under the water, a callused hand found hers and raised it up. His other hand held the ring. "This should be yours."

At her nod, he slipped the silver band onto her finger. It was surreal to see the slashed black circle, the symbol that had haunted her nightmares and marked her Eyes, on her finger. A soulshielder ring, she realized now, though it was a mystery how Joren had come to possess one.

When she looked back up at Ty, the intensity of his gaze pierced her very soul, and in the hazy depths of his green eyes, she recognized herself. Recognized the pain buried inside both of them. The pain of Joren Takkakus.

"What did Joren do to you?" she asked hoarsely.

Ty stiffened in her arms but didn't pull away. "Nothing worth remembering." He dipped his head until their foreheads touched. "But the catacombs? On Pledging Night? I can't stop thinking about you, Seren Moralis. That fire in you. It made me want things I haven't wanted in ages. It made me come alive."

When his thumb trailed along her bottom lip, her lips parted expectantly. A yearning surged through her for things she had never wanted before.

"We shouldn't be doing this," Ty groaned, but he didn't move away.

"Why not?" Her breath hitched. The last thing she wanted was for him to stop.

Ty squeezed his eyes shut. "Quinton wouldn't like it."

"Quinton was ready to duel you to the death." If that was Ty's only problem, Quinton could throw himself in a lake—just not this one. "I don't care what he thinks. I only care if you'd like to kiss me."

"I think you know the answer to that."

She did—wedged as close as they were, nose to nose. In response, she closed the barest distance between them. The kiss was soft and careful at first, teasing that heat inside her. A dart of his tongue. A graze of her teeth. He tasted of sweet clover, and something bitter. She couldn't quite place it.

The tenderness didn't last long. His need became more insistent, demanding that fire inside her rise as if he wanted to swallow it and consume her.

But she had her own demands. Her fingers threaded through his hair, desperate for some impossible angle that would unlock what they were both trying to find in each other.

Meanwhile, his hands had swept down from her face and over her shoulders before continuing their journey under the water. As they passed over her scar below her bandeau, she sucked in a breath. Ty didn't pause or recoil in surprise as if he'd known it was there, and she exhaled when his hands curved around the small of her back, melding their flesh into one. Only it still wasn't close enough.

He groaned into her mouth before tearing his mouth away. "I think we'd better stop."

Both of their chests were heaving, and she placed a hand on him to steady herself. Part of her was disappointed. Running away with Ty might have its advantages. As she pulled away, she repeated his words to her after their first kiss. "Easy come, easy go, right?"

Ty cursed and crushed her against him again in a tight embrace, his mouth sloppily connecting with her forehead. "That wasn't about you. That makes it sound worse, but I said it to hurt Q. So I'm still a right bastard." His hold loosened, so she could break it if she wanted to. But he looked her in the eyes, those keyholes of the soul, and he *knew*. "I hurt you, too, didn't I?"

She didn't answer. It seemed silly to admit that.

"Hurting you is the last thing I wanted to do, Tabby. I won't let you go so easily again."

She attempted a light smile. "Looks like we're stuck together—for a while at least. But I think that nickname needs to go."

Ty pursed his lips as if he might argue with her, but he let her glide away, the low position of the sun catching his attention. "We should head back."

"We should talk about my Inheritance first." After all, she'd promised, and who knew when they could steal another private moment? He waited, and she debated where to begin while she contemplated the lone cloud in the sky.

"Their taibhseir says I'm a seer like her. Do you know what that is? That I can enter Time's Flow and, with more training"

—she winced at her continued failure—"I could see the future. Maybe the present, too."

She didn't mention the nightmare she'd had of her uncle at her cradle. It might strengthen Ty's resolve not to return to Luminaria. And what use was past vision, anyways? The past was done. It was the future she had to look to.

"What have you seen of the future?" Tension coiled in his shoulders as if he were bracing himself for the worst possible outcome; yet there was no disbelief or revulsion in his features like she feared.

"Nothing useful yet." She hugged herself under the water, grateful Ty didn't press her further. "But I don't need Seersight to know the others will wonder what we're up to."

His usual smirk returned. "Oh, they'll have ideas about that."

To hide her flaming cheeks, Seren dove under the water and swam toward shore. In the shallows, Ty waded past her, water sluicing over muscled thighs, and she quickened her step to catch up, picking up her clothes on the beach lest she had to wonder where to look. Her gaze darted along the tree branches, scanning for spies. Brown birds, maybe wrens, chirped innocuously in the branches.

"So are you worried about being caught naked together or confessing you're a spy?" Ty asked casually over his shoulder as he used his damp cloak to dry his arms.

"Lower your voice," she hissed. She pulled her cloak out of her pack and wrapped it around her like a shield. "Thanks to you, the Felinae already think we're together," she said to his tattooed back as he dried his torso. Still, she had no desire to have anyone stumble upon them like this. "And despite your opinion about these Crescents being the weapon, I still believe Uncle Tarquin meant for me to infiltrate the Felinae. I may still be part of his plan."

And if she wasn't, that meant Uncle Tarquin truly thought

her a traitor. Which only meant she had to prove her loyalty all the more. When Ty didn't respond, she pressed on. "Whether he sent me doesn't matter now." Maybe if she said it enough it would feel true. "What matters," she said, throwing her borrowed shirt over her head, "is that we redeem ourselves in the eyes of Luminaria."

"What happened in the lake seems counterintuitive to that."

She shrugged. "The betrothal is a ruse." Somewhat dry, she shimmied into her leathers, refusing to look while he did the same. "Q doesn't want to marry me. He can barely stand the sight of me. And Luminaria will forget and forgive when he does—which is as soon as he finds someone else to occupy his attention." And by the time she and Ty returned, whatever this attraction was between them would be spent. He'd be ready to move on. But why not enjoy Ty's company while it lasted?

"Are you certain of that?"

For half a breath, she thought she'd spoken her thoughts out loud, and she fumbled the buckle of her holster where Vindicta lay, a reminder of her pledge to earn back Uncle Tarquin's esteem and have her revenge. But Ty meant Quinton and the betrothal. Still, she thought her plan over again as she laced up her boots, ears alert for any sign of others in the forest.

"I am. While Quinton can hold a grudge"—*the last ten years were proof of that*—"he doesn't want me as his wife. And I have a plan for us to earn Uncle Tarquin's forgiveness and be welcomed home as champions. Then we can deal with Joren."

He looked at her warily. "And what's your plan to win back our honour?"

*Praise Lumina, he's clothed again.*

She drew herself up to her full height, still a few finger spans shorter than him. "We assassinate the Felinae princes."

"Prince-s?" he repeated slowly, holding up two fingers.

"There's two," she confirmed. "The youngest is the crown prince. The eldest is in hiding after renouncing his title. We'll need to locate him, of course." She waved that off. "But both will need to be dealt with in order for the republic's conquest to be uncontested, and I doubt either will willingly surrender after all this time. There isn't time to alert the Legion. No, we have to do it ourselves once we arrive at court. It's our best opportunity to earn our honour back."

Perhaps their only one.

"*If* we succeed and live to talk about it." Ty finished tucking the tail ends of his shirt inside his leathers. "Or we spill our information on Tarquin and the Crescents to the regent in return for enough coin to live comfortably on the white sands of Cartarchaa for the rest of our days." He leaned forward as if to capture her mouth again. "Just the two of us."

She reared back in alarm. And it wasn't just the suggestion of lifelong commitment. "What kind of life would that be?"

A life without a House to their name? Without proving herself to Uncle Tarquin? Without vengeance against the Felinae or Joren Takkakus? No, the wrongs had to be righted. Justice meted. She'd do it by herself. Honour demanded it. *To the end*. But she realized she wanted Ty to say he wanted both the same things. That she wasn't in this alone anymore.

Gazing up into his light green eyes, she answered her own question. "It would be a life of exile, of a traitor. Returning home as victors is our only option, Ty. It's our duty to our House. Our honour demands it." She steeled herself for rejection, clutching his forearms tightly. "You are with me, aren't' you?"

Her heart thudded loudly as she waited for his response, and he tucked a loose strand of hair behind her ear.

"I'm with you, Seren. But let's give ourselves time to think this through. Your Inheritance, can you see if your plan succeeds?"

"No seer can see her own future," she repeated Drakori's words.

Tyberius raised an eyebrow. "What about the republic's future? Or these princes?"

"Nothing yet." She didn't want to admit Time's Flow hadn't let her back in. That maybe her uncle was right for not training her with his Crescents. Maybe she wasn't good enough, strong enough, clever enough to use her Inheritance properly.

Leaves rustled and twigs snapped as a thumping noise approached in the distance. Someone was tromping through the brush, and they weren't being quiet about it. Had their conversation been overheard? Hastily, she tightened the laces on her leather vest, and her fingers brushed the wanted poster Ty had given her.

"Seren? Tyberius?" Vesper's shouts rang through the forest.

Seren glanced over where her boots had been, at the clusters of tiny purple berries on the verge of ripening, and an idea formed in her mind. Stooping down, she picked a handful of the darkest.

"Watch you don't crush those in your hands," he warned. "Blackthorn berry wine has ruined more than one silk shirt."

*Perfect.* Seren laid the handful down on a flat rock, then used her knife to squish a few into a dark ink while Vesper came closer and closer. A glance at Ty's relaxed posture told her he hadn't heard the Swiftfoot. "Vesper—the others—are looking for us," she whispered. "We'll have to be quick." Hastily, Seren turned over the poster to its blank side.

Ty's shadow crossed over it. "How quick? Less than three eclipses won't do my reputation justice."

Her face burning yet again, Seren concentrated on keeping the knife steady as she wrote. He tapped his ear and winked. Ah, he was providing a reason for Vesper to stay away.

"Um, Seren?" Vesper called, closer this time, and Ty turned his head in the young Elusive's direction.

"We're almost done!" Seren hollered back, then almost died of embarrassment at Ty's smirk.

"Almost finished!" Ty bellowed. From her crouched position, Seren hit him in the knee with her fist, which elicited a grunt that only increased her mortification.

From the trees, maybe fifty paces away, there was a faint giggle. "I should hope so," Vesper called back. "The sealgair's patience wears thin. I'll return to alert him you're on your way."

The tromping noise receded in the direction of their tree camp. Seren's racing heart slowed as guilt kicked at her insides for the subterfuge from Vesper. She held up the half-finished note to show Tyberius and caught the flash of silver in his hand before it disappeared inside his jacket. When had he stolen the flask back from Vesper?

He caught her staring and gestured at the note. "A love note? For me?"

Seren dipped the tip of her knife back into the crushed berries to add her initials. "For my uncle."

## 28

Llion set a brutal pace to make up for lost time. Where he was leading them, he didn't say, but they traversed deeper into the Western woods, through flowering meadows and over lumbering hills. By the terrain and the direction of the sun, it was clear they were not returning to Clan Wolvair. They followed no path, yet Llion never wavered on which way to go, his winged confidantes lending him a bird's-eye view.

So far, there had been no signs of pursuers. But if Ty could track them, there was no reason another party couldn't, especially one with Inheritances and heightened senses. Unless Uncle Tarquin had instructed his Crescents to fail in their search, in order to protect her cover.

As they walked, Ty seemed to be the only with the desire to talk. He related how the City Patrol had turned Luminaria upside down in the days after her disappearance on the chance another House had abducted her. Valera had been questioned and was nearly charged with treason. At Quinton's insistence, however, the imperator had dismissed the matter. The plight of her friend pricked Seren's conscience, and she vowed to right any wrongs when she returned.

According to Ty, a tracking party—she assumed he meant these Crescents—had been sent after Seren only to returned weeks later with her horse, which was damning evidence that she had run away. It had sealed her fate as a traitor in the city's streets. The tawdry talk about Tyberius and her had surfaced soon afterwards.

It was a relief when Llion asked about more practical matters, such as the Legion's whereabouts and activities. The bulk of the Legion had marched north with Legatus Takkakus soon after Dobhran was arrested in Gull Harbour. Quinton, Seren gathered by what Ty didn't say, had stayed behind in charge of the remaining legionnaires on the wall and to coordinate with the City Patrol. Ty was careful not to implicate himself in the capture of Dobhran; otherwise, she suspected Llion would have far more pointed questions for him. Or, perhaps, Llion was biding his time for a private interrogation. That thought kept Seren's already worn nerves on edge for the rest of the afternoon.

Once dusk settled, and the stars began to dot the indigo sky to keep Lumina company in her full glory, the woods thinned into overgrown orchards of flowering chestnuts, apple trees, pear trees, and maythorns. Delicate white and pink petals carpeted the knee-high meadow grass, their sweet fragrant scents tickling her nose, and Seren hoped they wouldn't be sleeping in these trees tonight. In a circle of maythorns bursting with pinkish buds, Llion stopped to stare into the grasses.

"I knew that last creek looked familiar," Vesper cried, dropping her pack and staff. She blurred in and out of the trees in a sort of a skip-hop before stopping to lean against a trunk, cheeks aglow. "Are we home in time for the Night of Mair, Sealgair?"

Under her cloak, Seren fingered the piece of paper tucked inside her vest, while she surreptitiously searched for a spot to hide it. In the mountains, Llion had said the trackers had followed her scent—and if they were Crescents with Felinae blood working for her uncle, they would track her to these trees. She ran a hand over the ridges of the closest trunk, feeling for a crack the right size to fit the folded note while she watched Llion kneel in the tangled grass.

After divesting himself of his pack and bow, he glanced up at the full moon, then began digging with his hands. "Sionnach, keep a lookout. Llews, come here."

Would another enchanted door reveal itself? There was no scout, but Vesper had said she was home, so this was her clan, the Llewyn.

"Sealgair, should I blindfold the Prims?" Kanta asked, eyeing Seren and Ty. Ever since Silver had left to alert the other Elusives, Kanta had appointed herself Llion's second. Usually, Seren ignored her, but being blindfolded wouldn't do.

Abandoning the trees, Seren strode forward. "I thought we'd settled this, Urso. I just risked my life for"—*Ellus*—"all of you back in Luminaria."

"Lady Kanta of Clan Urso, right?" Ty sauntered over with a dazzling, self-deprecating smile. "I couldn't find my way back here if you drew me a detailed map, I assure you."

Many had melted under such attention. Clan Urso must be made of sterner stuff or uninterested.

Under her nest of tangled curls, Kanta's face took on the look of curdled milk. "I suppose Seren's told you everything she's learned about us then. Will I be on your list of targets, Secundo? Be warned, the Urso have claws."

Seren scowled to cover her unease at how close Kanta was to the truth. "If you had bothered to introduce yourself to him, I wouldn't have needed to tell him who you are. And if you feel like a fight, I'm ready when you are."

"Oh, you need not fight over me," Ty protested, neatly drawing Seren back a step by the wrist and then raising their entwined hands for a kiss. "I'm spoken for, Lady Kanta."

His declaration struck everyone speechless. As he grinned at her over their hands, Seren thought his misunderstanding a clever ploy to defuse the situation—until she realized everyone could plainly see the black circle on her finger.

There was a gust of wind, and then Vesper was shaking her by the shoulder. "You didn't say he gave you a ring."

"It happened at the lake," Seren murmured, her gaze drifting over Vesper's tawny head. At the edge of the tree line, Ellus lingered in the shadows. Guilt stabbed at her. She'd barely spoken to him since they fled Luminaria. And since Ty arrived, he'd kept his distance from them both.

"We don't have time for this," Llion barked. He pinched the bridge of his nose with dirt-encrusted hands as if a headache ailed him. A pile of dry brown leaves and meadow grass lay beside him. "Dobhran compromised the location of the entrance."

The dead man's name silenced them. Kanta and Vesper both darted furtive looks upward at the tree Thane had climbed. So they both knew how Llion had come by that information.

"Entrance to what?" Ty reached for a sword he no longer carried. When he didn't find it, he glared at Llion. "And if Imperator Moralis knows how to find it, why in Sol's name did you bring us here?"

"To warn Clan Llewyn they must vacate the den," Ellus replied, pushing off his tree to join them finally. Ty's sword hung from his waist, and he didn't offer it back. "Considering this new danger, the Throne will summon all the clans to Caisteal Dìomhair." He shrugged. "Or so I suspect."

Llion grunted in assent. From over his shoulder, Seren saw what the grass and petals had hidden: a pearlescent stone that shimmered in the starlight. She sucked in a breath. Like a piece of the moon brought down to earth.

A shadow flitted over it. Above, an owl flapped overhead; it hooted urgently, and Seren's palms tingled.

With a groan, Llion sank to his knees. His earlobes had turned black with the Goddess symbol again.

Ellus was beside him almost as fast as a Swiftfoot. "You can't keep in contact with all the birds in the entire forest." Concerned irritation laced his words.

"What's wrong with him?" Ty muttered to her.

"It's from overexerting his Inheritance," Ellus explained, as he helped Llion stagger to his feet.

The larger man grabbed Ellus's lean shoulders in a tight grip. "A tracking party is headed this way from the north."

These trackers weren't coming from the direction of the city then. Were they after the Felinae, her, or Tyberius? Or all of them?

It was then Seren noticed the heat of the afternoon hadn't dissipated. In fact, the temperature was climbing even as the shadows darkened, and a faint crackle filled the forest.

"Smoke! To the north!"

As Thane shouted from his tree, she saw the grey plumes rising above the green treetops into the stars. Too thick to be a cooking fire, and too loud. Soon Seren didn't need to strain her ears to hear the cracking and popping of wood as the unseen fire devoured the old trees at an alarming rate.

An unnatural rate.

She glanced at Ty, and his grim look confirmed his thoughts were the same: the Crescents.

"What do we do, Sealgair?" Vesper asked, wide-eyed. "Our orchards will be destroyed."

With a thump, Thane landed in a crouch, petals falling around him. When he rose, he unsheathed his stolen sword and gave it a considering look. "Prim blades are decent at spilling blood."

All eyes fastened on Llion, who stepped away from Ellus, spine straight. "It's not to our advantage to engage. Soon the air will be too thick with smoke to breathe. Swords out, but we should be inside the den before they or the fire reach us." *Should be.* He clapped a hand on Vesper's shoulder and gentled his tone. "The trees will grow again."

Vesper's thin shoulders drooped in acceptance as she knelt with him to clear more earth from the pearlescent stone.

Sweat had already broken out on Seren's brow, and her skin was damp from the rising temperature. Since the trackers hadn't followed them, then they wouldn't have come across her scrawled message tucked under a rock at the lake. This might be her last chance to have a message about her plan to assassinate the princes—and the fact there were two of them—conveyed to her uncle.

Seren glanced around the clearing, silently cursing herself for arguing with Kanta instead of hiding her second note—a duplicate of the first. Where would it be safe from the fire? Where might the Crescents, whom she was praying her uncle hadn't sent to retrieve her, find it?

"Why didn't your birds alert you earlier, Sealgair?" she grumbled. She refused to fight any more members of House Moralis or any other Prims. She was a traitor enough as it was.

"They were watching to see if we were followed—we weren't," Llion answered without stopping his work. "The trackers must have circled to head us off. Or come from another location."

That this move was made possible by the information Dobhran had given up went unsaid. Another possibility struck her. The girlish voice from her dreamscape—the other seer, who must be part of the Crescents—could she have directed the tracking party here?

"They may know where we are, but the enchantment of the door will keep any Prims or forest fire out," Ellus said in a reassuring tone. He still wouldn't meet her eyes, but he had joined their circle.

She forced herself to concentrate on what he was saying. Primordians would be kept out, yes, but what about the half-Felinae, like her? Could she open the door? And if so, then perhaps so could Uncle Tarquin's Crescents. But no, Ellus had said only a clan member could call the door to their clan's den. "Could a descendent of a clan member open the door?"

The question seemed to startle Ellus. "Maybe." He glanced at Llion. "They'd need to know the clan words, though. What about the group who attacked us outside the Wolvair den, Sealgair? Could these be the same archers?"

"If so, they've changed tactics." Llion gestured impatiently to the stone. "Vesper?"

Vesper placed her tawny hand on the stone and murmured strange words. Different, Seren thought, than the ones the Wolvair scout had said. One by one, silver swirls unfurled from under Vesper's hand, similar to the moon etchings on her cradle and the Wolvair door. They halted, however, before completely covering the stone, a thumb's length away from the edge of the stone and then withered like the dead vines of winter.

Vesper repeated the litany, more frantically this time. "Why isn't it working, Sealgair?"

"I don't know," he muttered as the swirls withered again. He placed his wide, roughened hand next to her slender one on the stone. Together, they joined voices, and Seren tried to commit the words to memory. A spark of silver pulsed along the brown tendrils but then stopped short again.

Ribbons of flame jumped to the maythorns around them, one by one. Thane and Kanta both had their swords out now to the forest, yet Seren hesitated to unsheathe hers. Sweat laced her palms, and Sila's eyes flashed before her.

Beside her, Ty held out his hand, as if understanding her reluctance. "Give me your sword, Seren."

She hesitated but passed it over. She was better to use Nightfall if needed. If only she had used it—done anything else —to stop Sila. If she had taken the time to think—

But there hadn't been time—or so she told herself.

Meanwhile, Ellus had sunk down in the tall grass next to Vesper, adding his hand and voice. As they finished the litany, a bright silver light flashed from the stone, and the three fell back, panting. It faded to reveal an intricate design of the phases of the moon on the stone door, similar to the Wolvair den, yet unique. In the middle, a silver pull-ring in the shape of a crescent moon had formed. With a heave, Llion opened it to reveal a dark hole below, the sides of which were lined in gleaming serendium and quartz. It would be a squeeze, the mountain all over again, and her chest tightened at the thought. But no, it couldn't be as tight as it looked if Llion expected to fit.

Llion nodded at Vesper, and she dropped through the hole first, her pack clutched against her chest. Kanta went next. With her back to the others, Seren drew out the folded square of paper from inside her vest. While Ellus and then Thane disappeared into the hole, she stepped back and knelt to fiddle with her boot. When she straightened, her hand was empty and the note was hidden in the grass. She prayed Llion didn't notice it.

"Go on, Morningstar." Llion had his back to her, staring out at the trees, bow in hand, ready to be sighted if someone should come running out at them, while Ty faced the opposite direction, her stolen sword in hand.

At the edge of the hole, she hesitated. It would be the

perfect time for Llion to eliminate a threat without witnesses. "You go first, Ty."

Behind her, Llion made an impatient sound, as if he read her mind.

"I'll be behind you," Ty said, squeezing her shoulder.

"Right behind me." She covered his hand with a squeeze before dropping into the grey darkness. She fell for a few seconds before hitting bottom and rolling on the hard ground. More serendium greeted her, but between the veins of rock sprouted the moon-like mushrooms that glowed the same pale hue as moonwood.

Ty dropped to the ground behind her, and she helped him up. "Cozy," he whispered. Then he grinned. "We need to stop meeting in dark tunnels, *amara*."

Seren nearly choked at the archaic Primordian endearment used in old ballads. But there was no time to discuss it. She tugged Ty out of the way before Llion landed on them. The sealgair murmured more words she didn't understand, and the light from above ground winked out, sealing them in. Tyberius's hand found the small of her back—a possessive touch, but one she found she liked for the solid presence at her side. As in the catacombs, she led him through the darkness, toward the faint strains of music.

The tunnel opened into an enormous high-domed chamber covered in sparkling violet and white crystals, and Seren's gaze darted between the mesmerizing ceiling and the sprawling floor filled with circles of dancing Felinae around tall bonfires of unnatural white flame. Moonwood, she realized. Branches of maythorn flowers festooned every archway, which was saying something since the dome was four tiers high with six tunnels on each level. No guards met them. It seemed Clan Llewyn trusted their safety entirely to their enchanted entrance.

*Fools.*

As Llion strode ahead, the revellers halted their dancing and bowed their heads. An animated murmur rose above the music, until it, too, ceased as if in obeisance to the sealgair. The other recruits followed in his wake, but Seren hung back with Ty, whose sharp gaze scanned the room. Which was what she should be doing to locate the exits, identify threats, and catalogue the numbers of Felinae.

Instead, her attention snagged on Llion's destination: a wooden dais with more flowers. In the centre stood a smiling, golden-haired woman of medium build. She wore a simple yellow garment that fell to her feet. It was fitted around her bodice and loosened outward toward the ground with long sleeves unlike the wraps favoured by Primordians. Each side had been slit and extra panels of brown fabric were added to give the wearer freer movement. A certain refinement in her stature and a delicate crown of pale pink blossoms separated her from the surrounding attendants. Faint lines around her cornflower blue eyes and her wide mouth spoke of burdens and worries, but they crinkled with warmth as Llion dipped down on one knee before her in homage.

As he ascended the steps of the dais, the woman captured him in an embrace, her forehead bumping his chin gently in her haste. "Llion! You made it back for the Night of Mair. What an unexpected but welcomed gift of the Goddess."

Llion held her awkwardly. "I'll dirty your dress, my lady."

She was too young to be Llion's mother. No grey infused her hair, though the freshness of youth had been supplanted by a confident radiance. Both had long blond hair, though hers was a rich, thick gold to his darker shade. Perhaps she was an older sister or a cousin? Which made sense, since his family name was Llewyn, like the clan.

The lady pulled back and wiped her eyes, not paying any mind to her clothing or her audience. To those kneeling, she made a waving gesture, and the music and dancing resumed. Llion visibly winced at the noise.

"Are you hale, my lord?"

He rubbed an ear before tucking his hands behind his back. "An earache is all, my lady."

"Gwenna said you were injured—"

"Arrow wound. Lady Fawn saw to that well enough," he interrupted sharply, looking around. "Taibhseir Drakori is here then?"

The lady's smile faltered, but she recovered quickly. "She arrived yesterday on the heels of her missive that the location of some of the dens had been compromised. We've also had word that the Throne has issued a formal summons to all the clans. We are to leave tomorrow morning. And yes,"—she held up a slender pale hand adorned with a single ring of thin gold wrapped around a yellow gemstone—"Gwenna informed me you would be followed here."

Seren couldn't keep her brows from shooting skyward. Why hadn't the Llewyn stirred themselves to stand guard outside the entrance then?

"And yet we are celebrating?" Llion frowned at the merriment before them.

At the censure, the lady straightened her shoulders. "Our people need more than the hope they place in your Elusives and our young prince. They need to remember why life is worth living." The lady smiled gently. "That is what we are fighting for, is it not?"

"I suppose if the taibhseir said we have the time," Llion replied tightly.

Seren's gut twisted bitterly. *If only Taibhseir Drakori had foreseen the rescue mission was a lost cause. We could already be at the Throne.*

In front of her, Ellus's back stiffened, and Vesper sent her a worried look over her shoulder. Had that slipped out?

"It is frustrating, relying on visions," the lady agreed, one hand on Llion's arm as if to stay him. "Taibhseir Drakori isn't privy to everything that is to come. We accept what the Goddess Seline gives us and act as best we can"—she lowered herself in an elegant curtsey, then raised her head—"Your Highness."

All the dancing halted again, the attention now solely on Seren. Row after row of Felinae dipped down on one knee or curtsied, following their lady's example.

Beside her, Llion shifted, clearly uncomfortable with the display. "Lady Llewyn, may I present Her Highness, Princess Seren of the Morningstars."

From the corner of her mouth, Lady Llewyn whispered, "It is me you should present to Her Highness, my lord."

"The pleasure is mine," Seren blurted. Anything to prevent drawing out this exchange, which was doing nothing to improve Llion's ire. She glanced askance at her kneeling audience. "Please."

Lady Llewyn inclined her head graciously, then rose. A moment later, her clan members followed suit. "The honour is ours, Your Highness. I had the privilege of meeting your father and his older brother, though I was a child when Queen Ellowyne wed Lord Lynus Morningstar. Be at home with us, Princess. And may I welcome your companion as well?"

"Tyberius Attica, my lady," he replied with a bow as the Felinae had done. "Thank you for your hospitality."

Lady Llewyn inclined her head with a smile. "Noa"—she indicated a woman behind her in a similar mustard yellow garment—"will see to your needs, and then I invite you all to partake in our celebration of Seline, the moon goddess, in both her Mother and Maiden forms on this Night of Mair." The formal invitation out of the way, a warmer smile suffused her face as her gaze lit upon her clan member. "And Vesper Llews, you've been much missed. Your mother will be so happy to see you, my dear. Now, off with you all or you'll miss the dancing."

At her kind dismissal, Vesper, Kanta, and Ellus dipped briefly to their knees before following Noa into the passageway, along with Thane. Ellus, it seemed, couldn't get away fast enough. But the promise of clean clothes and food wouldn't sway Seren so easily. The forest burned above them, and this lady wished them to dance and eat and drink? When legionnaires might come knocking on her door? Or the imperator's Crescents?

Instead, Seren lingered behind at the back steps of the dais, and Tyberius stuck close. He, at least, knew the value of eavesdropping.

"A late night before a long journey makes for a longer journey, my lady." Llion's tone was polite but terse as he stood by the lady's side, looking out over the dancing.

"Taibhseir Drakori would not let us leave without you, not that I would." The lady slipped her hand through the crook of Llion's arm and glanced up at him. "And it is sacrilege not to offer Seline her tribute on this night of new beginnings, dear husband."

Llion was married? To this kind and elegant, albeit slightly foolish, lady?

"But we are packed and ready to leave at first light, and Gwenna predicts a safe journey," Lady Llewyn reported. That penetrated the fog in her mind, and she stepped up onto the dais.

"Did she predict the raging forest fire above us? Have Drakori's visions never been wrong?" Her hard voice or impertinence earned her a startled expression from over Lady Llewyn's shoulder. She probably wasn't used to rudeness. Though she should be, considering who her husband was.

The dancing slowed, and Seren had the distinct impression that the Llewyn were pricking their ears to listen, which Vesper had explained was the height of discourtesy in Felinae society. But Seren supposed she couldn't blame them. Around two hundred of them had heard this new princess question their lady, the sealgair, and the taibhseir.

Maybe that was what they needed. Someone to question their heavy reliance on nothing but what one woman saw in her head.

Llion levelled a quelling look across the floor. The music, dancing, and whispers ceased. He let the silence swell before he addressed them.

"You should fear Tarquin Moralis, Princess, but you are under the Throne's protection. That means you are under Clan Llewyn's protection. We are not as defenceless as you assume. As history has shown us," he said, voice rising, "Prims cannot fight what they cannot find!"

Hearty shouts of approval pierced the cavern. They died when Lady Llewyn spoke, her voice calm and measured. "And for almost two decades, the ancient knowledge of the Keepers, returned to us by our esteemed taibhseir, has kept us and our dens safe."

More cheers burst from the crowd, and Llion swayed on his feet, leaning more heavily on his wife's arm. With a wave from Lady Llewyn, the musicians placed their pear-shaped instruments at their necks and struck up a lively tune by passing something akin to a bow across the strings.

Quickening her steps, Seren cut off Llion and Lady Llewyn's retreat. "I do not fear my uncle's legionnaires," she hissed lowly, "but I am familiar with what fate awaits traitors in Luminaria." And if she and Ty were captured now, they'd have little to prove they weren't traitors. "The sealgair's protection is conditional until the Throne makes a decision. If Prince Alban refuses my petition for sanctuary, both Ty and I will be thrown at the mercy of my uncle, the imperator. So forgive me if I find it foolish to risk our lives on a vision of a *possible* future."

Llion's eyes hardened into a cold, flat expression that told her he knew about her hand in Dobhran's death. At that moment, she understood if he had his way, neither she nor Tyberius would be granted sanctuary. It was a good thing she wouldn't truly need it.

"My lord, is this true?" The lady's tone held genuine bewilderment. "Why hasn't Prince Alban granted his cousin asylum?"

"Riaghladair Boreal cautions against haste in such matters," he replied stiffly. "Loyalty does not depend on blood, my lady. It must be proven."

"Indeed?"

"Come, Lenore. There is more to discuss in private with the taibhseir."

Turning on his heel, Llion swept Lady Llewyn off the dais in his haste. Left behind, her attendants eagerly joined the dancing circles as the pair disappeared into the dark passageways.

A plan began to form as Seren made her way to Ty, who leaned against the archway in the shadows, completely at ease with the revelry around them. But then he'd never shied away from the moon balls, either. As she approached, Ty tore his attention from across the cavern, where the uncorked barrels of drink flowed freely. With barely concealed thirst, he drank her in with his eyes instead.

"You have a dangerous glint in your eye, *amara*."

She took a step backward into the shadows, then crooked her finger. "Care to explore more tunnels with me, *amaro*?"

## 29

Moonwood lit the deserted tunnels along with glowing mushrooms, enough that Ty didn't need to hold on to her. Yet he stayed close, matching her purposeful stride.

"We could simply ask for directions to our rooms." Fingers ghosted across the nape of her neck.

Seren hesitated, tempted to abandon her search for more of his touch. But although she didn't know what she was looking for, it seemed a waste of an opportunity not to explore the Llewyn den while everyone else was occupied.

The warmth of his touch receded when she didn't respond. "You truthfully meant explore the tunnels then?"

"There could be valuable information here." She didn't look at him as she reached a door. It was locked. "We can use the same excuse as the catacombs if we're caught."

He said nothing else, and neither did she as she tried door after door set into the serendium walls of the den. Some were locked. Others opened into rooms half emptied of their contents. One room held shelves upon shelves of preserves. Another had crates of linens and clothes. Another, shovels and tools for digging. An adjacent passageway led them into a wing of living quarters. Rooms with simple wicker beds, at the foot of which sat packs and bundles ready for the early morning departure.

This room also had a worn desk with a holder for a quill. Seren pulled out the drawers, but someone had thoroughly emptied them. The Llewyn had left nothing valuable about as if they were never coming back or on the chance their enemies infiltrated their subterranean fortress, she supposed.

"What do you hope to find?" Ty leaned against the closed door, arms crossed, forehead glistening with sweat despite the cool, damp air.

"Something," she muttered, before turning to the crates in the corner. She pushed the lid off one. Threadbare linens. She dug into the box, feeling around with her hand. "You could help, you know."

"Rifle through bedsheets?" The idea seemed to amuse him. "I'm afraid any secrets they once held are long gone."

She shot him a scowl over her shoulder while keeping an ear out for any approaching footsteps. They should probably rest before the journey tomorrow, but something akin to desperation drove her onward. Maybe in the next room she'd find something she could use against the princes.

Then her fingers closed around a hard object. She sucked in a breath and pulled the folded sheet out. Three books tumbled out.

"What is it?" Tyberius pushed away from the door. He'd brought the moonwood branch from the hallway sconce with him, and he held it up to see.

She picked up the first dull leather-bound book and flipped through it. The words made little sense to her, but maybe Ellus could read them. The next book was the same, except its pages were illuminated. One was a portrait of a king and queen painted in cerulean and crimson. The parchment seemed too old to be Queen Ellowyne and King Lynus. A large cat with tufted ears and luminous eyes slept at their royal feet, and two moons hung behind them.

She returned the book to the crate, which left a slim volume with gold leaf on its spine. When she picked it up, a low hum started in her palms, and she almost dropped it. In her fumbling, the book fell open to an inked drawing of the Goddess mark. It was a complicated, knotted pattern of lines that made a circle with a diagonal slash. At the bottom of the page, she recognized one word: *Unamkhara*.

"That mark—I've seen it on Crescents. And it's the same as Joren's—as your ring," Ty observed from over her shoulder.

"It's the mark of the Goddess. It appears when we use our Inheritances. But this word here means soulshielder. They're like sword brothers or sisters, except the responsibility to one another runs deeper than the flesh." She hesitated. "My father had a soulshielder, not that it helped him in the end."

"Soulshielder." Tyberius tasted the word while she stood and tucked the book carefully up the back of her vest and then arranged her cloak so no one would see it. "Like a protector of your soul instead of your back?"

"For body, heart, and soul I think." Guilt washed over her. Quinton had been his sword brother. How much of their quarrel was her fault? Valera would say none—that they were solely responsible for their own actions. It was difficult to believe they would both toss away years of friendship when she knew her cousin had not a single romantic feeling for her.

"What went so wrong between you and Quinton?"

She watched him carefully as he paced over to the door. While it was difficult to make out colours in the low light, a clammy pallor had taken hold of Ty. Perhaps he had caught ill in the tower?

When he finally spoke, his voice was flat. "It's been a long time coming. We've drifted apart the last few years." He shrugged. "Since we returned from the continent, we've held differing opinions on the company we each keep, you could say. That doesn't mean I want him to come to harm." He seemed to tremble at the thought. "Certainly not by my hand."

Which was why he had left Luminaria.

"You don't approve of his involvement with the Crescents? And he doesn't approve of . . . " Her cousin's words came back to her. *Another lover's token, Ty?* "Of your activities?"

"Does it matter? We both know once Quinton gives you the cold shoulder—" He broke off and shrugged.

He didn't trust her completely, and it stung for some reason. She had shared her most damning secrets with him. Except for one. *Sila.*

*He came to me after Quinton betrayed him.* Ty trusted *her* with his life, if not his secrets yet. And she didn't regret that he held hers. Secrets, she was learning, were exhausting.

"We should head back," Ty said, shaking her out of her reverie. "And I could use something stronger than water. These last few days have been hell."

Likewise, the motivation to search had left her. In silence, she retraced their steps through the empty moonwood-lit passages. Not far into the labyrinth, the Eyes on her palms tingled at the juncture of an unfamiliar passageway. Deciding to follow them, she led Ty into the new section, and soon familiar whispers pricked her ears. Maybe her Inheritance wasn't completely useless after all.

With her hand, she motioned for Ty to stay quiet. Then she slunk forward as silently as possible. The closer she came to the low voices, the more frenzied the tingling. She stopped forty paces from the door with the light spilling from under it —close enough to hear clearly. There was an adjacent tunnel, and she ducked down it. Out of the corner of her eye, she saw movement, like the flap of a cloak, farther down the passageway. When no one appeared, she relaxed to concentrate on the conversation.

"If Istra insists on the marriage to Lady Fawn," Lady Llewyn said in a low tone, "it will position Clan Wolvair as powerful advisers to the Throne. I fear their alliance with Clan Ermine may adversely influence the young prince."

Warm breath on her neck sent a different tingle down her spine. Tyberius had followed her, and when he pressed his lips there and murmured her name against her skin like a question, she almost missed Llion's reply.

"The prince is in no hurry to marry."

"Be that as it may, Prince Alban does desire to be crowned," Drakori said gravely, "and mayhap to slip the yoke of his aunt through marriage. We can no longer keep our eyes veiled when it comes to Istra Boreal." A banked anger simmered in Drakori's voice. "After ruling for so long, I fear she won't step back gracefully. And if she remains the power behind the throne, she will lead us on a path to ruination. The young prince must be informed of her perfidy."

"He won't accept less than absolute proof of her treason," Llion replied. "And we'll lose any advantage we have if he confronts her with our suspicions."

Unaware of the discussion taking place behind the door at the end of the passageway, Ty silently kissed a trail up her neck, and her palms tingled in a frenzied manner. Seren raised her hand to push him away; instead, her traitorous fingers delved into his soft hair and pulled him closer when he reached the sensitive spot below her ear.

While she surrendered her mouth to Ty, she strained to eavesdrop. Even though Ty was taking pains to be quiet, she hoped if any of the Felinae overheard them, they would dismiss them as a couple who had snuck away from the celebrations.

"Perhaps it is time for the eldest prince to present himself to the Felinae," Lady Llewyn suggested.

There was an inner pop—a loosening of pressure inside her —and suddenly she was looking down on two blond heads— one dark, one light—and one head of grey. Llion, Lady Llewyn, and Taibhseir Drakori. Hovering above them like a wraith; yet no one seemed to notice her. And her body was still in the tunnel, on the receiving end of Ty's heated mouth, which she could still feel, if faintly. Occupying two places at once—it shouldn't be possible.

"I am sworn to Prince Alban." Llion stood stiffly in the small room with earthen walls and wicker furniture far too small for his frame. "I will not act against him."

On a divan of faded yellow sat his wife, impeccably straight as if presiding over a formal affair. In comparison, Drakori, still in her grey travelling clothes, slumped in an armchair on the other side of a low table, adorned with a finely worked piece of lace and a stout candle to ease the dullness of the room.

"We would expect nothing less from you, my lord," Lady Llewyn replied evenly, pulling her wool shawl tighter around her shoulders in the dampness. "But it may not be in Prince Alban's interests to sit the Throne—if Istra proves resistant to stepping down."

"He has been raised for the responsibility since birth." Llion's hand clenched by his side. "He is suited to it."

"Is he? Or has he been raised to be her puppet?" The taibhseir stared into the black gemstone on her staff as if it might hold the answers she sought. "Raised in a foreign court, away from his people." She stamped the staff on the floor, eyes flashing. "I never should have gone along with it. And now Istra has pulled the wool over our eyes with this unhallowed alliance."

"Do we have any insight into what Boreal and Takkakus are planning?" Llion asked. "Any proof of her treason beyond your visions? Witnesses or letters to Legatus Takkakus?"

*Takkakus.* It was a grim and frustrating satisfaction to hear the dishonourable actions of Joren were echoed in his House and father. She had assumed Joren abhorred her for being half-Felinae. But his father's treasonous alliance with the enemy pointed to the long-simmering rivalry between their Houses.

Whether or not his attack on her had been personal or part of a scheme of his father's, if Calvus was aiding the Felinae regent, the fissures of treachery in House Takkakus now ran deeper than a House vendetta. It was treason against the republic, and her uncle needed this information before Takkakus and Regent Boreal put their plan into motion.

"We do not yet have proof to bring before the clans," Drakori admitted, sourly. "If Istra has dared to do this behind our backs, there may be more stains of betrayals in her past. But the soul of the one who sits the Throne must be unblemished if we hope to restore the Elusive Mysteries of the Keepers."

On that enigmatic note, the conversation inside the room moved to the preparations Lady Llewyn had made for the journey tomorrow. Seren's consciousness floated back inside her body, where she found her lips stinging and her chest heaving against Ty's.

He stroked her cheek, concern etched in his soft green eyes. "Where did you go?"

Her gut clenched at what he could have seen. But her hands had been on his neck, sloping down his shoulders. No chance for him to see the Goddess mark. Afraid that they might be overheard, Seren pulled him down the tunnel by the hand. "Where could I have gone?"

"I would rather we didn't lie to each other." He dug his heels in, forcing her to stop. "If you don't want me—if you don't want me to kiss you, you can say no."

The careful way he held his expression made her want to prove her interest by dragging him into the next empty room. Instead, she grabbed a handful of his shirt to pull him closer. "I do want you. And I'm sorry I was distracted—I'll explain, but it's not safe here."

The lines around his mouth relaxed in a way that made her chest loosen. For whatever reason, she did not care to see Tyberius in pain. "All right, but next time"—his voice dropped, and amusement danced in his eyes—"you don't need to lead me into a dark tunnel to kiss me, *amara*."

*Of all the nerve.* He had kissed her.

In their haste back to the main tunnel and with the thundering of Seren's heart in her ears at what she'd overheard, they almost knocked over a round-cheeked woman in a yellow dress. Noa, one of Lady Llewyn's attendants.

"Lost in the tunnels, I see." Noa uttered the firm admonishment with a shake of her brown braided head, presumably at their dishevelled appearance. "Come along, Your Highness. My lord. You'll both need a bath before you're presentable."

———

An hour later, the dancing hadn't subsided. The Llewyn circled the strange white fires, their feet flying in an intricate, fast-paced dance while their shadows climbed the walls as she and Ty stood to the side in their borrowed finery.

Part of her wanted to find a secluded spot to tell him what she had learned about Takkakus working with the Felinae regent. But then she'd have to explain how she'd been eavesdropping out of her body while he kissed her. Which might hurt his feelings all over again. He appeared to have forgotten about it, becoming more focused on getting to the bottom of his cup of wine.

Not for the first time, she wished Valera were here. Her friend seemed to have her finger on the pulse of power and influence at the Lyceum and nobilis society at large. And Valla's insight into the mind of her former patrius would be invaluable. Politics were not Seren's strong point. Anticipating an opponent's moves in a fight—that came naturally.

*What should I do, Valla?*

A memory of playing Conquer rose. Seren had been on the verge of losing all her troops to a fellow cadet who had been dared to challenge her, when Valera had whispered in her ear, "Flip the board. See what she covets of yours and use her desires and fears against her." It had made all the difference, and her opponent had been forced to surrender.

So Seren took her absent friend's advice and flipped the board. The alliance between Regent Boreal and Legatus Takkakus must involve the Legion since it was the greatest benefit to allying with Takkakus and the greatest threat against the Felinae Dominion. However, it was inconceivable that Takkakus could convince five hundred legionnaires to break their oaths. Of course, simply keeping the Legion out of a battle or leading them into a trap to weaken Luminaria's defences might be enough to turn the tide of the war.

But what did Takkakus gain? Nothing short of her uncle's office and title would be worth such vile treachery, for if Calvus Takkakus's betrayal of the Laws came to light, her uncle would execute him as a traitor—as well as his heirs and any other nobs who had knowingly colluded with the enemy. The Consul or Imperator might even dismantle their House for their dishonour.

From her uncle's standpoint, the division of loyalties in the Felinae court made it ripe for conquering. If the eldest prince was to come forward, he could make a claim to the Throne and pit the clans against one another. Boreal would support her chosen one, the younger prince. She and the prince would have Takkakus backing them. Which would then divide the Houses in Luminaria—those who sided with Exiler House Takkakus and those for House Moralis and the imperator. The Exilers might throw their support behind Takkakus despite his treason, after chafing under the more prosperous Founding Houses. Civil discord within the republic could be Boreal's secondary intent in forming this alliance with Legatus Takkakus.

Above this cavern, however, possibly at this very moment, her uncle's Crescents were searching for her. Should she try to leave through the same enchanted door and warn them of Calvus Takkakus? Or should she stick to her mission—her new mission—to assassinate the princes with Ty?

Unable to come to any sort of decision, her attention returned to Ty—another fine sight. Some colour was back in his cheeks, likely the wine, but she was relieved he no longer looked ill. After Noa had found them, they'd been separated, each to their own room to bathe and dress for the celebration. The former legionnaire cut a dashing figure in his black leathers and a borrowed grey silk tunic, embroidered with swirls like the ones on the enchanted door, and she caught more than one friendly glance his way.

The mark of her Inheritance pulsed underneath her palms as if in agreement. Did it mean something more than the wild way her body responded to him?

It wasn't just Ty that her Eyes responded to, though. Around Ellus, the Eye on her forehead tingled. Did that mean Ellus had something to do with her future? And Ty, her present?

But he wasn't the one she needed to find. Neither of them were. Her hands curled into fists. Some Inheritance.

*The princes, the princes. Tell me where the princes are.*

Nothing except the continued tingle of her Present Eye.

In disgust, she rubbed her offensive palms on her borrowed skirt. It was as black as the night sky at her waist, but it faded to an indigo. Because of her height, the hemline hit at the knee. The soft material flowed outward with slits up the sides for free movement. Black leggings underneath were a soft caress against her skin.

"All the better for jumping," Noa had said mysteriously as she cinched the skirt around Seren's waist.

The upper bodice was black and covered with crystals, like tiny stars, that were concentrated at her waist and became more diffuse near her bosom. It tied up in the back with laces that had to be tugged on to tighten until Seren swore she'd cut it with her knife if Noa and her young assistant didn't stop. Still, she'd caught Ty staring more than once. It was at the same time the most beautiful and most comfortable clothing she'd ever worn.

A loud clapping tore Seren from her thoughts. At the nearest bonfire, a blonde woman in green skirts approached the white flames, which were easily a few feet taller than her. She took off running, pumping her arms furiously; then, with a two-foot spring, she was airborne. Time seemed suspended while she flew over the flames, her yellow sash flowing out behind her like the tail of a shooting star. The woman landed near the edge of the embers and rolled into a standing position. Fire caught on the end of her skirt, but with practiced swiftness, her friends slapped the nascent flames with their skirts or woollen jackets. The crowd roared and carried the beaming woman off to celebrate her victory.

"Did you see that?" While dancing the moondance had taken her to some new heights, Seren had attempted nothing quite like this.

"Hmm?" Ty squinted into his empty cup. He seemed completely unfazed by the unnatural feats around him, his gaze unfocused. She frowned at the sweat glistening on his forehead when a tingle began on her own.

The merry dancers parted, and a familiar lean silhouette emerged.

**30**

───────

If Ty was dashing, Ellus was elegance refined. Cerulean pants, tucked into gray boots, and an ice blue tunic-styled jacket, decorated in silver embroidery and worn over a pale blue silk shirt, caressed his lithe form. Silver buttons at each wrist and a silver silk sash tied around his narrow waist completed the outfit. The fit was perfect and did wonderful things for his shoulders as if the suit had been tailored precisely for him.

"Reul." Ty raised his wooden cup at Ellus, excusing himself. As he weaved across the cavern, more than a few Llewyn tried to entice him into the dance, but Ty stuck to his goal—the wine and mead barrels. It was only his second cup, yet overindulgence, while surrounded by their enemies, was unwise.

Ellus bowed stiffly before her, drawing stares. "Would you honour me with this dance, Your Highness?"

It was all wrong. His whole mien. The frosty distance. It hurt, more deeply than she cared to admit. "I thought we were friends, Ellus. I thought I didn't have to justify myself to you."

Surprise softened his features. "We are. I thought—" He cut himself off, and his gaze darted to the ring on her hand.

Maybe he'd thought she'd lied by omission to him, and guilt stabbed her all over again because she couldn't explain she hadn't known Tyberius would show up, pretending to be her lover.

Then Ellus took a deep breath and let it out slowly, pulling at his standing collar. "You're right. You don't owe me an explanation. May we start over?"

She nodded, not sure if he meant the night or the entire course of their acquaintance. But Ellus didn't seem to know what to say next, and neither did she.

In the silence, she marvelled at yet another display of height-defying acrobatics, the likes of which she'd never seen. There seemed to be no wrong way to do this leap of faith. "Does this dance require jumping over the fires?"

"If you want." He inclined his head with a warm smile and held out his hand, more like himself. "Do you wish to dance?"

She inclined her head, and he steered her into a circle of dancers promenading with their partners, side-by-side around a white bonfire.

"It's called a fire reel. We dance them on the night of the full moon in hopes the Goddess will see our efforts to honour her. Do Prims have such revels?"

"The moon balls are similar if you take away the fires." *And the good-natured rowdiness.*

Though nothing untoward was taking place besides a few lusty kisses in the spirit of the Night of Mair. Under this full moon—Maiden's Moon, as Prims called it—Lumina was known to bless the fruitfulness of such unions, and she remembered Lady Llewyn's joy at Llion's arrival.

"We're not so different," Ellus mused, cutting into her thoughts.

"You and me?" They were and they weren't.

"Primordians and Felinae. We both dance. We both can be jealous, angry, and sad. Yearn for something out of our reach. Strive to keep those we care about safe."

Before she could reply to those bewildering statements, he pulled her right arm straight across him, and his gaze snagged on the ring on her finger. At that moment, she desperately wanted to tell him the truth about *everything*.

But she couldn't without ruining everything.

With a gentle touch, he set her left hand on her hip over his own left hand like the other dancers. The steps were like little hops, and soon she got the hang of it. Ellus swung her around in a circle, and they switched directions with the other dancers in the circle.

"The ring Secundo Attica gave you, it's a Felinae unamkhara ring."

She'd suspected so. "And?"

Abruptly, they switched directions again. "It's exchanged between soulshielders. Are you his soulshielder?"

She frowned. "Primordians don't have soulshielders."

The possibilities of what else the ring could signify hung between them. Vesper had reacted like it meant they were betrothed. So had Ty, and she hadn't refuted that belief. Is that what Ellus thought?

In Luminaria, rings signified one's station or office, or they could commemorate a victory or the sealing of a contract, including marriages and sometimes betrothals. The lack of a ring at her betrothal to Quinton further strengthened her belief that it was a ruse.

The promenading stopped and Ellus began stamping one foot on the spot, while she copied as best she could. "How did Attica come to possess it?"

Of course. Ellus was concerned about the ring's origins, not the reason Ty had given it to her. He had admitted he was all but spoken for with his aunt pressuring him to accept her chosen bride.

"Ty won it from another Prim named Joren Takkakus," she said at last, not wanting to go into the details. "How Joren came by it, I'm uncertain."

House Takkakus was working with the Felinae regent—did their alliance go back almost four years? If so, it wasn't so farfetched to think somehow an unamkhara ring had made its way from Regent Boreal to House Takkakus.

She watched to see if Ellus reacted to the name Takkakus, but his expression was unreadable. Concentrating on the dance steps and Ellus's questions at the same time was challenging, and she prayed he would let the matter drop.

To her relief, the promenading started again. They were halfway around the fire when he spoke again. "Are you certain of Secundo Attica's trustworthiness? I ask because this breach between Attica and your cousin could be a falsehood, a convenient reason for his sudden appearance, and a way for the Legion to spy on us. Your feelings for him may conceal his true motives from you."

Seren's blood chilled and then flushed hot with warring emotions.

He thought her so besotted with Ty she couldn't think for herself. That cut deep. Yet his suspicions about the spying were too near the truth. How ironic that he couldn't see that *she* was the spy. Possibly because he thought her too infatuated to be a threat to anyone.

Her anger flared. Ty had fought for her, punished the man responsible for the red scar on her ribcage, and brought her his ring. She could trust him. Yet . . . Ty had made it plain he wasn't loyal to Tarquin Moralis, and he hadn't explained his reasons for spying on the Consul.

She pulled away so swiftly that Ellus stumbled after her in an attempt to avoid colliding with the other dancers. She put out a hand to steady him and then just as quickly withdrew it. "I can take care of myself, Ellus."

His shoulders drooped as he brushed the fiery strands of red off his forehead. "Forgive me, Seren. You don't need me to win your battles for you as we both know. But as a leader for my people, I must ask you to consider if you may be a means to an end for him."

The remorse in his sapphire eyes soothed her ruffled feelings. She wet her lips and took the hand he offered, her forehead tingling as she did. "I'll keep it in mind."

The next part of the dance required that they switch partners, the inside circle rotating clockwise, the outside, counter-clockwise. When she finally returned to Ellus, she was ready with her own questions. She'd always thought the small talk Valera had engaged others in at balls was so tedious. Now she wondered how much information her friend had gleaned from such turns around the floor.

"Tomorrow, we leave for the Throne. Are you looking forward to returning to court and your impending marriage?"

As they whirled around, his eyes glittered like the crystals hanging above them. "I am not betrothed yet. Sometimes I wish I didn't need to return."

That was interesting. The dancers paused. A stout man in a yellow vest was readying himself to jump the fire. Everyone moved back to give him room, and she and Ellus sank back into the clapping crowd to watch.

"Tell me, is the prince well-loved among the clans?"

"So I am told."

She gave him the tiniest of frowns. Valera would've been proud.

"Why?" he asked, taking the bait. "Has someone given you reason to believe otherwise?"

"I overheard a strange conversation tonight. You said the return of the prince's brother isn't widely known, but"—she paused to see if anyone was paying attention to them, lowering her voice—"Lady Llewyn and Drakori were calling for the elder brother to take the Throne." She left out the part about the regent conspiring with Legatus Takkakus lest he think Ty was somehow involved.

Ellus stilled, and the white light gilded his mahogany hair, highlighting the deep ruby jewel tones. "Were they?"

"Do you think that the clans might be torn between the two princes?"

"I highly doubt it," he replied, dashing her hopes of a divided dominion. The music swelled, and they returned to the circle. A grin chased the sombre look from his countenance. "But anything is possible. After all, who would have thought I'd be dancing with a princess on the Night Mair?"

"Would your aunt consider marriage to a princess a good match?" The question tumbled out before she could think better of it.

His eyes widened before he chuckled. "I'm afraid she's already set her mind on someone else." Then he gave her an unreadable look. "But perhaps."

Then Ellus bowed his head and knelt on one knee. "Dance around me now," he whispered.

Those in skirts swished them, circling their partners, and Seren copied their movements. As she rounded in front of Ellus, her eyes locked with his sapphire blues, and she nearly stumbled at the yearning in them. For her?

Her heart sped up and out of rhythm. The quick notes of the fiddles slowed, then faded. The other dancers seemed to disappear around them. Time was spinning slower—or maybe it was her feet. The heat from the flames spread through each of her limbs, culminating in the mark on her forehead, which pulsed along with their pounding hearts, each an echoing beat of the other. Soon she lost herself in the story their bodies were telling together, one as ancient as the beginning of time.

Then she was rising in the air, Ellus's hands on her waist, and she was spinning like autumn leaves caught in a swirling wind eddy. She flung out her arms and threw her head back with reckless abandon.

"Faster!" she cried, and he obeyed.

The shadows of the dancing Llewyn melded together on the walls of the cavern, reaching for the crystals studded in the dark serendium above, now motes of light in a night sky.

It was dizzying. *Freeing.* And Seren never wanted it to stop.

Eventually, the whirling slowed.

Breathlessly, she slid down in his arms as he lowered her to solid ground again. While the world continued to spin around her, he was her anchor, and she was safely moored in his embrace. Just like he had been her tether on top of the mountain.

His mahogany fringe was mussed, and a sheen of sweat covered the dip above his lip. The heat of the nearby fire—twice as tall as her—barely touched her, she was so fevered from their dance.

"Seren—"

"Jump with me?" Unable to wipe the wide grin from her face, she held out her hand.

Surprise lit his eyes, but his warm palm clasped hers, sending a jolt of tingling to her forehead. Together they backed up, eyes locked on each other. Around them, the clapping began.

"Ready?" he asked.

In answer, she started running, and he took off in tandem with her, their hands locked together. Right before he leaped, his hand squeezed hers. She jumped, and then they were both vaulting over the fire to a chorus of shouts. Ellus flew ahead, their clasped hands stretched out between them.

At the highest point, there was a feeling of weightlessness. At that moment, time seemed to slow and stretch, and Seren knew what it was like to be a star, hanging in the night sky. A star but not alone. Every clan member down below was a spot of shining light, and she and Ellus were but two in the sky of many. Her heart overflowed with a crushing affection until a joy too large for her body burst from her. For the Llewyn. For everyone. For her.

Even as she coasted along on the wave of exhilaration and blissfulness, it made little sense. The Llewyn were nothing to her. Where was this feeling coming from?

Another wave of warmth engulfed her; this one infused with tenderness and a tinge of something deeper—sharper.

*Desire.*

The air shifted, and they began descending. Ellus landed first on the other side of the fire, with her on his heels. He took several large steps to slow their momentum, and their hands tore apart. Abruptly, the feelings she had sensed from him were severed. He halted mid-stride to look back, and she bowled him over in a heap of skirts and silk.

As he lay unmoving beside her, her heart, already frantic from the rush of the jump, skipped a beat. "Did I hurt you?"

Then his chest spasmed, his laughter ringing loud and full for several breaths. "Only you would jump high enough to miss the flames, yet still manage to ruin our clothes."

"If you're so worried about your silks, you shouldn't have worn them." Her finger stroked the lustrous material of his sleeve, and he stilled under her touch.

"I confess I didn't expect to be jumping a fire tonight." He paused, and the amusement fled his features but not the warmth. "It was my first jump. And I'm glad it was with you. Was it everything you were hoping for?"

Before she could respond, Llewyn dancers enveloped her and Ellus in congratulatory cries and embraces. Squished against Ellus, she hung onto his shoulder to steady herself, and he brought her in close. Her lips brushed his ear. "It was . . ."

*Sublime. Exhilarating. Decadent. Addicting.* When she was with Ellus, he seemed to take her soul to new heights.

From over his shoulder, she spotted Ty bearing down on them with a cup in each hand. His coppery hair was tousled, and he had a high colour to his cheeks as if he had been dancing, too. When Ellus stepped back from her, some of the overwhelming feelings receded.

Ty whistled low in admiration as he handed her a cup, his fingers brushing hers, sending tingles to her palm. "I've never seen you move like that."

She didn't know how to feel about Ty having seen her jump the fire with Ellus. She was completely out of her depth, so she took a gulp of the spiced mead, which set her coughing as it burned her throat.

When she recovered, she found Ellus giving her a puzzled look. "You haven't seen her moondance then, Attica? It is a sight to behold."

At the compliment, her ears burned. She didn't know how to respond, so she took another sip. Tyberius had never witnessed her moondancing, nor did he know anything about her training with Master Kai. When she glanced at him, it was to find him staring at her intently, his pupils dilated.

"Why don't I see you dancing at moon balls, *amara*? You're magnificent."

She flushed at the awe in his tone, then shrugged to hide her embarrassment, which only made her more uncomfortable in her tightly bound bodice. It was far too hot in the cavern. "Maybe you would if there were fires to jump over at moon balls, or if you asked me to dance. But you always disappear when it's time to dance, don't you?"

She must have said the wrong thing, because a strained awkwardness descended upon the three of them as they stared at each other.

"Haven't you had enough tonight, Attica?" Ellus finally

asked, tone clipped, as Ty drained his cup. "We'll be leaving at first light."

"Someone should inform Urso and Sionnach of that." Ty smirked widely as he wiped his mouth with the back of his hand, then gestured to one side of the cavern. "I think they've got a bet on who can hold their mead better. And Vesper has been whirling around like the winged seed of an ash tree."

Seren looked around for her young friend. Her disappointment at missing the chance to dance with Vesper dulled the last of Seren's euphoria, and the emotional fatigue of the day swept over her like a heavy, wet cloak.

"Where's the sealgair?" Ellus frowned at the boisterous crowd, likewise searching for Llion and their companions. "He knows better than to let Vesper burn herself out again."

"Busy with his beautiful wife, I suspect." Ty shrugged like there wasn't a solid bone in his body, his grin just as lopsided. That was definitely more than his second cup. And she should've sought Vesper out before this and checked on her.

"I'll collect the others then." Ellus ran a hand through his mahogany locks, avoiding her gaze. "I think it's best we all turn in."

"Agreed," Seren said, quickly taking the empty cup from Ty's hand, then linking her arm through his. He didn't resist. In fact, he seemed all too happy to lean in and rest his head against hers.

Ellus began to bow again, then stopped. "Please give thought to what we discussed, Seren."

"I will. Goodnight, Ellus."

"Goodnight, El-lus," Tyberius chimed in, giving a sloppy salute.

Seren sighed as she propelled him toward the tunnels. If Ty's decadent behaviour was part of some master plan to lull her into thinking he was more dangerous to himself than her, then Ty was by far the superior spy for she was entirely fooled.

---

SOFT SNORES FILLED the small dirt-walled room that had been assigned to Ty. As soon as his boots came off, Ty had lain down on the thin mattress and nodded off. His fine tunic would be rumpled in the morning, but it was too late to try to get it off him. At least it wasn't stained. The same could not be said for her dress. Seren tucked a wool blanket over him, then glanced from the water basin to the smears of dirt on the velvet skirt. Back home, a serv would see to her clothing. Perhaps Noa would look after it tomorrow. Except they were all leaving for the Throne in the morning.

All at once, exhaustion took root in her, and the thought of sleeping in a proper bed buoyed her toward her own room next door, dirt stains be damned. But she hadn't gone more than a few steps in the empty passageway before a tingle broke out between her shoulder blades.

*Eye behind, past in mind.*

Sharp pain exploded from her Past Eye, and her back spasmed. She staggered, trying to keep upright as the pain intensified. *So hard to breathe.* Her knees hit the ground, and she realized how vulnerable she was. Anyone could come along while she was stuck in this vision, and if she lost control of her body again, it would be easy for Llion to suffocate her without a soul knowing otherwise. Or for Thane to steal her secrets. Solfire, she was surrounded by enemies. Now was not the time to be taken by a wild vision.

She tried to call out to Ty. Nothing but a strangled whimper came out. Her back bowed in agony, the pain refusing to abate. *I am a stone.* She closed her eyes, trying to block it from her mind. She had to get to her room before someone found her like this. Digging her fingers into the packed dirt as much as she could, she pulled herself along the ground. It wasn't far to the door, but then she had to claw her way back up to her knees to reach the knob. Part of her thought dying might be easier.

*Pain is life. Both shall end.*

The familiar mantra gave her the strength to push through the pain. Finally, the door pushed open, and she pitched forward, unable to stop herself from falling. If she would be forced to have this vision, this pain, at least she was in the relative safety of her room. Lying in the dirt, she inhaled the earthy scent and gave herself over to it. Then, as swiftly as it had come, the pain vanished.

Sun scorched her skin, and her mouth felt as dry as the Cartarchaan sands. Everything was hazy. A crystal blue sky and a jeering crowd of spectators slowly came into focus. She knelt on a wooden platform before thousands of motley faces, with her arms secured behind her.

A shadow fell across her. An unfamiliar Primordian centurio, adorned in a black-plumed helm and black breastplate, loomed to her left with his sword in hand. The bright sun behind him obscured his features, but his occupation was all too clear.

The Legion's executioner.

A primal terror known to every living creature held her tight. Her legs wouldn't respond, nor would her hands test the scratchy rope that chafed her wrists. She had failed. Failed Uncle Tarquin and her House. Failed Ty, too. That last thought cleared the fog from her mind.

*Seers aren't given visions of their own futures.* This was a wild vision. So this wasn't her future, but someone else's past? The tingling and pain had been concentrated in her Past Eye. Still, deep down she knew this could be her future if she returned to Luminaria without atoning for her broken oath.

Just then the executioner raised his sword, and the sun glinted off the metal. Seren caught her reflection—the reflection of a man with medium brown skin, dark curls, hollowed cheeks, and sombre hazel eyes. She had seen a likeness of her father's face once, in a book she'd found as a child. The book had been taken from her by her nurse and burned while she watched.

"Prince Devan of the Morningstars, Ambassador of the Felinae Throne." The sword lowered, and the centurio addressed her father in the accented voice of an Exiler. "You kneel here convicted of siring a child on Nobilis Adalyn Moralis, an act that broke the good faith and Accord between our peoples."

Dizziness assailed her. This was her father's execution.

Seren tried to move her body—her father's body—but she couldn't. And it wasn't the shackles holding her back. She couldn't control his head or the direction of his gaze. Just like with her vision of her uncle at her cradle.

What had the taibhseir said about uncontrolled visions of the past? The seer's temporal spirit could become trapped in one . . . and die. What if the body she inhabited died? Would she die, too? Is that what Drakori meant?

"You have the privilege to beg for forgiveness from the Goddess before you die," the centurio continued.

Seren's lips moved involuntarily, and a low, hoarse voice answered. "Good faith? If there was ever good faith between our peoples, it was broken by Tarquin Moralis. If I am guilty, it is only of protecting my unamkhara. And I do not regret that. For him, I would die a thousand righteous deaths." He paused. "But this is not one."

A flash of interest crossed the centurio's blunt features. The booing of the masses reached a crescendo. It was doubtful anyone but the executioner had heard her father's last words.

"Get on with it," muttered a familiar iron voice from the sidelines. A younger Tarquin Moralis in City Patrol black stood off to the side, a pomegranate cape secured at one shoulder with a silver eagle.

Her gaze—or Devan Morningstar's—locked onto him. "Lord Startaker won't forgive this."

It was uttered as both a promise and a regret.

"Yet I don't see him here offering to take your place," the younger Tarquin replied calmly. "I suppose the hearts of soulshielders are as fickle as the hearts of princes."

The centurio raised his sword with both hands.

"Forgive me, Kyn," Morningstar murmured through her lips. "I did my best for them. For you."

The cold blade bit through the back of her neck, yet the world didn't fade to black. She was floating. Rising above them all. She prayed to Lumina she was returning to her corporeal body, and not dissipating for good.

No one noticed her, their attention on the body of the broken prince below. While the masses roared their satisfaction, the executioner removed his helm in an odd show of respect, knelt beside the headless corpse, and took her father's lifeless hand in his own.

The blunt nose and thick neck of the executioner reminded her of the boy in her nightmares—Joren Takkakus. This must be his father, a younger Calvus Takkakus, who was tugging on the dead prince's limp finger. Seren fought against the pull of Time to swim back down and see her father's unamkhara ring gleam in the high sun as it came free.

# 31

The next morning, moonwood torches glowed brightly, but the Llewyn did not. Piles of sand covered the firepits of last night, and the long tables had been rearranged into neat hedgerows through the spacious cavern. To the side was a subdued line of Llewyn shuffling toward several cauldrons of something being ladled into bowls. Their finery had been packed or left behind for more serviceable travelling outfits.

*More porridge,* her nose informed her. Her mood already sinking, Seren joined the line with Ty, and soon they each had steaming bowls in hand. Neither of them spoke as they settled side by side at an empty table. Ty seemed incapable of conversation or eating. With his elbows propped on the table, he cradled his head in his hands like it was a fragile egg. Among the yellows and greens of the Llewyn, he was a storm cloud of black leather.

She could muster little sympathy for his self-induced plight. After her wild vision last night, her sleep had been fitful, and the moment her father lost his head repeated over and over again in her dreams. She pushed the memory away and swallowed another thick spoonful. It could be used as mortar between bricks, though the spices made it slightly more appetizing than the gruel Llion fed them. But who knew how much there'd be to eat on the long march north to the Throne?

A comely young woman, dressed in the mustard-yellow woollen vest and green skirt the Llewyn favoured, appeared at their table with a cheerful smile with a tray of steaming mugs. She set one in front of Ty. "Lord Attica."

Seren's mouth watered. *Khava.*

Ty encircled the mug with both hands before looking up with a genuine smile. "Jana, you're a gift from the Goddess for remembering my request. And a fine dancer, too."

A blush crept up Jana's neck as she set another mug for Seren. It seemed Ty had done his own share of dancing last night. And requested khava for the morning after?

Unsure how to feel about that after her own dance with Ellus, Seren inhaled the rich aroma instead. Lumina, she hadn't had a taste since she'd run away. *Embarked on her mission,* she corrected herself. When the ships from the continent docked, there was always a reason to celebrate in Luminaria.

Seren scowled at the dark brew. For Lady Llewyn to procure the beans, someone must be supplying the dens with imports. Or perhaps it had been stolen from Gull Harbour.

Since the khava was too hot to sip without milk, she blew on it. The scalding temperature, however, didn't deter Ty from a long gulp. She hoped it revived him enough for the long journey ahead. At the end of which Llion would bring them before the crown prince and his regent. That was what she needed to focus on. The mission.

"Lord Attica said you liked it sweet, Your Highness," Jana said with a tentative smile for Seren as she set a small pot of milk on the table.

Seren's hands tightened around the mug at the unfamiliar

honorifics. "He's a secundo, not a lord, and I'm a bastard, not a princess."

"You certainly are in the morning." Thane stepped around Jana, pilfering a mug from her tray before sliding onto the bench next to Ty. He smirked at her. "Little sleep, Princess?"

While Jana mumbled her apologies with a curtsey, Seren thought about throwing her drink at Thane. But that would be a waste of good khava, so she settled for a scowl. In Jana's wake, Ellus, Kanta, and a yawning Vesper, all wearing their travelling cloaks, claimed the other side of the table. Fortunately, Thane was too busy eating his and Ty's porridge to say much else. The same with the others. Teapots were brought over, which seemed the favoured morning beverage choice among the Llewyn and other Elusives. When yet another Llewyn addressed Ty as Lord Attica, Seren's scowl sent him scampering away. It didn't have the same effect on Ty, however.

His mouth pulled up in a twitch of a grin as he stirred some of her milk into his second cup. "I could get used to being 'Lord Attica.' It has a certain cachet around here, and I doubt the imperator will let me keep my rank since he's intent on not letting me keep my head."

He knew she had a plan for that: assassinate the princes and return home as honoured warriors.

"The sealgair informed you then, Attica?" Ellus interrupted, raising his head from his bowl. The dark red strands of his hair were more muted without the bonfires. Gone were his silks from yesterday, but his usual cream undershirt and leathers had been cleaned and a soft green wool tunic thrown over them. She preferred the simpler garments. He looked more like the carefree young man she'd trained with in the mountain, except his expression was anything but.

"Informed me of what?"

Ellus glanced around the crowded tables. "I suppose everyone will know soon enough. A note was left on the entrance to the den last night, after the trees around it were scorched to ash."

"A note?" Had her uncle's Crescents found her note and responded?

"It bears the seal of the imperator and demands Clan Llewyn hand over the Prim traitors to be executed." Ellus looked from her to Ty.

"Or what? He'll declare war on us?" Next to Ellus, Kanta rolled her eyes while licking her spoon. "Oh wait, too late."

Ellus's expression thinned. "If we deliver Seren and Attica to him now, Moralis promises to spare Clan Llewyn in his conquest."

"We can't hand them over!" Vesper exclaimed from the other end.

"And if Lady Llewyn doesn't?" Ty asked sharply. A pall of future death and ruin spread over the table. No spoons rattled against bowls. Not one Llewyn in the large hall dared to breathe.

Across from her, Ellus's hands tightened around his mug, the only sign of emotion. "Every Llewyn, young or old, will be put to the blade. Any clan known to have harboured you will bear the same fate."

"If the Legion can find us," Kanta snarled, echoing Llion's words from last night. "And even then, we won't be so easy to execute."

"Mass executions over two lives?" Seren swallowed back the rising lump in her throat. It didn't make sense. "I don't believe it."

It seemed inconceivable that the lives of those she sat with, those she had danced with last night in celebration, would be forfeit if they didn't meet Uncle Tarquin's demands. Demands that only made sense if Uncle Tarquin believed her to be a traitor—not a spy.

Even so, it was still hard to wrap her head around her

uncle's threat. While bringing the Republic's rule of law to the isle had long been his goal, never had she heard him speak of annihilating the clans before.

Was it the desire for retaliation? There were at least as many Llewyn as the Prims burned in Gull Harbour. Some might argue it was a balancing of the scales. Once, she might have supported that argument. But not now. Dobhran was dead, by her hand, yet those who had died in the burning of Gull Harbour were still gone. And instead of feeling victorious, Seren felt hollowed out like the discarded white rind of a pomegranate.

Ellus had said something similar to her. *We can't settle the debt for the dead—not with more death.* But somehow the debt would need to be settled.

The sound of Ty's empty mug hitting the table scattered her wayward thoughts.

"Wake up, Seren. You left House Moralis and the imperator's son behind for your family's sworn enemies. I escaped from a cell, and I'm assumed to be consorting with you, a known traitor. We are enemies of the republic. We've made the new imperator look like a fool, and he wants our heads for it. The only reason he prefers them attached to our bodies is so he can drive his sword through us in front of all of Luminaria."

Her face reddened, and she looked away, the thought of being so worthless to her uncle unbearable. No, not worthless. Apparently, she was worth the death of over three hundred souls.

A gentle touch on her hand, still clutching her mug, made her glance up. "Lady Llewyn won't agree."

Seren pulled her hand back from Ellus. "Then she's a fool. We are not worth Clan Llewyn's lives. When did my uncle say the delivery was to take place?"

Ellus scrutinized her like she was a puzzle he was eager to solve. "By dusk."

Was it an opportunity to report her information to him so far? Then she and Ty could "escape" and return to the Felinae to finish her mission. Because the princes had to die if there was any hope of conquering the Felinae with little bloodshed.

Her Primordian ancestors had a saying: *Destroy the throne, take the kingdom. Destroy the kingdom, take a hollow crown.*

Except Ty was convinced that Tarquin Moralis would hang him upon sight—or force him to duel Quinton. And there was no guarantee that she could find the Felinae again once they left. It was too risky, she decided, to give Ty and herself up to these Crescents. If they didn't believe her mission, she and Ty would end up on their knees in the Amphitheatron like her father.

"The Throne doesn't recognize ultimatums," Ellus said in response to something Kanta had said. "And handing Seren and Secundo Attica over will not protect the lady's clan from the imperator's agenda. We all know he's not to be trusted. She'd never consider it."

"You seem very certain of that, lordling," Thane mused.

Twin spots of colour brightened his cheeks. "I was there when the lady and sealgair discussed it."

Vesper stirred her porridge absently. "I thought the Legion was headed north."

Everyone looked at Ty, and he shrugged. "Last I heard. Maybe a few cohorts were kept behind."

But it wasn't legionnaires above the den, it was her uncle's Crescents.

Thane rolled his shoulders, his mouth slung in a cocky grin that put Seren's teeth on edge. "We did fine against Tarquin Moralis's guards, especially with our Swiftfoot. Maybe we and the Llewyn should give the Legion a welcoming in return. What do you say, Vesper?"

Vesper paled, her hair falling over her face as she looked into her bowl. No, the Swiftfoot didn't have a mercenary bone in her body.

Ty rubbed his temples in exasperation. "You won't find this force as easily defeated as those House guards. Nor will you catch them unaware. You were lucky Tarquin's elite guard of seasoned legionnaires had escorted him to the Observatory that night. And the ones he's sent after us will expect your Inheritances and be prepared to counter them."

Seren noticed Ty hadn't mentioned the Crescents by name or their unique heritage. He must still be hoping to use his knowledge as a bargaining tool with the regent.

"We disarmed you easily enough, legionnaire," Kanta said with her usual tartness.

"I had no desire to fight you, though I suspect it would've gone badly for me had I tried," Ty replied, earning him an unladylike snort. It struck Seren that Tyberius regularly let others underestimate him. Only Ellus—and maybe Llion— considered him a threat.

"You and your legionnaires are seasoned in wars that do not concern them." Ellus's voice, uncharacteristically harsh, sliced ruthlessly through the banter.

"I won't argue with you there." Ty's admission stunned Seren. She hadn't considered whether the Legion should or should not be on the continent. "Though I doubt you'll be pleased to hear the imperator has recalled all the cohorts not locked into contract. Their ships should be almost here by now."

"We should leave," Seren interrupted. She stood, unease trickling through her. Takkakus didn't have the entire Legion with him—a relief—but how quickly could her uncle marshal the incoming legionnaires? A searing sensation burned her forehead, adding to her foreboding. "Is there another way out of the den?"

"You see?" The brusque voice of the taibhseir scratched uncomfortably against Seren's marks, while the serendium in the woman's staff seemed to amplify her feeling of dread. "Even now her Eyes are trying to tell her she needs to leave, but she won't open herself up to the why or the where."

————

THREE PORCELAIN BOWLS and a silver tea tray sat atop a white cloth embroidered with buttercups around the edges. It was hardly a spread for the leader of the clan, yet Drakori had obviously brought her to Lady Llewyn's private dining room. Yet the lady was absent. Llion sat before one bowl, his hands steepled and brow furrowed. Dark circles ringed his eyes, the strain of the last few days—or grief, she supposed—having caught up to him. But for all appearances, he was prepared for trouble. His brown leather cuirass, cleaned and oiled, covered a fresh linen tunic, which was tucked under sturdy bracers.

Taibhseir Drakori lowered herself into a seat at the other end of the round table. The empty spot between them must belong to Lady Llewyn.

"You said if I came with you, we'd leave the den faster, so I'm here," Seren said to break the roiling tension in the room.

"Tell me"—Drakori tipped her empty teacup toward Seren —"what do you see, child?"

Mushy black leaves had congregated at the bottom. To Seren, it didn't look like much. Some of the detritus in the shadow market did tea readings. Not that she'd partaken of such charlatanry.

But an arched shape, a half moon, jumped out at her. She strove to keep her breathing even. A crescent, plain as day— only it was upside down. Did it refer to the Crescents?

Llion's gaze flicked impatiently from the cup to Seren. "I see arrogance and wrongheadedness, nothing more."

"You mistake the teacup for a mirror then," she shot back.

Llion's chair scraped back, but before he could rise, Drakori spoke. "You could both benefit from some inner reflection. On more than one subject." Her gaze pointedly rested on the empty chair. "Perhaps on your journey together, you'll find you have more in common than you suppose."

"So let's move out." Impatience wet Seren's tongue. "Your vision of our safe arrival or not," she said to Drakori, "while we eat porridge, the Legion"—*or Crescents*—"are preparing their next attack."

A growl rumbled in Llion's throat, but Drakori simply righted the teacup. "You resent me for my Inheritance, even though you have the same gifts. I did not ask for my powers any more than you, child. But the Goddesses gave them to me and the responsibility to use them wisely for my people. And you have the same responsibility. Yet you fight against what the Goddess wishes to show you. Tell me, do you use your Inheritance, or does it use you?"

The truth stung even if Seren lied to herself that she didn't care. But if she could use her Inheritance, maybe she could avert a war—save the Llewyn from the fate promised at her uncle's hands.

"Her Eye did locate Dobhran for us," Llion bit out through gritted teeth.

A single grey eyebrow rose. "Did it?"

She might have fooled the others, but somehow Drakori knew. Before Llion could question her story about using her Inheritance, she retorted, "Why should I trust the visions of someone who's been playing around in my mind?"

"I was never in your mind, child," Drakori admonished. "It was a meeting on the temporal plane between seers. One you were unprepared for, I'll admit, and on purpose. Riaghladair Boreal ordered a thorough examination of your loyalties." The seer raised a hand in anticipation of Seren's question. "And, no,

I cannot force you to meet me there—if you strengthen your temporal shields. I promise, however, not to enter uninvited." Her bushy brows drew together. "The waters swirl with troubling futures shrouded in shadows. You must master your Eyes, Seren. Your future, and possibly the Felinae Dominion's, depends on it."

"According to your visions." Though her Future Eye tingled as if in agreement. Her chin lifted of its own accord. "You've been wrong before."

The silence confirmed her suspicions. Drakori absently turned the dainty teacup by its handle. Her words came slowly. "A past vision shows what happened at a particular time and place. The margin of error is least there. A present vision may show you where something or someone is, but not necessarily their precise location, which can invite mistakes. A future vision, however, reveals but a potential fate, though with time you'll get a sense of how possible it might be."

The heavy weight of one who had grappled with the quandaries of Time settled in Drakori's hooded eyes. "All seers choose future currents that dissipate or flow into other stronger ones in the end. The more we apply our Inheritance, however, the more adept we become at following the strongest currents in Time's Flow, the ones with a better chance of coming true."

"So we're nothing more than gamblers playing the odds." Seren grimaced. No wonder Silver held scrying in contempt.

Llion came to Drakori's defence. "Every successful legate in Primordian history has used information at hand to calculate their enemies' line of attack and shape their battle strategy. This is one more strategy."

"Fine," Seren conceded, crossing her arms, "but your teachings haven't helped me foresee the future. What more can you do, Taibhseir?"

"Have you experienced a wild vision yet?"

"No." She still didn't completely trust Drakori. Until she did, she'd keep those past visions to herself.

Drakori's gaze narrowed, but she didn't argue. "You are blocked, Seren Soul-Marked. At first, I thought someone had done it to you. Now, I suspect you're holding yourself back. That's why you won't be continuing on with Clan Llewyn. You will travel to Unkat Axstrida before heeding the summons."

Seren gritted her teeth at another delay. "Is that another den?"

Drakori shook her head, and Seren scowled at the seer's obliqueness.

"Won't you be coming with me, Taibhseir?"

"As you've pointed out, I've taught you all I can. And it's clear you don't trust me." Unbothered by this, Drakori poured herself another cup of tea. "Now, you must look inside yourself for Time's Flow. The Unkat Axstrida will aid you, and the sealgair and Thane Sionnach will watch over your corporeal body while you enter the temporal state."

Seren chewed the inside of her cheek. If she could control her Inheritance, it would turn the assassination of the crown prince and her subsequent escape into a manoeuvre even a first-year cadet could pull off. She would also have a better chance at ferreting out the eldest prince and eliminating that path of succession. As impatient as she was to reach the Felinae court and accomplish her mission, it didn't make sense to snub this opportunity. And it didn't look like she had much of a choice.

"Collect your pack, Morningstar," Llion barked, already striding out without looking to see if she followed.

It was clear the sealgair wasn't pleased about the change of plans. Not that there weren't reasons enough for Llion's distemper with her, but she remembered how he had fought Silver bitterly about separating himself from his recruits—Ellus in particular. Perhaps Llion considered Ellus the weakest fighter or the more politically valuable hostage in her uncle's hands? Though Kanta was from the Felinae nobility as well. No, there was something else at play.

At the door, she paused. "And what of Tyberius and the other recruits?"

She wasn't keen on leaving Ty alone with him looking ill. Yet he'd spoken with such contempt for her uncle and his Crescents that she hesitated at having him by her side while using her Inheritance. Knowing she had one and seeing it were two different things.

Drakori rose stiffly from her chair with her staff. "He'll accompany me, the other recruits, and Clan Llewyn to the Throne. Lady Llewyn pledges no harm will come to him. And there is no other current in which I see otherwise on his journey north. He will be safe."

Seren's Eyes pulsed in comforting tingles as if feeling the truth of Drakori's assurances. Despite her hesitancy to trust Ty's life to visions, tension loosened in her chest. "Good."

Before Seren could leave, Drakori's hand snaked out and caught her wrist. For a woman in her fifth decade, she was strong. "You must make peace with the Warbler and the Lockpick."

Seren could've broken the hold, but she hesitated at the gravity in Drakori's mien. "Why?"

Drakori pressed her lips together, then relented. "The future of the isle, and perhaps the realm, depends on it."

Seren's eyes narrowed. It wasn't her fault Llion and Thane despised her. Maybe the isle's future—and their lives—depended on her benevolence when she handed the Felinae Dominion over to Uncle Tarquin. She yanked her hand free. "Maybe it depends on them making peace with me."

———

THE CHURNING FEELING in Seren's stomach, not her Inheritance, warned her that Tyberius wouldn't like the altered plan.

She found him wearing a path in the earthen ground on the far side of a busy cavern, not far from where Ellus, Vesper, Kanta, and Thane waited with their cloaks and packs to join the march. She supposed Llion was making his farewells to Lady Llewyn, who was also absent. Groups of Llewyn made a long line from where they were departing into a tunnel with what belongings they could carry. From the surrounding chatter, Seren gleaned it was a subterranean route that would emerge in the northern edge of the Western woods, away from the fire. From there, the Clan would travel on foot to a hidden underground pass in the Selinen mountain range. The pass would take them under the mountains to the Northern plains, from where they would trek the last miles to Caisteal Dìomhair, the seat of the Throne.

The lines around Ty's mouth relaxed as he took in the sight of her. Under his gaze, her palms tingled and her stomach tightened. Did that mean she shouldn't leave him or simply that she was nervous?

"Ty—"

He raised a finger, then took a moonwood torch off the wall and led her down a side passage, away from the hubbub.

"Can you hear anyone?" he whispered, stopping in front of a wooden door.

She shook her head and followed him in. Shelves with musty odds and ends lined the cramped closet with a broken wheelbarrow overturned in the middle with crates of what looked like broken hammers and pickaxes.

"I'm not travelling with you to the Throne," she blurted to his cloaked back.

"I heard." He rummaged around before placing the moonwood torch in a tin pail before turning to face her. "I don't like how they're separating us, Seren. Anything could happen."

*To you.* That part was left off, but Seren heard it, loud and clear.

While her moondancing was a secret, she was a trained Lyceum graduate. Her chin lifted. "I can take care of myself. If Llion wants me dead, he doesn't need to bring me into the woods to do it. He's sealgair and lord of these people."

"Unless he doesn't want witnesses." Ty raked a hand through his coppery hair that stuck up down the centre of his head. "You'd be safer with Lady Llewyn and the clan around to hold him accountable."

"Sionnach will be with us." And while she wasn't Thane's favourite person, neither was he Llion's favourite. "Besides, it wasn't his idea to take me there. Drakori says visiting the Unkat Axstrida will help me harness my Inheritance. Think about what I can do if I can see the present or the future. I could end the war."

Maybe that was what her Felinae nursemaid had foreseen.

"Don't you see, Seren? Like Tarquin uses his Crescents, the Felinae will use you for their own advantage. The more powerful you become, the tighter they'll hold on to you."

Fire burned in her belly, and a growl of frustration erupted from her. "My uncle isn't using me. It's my duty to follow our patrius—our imperator's—orders. Whether or not he sent me here. But how could you think I'd let the Felinae use me against the republic?" She held up a hand to forestall any argument. "It doesn't matter. The Felinae don't need me to locate the Legion's whereabouts or Uncle Tarquin's war plans. They already have Taibhseir Drakori."

And Belden Buhair, and perhaps more. However, their scryings of the future must have been less clear than the princes wished, or Seren suspected Drakori wouldn't be so adamant for Seren to travel to Unkat Axstrida.

Ty didn't seem to hear her as he closed the distance between them, his green eyes filled with worry. There was only so much room in the closet, and it all seemed to be filled with him. "When you ran away, you drew the Felinae out of hiding, Seren. And the Felinae will do the same—use you to lure the Legion or the Crescents into a trap."

His hands settled over on her hips above her belt and puller her closer, and her hands curled into the leather of his jacket. For once, her palms didn't tingle. Did it mean she shouldn't stay with him?

"I won't let them," she whispered.

His head tilted down toward hers. "I don't care about them. I care about you. In danger once again. And me not able to do anything about it this time."

*Again?*

"I'm not so naïve about the Throne desiring my abilities," she murmured, her hands absently trailing down the hard planes of his chest covered by supple leather. "My Seersight might be limited right now, but I can *see* that." And truthfully, it didn't seem that bad compared to her own betrayal of them. "But I'm also a weapon for *us*."

His eyes heated, and his hands slid up her waist under her jacket. "All the more reason for us to stay together. Runaway together."

Blood rushed to her cheeks. He thought she meant her and him, not House Moralis or the republic. "I can't."

The air sparked with frustration. So much fire between them. Would they burn each other into ash?

"Please, Seren." His mouth dipped low toward hers, but she couldn't surrender to whatever this pull was between them. Not right now.

"I must master my Inheritance so we can track down the princes," she said shakily, holding onto her self-control by a thread. "I must find out when and where they'll be vulnerable."

Ty let go of her and stepped back. "So you're sticking to this childish revenge plan? I told you, you're not the weapon."

Her chin snapped up. *Childish?* "It's justice—for Gull Harbour, for the breaking of the Accord." Her reasons rang hollow in her ears. Dobhran and her father had both paid for those mistakes with their lives. Neither of *these* princes had anything to do with the breaking of the Accord. Maybe Gull Harbour hadn't been their idea either. "We need to restore our honour so we can return home. Don't you want that, Ty?"

"Sol's hells," Ty hissed. "You and Q both need to pull your heads out of the sand. There are death orders out on us. I was in the room with Quinton while his father questioned Valera on your whereabouts. The man's cold outrage wasn't an act. He didn't send you on this revenge mission."

"So he made you think." Yet the conviction in his voice made her chin tremble.

Ty's drawn-out sigh dashed her hope that he would come around to her way of thinking. "Then I'm coming with you to this Goddess-forsaken place in the woods."

Fear blossomed in her belly. "You can't." She licked her lips searching for a reason—any reason—why not. "You need to keep an eye on Lady Llewyn and Drakori. I think they may be planning to overthrow the crown prince."

"Don't you see? Divide and conquer is the oldest trick on the Conquer board because it works." Ty took a step closer. "Insist I come with you. You're important enough to their plans that they'll agree to it."

She doubted she could persuade Llion of anything, but the thought of Ty seeing her use her Felinae Inheritance made her feel nauseous.

"I can't protect you if I'm not with you," he murmured. His hand reached to cradle her cheek, and she relaxed under his touch despite her resolve. "Just let me keep protecting you. Please."

"I don't need or want your protection. Never have. And I don't need your help with the princes—but I want it."

He winced. The tentative expression on his face made him look younger. "Maybe I want nothing to do with the republic or the Felinae Dominion. Maybe all I want is you." His hand fell away, and she mourned its absence. "Tell me you want me with you, Seren. That's enough for now."

Truthfully, part of her wanted exactly that. But then he'd see her using her Inheritance, something he saw as a liability—a reason for the Felinae or her uncle to yoke her under their control. Maybe she had seen it that way, too, at the beginning. But it was *hers*.

What had Ellus told her?

*There's more power in you than you might ever know.*

All from Inheritances that Primordians had scorned and, if it came to open battle, would fear. How could Ty not feel the same when he saw her for what she was?

"We could leave," he whispered in her ear. "Take a ship for Cartarchaa or the continent."

He might want to leave Luminaria behind, but she didn't. "I know I've broken my oath"—she swallowed down the guilt of Sila's death—"we both have, but I can't abandon House Moralis—our families, our friends."

Ty recoiled physically from her unspoken accusation that he had done so, and his hands dropped listlessly to his sides. She hadn't meant to hurt him. "Ty—"

He raised a hand. "Once you track down the princes, pray tell how you'll take their lives? You're not the heartless killer you think you are."

"I am." She might have had a heart once, well-hidden behind her scowl, but it had cracked and fissured after Dobhran and Sila—maybe even before. So she would harden it, turn it to stone as Uncle Tarquin had his, and she'd steal the lives of these princes. If the Felinae surrendered to the republic, untold lives would be saved. In a sense, she was also protecting Vesper and Ellus and Kanta and Thane by removing the need for them to fight. And after her uncle realized she wasn't a traitor, he'd spare Clan Llewyn from his ultimatum.

Her last hope that Ty would understand why she had to do this was fading along with the sliver of hope that he could forgive her, though she didn't deserve it. "Back at the villa, I killed Sila Utticor with a sword through the heart. That was after I slit the throat of Alphonius Luther. I am as heartless as they come, Tyberius."

He blanched, then shook his head as if he couldn't believe it. Didn't want to believe it. "You're not the first to defend yourself with deadly force. It is regretful—"

"I wasn't defending myself. He was a traitor. It was no less than he deserved." And so was she. But not in her heart. That must count for something.

"And Sila?"

That kill she couldn't begin to defend. "I don't know—she was coming at Ellus, her sword ready for a killing blow—" Her voice broke. "I reacted. I do regret that I took her life, but not that I saved his."

Ty rubbed his face as though his head ached. "Battle fever. It happens." A muscle twitched in his jaw. "But this petty revenge will only end badly. Can't you see that?"

"Honour is not petty," she snapped, her fury rising. "Honour demands I end what my parents started."

"Does it? Is that what 'honour' demands?" Ty's voice rose to meet hers, his arms flying out wide. Maybe this was how they'd burn each other down. "You can walk away—their story does not need to be your end."

The doorknob was cold in her hand. She glanced back, giving Ty one more chance to understand how much she needed to see this through.

Honour separated the worthy from the unworthy. The honourable from the detritus. It would allow her to rise above the stain of her parents' mistakes. It was honourable to end a war, wasn't it? Without her honour, broken though it might be, who would she be?

"Honour is all I have. Can't you understand?" It wove around her like the bandages the silent moon sisters wrapped about her broken body after she was found bleeding in the alleyway; honour held all her broken pieces together. When he'd held her in his arms as she broke apart in the lake, she had thought maybe Ty could do that. Heal her broken pieces. But she was wrong. She had to do it on her own, as she'd always done.

As she walked away from him, his parting words drove into her back with a ruthlessness accuracy that she didn't expect from him. "Honour isn't all you have, Seren. It's all you want."

**32**

———

Daylight and fresh air—not smoke and charred tree stumps—greeted her when Seren at last emerged from the tunnels, through a different enchanted door in another part of the forest. She wondered if the magic of the doors had somehow prevented the fire from spreading, but since Llion wasn't speaking to her, there was no point in asking. The sweet notes of wildflowers and the twittering of the woodland birds, however, did little to soothe her foul mood after her parting with Ty. Her bravado to him aside, she was relieved not to be alone with Llion; although she had no particular desire for the Lockpick's company, either.

Since leaving the Llewyn den, the sealgair had barely acknowledged her presence, which suited her fine. If he wasn't bound by his oath to deliver her safely to the Throne, she suspected he'd do more than scowl whenever he looked at her. Which wasn't much, given that he led the trio. Thane wisely trailed at a distance, lest the sealgair turned his temper on him. And she lagged farther behind him, wary enough of what both men were capable of to keep them in her sights.

Not that her wariness meant she would admit that Ty had

376

been right to demand to come with her. Thinking about their last exchange made her blood heat all over again. The arrogant nerve to accuse her of valuing honour too highly. Honour was the backbone of the republic. If one didn't honour and serve their House, the republic would descend into anarchy—wouldn't it?

War brought disorder as well. That was why Legion legates throughout the histories chose swift invasions over drawn-out negotiations and sieges. The Burning of Gull Harbour had sealed Dobhran's fate. A fate he deserved for taking the lives of so many innocents. But if Ty was correct about Uncle Tarquin desiring both their deaths as traitors, then she had jeopardized the lives of Clan Llewyn for harbouring her.

Those deaths to come—all four hundred and eighty-eight—along with Dobhran's and Sila's, lay heavy on her soul. She could feel the weight of it like an abscess eating at her flesh and spirit.

Or was that something else?

A giggle had Seren whipping around to face . . . a trickle of a stream over an outcrop of rock?

"Who's there? What do you want with me?" Seren demanded of the forest.

Another giggle. Mocking. Like the girlish voice who had interrupted Drakori's dreamscape with Seren. Then the giggle hadn't come from a corporeal body. It had to be the untrained seer that Drakori had mentioned to Wolvair.

After she checked to make sure Thane and Llion were out of sight, she closed her physical eyes and concentrated on the ones etched under the skin of her palms. Immediately, they tingled, and the bubbling of a meadow brook filled her mind.

*Is this your pitiful attempt at a dreamscape?*

The condescension sounded odd in the childish voice, like how Quinton used to parrot the scoldings of their tutors back to her. *Who are you?* Seren's feet splashed in the shallow water as she searched upstream for the other seer.

*You're rather dull, Seren Moralis.*

Seren scanned the embankment for a temporal body hiding in the tall grasses. *Meet me in the flesh and you won't find my knife dull.*

*You'll have to catch me first!*

Something splashed behind her. Seren took off after it, following the meandering curve of the widening stream. A flash of a pale foot belonging to a white shift and honey-blonde braids disappeared around a grassy bend, but the young seer was gone by the time Seren rounded it.

*Give up already. You'll be too late.* The taunt was delivered in a sing-song voice.

*Too late for what?*

There was no answer. The temporal stream dried up, and once again Seren was back in the forest—alone.

*Ellus, why aren't you here?*

When no answer came, she adjusted her pack and trudged onward. It was then that she realized she'd been expecting one—hoping for him to answer. Somehow. There was no one she could talk to about her untamed Eyes or the mysterious seer. No one else who would listen so well. And she didn't want to unload her problems onto Vesper's young shoulders.

*You don't have to justify yourself, Seren. Not your existence, not your decisions. Not to me.*

Recalling Ellus's promise to her fanned her irritation with Tyberius, which had rubbed her like the blister on her heel since leaving the den. He'd acted like her mission was nothing more than self-indulgence, as if it weren't vitally important to the peace of the republic.

She crested the hill to enter a meadow of yellow, red, and purple wildflowers. On the horizon, a line of broad, old pines rose like a fortress into the sky, their tips piercing the three-quartered moon still visible in the afternoon.

As she approached, it became apparent the trees, the size of ship masts, weren't in a line but a ring. Llion and Thane stood on either side of the largest white pine with their backs to her. Whatever they were looking at held their absolute attention.

On the other side of the trees was a massive, round sinkhole. The depression was at least four of Seren's body lengths deep, and the sides were covered in twisting tree roots and vines. At the bottom was a circle of tall black stones with etchings that reminded her of the doors of the Llewyn and Wolvair dens. More precious serendium. The stones were evenly spaced to form a circle, and in the centre a flatter slab was raised up, higher than the rest. The gleaming black stone cut across the circle on a diagonal like a sundial.

Absently, Seren touched the smooth metal of her father's ring with her thumb. "Is this the Unkat Axstrida?"

Thane snorted. "Not grand enough for you, Princess?"

Seren didn't know what she had expected. A temple with another seer?

Llion scratched his chin as if coming to some decision. "We'll be back for you at dawn."

"Wait!" Seren grabbed him by the bracer as he turned to leave. "What am I supposed to do here?"

The full force of his stare hit her, and she let go of him, ashamed to have whined like a child. "Find your Seersight. You have one night. Then we head out to rejoin the Llewyn before they get too far from us."

"But what if I can't—"

"I'll not leave them undefended for the entire journey back." Llion's harsh tone brooked no argument. He stalked away, but Thane didn't follow. Instead, the Lockpick leaned against a wide trunk with an insufferable look on his face.

"Do you need an invitation to leave?" she asked at last.

"Seems like you accepted yours rather swiftly." He raised a dark brow. "Your legionnaire showing up wasn't part of the plan, was he?"

The unwanted insightfulness—from Thane, of all people—rankled. "I beg your pardon?"

But he took her scowl in stride. "You know, your plot to marry the crown prince, kill him on your wedding night, and steal the kingdom out from under our noses."

She didn't have to act surprised. Marriage had never been part of it. "I fled one potential husband. I have no 'plot' to acquire another."

Thane's dark brows shot upward. "If that's true, once you swear allegiance to the Throne, do you honestly believe Regent Boreal or Prince Alban will leave you alone to make your own choices, Princess of the Morningstars? I thought you had more sense than that."

She cupped her hands in a rude gesture she'd seen him use, and his eyes crinkled in patronizing mirth. Before she could wipe it from his face, there was a distant bellow from Llion. Under her baleful glare, Thane reluctantly left with a mocking Primordian salute to her.

So much for making peace with the Lockpick.

Turning her mind back to the task at hand, Seren surveyed the Unkat Axstrida below. Circles within circles had been carved into the gleaming serendium stones.

What did it all mean? Drakori wanted her to access Time's Flow, but she hadn't mentioned stones. And now, because of Llion, she had only one night to figure her Inheritance out.

Seren gazed up at the moon hanging in the patch of blue afternoon sky, framed by the tips of the pine trees. *Lumina, can you tell me what I'm supposed to do?*

A few birds twittered in the silence, and Seren sighed. The Goddess had never answered her prayers before. Why would she start now? But she had to try something.

She took a deep breath. *Seline, will you help me?*

If Lumina had a sister goddess, she didn't answer either.

At a loss, Seren sat down in the cool shade of the trees, dangling her legs over the edge, and stared at the mysterious, silent stones. She stared at them for what seemed like an age without any idea how to proceed. But if she could use her Seersight to see the present, then ambushing the princes would be as easy as hitting a throwing target with her knife.

*Only it won't be a wooden target you're skewering.*

She shuddered as the feeling of her sword sinking into Sila's flesh reverberated through her. In an attempt to outrun the memory, she jumped over the ledge. The tangled roots flew by her on the way down until she landed in a crouch, narrowly missing a stone as she rolled to her feet on the scrabbly grass.

Slowly, she rose. Nothing happened. The ground didn't open up and swallow her. Not a tingle, not an itch, not even a wisp of a vision. Irritated now with her caution, she walked around the outside of the stones, running her hand over their smooth surfaces. Unlike the rocks near the waterfall, no moss or lichen scaled their surfaces. Did some hermit clean them?

Once she had completed the perimeter, she strode into the circle, to the centre one, which was positioned horizontally like a table for an offering to the goddess. Eyes closed, she touched the last stone and braced herself.

Nothing. No tingling, no sense of power, no voices or images. Desperately, she climbed on top and surveyed the stones, unsure what she was searching for.

But the silent stones didn't give up their secrets. Disappointed, hot, and sweaty, she flopped down on the stone and closed her eyes. It was the first time she'd been truly alone since she crossed paths with Llion. No one to look at her with suspicion, derision, contempt, disappointment or hurt. It should've been a relief.

It wasn't.

Neither was there anyone to look at her with camaraderie, friendship, or trust.

She missed Valera so much her heart might burst like a bruised plum. It wasn't only Valera she missed, however. If Vesper were here, she'd be darting around, gawping at the stones and probably telling stories she'd heard about such things. Ellus would be studying the concentric circles and recounting how the Keepers had constructed the temple and its use from some old books he'd read. Kanta would pick an argument about how the Legion would destroy this place and how it would be all Seren's fault.

Seren bit her lip at the pang of guilt. Whatever this place was, it felt like hallowed ground, and it shouldn't be destroyed. Tears pricked at the corners of her eyes. At that moment, she'd even welcome Thane back to exchange barbs with, if it meant she wouldn't be here alone with her tumbling emotions.

Oh, why had she scorned Ty's offer to accompany her? Because he had wounded her pride by declaring her plan petty and childish?

Partly. His condemnation had stung, yes. But if she was honest with herself, she'd been nothing short of terrified of him seeing all of her, the weak parts hidden under the strong front she put up for others. Of seeing her fail to use her Inheritance. Had it been only yesterday he'd kissed her in that lake after she fell apart in his arms? And here she was falling apart again, all because she had to face her failure to use her Inheritance, and it was her own damn fault he wasn't here right now.

She hugged her knees to her chest and scowled at the offending stones. The enclosure was unnaturally quiet to her sensitive ears—no birds twittering, no breeze rustling through the trees. Only her noisy thoughts crowding her head. At the Lyceum and House Moralis, she had been surrounded by people but often alone. House members and cadets alike had refused to acknowledge her presence unless she made them, and Quinton had avoided her as much as possible. And to think, all the while he hated her, he'd been training Prims like her. Prims with Inheritances.

Now he was probably hunkered outside the Llewyn den with the Crescents, waiting to accept her surrender. Or perhaps, he was tracking the Llewyn north to the Throne on the heels of the Legion in anticipation of their quarry—the Felinae—being flushed out into the open. If the seer had foreseen the summons to the Throne, Quinton might very well be headed north. It was humbling that until Dobhran's capture, the dens of the Felinae had remained hidden for almost two decades by some enchantment. Invisible doors with the same circles as these stones, the same polished substance.

*Circles. Moons.*

Of course. The Unkat Axstrida must be a shrine to the Moon Goddess—one of them, at least. The moon was an orb. It travelled in a circle. The concentric circles on the stones. Circles held power. The unamkhara symbol had a circle with a slash, too. She didn't know how she understood, but she did.

She looked at the sinkhole and stones again through fresh eyes. It was serendium. *Seren* meant star. *Star rock?* Rock from the sky?

One of Drakori's fireside tales came immediately to mind. In a fit of jealousy, Lumina had unwittingly destroyed her sister—the pieces of Seline's body flung into the sky to create the stars. If some of those pieces had fallen to the mortal realm, like Ellus had claimed, then Seline had been protecting the Felinae all these years with pieces of her celestial body.

That's what Vesper had meant about Seline being all around them; the goddess was in the sky and here on the earth. In the rock.

The possibilities awed Seren, but the pragmatic part of her needed to figure out how to access her Eyes. Maybe the stones would add their celestial power to hers, like an amplifier. Or they could be a doorway to Time's Flow or the Goddess. Only one way to find out. And the sooner she found Prince Alban and his long-lost brother, the sooner she could restore her honour and return home. Goal firmly in mind, she closed her eyes, straightened her spine, and placed her palms facing upward on her knees. As Master Kai had taught her, she took four slow, cleansing breaths, one for each direction, and exhaled her thoughts and worries to focus solely on the inner light Lumina had placed inside her to ignite her mortal body.

The nascent blue flame tripled under Seren's tending until it lit up the dark depths of her soul, sending a crackling warmth through her. *Now to find Time's Flow.* Her ears picked up the faintest gurgling sound, and her temporal self followed it. Blue flame parted to reveal a woodland stream. It beckoned her closer with its murmuring until she crouched at the edge of the running water.

*Show me Prince Alban.*

The stream continued to gurgle along merrily. She had the unreasonable desire to grab the temporal water and shake it until it showed her what she wanted. But Master Kai had taught her that water couldn't be threatened or coerced. Neither could a goddess, she supposed. Since her Inheritance was a gift from Seline, perhaps she should temper her words.

She waved a hand over the temporal water as if it were a jittery horse and she might stroke its withers. *I seek Prince Alban. Can you please help me find him?*

Her request echoed across the stream, like the skipping of a flat rock, and she followed until it sank below her. At once, the water surged in a ripple around her, rising both in Time's Flow and in the sinkhole where her corporeal body sat, until the stones were underwater and a dark sea licked at her crossed legs. If she plunged into the temporal, her body would be left behind, completely vulnerable. Llion and Thane were supposed to be guarding her, but they'd left and were probably setting up camp or hunting. If the water rose much further, she'd drown.

She pushed the fear and doubt away. She'd have to trust the taibhseir, the waters, her Inheritance, and the magic of this place. Although she couldn't see the black stones anymore, she felt their ancient power thrumming in her bones. It pulled and grabbed at her with every step into the temporal stream, a greedy undertow that buckled her knees. This time, she didn't fight it.

When she was up to her chest in the swirling temporal waters, she could sense the ring of stones thrumming with the force of a typhoon, and her Eyes and the unamkhara ring pulsed in tandem as an unearthly blue light erupted from all four. Instead of drowning, she found herself standing firm on the slab of rock, in the storm's eye. A vessel for the power coursing from the stones through her.

*By the moon, the power!* She was invincible, a goddess. And the power of the Unkat Axstrida, hers to command. A laugh of wonder bubbled out of her as she stretched her hands out to her sides to call on the stones.

In an instant, the winds receded, leaving behind a calm, deep pool at the edge of the rock. She could no longer separate the temporal waters from the Unkat Axstrida. Maybe they were one and the same.

*Is Prince Alban of the Fallenstars the one you seek?* crooned the stones.

*He is.*

*Come and find him, Thrice-Marked.*

Without another thought, Seren dove into the black depths.

**33**

———

Someone stepped right through her.

Seren gasped at the bone-chilling feeling as the cloaked woman blithely continued following the line of travellers in mustard yellows and grassy greens meandering through the forest. A black circle with a slash on both Seren's palms confirmed Time's Flow had brought her to the present. Next, a man approached, pulling a handcart occupied by two young children and a swaddled baby. A pointed hat with a feather in its upturned brim was worn low over his face. Could this be the prince?

Before he could walk through her, Seren moved behind a sturdy oak. It was a relief to find she inhabited a temporal body of her own, one she could direct as she wished. But her heart plummeted as the man and cart trundled past. He was far too old to be the prince—nor would she find him here amongst the Llewyn—for that's who these travellers were.

After all that ancient fanfare, her Inheritance still hadn't worked properly. She wanted to scream. Had her uncle somehow known how useless she would be? Was that why he hadn't trained her with his Crescents?

386

But there wasn't time to dwell on her latest failure. Familiar voices tickled her ears. A stone's throw away, Kanta, Vesper, and Ellus walked in file, their packs bulkier than before. Lumina, it was good to see them even if they couldn't see her.

She scanned past the trio and was rewarded with the sight of coppery hair and the scent of sandalwood and lime. Tyberius—unharmed and looking not much better than earlier that morning—trailed the Elusive recruits at a distance. None of the Llewyn following behind seemed inclined to pass the Primordian.

Seren fell in step with him. It might have been her imagination, but she thought she saw Ty's hand twitch beside her. When she tried to take it, her fingers slid through his as if she were made of air, but a tingle ran up her arm from her Eye.

"Did either of you meet Prince Alban while you were at court?" Vesper asked in response to something Kanta had said about tutors.

Maybe Time's Flow had brought her here for this? Any information about the prince would be valuable.

"I have spent little time at the Court of Isles," Ellus said, his tone flat, and Seren recalled how he had lived at the Ice Court.

Kanta pointed to a stream close to the path, and the group followed her there. She dropped her pack and crouched at the edge to fill her canteen. "I met Prince Alban when we were younger. He's been away for many years, but he is expected to return to court any day now." She took a swallow, then grinned mischievously. "This summons may also double as a betrothal celebration for our young prince."

A pang of sympathy for her royal cousin echoed through Seren, and she squashed it. The man would be dead by her hand; it didn't matter if he had a choice or not in his betrothal. But if she wasn't her uncle's weapon, the alternative was that she was truly betrothed to Quinton. Or had been before she was declared a traitor. She glanced back at

Tyberius. He had stopped to fill his canteen farther down the stream. It was incredible how their lives had become so intertwined so quickly after one kiss. She wondered if he would've stood aside and watched her marry Quinton if she hadn't run away.

"Is it true the prince is as learned as any scholar?" Vesper crouched in the sandy banks of the creek, canteen in hand. "They say his mind is sharper than any rapier ever forged."

Kanta snorted. "Who is 'they,' exactly?"

"Lady Llewyn's attendants." Vesper ducked her head sheepishly. "I overheard them at the Night of Mair."

"I suspect that is an embellished rumour." Hiding a grin, Ellus tucked away his filled canteen on the side of his pack. Then the grin faded as his shoulders sagged. "And it hardly matters since Prince Alban cannot win against the Primordians by spouting philosophy."

"Not all wars are won with swords," Tyberius muttered from farther down the bank. He sat under a cedar tree, forearms resting on his knees, gazing out at the stream. "Words can carry the day."

"Says the man who ran away from a duel," Kanta huffed, and Ty flinched. "Guess you couldn't talk your way out of that one. No surprise. Prims only understand one philosophy—the might of the sword."

"What then is your impression of our crown prince, Lady Kanta?" Ellus asked, drawing the attention away from Ty so effectively, Seren almost thought it was on purpose. "They also say he is no warrior."

A light breeze rustled Kanta's messy curls, and her bearing took on a contemplative air. "Prince Alban is loyal and just and clever. We can rely on him to be the king we need and to choose a worthy queen to lead us."

The lines of tension around Ellus's mouth smoothed out, as if Kanta's opinion acted as a balm.

"And what does your lord father think of Prince Alban, Ellus?" Vesper asked.

Ellus flinched. "He died along with my mother on the Night of the Broken."

Vesper's hand flew up to cover her mouth. She looked like she'd give anything to take back her question. "Oh, Ellus."

A dull pain exploded inside Seren's chest, like her heart was being scraped against stone. Then an overwhelming loneliness swallowed all the breath inside of her.

It wasn't her own.

*Ellus?*

His head snapped up to scan the trees, but his gaze passed over her unaware. He hoisted his pack. "Many died that night. I'm not the only one who lost family."

It was Vesper who did what Seren wished she could, squeezing Ellus's arm in comfort. "May you meet them again in the Mists."

"And the regent? Is she as frightening as I've heard?" Tyberius sipped from his flask from under his tree. Behind him, the line of the Llewyn was dwindling.

Kanta snorted. "To Prims, I'm sure she is." She glanced at Ellus, but he didn't offer his own thoughts. "She is not known to suffer fools. Come on. Last into camp will be last to eat."

While Kanta and Vesper helped hoist each other's packs up, Seren let her gaze linger on Ty as he waylaid Ellus. His cheeks looked hollow and the black of his clothes brought out the shadows under his eyes. Something painful ailed him, and she wished she hadn't left him behind.

"Reul, you're her friend. Do you think Regent Boreal and the prince will grant Seren asylum in the Felinae Dominion?"

For a long breath, silence hung between them.

"Our riaghladair will act in the best interests of the Felinae, as will the prince," Ellus murmured, and it was her turn to flinch. Her mission was in the best interests of the Felinae—

just not the best interests of the Felinae princes. But if they truly cared for their people, they'd surrender. And yet, they hadn't done that. They'd burned Gull Harbour instead. A foolhardy taunt at their enemies.

Ty nodded before clapping the side of Ellus's pack. "I can work with that."

The roar of water overtook her senses, and Seren felt her temporal body being sucked away in a whirlwind.

Her eyes opened. Once again, she sat on the slab in the stone circle at the bottom of the sinkhole. She and all the stones and tree roots were as dry as a field in drought.

———

Darts of fire from the fleeing sun swathed the sky when Seren settled once again with her palms on her knees on the centre slab. She'd thought about what to scry for next while savouring her portion of the roasted pheasants that Llion had shot with his bow for supper and Thane had cooked over the fire. This time, she would try her luck with the eldest prince. She'd also call to her Eye before calling to the water and the stones to see if that made a difference. As exhilarating as the wild power of the stone circle had been, it had also been exhausting, and she hoped she could simplify some of the steps. Once the blue flame inside her was burning bright again, she called out.

*Eye on hand, sift the sand.*

Her flesh burned at the site of the marks. A glance confirmed a circle with a diagonal slash on either palm, lit by bright blue light. Lumina's or Seline's light.

Now, the pool. The water rose at her beckoning, faster and less turbulent this time, until it surrounded her on the slab. Still, strands of her hair whipped free of her braid in the whirlwind. The stones thrummed to life with the ancient power, and she felt its echo in her veins.

*I seek the eldest prince of the Felinae. Do you know him?*

The stones remained silent. Maybe she needed his name? She didn't know it, but she knew his mother's.

*Eye behind, past in mind.* The mark on her back seared her skin between her shoulder blades. *I seek Queen Ellowyne of the Fallenstars and her sons.*

Her request sank like a stone beneath the churning waters. The wind dropped her hair and the pool became placid.

*Come then, Thrice-Marked.*

Leaning over the stone, Seren plunged head-first into the icy temporal waters.

---

THE HEARTH generously warmed the small sitting room of grey stone, casting a glow on the woman with long, shining red-gold hair that stood facing it. She was clad in a loose light-blue dress much like the one Lady Llewyn had worn on the night of Mair with long sleeves and a skirt that flared outward. In her arms, she rocked a swaddled babe while crooning a soft lullaby. Behind her, a boy in a blue tunic and sash with curling locks of dark blond crept closer on all fours around the divan. He jumped out in front of her with a loud roar. The baby let out a wail while the woman startled in false surprise, to the boy's delight.

"Your brother was almost asleep," she admonished him, affectionately. The boy jumped around the vacant rocking chair, roaring until the baby's cries grew louder. But as soon as his mother lowered the babe to see his brother's face, he quieted. The boy made a softer roar, and the baby gurgled in response, his bright blue eyes fixated on his older brother. The woman ruffled the older boy's curls with her one free hand, and her breath hitched. "My precious children."

The boy squirmed under her hand. "Mama," he protested, but the woman held on.

"Promise me you'll always be there for each other." Her hand slid to his cheek. "And for your sisters."

The boy stilled, his honey-brown eyes solemn. "Yes, Mama. Who else will fetch the frogs out of Lorie's and Rin's beds?"

Love lit up the woman's entire being as she kissed his forehead, the babe nestled in her arms between them. A shine encompassed the three of them together, so bright Seren had to look away.

"Scamp," she chuckled. "You're the one who puts them there. But I'm serious, darling. You four are stronger together, but the taibhseir sees a great strength in you. Protect them, my love."

He nodded. "I promise then, Mama. Now can I go play?"

Guilt sunk its sharp claws into Seren, the intensity of the moment ripping at her heart as the roar of rushing water heralded its end.

With the vision and waters gone, Seren was left alone on the hard stone with a heavy emptiness. *Do the princes deserve death at my hands?* Their sisters, their parents, were already gone.

Seren hesitated. Maybe Ty was right, and she wasn't as heartless as she thought. Maybe Ellus's idea of peace wasn't so laughable. Could the Primordians and Felinae unite under one ruling consul? Not as conquered subjects, but as . . . equals? Would either side agree to it? If so, maybe there was another way to end this war and restore her and Tyberius's honour.

She shook her head to dispel her troubled thoughts. At the movement, pain blazed through her temples, and she slid helplessly off the stone.

The stars blurred above her as her forehead pulsed. She

must have hit her head somehow. A thud sounded nearby, and the ground trembled around her. Was the sinkhole sinking? She reached out an arm for the stone—anything—to help pull herself up. *Up.* She had to get up, but she could barely think through the pounding in her head.

Then—suffocating heat burned around her. Shouts of alarm and wailing children assaulted her ears as flames lapped at the dawning sky over unfamiliar thatched roofs. Those that had escaped the burning dwellings rallied around the well in the main square, where a line of townsfolk waited for a pitifully small bucket to be hauled up and passed along.

A mother pried open the fingers of a frightened babe who clung to her nightgown and dropped him in the well. A chance, at least. And if not, better to die in a watery grave than burn alive.

---

"Well, she's breathing."

The voice was familiar, but her eyes refused to open. After another late-night training with Master Kai, she was exhausted and waking up for Soronius's history class was a poor incentive. The scholar could make any battle boring.

Someone shook her shoulder, roughly. When she moved, her head pounded like she'd drunk too much Ambrosia. She tried to tell Valera to go away, but her tongue was stuck to the top of her mouth.

"Morningstar, wake up."

The commanding tone jolted her awake. Two blurry faces hovered over her along with a few twinkly stars. Night had fallen. Her fingers twisted in the cool grass at her sides as it all came rushing back—the flames, the shadowy figures, the smoke. She sat up in haste, almost butting heads with Thane and causing a wave of dizziness. "What happened?" she mumbled.

"You were having a vision," Llion said curtly. "Then blacked out and fell."

An owl hooted in the trees. So he'd been observing her through his Inheritance. For how long? In order to know she'd had a vision, he must have seen the Eye on her palms or forehead during it. So the fire hadn't happened in the past.

Thane moved to lean against a tall stone, as if he'd rather be anywhere else. But she could tell he was watching her closely. "Do you always blackout when you have a vision? Seems tedious."

"No—" It hadn't happened when she scried for the princes. "I don't know. It's happened a few times with wild visions."

"When you had the vision of where Dobhran was?" Thane asked sharply.

*Right.* The vision she'd pretended to have. Ignoring Thane, she focused her attention on Llion. "How long was I out?"

Neither Thane nor Llion offered her a hand as she got to her feet. Not that she'd have taken it from either of them. Lumina, she hoped it wasn't too late. Had this vision been of the present or the future?

"Not long," Llion said. "What did you see?"

"You saw the mark on me? Where?"

Llion raised his hand and touched his forehead, and the tension in her body released in one deep heave. *Eye on head, future read.*

"Future sight. There's still time then." Relief swept through her as she covertly leaned against the centre stone to keep her balance. Everything was still fuzzy from using her Inheritance it seemed. Or the fall.

Thane scowled. "Time for what?"

"Is there a Primordian village near a beach nearby?" she demanded of Llion.

Thane snorted. "Why? You want to turn yourself in, Princess?"

"No," she ground out, keeping her gaze on Llion. It was him she'd have to convince. "Lives are in danger. Fire. I saw a village on fire."

Llion didn't respond immediately, and the sounds of various night insects filled the air. "Ultima Thule is half a day's walk. We'd be lucky to get there by morning if we walked all night. And your vision might be days or years away."

"Or it could be tomorrow at dawn." Would it be enough time? She pushed off the stone and wobbled. "We need to leave now."

Then Thane was in her face. "So you can lead us into a trap in some backwater Prim outpost? I bet the Legion will welcome us with open arms."

Closing her eyes against another wave of dizziness, Seren turned away from him and the fight he offered. Hitting him, as much as she liked to, wouldn't win this argument.

"Quiet, Sionnach," Llion ordered. "Tell us what you saw, Morningstar."

Images from her vision flickered in and out. She didn't suppress her shudder. "Flames and death. And if we waste time, a whole village will burn."

"Why should we care if they die?" Something akin to fear flashed in Thane's eyes before they turned flinty. "Why should *you* care? Don't they consider you a traitor?"

Ignoring him, she took a step toward Llion. He had to believe her. "Aren't you curious who starts the fire?"

"An untended hearth is my guess." Llion scratched the day's scruff on his chin, uninterested.

It took all her patience not to do something reckless. Instead, she settled for one of her infamous scowls. "It's not a hearth fire, and you wouldn't dare send your Elusives with the Legion somewhere in the north."

Except he would. He had given Dobhran orders to burn Gull Harbour. Why did she think that the thought of having all those deaths on his hands would bother him? She needed some other way to persuade him.

"Maybe I will." He seemed to be warming to the notion. "It would serve as a diversion to keep the Legion away from Clan Llewyn, who will out pace us to the Mountain Pass if we detour to Ultima." But the gleam in his eyes told her it would be revenge for the death of his operative.

*Flip the board.*

"But that's no way to treat the suppliers of Clan Llewyn, is it?" At his sour grunt, she knew she'd guessed correctly. The Prim village on the coast was the closest settlement. They had both bounties from the sea and the fields to offer the Llewyn in trade.

"That does not compel me to save them. Are you beholden to rescue the person who cobbled your boots?" He scoffed at the silent stones as if he doubted their power, yet she noticed he refrained from brushing against them. "If your vision even comes to pass." *Bastard.* "No, we should continue to meet up with Clan Llewyn. Come. We'll sleep a few hours before heading out."

*Sleep?* She couldn't sleep with visions of burning people in her head. "Would any of your Elusives act without orders?" she pressed.

It wasn't the only explanation for the fire. But it was the one she hoped for. Llion, however, bristled at the insinuation.

"Even if one might act alone, by now Silver will have sent them on to Caisteal Dìomhair."

She'd forgotten the assassin's mission. Then Llion's threat of an attack was an empty one, at least.

"Odds are it's the Legion burning out traitors or looking for us." Thane yawned, with a nonchalance that was more affected than real, she suspected. "Both are good reasons not to go."

She should have known Llion and Thane wouldn't care about the deaths of Prim children and families. Not after Gull Harbour. But the urgency of the situation compelled her. "It's not the Legion."

"Then who is it?" Thane threw his arms wide in frustration. "We've run out of culprits, haven't we?"

"I don't know." That was a lie. The Crescents had one who controlled fire. The one who had set the forest on fire around the Llewyn den. But it didn't make sense for Uncle Tarquin to burn a Primordian village—unless he knew they had been selling their wares and food to Clan Llewyn? From Dobhran maybe?

An hour ago, she might've condemned the villagers to such a fate; however, their cries for help lingered with her, along with the smell of burning flesh. And could she truly fault Ultima Thule for providing food and materials so Vesper and her clan could survive?

"You say it's not your Elusives, but in my vision I was inside the body of the one who lit the fire, someone who couldn't be from the village or the Legion."

It came to her then that Drakori had called her father's soulshielder a Sparker and spoke of fire in his soul. Kynden Startaker was dead, and this Sparker was someone else entirely.

Llion stilled, one hand on a vine to climb upward. "How can you be certain, Morningstar?" There was a curious note in his gruff voice. Even Thane looked mildly intrigued.

"Because the flames started here, in the palm of my hand."

# 34

Seren pounded on the rickety door of the first hut, her heart as loud as her fist on the rotting wood.

It'd been a gruelling pace, but Llion's curiosity about the unknown Sparker—who might be the same one who had set the forest around the Llewyn den on fire—had brought them to the village river in time to see the mill go up in a blaze. The sight had convinced both him and Thane that her vision had come true. There'd been no question then of warning the inhabitants. Llion had sprinted off to the outlying farms, while she and Thane had run up the hill, toward the sea cliff lined with rickety fishing huts. No smoke rose yet from the village farther up the craggy rise.

*There's time.* However, the huts were so closely clustered together with straw-thatched roofs they might as well have been kindling. One spark and they'd go up like the bonfires at the Llewyn den. As she knocked again, she kept her eyes peeled for movement. The Sparker could already be hiding between them.

When there was no answer at the door, Seren moved to the

lone window. It was shuttered with ill-fitting boards, which she tore open easily. "Wake up! Fire!"

From under a pile of patchwork blankets, two women in loose sleeping tunics with brown braids roused themselves. Neither panicked at a stranger at their window. With purpose, they woke or picked up the smaller sleeping forms around them.

At the next hut, Seren rammed her shoulder into the door, and it gave way. "The mill's on fire! Your homes may be next!"

The sleeping woman and man bolted upright on their sleeping mats and stared at her, dazed. At the woman's side was a woven reed basket with a sleeping babe. Seren picked up the basket and walked out the door. The woman flew out after her, black coils of hair flying out from under her sea-green head wrap, and Seren thrust the basket into her well-defined brown arms before running to the next hut.

She banged on that door, yelling fire until the inhabitants roused themselves. Out of the corner of her eye, she saw the woman hand her baby to one of the older women who already had a trio of sleepy children in their nightclothes clutching the ends of her faded orange tunic. As Seren ushered an old man and his son out, the lithe woman caught up to her. "Hadi and I will help you wake the others."

The man behind her, in a simple brown tunic like his wife's, nodded grimly. "After that we must protect the boats, Yara."

Some of the tension in Seren's chest loosened as Hadi and Yara ran to the next hut, alternating with her. Soon someone began beating a gong-like pot with a stick, and Seren had to spare a few breaths to focus her hearing elsewhere. She pounded on a few more doors until the awful din awakened the rest of the fisherfolk. Prims of all ages emerged, wrapped in blankets and shawls, blinking in the growing daylight and coughing at the acrid smoke in the air.

There were shouts of alarm at the mesmerizing inferno

across the river. Flames engulfed the mill's wheel, leaving the stone tower blackening against the creeping blush of dawn. The crowd around Seren swelled, jostling her about as she waded through. She should warn the village up the hill, but she couldn't find Thane in the sea of bodies around her.

Had the Sparker found him? Bile rose in her throat at the memory of the acrid scent of burning flesh.

"Let me through!" she yelled, shouldering her way through to the end of the huts, checking between each. She rushed around the corner of the last hut and skidded to a halt. Thane knelt on the back of a black-clad figure, who lay unmoving on her stomach in the scrubby grass. Her hood had fallen back to reveal brown hair, a long nose, and parted lips. She was still breathing. But who was she? An Elusive or a Crescent? A Felinae or one of the Moonlight children?

One of the Sparker's arms stretched out past her head, nearly touching the stick-lined walls of the hut. *Lumina*, it had been close.

Thane slid off the young woman. In one hand, he held a stone from the river; with the other he checked the Sparker's pulse in her neck. She shuddered. *Skin to skin*. Then he tossed away the stone toward the cliff, jaw clenched. "Awake, she could light a fire. And not all of us know your fancy neck strike, Princess"

Was he upset she hadn't taught him? No, it wasn't that. He'd seen her shudder. Knocking the Sparker out was a good defence against her Inheritance—if that's all it was.

"Or is it just my touch you find nauseating, Princess?"

She licked her lips, uncertain what to say. Then a glint of metal drew her eye to the grass near the woman's gloved fingertips. An ordinary flint box.

*Solfire.*

Thane spotted it as she bent to pick it up. "So this wasn't the Sparker from your vision?"

Why was he asking her? "Don't you know that and all her secrets?"

Hurt flashed across his features. "I know I've been a bastard to you." He stepped in close, lowering his voice so as not to be overheard by the gathering fisherfolk. "But I don't go around ripping secrets from everyone I meet. Like a soul-damned thief."

She faltered at his indignation. "I saw a hand, not a face. The Sparker must still be out there. We need to warn the villagers." She glanced at the woman. "So you won't take her secrets to discover who we're up against here?"

"She's unconscious, Seren." He gaped at her, like what she was suggesting was outrageous, and maybe it was. "Besides, my Inheritance won't work unless she's awake."

Good to know the Lockpick couldn't steal her own secrets in her sleep. Something she hadn't even considered.

A murmuring grew around them, and Seren shifted away from him under the gaze of their audience, whose attention was diverted from the fire to the three outsiders in their midst. She tried to see Thane as they might. With his pale skin and dark hair, he looked more like Quinton's cousin than she did. But Prims were a varied lot, the consequence of half a millennium of conquest and alliances across the continent. The crowd was quiet—too quiet. She didn't know if nobs from the city were any more welcome here than the enemy. Or had they heard Thane mention her vision?

Thane nudged the unknown woman with his boot, then directed his own levelling stare back at their audience. "Citizens of Ultima, we've tracked this detritus from Luminaria. She set the fire on the mill. She may have accomplices."

Even though she'd heard his impeccable nob accent before when he was impersonating a House Moralis guard, it gave her pause. There was definitely more to Thane than picking locks and stealing secrets.

"Something to tie her up with would be useful while we track down the others," she added.

Netting was produced, and Yara and Hadi kept the curious crowd back while Thane secured their prisoner's hands and feet. Her identity still puzzled Seren. While she didn't recognize the young woman from the Lyceum or nobilis society, that didn't mean she wasn't a servilis member of the one of the Houses or one of her uncle's Crescents. Or maybe Llion would know her, despite his belief that rogue Felinae weren't involved.

The crowd parted, and a woman with black ringlets streaked white and a fishnet shawl the colour of the ocean approached them with purposeful strides. "I am the matrona of our community." She touched the spot over her heart with two umber fingers. "You have our gratitude, strangers. Even up here in these desolate rocks, we've heard about the burning of Gull Harbour. Are you both legionnaires sent by the imperator to protect us?"

Shouts and the peal of bells split the air from the direction of the village, and Seren was saved from lying. Above the rooftops, a trail of smoke was rising into the red morning sky. Her heart sank. They'd failed to stop the Sparker.

Then out of the smoke came a blur of brown. An owl. It swooped down over her head, and she ducked. It came back again, screeching, and tried to rake Thane's cheek with its talons as he rose from binding the hostage. "For Lleufer's sake!"

It screeched and flew back toward the village. Seren exchanged a heavy look with Thane, her stomach clenched with a sense of foreboding that had nothing to do with Seersight.

———

As she ran down the busy main road, alongside Thane, Seren strained her ears amid the cries and shouts of the townsfolk as they streamed out of their wood and clay homes. She had never been to any of the coastal villages. The dwellings here were unlike the grand villas of the city, and she wondered if Ultima had originally been a Felinae village. "Do you see the owl?"

With such commotion in the narrow cobblestone streets, none of the townsfolk spared more than a cursory glance at the two strangers in their midst. Once the fires died away, however, they would look for someone to blame. Someone like an outsider—or three.

"No," Thane said curtly, not breaking stride. "But it flew this way."

Most of the townsfolk were headed the same way. Not out toward the bay and river, but farther into the village. Soon the street widened into a square. She slowed as the crowds became as thick as Kanta's porridge, and Thane took the lead, weaving around people like someone familiar with busy streets. But, of course, he couldn't be familiar with such a thing. She followed until he disappeared behind a wall of townsfolk. It was a water line. Buckets and pots of all shapes and sizes were being filled at the round well, then passed from person to person down the line to be thrown on burning shops and houses.

On the other side, she found Thane in front of a crooked, blooming pear tree that was growing out of a raised stone bed. A glow in its branches caught her eye. Moonwood?

Seren blanched. The luminescence wasn't moonwood but a filmy substance smeared on a well-charred leather apron, in the shape of a crescent moon. An apron worn by a man, hanging limp from the rope around his neck. She swallowed. In their frenzy to put out the fires, the townsfolk hadn't noticed the hanged man yet.

Thane made a noise in the back of his throat and turned away from the sight. "Do you hear Llion?"

It was all the excuse she needed to close her eyes. There

were so many distracting noises to sift through. Then, above the tumult, rose a familiar roar.

———

"HE'S IN THERE?" Despite the disbelief in Thane's tone, it wasn't a question.

Llion's shouts had drawn them a few blocks away from the square and crowds to a brown and white two-storey house engulfed in Sol's fiery hells. Above the burning pitched gables circled the owl. When it saw them, it hooted as if to say it was past its bedtime, then flew away. The front overhang of the second storey and part of the burning roof had fallen to the street, blocking the heavy oak door and much of the side yard. Along with the debris lay a half-burnt sign with a painted anvil, proclaiming the place as the iron-forger's. The upper half was consumed, though the flames pouring out of the barred window casement on the bottom floor pointed to a ground start. It was a corner lot with a small, fenced-in yard on one side separating it from the next dwelling, which had not yet caught fire.

Seren bit her lip in consternation. The fire had spread remarkably fast through the house. Unnaturally fast.

A faint, high-pitched wail from inside interrupted her thoughts. She rushed to the open window, where smoke bellowed out from between the iron bars—a security measure she'd not noticed on other houses. Coughing, she covered her mouth and nose with her shirt. "Llion? Are you in there?"

From the smoke emerged a sooty, sweaty face surrounded by braids. Seren heaved a sigh of relief.

"Where's Sionnach?" Llion croaked before falling into a coughing fit. "He wasn't to let you out of his sight."

A wave of heat washed over her from the house as Thane

stepped up behind her. "I believe you said 'if she dies, you die,' but we're not the ones trapped in a burning house."

Seren couldn't stop her brows from rising at the strangely protective orders. But then Llion had sworn an oath, and for all his faults, the sealgair was a man of his word.

"There's a child and Regul's apprentice trapped with me." Llion coughed. "The front collapsed while I was in here—"

"We saw the door's blocked," she cut in, examining the window. The iron bars divided it into five rectangular slots, each one not much larger than her foot. "Can the children fit through?"

Llion lifted up a child around six years old to the window for fresh air. Wide brown eyes stared back at Seren, while tears, sweat, and ash streaked the stringy honey-brown hair plastered to her flushed cheeks. There was no hope the poor thing could slip through the tight space.

Seren bit her lip, gazing upward at the flames licking the roof. "Could you jump from the roof?" Part of it was still intact. The height would break a Prim's legs, but she'd seen Llion scale a mountain.

"The staircase is impassable," he said, dashing her last idea. "But these bars are heating up. If they get hot enough, they might bend enough to get the children through."

With a frown, Thane leaned in to inspect the bars. "Move away."

Once Llion complied, Thane delivered a forceful kick to the bars. Then another. They barely budged. *Solfire.* They might be bendable if heated long enough, but not before Llion and the children roasted inside. If only they had arrived earlier and caught the Sparker.

"We'll need tools to dislodge them." Thane wiped his sweating brow with the bottom of his shirt.

There was a coughing sound from the window. "Tools?" A dark-haired boy, features round and soft and glistening with sweat, came forward then to breathe the air in desperate gulps. "Look around Pater Regul's forge in the yard."

At once, Thane took off around the side of the house.

If Thane couldn't dislodge the bars . . . "Get as low as you can, away from the smoke," she said to Llion and the children all huddled by the window. "I'll bring help."

Then she ran as fast as she could back to the square, ignoring Llion's shouts behind her. He and those children didn't have much time. But it would take time all the same.

In the square, the townsfolk were up on ladders that leaned against the cooper's and the chandler's shops. Each had a pole to drag the burning thatch off the less well-to-do businesses. When it fell to the ground, older youths rushed over to stomp on it or douse it with sand from a barrel. Seren reached two boys stomping on a chunk of burning thatch first.

"There are children trapped," she said, tugging on the taller one's sleeve. He looked at her. They were children, too. She shouted at a man lugging a bucket of water toward the cooper's, but he sidestepped her, paying no heed.

Someone yanked on her arm from behind, and her hand shot to her knife. "We need you in the water line," said a buxom matrona before registering the knife in Seren's hand. She had an azure blue shawl tied around her like a sash, and from within its folds, an infant blinked up at Seren.

When the woman let go of her, Seren sheathed Vindicta. "There are children inside the iron-forger's. Please, they need help. My friend is trapped with them." What else could she call Llion?

The woman noted her leather garments, knife, and nob accent. "You knew Pater Regul?" Her gaze flicked to the pear tree and the corpse, which wore what Seren realized was an iron-forger's leather apron. "May Lumina bless his soul in the Vale."

"My friend knew him. Can you help them?" Seren's chest

tightened. She didn't know why she cared so much. If anything happened to Llion, it would be a blow to the Felinae's war effort. But there were two children with him, children who he must have gone in to save.

The matrona studied her for a moment, then hollered at the tall man in a brown tunic halfway up the nearest ladder. "Brandus! Those orphans are trapped at Regul's. Start a new line!"

Brandus slid down the ladder. The matrona caught the ear of the boy who'd ignored Seren and ordered him and his friends to bring what was left of the sand barrels. At the sight of the water line reforming to reach the iron-forger's house, Seren let herself feel a glimmer of hope.

But the house was down the hill, a few blocks away, and the line would be too short. Townsfolk ran past her with their fire hooks, but without the water...

Suddenly, the line was swarmed with newcomers. Their clothes were shabbier, their bodies thinner and tanned by the wind and sea. A familiar face under a sea-green head wrap approached her. Yara squeezed her arm. "Need a few more hands?"

Tears pricked at Seren's eyes as she looked from Yara to Hadi. "They would be most welcomed."

Hadi nodded, a hand on his wife's thin shoulder as if he were grateful they were both alive. "You saved our homes, now we try to save theirs."

Together, they led the other fisherfolk, with their wooden bowls and buckets, to join the line. This hadn't happened in her vision. The future had changed. With that realization, the tightness in her chest loosened, and she took off running back to the iron-forger's on the heels of a few townsfolk with fire poles. But a flash of black leather down an alley slowed her feet.

Thane or the Sparker? On instinct, she ducked into the alley.

From the side, a large body crashed into her, and her chest hit the wall of a shop. Before she could catch her breath, her arm was twisted behind her and a hand encased in leather clamped over her mouth. It wasn't Thane.

She tried to break free, but the bruising hold was too tight. Whoever he was, he out muscled her. She landed a stomp on his instep, but he didn't drop her. Instead, he dragged her farther into the shadows, where blood dripped like angry slashes from the plaster and timber walls.

*Prims Go Home.*

*All bow before the Prince.*

She threw her head back to crack her assailant's nose, but at the last moment, he let her go and sidestepped. So she spun around with a high kick to his face, in the moondancer way. He took the kick but grabbed her leg and used it to wrench her off her feet. The air whooshed out of her as she landed on her back. Gasping, she forced herself to roll out of striking distance, but it put her with a wall to her back.

She scrambled to her feet, hand going for her knife. If this was the Sparker and he was with her uncle's Crescents, she had to tell him she was on his side before he used his Inheritance. "Who sent you?"

In the tussle, his black hood had fallen back. Two storm-grey eyes stared back. Soot was smudged over his features to obscure them, but under the ashes, she scented cloves and cinnamon and blood. It was a knife in the ribs as she recognized the cruel curl of his full upper lip.

"The imperator. Any last words before you die, traitor?"

## 35

Seren's jaw went slack. "Why are you here, Quinton?"

Moon mother, could the Legion be here with him, too? She skimmed the shadows of the alley, but it was empty save for a discarded skein in a puddle of blood.

"I promised you death the last time we met." With his usual grace, he drew his short sword. Blood smeared his gloves. She'd interrupted his work.

Despite the heat of the burning buildings nearby, ice pooled in her belly. His blatant loathing chilled her, and perhaps that was why she focused on the blood-marked walls behind him. Beneath the anti-Prim slogans were four slashes in red, like four claw marks. What everyone in Luminaria recognized as the signature of an Elusive attack.

It didn't make sense. "You're an Elusive?"

"I haven't broken my oath to House Moralis," he scoffed, disgust dripping from each word as he backed her up against the wall with his sword.

Hot anger flared through her melting the ice as the blade neared her throat, but she didn't pull her knife. "Neither have I.

Do you think your father would tolerate my betrayal if he hadn't sanctioned it?"

She didn't know if she was telling the truth anymore, but it was all she had.

"Tolerate?" Quinton echoed, brows rising. "He's declared you and Ty both traitors. Death awaits you in Luminaria. Or here." A muscle bulged in his square, stubbled jaw as his gaze locked onto her hand on the wall behind her. The ring Quinton had mistaken for a token from one of Ty's past lovers now on hers.

"Tell me, is my sword brother worth it? Are his charms worth your honour?"

Her nostrils flared in indignation on Ty's behalf, the feeling followed swiftly by guilt. Despite their last words to each other, she could see now that Ty had only been looking out for her. She touched a finger to the ring on her hand. "Tyberius is worth . . . a thousand of you or me."

Quinton recoiled as if slapped, and she pressed her advantage. "Do you have so little faith in your father's hold on the city to think Ty and I escaped without his permission? Because I do not."

Quinton's jaw sagged along with his sword, and her heart burst with satisfaction at flummoxing him. For ten years, he'd thought her unworthy of being his cousin, his friend, and now he thought her unworthy of being his father's spy. And there was still a slim chance Uncle Tarquin had put his faith in her.

But then Quinton slowly shook his head as if he pitied her. "You killed Novitius Utticor, your own House sister, to protect one of those spineless cowards."

"That was a grievous mistake in the heat of battle." It was a pathetic excuse, and the shame of it pierced her. "One I deeply regret, but I had to protect the Felinae Elusive in order to keep up my subterfuge. He's important. A lord."

She didn't know how she knew—but she knew. If Ellus had

died that night, Llion would've cut her down where she stood, then gone for Uncle Tarquin's head. There would've been no mercy in him. *That's not why you saved him though.*

Cold, flat steel pressed against her throat. "*Lies.* Father ordered me to bring you back home should our paths cross. By any means necessary."

"Listen for once, will you? I left House Moralis on a mission to infiltrate the Felinae and their hidden dominion. To spy for your father." True. Even if Uncle Tarquin hadn't sent her that was why she left. "My companions and I are on our way to the where the princes and regent are hiding."

Quinton gave her a sharp look over his wavering sword. "Tyberius is here?"

"He's travelling ahead with Clan Llewyn."

*Out of your reach.* Out of hers, too.

"And Father knows about your mission?"

She hesitated. Her doubts crowded in together, stealing her confidence. Ty was convinced that the Crescents were the weapon. Yet he had offered no proof beyond his interpretation of her uncle's behaviour. But then there was the fact that Quinton had orders to capture her; that he'd been training these Crescents, and was now leading them—against Prims, though.

"On Pledging Night, Uncle Tarquin told me to follow him into that Consul meeting where he boasted of his secret weapon. I was hiding in the gallery. I assumed he meant me until—"

"Until our betrothal." Quinton lowered his sword enough she could look away to avoid seeing the scorn in his eyes.

She gathered herself and scowled at him. "Why did Uncle Tarquin send you here with his Crescents to set fires? Our people aren't the enemy."

*Maybe the Felinae aren't either.*

Surprise at her knowledge flitted across Quinton's face

before it hardened. "This village is treasonous by association. They've been supplying your companions with food and weapons. The iron-forger confessed—" He licked his finely-drawn lips, and she tried to forget the dead man hanging in the square. "What do you know about the Crescents?"

"They have unnatural Inheritances from their Felinae blood." Tyberius was right that others may try to use her, and she decided not to reveal hers to Quinton yet. "And you've been training them to fight, honing them into an elite unit."

*When you could've been training me.* Fighting side-by-side with Quinton—it was a dream she'd long given up on. Once, she'd been incredibly jealous of Ty for being Quinton's sword brother.

"Ah," he sneered, "then I suppose Tyberius has whispered all my dirty secrets to you."

A chasm of questions and secrets from years of estrangement opened between them. Yet Time's Flow pulled at her. *You have somewhere else to be.*

"Oddly enough, we don't spend our time together talking about you."

Crimson dusted Quinton's cheekbones, and she had the feeling he was remembering how he'd caught them kissing. "Enough of this. I'll take you back to the imperator—he can decide if you're truly a traitor."

Her knees went weak; then she snapped her spine straight. "Do that and you squander a lucrative advantage in this war. Whether your father sent me to spy is irrelevant. I am now trusted by these Elusives." By a few, at least. "Enough for them to bring me to where they've hidden the crown prince. I, and Tyberius, can be of great use to the imperator in our position."

"If that's true, what do you have to report to my father, cousin?"

This was her opportunity to set him straight. Yet she hesitated, the memories of Clan Llewyn leaping over bonfires filling her head. Fire, everywhere fire. Gull Harbour, the Night of Mair, here in Ultima. Elsewhere . . . She shuddered. Another vision had assailed her before dawn, but there wasn't time to dwell on what she couldn't change.

"You're headed back to Luminaria?" she asked instead, surprised. "No more backwater villagers to terrorize? Or Legion to report to?"

*Not following Clan Llewyn to the Throne*, she prayed.

"They're the ones terrorizing us. This?" Quinton gestured at the fire raging on behind her. "This is justice for fraternizing with the enemy."

*Justice*. The word struck her off-kilter for a moment. Hadn't she used the same argument for assassinating the princes to convince Ty? A kernel of doubt reared its head. But whatever Quinton was doing here, it wasn't justice.

"Funny how justice looks like burning houses with Primordians both young and old inside. What happened to bringing traitors before a magistrate? What happened to Aequitas for honour?" Her gaze wandered back to the blood-spattered walls, and she bared her teeth. "You're not even taking responsibility for this *justice*."

Tomorrow, after the smoke was gone, the townsfolk would see the painted claw and slogans and assume the Elusives had attacked them. There would be no more provisions or weapons from Ultima Thule for Clan Llewyn. In one politically savvy attack, Uncle Tarquin had punished Clan Llewyn's suppliers and blamed it all on the Felinae as well.

"I'll not repeat myself," Quinton said, coldly. "What do you have to report?"

"I told you there's been a summoning of the clans to the Throne." Here was the crowning blow. "I am to be presented to the crown prince and regent to make my petition for asylum. Meanwhile, Ty and I will use the earliest opportunity to assassinate the princes."

"Princes? Both live?"

"The eldest has been in hiding for almost two decades. Very few Felinae know he lives while the younger Prince Alban has been overseas. His arrival is expected any day, along with his forthcoming marriage and coronation." The memory of the golden little boy roaring at his baby brother surfaced in her mind, but she hurriedly pushed it away. "Of course, neither he nor his brother will draw breath long enough to utter any vows."

"Until you commit the deeds, these are all empty promises. You must have locations? Ideas of their next attack?"

"The sealgair doesn't exactly consult me on his war strategy." She hesitated, edging closer to the alley's entrance. "I get the feeling they are waiting for something. The summons, perhaps."

"Empty words."

"There's an underground den, a two-day trek from the city, northeast of the Aegis," she blurted, desperate to prove something to him. "The entrance hides in a cropping of silver birch. The door"—she hesitated—"is enchanted. To open it, a Felinae from that clan must touch it and say some words."

Unless one of the Crescents' ancestors was a Wolvair, she didn't think they'd be able to perform the same ritual. And even if they could, Lord Wolvair and his clan would be long gone to the Throne. There was no harm in giving away the location, since Dobhran had already compromised it.

Quinton took her mention of enchantment in stride, but then he'd been training Crescents with who knows what kind of Inheritances. "Is that where you've been? Can you open it?"

"Briefly, and no. Their sealgair—their legatus—trained me and some other recruits inside a mountain on the Eastern coast, near where your father's Crescents lost me."

That was a guess as well, that her tracker had been a Crescent.

Quinton's sword came back up. "You mean where Markus died. Peri barely made it back with your horse. She shouldn't have wasted her strength on saving the damn animal, only she thought you were still astride it."

"Who?" Outwardly, Seren forced herself to remain calm. The names weren't familiar to her, but Quinton said them like they were under his command. Like they were friends. And Bay was alive because of a Crescent, while Llion had tricked her. He'd taken her cloak with her scent, not to give a false trail but as a lure. And he'd taken a Prim's life for doing nothing more than following him to the cavern. Bile burned her throat.

"I need to go before I'm missed." She couldn't tell Quinton the man in charge of the Felinae's Elusives, who had most likely killed Markus, was stuck in a burning house. She needed Llion alive to take her to the Throne, no matter his atrocities.

"When will you be done with your 'mission'?" The doubt in Quinton's voice lashed her like a whip as he moved to block her exit.

She felt her temper rise in kind. "Why is it so easy for you to believe I'd betray you and your father? You're family."

Her words seemed to suck all the air from the alley. Quinton's gaze drifted over her shoulder. "Because it's what I would do, if what had been done to you, had been done to me."

What did he mean? The betrothal?

Then his free hand curled into a fist. When he looked up at her, it was with a fire that consumed him from within. "But you couldn't just leave. You had to take him with you."

And here lay her most unforgivable betrayal in Quinton's eyes.

Seren snorted. She hadn't 'taken' Ty anywhere. "You didn't make it difficult for Ty to leave. A cell in the tower? A duel to the death? Is that how you repay his love?"

Hope widened in his eyes, dousing the flames of his fury. "He—?"

Her heart softened. "He didn't say anything, but I can tell he's hurting." And Lumina knew she was partly responsible for that hurt. "What happened between you?"

Quinton braced himself with a hand on the wall next to her, his sword lowered to point at the ground. "He refused the imperator's direct order to interrogate the traitor in front of me and my guard. That alone is a treasonable offence." His shoulders slumped. "I reacted. Badly. The rumours about you and him didn't help."

"For Lumina's sake, we didn't have a tryst behind your back —but if we had, it wouldn't have been any of your concern since neither you nor your father informed me of the betrothal." A thought dawned her. Unless . . . "You and Ty weren't together, were you?"

He made a slashing motion with his hand. "We haven't been for some time. And are you two involved now?"

"It's still none of your concern." Her cheeks burned at the memory of their kiss in the lake.

He nodded dully. "That's what Ty said—that it had only been a kiss—but I refused to believe him. That was an insult he couldn't let go. When he swung at me, I didn't dodge on purpose. I wanted an excuse to hurt him as much as I was hurting." His throat bobbed. "And when Father ordered him chained in the tower, it was my guards who locked him up. Afterward, I tried to smooth it over, but neither Ty nor Father would listen." Quinton chuckled darkly. "I'm a disappointment to them both. And to you."

Seren heard the bruising self-loathing in his voice; it spoke to a tiny corner of herself. She'd pushed Tyberius away, too. If anything happened to him while he was with the Felinae, she'd never forgive herself for abandoning him.

His shoulders straightened before he pushed off the wall. He nodded toward the bustling street. "Don't repeat my mistakes. If you love him, keep him safe. Please."

"I—I'll try." She didn't know if was in love with Ty. She might be falling for him, and she took Quinton's words to heart. "I didn't mean to take him from you."

Quinton smiled wanly. "He was never mine to begin with."

Of course. Ty was his own person. And when this was all over, and if they weren't pretending to be lovers, would he choose her? Did she want him to?

At the street corner, she glanced back into the alley. "Keep an eye on Calvus Takkakus—he may be colluding with Regent Boreal to betray Imperator Moralis."

"Heads will roll if that is true." From the shadows, Quinton saluted her, fingers splayed in a V over his heart. "To the end, cousin."

———

A FEW STEPS from the alley, Seren's boots skidded along wet cobblestones and right into another figure in black leather who grabbed her. Her heart stuttered.

"*Lleufer*, what happened to you? Did the Sparker find you?"

Her hand rose to her face. It was scratched from hitting the wall. She met Thane's eyes, expecting derision at failing to capture their target. Instead, she found an irritated concern that sat awkwardly about him. His hold on her upper arms relaxed, and she pulled back even though sleeves covered her arms. Although her secrets seemed safe, Felinae hearing was another matter. Had Thane seen Quinton? Overheard their conversation?

"He got away," she lied on the off-chance Thane had seen her in the alleyway with Quinton. "Llion and the children?"

"Still in there. I couldn't get the bars off. But he ordered me to go find you when you didn't return." He ran a hand through his tousled, ashy hair. "You took off without—"

"Come on." Before Thane could question her further, she

ran down the hill to the iron-forger's, following the water line. Within a few steps, Thane fell in with her. The street in front of the house swarmed with those fighting the fire with sand and water and poles.

Seren weaved her way through the tumult. In her absence, the townsfolk and the fisherfolk had been busy. Those with pole hooks had pulled what was left of the burning overhang down and away from the elaborately wrought iron–hinged door that proclaimed the owner's skill. Others threw buckets of sand or water through the lower windows and on the door—but the intervals between buckets were too long.

Thane joined her near the window. "Why, for Goddess's sake, did Llewyn go in there?"

"He must have been trying to warn the iron-forger." Or to save the children.

It made sense that if Clan Llewyn was in trade with Ultima Thule, they would want items from the iron-forger. Regul must have been their contact. Somehow her uncle had learned of this arrangement and ordered the iron-forger's death and his house set ablaze. Perhaps Llion hadn't seen the dead man in the square.

With the area clear of burning debris, a group of townsfolk approached the door with a large tree trunk with the branches shorn off. One side had been carved out—probably, it was intended to be a water skiff. She got as close to the window as the blistering heat would allow. "Llion? They're breaking down the door!"

There was no answer. Smoke permeated the inside of the wooden house in a thick cloud, itself as deadly as the flame that burnt flesh and bone to ash. There was a boom as the impromptu battering ram hit the reinforced door, barely making a dent. Seren cursed under her breath.

"Hold up!" Thane called, running over to the group with a leather satchel she hadn't noticed until now. He began examining the hinges, being careful not to touch them. "The door's reinforced with iron. It will be faster to remove the hinges, if they haven't fused together." He retrieved a pair of long metal tongs from the satchel—Pater Regul's tools, she supposed.

The pins wouldn't budge, however, and Thane resorted to swinging a sledgehammer at the hinges. The clang of the iron hitting iron made Seren wince. Then a burly man almost the size of Llion stepped forward. In a couple of swings, he made quick work of Regul's smithing.

There were cheers of triumph as the door gave way under the battering ram. Clouds of thick smoke billowed out from the house, obscuring the view inside. Then flames lashed out, eager to snatch at anything that would burn. The villagers hollered into the house for the children by name, but no answer came. Seren exchanged a worried look with Thane before she added her voice to theirs.

The water line adjusted to throw water inside the door, but the water was coming slower now. A tall girl, in a blue wrap with a corded belt around her waist, waited for the bucket to come her way. Around her, townsfolk were leaving to go to the next home or shop in need of succor. No doubt the well was running low, too.

Closing her eyes, Seren strained her ears for sounds of the living inside the house, using all her concentration to filter out the surrounding din. Still, she couldn't hear anything but the crackle and hiss of fire. "I don't hear them."

Wiping the sweat from his forehead, Thane shook his head. Neither did he.

Time had run out. If Llion were alive, he'd most likely blacked out from the lack of air. Him and the children. She had one last idea, but it was a gamble.

Seren caught the tall girl's attention arm and whispered in her request. The girl nodded vigorously and then took off running. Mind made up, Seren made her way to the smoking doorway, Thane at her heels.

"I don't think anyone here would blame us for not going in," he murmured. "Honestly, it's in both our interests to let this be, Princess."

She faltered. The cold-hearted sentiment from Thane didn't surprise her. She'd rather not burn or die, either; and there was no love lost between him and Llion, though she didn't truly understand why.

Or did he mean it was to their advantage not to let Llion live?

True, Llion would be an obstacle between her and the princes, sworn as he was to protect them. But Thane still suspected her of duplicity—his latest theory being that she was planning on marrying Prince Alban to steal the Throne. This could be a trap for her. Furthermore, showing up before the regent and princes without the sealgair didn't seem wise.

"You're not scared, are you?" She managed a wry grin, ignoring any other meaning in his words. "It's no more dangerous than attempting a rescue from under the imperator's nose."

Thane pushed back his dark hair, dusted with ash and damp with sweat. "As I recall, we failed at that."

Tears pricked at the corner of her dry eyes. For once she wished they had rescued Dobhran and never ran into Sila. Maybe that's why she couldn't give up now. "The villagers may not blame us, but others would. Silver will hunt us to the far corners of the realm if we let Llion perish. Also, can you get us to the Throne from here?"

He sighed. "You make a sound argument."

"And I would blame myself." Her own words startled her, but they were true. And she had enough blame to carry already. "I convinced Llion to bring us here. It was my vision. This is my responsibility."

"You didn't make him enter that burning house."

"He risked his life for the children of his enemy. I respect that." It didn't make up for Gull Harbour, but it was something.

Thane asked no more questions. He intercepted a bucket of water from the line, which he placed at her feet. Stripping off his leather jacket and his shirt, he dunked the latter in the water and fashioned it over his mouth like a scarf. Then he put his jacket back on. Quickly, she followed suit, unconcerned in the desperate moment about displaying her scar. Her vest she handed to Yara, who had appeared at her side to wish them the blessings of the moon.

The crowd moved back for them. No one else volunteered to go in. Seren couldn't blame them. They'd already done more than she'd expected. Indeed, most of the townsfolk and fisherfolk were more concerned now with putting out the roof fire to stop it from spreading to other establishments.

"That vision you had while crossing the river here," Thane began, the words muffled through his soaked shirt. The heat intensified as they near the doorway, searing the air. "You didn't see us dying in here, did you?"

"It wasn't about Ultima." In all the mayhem since arriving, she'd forgotten. Somewhere, farther north, a Felinae clan was burning in a simultaneous attack. Her recent promise to Quinton aside, guilt for those she couldn't save tore at her heart. She couldn't help them, but she could help Llion and the children in this house.

"Well," he said, clapping her on the shoulder, "that's something, at least."

When she didn't recoil, his hand lingered there and his dark eyes, the only visible part of his face, softened. "Princess, there's no point in both of us dying in there. Listen for me. I may need you to yell insults at me so I can find my way out."

The last part was said with a smirk in his voice. Yet his selfless offer startled her, especially since he'd insinuated that they should leave Llion to die. But Thane couldn't do this by himself. Neither could she.

"You can't carry Llion and two children out by yourself, neither can I. We go in together."

Surprise flickered in his eyes before he inclined his head, but a shout from behind her made her look back.

"Mistressa! I found what you wanted!"

The girl had returned, coils of rope in her arms, the same as her belt.

————

THE HEAT WAS a hundred times hotter than she imagined Sol's hells to be.

Seren entered the house behind Thane, both of them tied together by the rope around their waists, the other end held by the girl outside. Two tradesmen had offered leather gloves so she and Thane could crawl on their hands and knees under the smoke. It stung her eyes, and she coughed despite the wet cloth of her shirt around her mouth. "Llion! Where are you?" she choked out.

From the dim light penetrating through the thick clouds, they must now be near the window where she'd last seen him. Water hit her as another bucket was emptied into the room; it evaporated into steam immediately.

"Sealgair?" Thane called. "Anyone?"

*If only my Felinae Inheritance was talking mind to mind instead of—*

Seren cursed her own dullness. "Stop moving. I'll use my Inheritance to find him."

Thane coughed. "Make it quick, Princess. It's hot."

Sending up a quick prayer to Lumina or Seline or both, she closed her eyes and searched for the light inside her. Right away, the temporal waters swirled, and it felt like her whole body was tingling. It wasn't as overwhelming as inside the Unkat Axstrida, but hopefully an echo of the stones' power was all she needed.

*Eye on hand, sift the sand.* Her palms burned. *I seek Llion Llewyn. Please,* she added, *his life and others are in danger.*

Most of the smoke vanished. The room was dark and damp, the air musty, and her feet sank into soft black earth. Three large barrels lined the far end, a tall pile of earth in front, and above them hung shelves of pickled fish and preserves. A root cellar of some sort. Was she anywhere near Llion and the children?

The mound near the centre barrel shook. Hope swelled in her heart as a glint of blond hair peeked through the dirt. That's where they were hiding from the flames.

She was about to leave the water to tell Thane to find the cellar, when up rose a child's face but with the proud nose she knew so well except it was straighter. His cheeks were softer and not as tanned. His hair was shorter and curled about his shoulders.

The spot between her shoulder blades burned—this was her Past Eye now. And this was Llion, but around the age of ten or twelve.

Seren gawked at the frightened young Llion in her vision, hiding in the dirt in some other house, some other fire. Although he was solemn and skinnier, he was the spitting image of the laughing child she'd seen hanging onto the queen's skirts. Her eldest son.

Seren's heart skipped a beat as the vision faded into smoke. "Found you, Your Highness."

## 36

Tonight, the sun god would have company as he disappeared under the watery horizon in a fiery blaze. Seren braced herself against the ship's railing as *Juakali* sailed toward the setting red orb. Around her, the largely Cartarchaan crew, in loose colourful tunics and billowy pantaloons of their land, went about their duties on deck and high in the lateen sails. Some humming a melody, as if they were singing the ship to sleep.

Though her bones ached with fatigue, slumber was the last thing on her mind. Since dragging an unconscious Llion out of the fire, the world had taken on a dream-like quality, including the timely arrival of Captain Halle and her two-masted vessel—courtesy of a message delivered by seabird during the night at Llion's bequest—to sail them north to the Throne.

A stooped sailor paused amid coiling rope to explain in Low Prim that the sky fire meant a favourable journey. The rich brown skin around his eyes crinkled as he smiled. She supposed he meant to reassure her, but it was too soon for Seren to take any comfort in Sol's flaming display. While the fire had been contained in Ultima, the wrapped dead, laid out

424

on the beach next to the burnt hulls of fishing boats, were a testament to her failure. Bundled in sheets or blankets, they waited for Lumina to ascend and carry their souls to their celestial rest. Perhaps to the Vale of Stars if Lumina deemed them brave and honourable.

It was some solace that the child and the Regul's apprentice had both survived, huddled with an unconscious Llion in the damp root cellar, away from the smoke and flames. Their guardian, however, hadn't been so fortunate; his body was indeed the one hanging in the town's square. *Justice* Quinton had called it for the betrayal of the republic. But she wasn't so certain it was.

She should be outraged that Pater Regul's blades, in the hands of Llion's Elusives, had spilled Prim blood. However, after Sila's death, she had no moral high ground left with which to blame the iron-forger. How she desperately burned to know Regul's reasons for aiding Clan Llewyn as much as her uncle's for condemning the iron-forger to death and Ultima Thule to the flame without trial.

One thing was clear to her: she wouldn't stand by and watch the Legion slaughter Clan Llewyn when the time came. Or gentle Vesper, who trusted her. Or even Thane or Kanta, and certainly not Ellus. At the thought of him, a strange yearning in her soul rose within her.

Lumina, she'd already killed once to protect him, and though her head knew it was all sorts of wrong, her soul accepted she would protect him with her blade again and again.

It was a disturbing realization. But it made her more determined to complete her mission by eliminating the princes and ending the war with as little bloodshed as possible.

Unless she could convince Prince Alban to parley? And he could convince his brother? But could she then persuade her uncle that a new accord of peace was the best path forward? His enmity for the Felinae after how Prince Devan had treated his sister ran deep. She shivered, remembering her pledge to seek vengeance on the Felinae. No, Uncle Tarquin would never forgive and forget the past.

But capturing Prince Alban, either personally or with the help of the Legion, to force a surrender of the Felinae no longer seemed possible, either. There was little chance that Llion, as sealgair or as prince, would surrender his dominion in exchange for his brother's release. He hadn't tried to negotiate for Dobhran's freedom; he'd simply gone in, sword-swinging, against the odds to save him. So he would do no less for his brother.

Seren sighed to the rippling water. Peace would need to be achieved by other means. In the grand scheme of the war, two lives were a small price to pay, weren't they?

*A small price for your honour?*

Seren shoved that unwelcomed thought away by focusing on her plan. First, she'd have to take care of Llion, the eldest living heir of Queen Ellowyne and King Lynus.

*Your cousin.*

From what she'd overheard, he was the greater threat than the crown prince. And all this time, he'd been right in front of her. The irony of it almost made her laugh. Who would've ever guessed the rough mercenary was of royal blood?

The polished wood bit into her clenched palms as her amusement faded as swiftly as it had come. She meant what she'd said to Thane. She respected Llion for risking his life for the iron-forger's wards. It shouldn't make her balk at the thought of ending his.

Somehow it did.

*But this is war*, she reminded herself. That he had saved two souls didn't wipe his blackened slate clean, not after condemning so many more to death in Gull Harbour and elsewhere. Just as saving the fisherfolk didn't absolve her of

Sila's or Dobhran's death. They were both still dead at her hand. Maybe there was no such thing as balancing the scales of life and death.

Moral quandaries aside, a warrior such as Llion would be a challenge for even a seasoned legionnaire, especially when she suspected many had died trying. Despite all her training for battle, Sila had been Seren's first kill. In the middle of Llion and Quinton's sword fight, with the threat to Ellus's life, she had reacted in the moment to protect him. The brutal ruthlessness of it still shocked her.

Of course, her Lyceum training had covered how to strike with deadly force, but not one instructor had explained the hollowness that would take up space inside her soul, a shackle of its own.

And two more shackles must be added. No matter the cost to herself.

And it had cost her something to free Dobhran of his mortal bonds. Some might argue her act had been merciful. Not her. There had been no mercy in her heart when she had taken it upon herself to be his executioner, just as Uncle Tarquin had decided Regul and Ultima Thule must pay.

*A burning for a burning.*

Seren pushed the grim comparison away, unwilling to face how much the Burner of Gull Harbour and the Burner of Ultima Thule might share in common.

Here, before the waves and the white motes that were the distant cliffs of Ultima, her resolve hardened. Capturing Prince Alban would not suffice. Llion would never surrender, never give up without a fight. She must assassinate the princes. If it meant ending the war—if it meant she and Tyberius could return to House Moralis, it was worth the cost to her soul.

The nobilis would toast her as *Seren Victoria*. Upon her arrival, laurels would be strewn in the streets. Uncle Tarquin would forgive all her broken oaths—Tyberius's, too.

The promising future vanished with the tang of copper on her tongue. She'd bitten through her lower lip. Blood, it all came down to blood—the blood that tied her to both the princes and House Moralis. The blood she'd already spilled. The blood she would yet spill.

Her empty stomach rumbled in concert with the choppy seawater, reminding her she had missed supper while she had collapsed, exhausted, in a vacated bunk. By now, the others must have already eaten, so she could slip below decks and avoid Llion a little longer.

Though everything still smelled like smoke, she caught the hint of something savoury and followed it below, through the narrow passageways.

"Ale not to your liking, Shade?"

The low voice with a melodic lilt dashed Seren's hopes of solitude, but her stomach and her curiosity propelled her onward. Silver had also called Llion by that name.

Through a broken knot in the wood bulkhead, she could glimpse the profile of a Cartarchaan woman in an indigo tunic, her black shoulder-length hair in tight braids, much in the same style of Llion's. She sat at a long plank table in a room so narrow, the benches touched either wall.

*Captain Halle.* They'd briefly met in the streets of Ultima, after she and Thane had hauled Llion out of the fire. The captain had arranged the rest, including the rowboat that had ferried them back to *Juakali.*

Across the table, Llion leaned back against the wall, his hulking size taking up most of the bench. Consciousness was an improvement from the last time she'd seen him. Yet he looked like he'd keel over without the support. The sleeves of a fresh emerald tunic were rolled up to his elbows, revealing his burns had been wrapped in strips of white cloth. The soot and ash had been washed from his sun-browned face, and his singed braids were tied back.

Had he heard her approach or scented her? She stank of smoke and burnt hair. But then, so did he. It was unlikely his nose would be able to distinguish such subtleties at the moment.

"My head already feels like I drained your last barrel," Llion rasped, pushing the mug in front of him away. "You don't know how good it is to see a friend. To see you, Halle."

"Then stay. It's been nearly ten years since you left *Juakali*," she chided.

"I was here trimming sails last summer, wasn't I?"

"Bah. A few days." She gave him a half-hearted scowl over the rim of the mug before taking a swig. "I never should have let you leave all those years ago in her company."

"I don't remember asking permission," Llion replied evenly. "And it wouldn't have changed my destiny. If Istra Boreal found me on the continent with Silver, she would have found me out at sea. This is my life now."

"*Hhmphf.*"

A glint of fire flashed in Llion's eyes as he pressed both his palms down on the table. "Don't ask me to regret my time with her. I regret too many decisions I've made." Before the woman could respond, he plowed on. "Speaking of regrets, do you know I had Tarquin Moralis's heir at the end of my sword? And I let him walk away." He pushed back from the table, disgust twisting his features. "My parents and sisters are dead because of Moralis—and now Dobhran is, too. I should've protected him better after Gull Harbour."

A black-brown, sea-roughened hand covered Llion's tanned, scarred one. "The sands of Cartarchaa whisper their wisdom to those with ears to hear. They say leave the dead to Death, for he alone can care for them. Turn toward the living while they still belong to you." Halle's fingers tightened over Llion's as she leaned farther over the table, voice lowered. "Revenge has never restored the dead to life. Only fed more bodies to the sands of Time."

The hollow places inside Seren's heart felt exposed to the light. It wasn't the same. She wasn't trying to bring anyone back. Certainly not her father. Her mission had started as a way to atone for her father's misdeeds—to prove herself worthy—and now it was essential she restored her and Ty's honour—which suddenly struck her as a completely selfish desire in light of the loved ones Llion had lost. And Ellus had lost his parents. And Vesper had lost her father, though there was still hope father and daughter could be reunited.

"I understand my responsibilities lie with the living, Halle. But can't a man grieve?"

A soft footstep sounded behind her. Seren whirled, hand going to her knife. Thane stood in the shadows of the passageway. Except for blood-shot eyes, he didn't look any worse for crawling through a fire. Like her, someone had lent him a tunic with a square-cut neck to replace their own burnt and smoky clothing. His was the colour of warm seas, while hers was the scarlet of solfire.

*Hungry?* he mouthed, rubbing his stomach.

Since she couldn't think of any other response, she nodded. Then he was entering the galley, stomping his boots to declare their arrival, before she could stop him.

"Seren missed supper," he tossed out in greeting before he slid in next to Captain Halle on the short bench. This must be where the captain and her mates dined.

There was no choice then but to follow and squeeze onto the end of the bench next to him. Sitting beside Llion was out of the question. If he suspected she knew the truth about him —well, she didn't want to be within easy reach. Though she half-wondered if that was the reason he'd been so intent on hurrying her out of the Unkat Axstrida. To stop her from learning how to use her Inheritance and from discovering who he truly was.

But she saved his life. That should make him less suspicious of her.

As she studied him over the plate of round flat bread Halle offered, his expression became inscrutable.

"There's *kpati* aplenty"—Halle lowered her voice—"but I wouldn't recommend it without the soup." She banged a fist on the back wall near a square flap of leather. "*Bakul mili*, Cook."

The flap opened to reveal a skinny, dour-faced man with a patch over one eye, his skin as dark as serendium, with grey touching his temples. Behind him was the galley. He muttered something in Cartarchaan to Halle, who said a few words in a conciliatory tone before he the disappeared with a *harrumph*.

Halle's deep brown eyes looked up at the ceiling, as though she prayed for patience, before her gaze settled on Seren. "You're the seer then?"

"I am," Seren replied warily. She half-expected Drakori to appear or Llion to call her a liar. But her scrying *had* led her to the eldest prince, twice. Once with his mother and brother, and once hiding in the cellar. And her vision of Ultima, wild or not, had come true as well.

"I'd like to hear how you saved Ultima Thule." Halle glared at Llion before he could protest. "From someone who was conscious."

Seren pressed her lips together, having no desire to relive it so soon. Whether it was her scowl or Thane's proximity to Captain Halle and her cutlass, which she'd taken out to shine on the table, he took up the tale, beginning with her vision of the fire. When he came to the part where they had crawled into the burning house after Llion, her palms began to sweat. After her vision of the child-Llion, the rest had been such a blur.

Vaguely, she remembered pulling Thane by the rope to the

trapdoor of the iron-forger's cellar. Of finding the children desperately trying to dig their way out with an unconscious Llion spread supine before them. Of carrying the young girl in her arms, while Thane took the youth on his back. Then, she and Thane had gone back in and together dragged Llion out by the arms, which was probably when most of his burns had occurred.

Two bowls of fish soup arrived through the flap—lukewarm but flavoursome—and Seren devoted herself to sopping it into her mouth with the kpati while Thane finished the tale. She was almost done the salty goodness when Halle's low whistle broke her reverie.

"I'd say many owe you both a debt of gratitude, including me for saving one of my former crew." Halle shot a long look at Llion which expressed her feelings on his reckless behaviour.

"I couldn't abandon them," he murmured, his back stiff.

Halle softened and something passed between the two of them. "I understand." The private moment over, the captain's attention swung back to them, her cutlass forgotten on the table. "If ever you need a haven, *Juakali* will welcome you both."

The captain's generosity underscored the absence of Llion's. Not a single word of appreciation had passed his lips yet. Maybe he considered it their duty as recruits to rescue him.

*Yes, but it was your cousin and his Crescents who put those children in danger.*

What was right, what was wrong—Lumina, it was all a jumble. Her stomach twisted at the reminder that the Crescent she and Thane had caught had escaped while most of the fisherfolk had been aiding the water line in town. Was that a good turn of events? It must be if it prevented Llion from learning of her uncle's true secret weapon—Primordians born with Inheritances.

"It was all Seren." Thane's voice sliced through her moral quagmire. "Any gratitude or boon should lie with her."

Smoke must have damaged her hearing because it sounded

like the Lockpick had praised her. "You were with me every step of the way."

"It was your vision that brought us there to help. Your vision that led us to find the cellar." He pointed at her with a piece of soggy kpati. "You were determined to rescue the sealgair. You saved those children."

"I thought all Prims deserved to die?" The absence of his unfailing scorn flustered her, and she wished he would snap something scathing back. Instead he stared into his bowl.

"You forget I've seen Gull Harbour through Dobhran's eyes," Thane murmured. "No one deserves death by flame."

Halle made a circle with her little finger and thumb and murmured a prayer to Sol, and after crawling through the burning iron-forger's house, Seren could imagine how torturous burning to death would be. "But you were against warning Ultima Thule."

He drained the last of his soup, then wiped his mouth with the back of his hand. "I was against walking into a trap with the Legion. First, and foremost, I am about saving my own skin. You should always remember that."

Of course.

"So who is responsible for Ultima's burning?" Halle asked.

"Not Elusives," Llion said firmly. "There were no familiar scents, and the Llewyn would not harm Ultima's citizens."

"That doesn't rule out another clan," Seren countered.

Thane muttered under his breath, pushing his empty bowl away. "It makes little sense for the Felinae to burn a source of trade except if they have no more need for supplies. If the Legion could be blamed, and the Felinae positioned as Ultima's saviour, it might go a long way to bring the coastal villages onto the Felinae's side." He looked pointedly at Llion. "Whoever could do that would gain favour among the clans."

By the Goddess, this was nearly the exact opposite of what had happened. But it wasn't unconvincing. The question was, why was Thane trying to throw suspicion on Llion and his own people?

"Who are you insinuating was behind this attack, Sionnach?" Llion's low voice made the hairs on her arms stand up and her body tense. Her hand crept down to Vindicta, and she wished she hadn't given her sword to the Llewyn.

"Burning is the Elusive way of doing things," Thane retorted before drinking the rest of his soup.

Moon above, if he kept this up, he'd goad Llion into a fight. Did Thane blame Llion for Gull Harbour, too? She frowned. Perhaps Llion wasn't the only one he was goading tonight. If she hadn't run into Quinton, she might've believed Thane's argument that this was some plot of the sealgair's.

"I learned of Ultima's fire the same way you did," Llion returned evenly. "Without Morningstar's vision, I wouldn't have been there."

With efficient briskness, Halle sent their bowls back through the flap, and now she pushed the mug of ale toward Thane. "A good thing you all were."

"There's only one group that benefits from eliminating Clan Llewyn's trade with Ultima and tarnishing the Felinae," Llion growled, his gaze fixed on her. "If the Legion isn't behind this, I'll cut my hair."

Seren kept her face expressionless, while her chest eased with relief that Llion didn't know about the existence of the Crescents.

But how could she have forgotten about the Legion and the traitor Calvus Takkakus? If Drakori was correct and Legatus Takkakus was in political bed with Regent Boreal, then destroying a Prim village that had been supplying a Felinae clan made little sense.

*Think who benefits, Seren*, Valera's voice chided her.

Regent Boreal knew who Llion truly was—Llion had said she found him on the continent. She must suspect that Clan

Llewyn and Lady Llewyn would support him over Boreal's chosen one, the crown prince. If Llion put himself forward for the Throne, the two princes would divide the strength of the clans. That made Llion a liability to the regent and crown prince.

The arrow attack outside the Wolvair den—it had been meant for Llion. Either to scare him or kill him. She was certain of it now. Wolvair was part of Boreal's cabal with Takkakus.

So was it a coincidence that Quinton and the Crescents were targeting Ultima Thule? Or had Legatus Takkakus leaked the information of the traitor Regul to Uncle Tarquin on behalf of Boreal, to orchestrate the attack on Ultima?

And what about the second attack? Was Boreal targeting her own clans, too? In light of Seren's second wild vision, it seemed more than likely that Takkakus also had a hand in this.

"You've gone pale." Thane peered at her from under thick lashes. "Was that what your other vision was about? The Legion?"

"Other vision?" Llion's scowl deepened.

Until now, she had forgotten about it, and she winced at the casual cruelty of that. "It was already too late."

Below the table, Seren's hands twisted around her wrists. Llion had to believe her. She didn't know why, except the horror of it was too great.

Halle's low but gentle voice led her back from the horror. "What did you see, seer?"

"It came upon me at Ultima's river, after you departed for the farms. It was a vision of the present. I had no forewarning of it."

There was nothing Llion could've done, but there was little chance he'd see it that way.

"No forewarning of what?" Llion growled.

Brought forth from the recesses of her mind, the vision unfurled in dreadful vividness.

"It happened before sunrise in a forest, far from here. Men and women and children lay asleep under blankets and furs. So cold." Her own hands were ice, and she paused, wanting to stay in this last peaceful moment. "Out of the pines and fog crept two figures carrying amphoras from which they poured what looked like oil over the carts and"—she shuddered—"over the huddled forms. A flint was struck, and the oil went up in a green flame, hotter than Sol's hells."

She closed her eyes, trying to banish the images of chaos that ensued—the faces twisted in agony and fear as the flames consumed them at an unnatural rate. Arrows hitting any who tried to escape. At Ultima, she hadn't the time to dwell on the vision. Now her soul screamed in horrified thrall.

There was a bang on the table, and she jumped in her seat. Llion's burning eyes fixed on her. "Were they the same figures in black you saw in your vision of Ultima?"

The lie wouldn't come. She owed him this much. "These were legionnaires."

Again, she closed her eyes, this time to avoid the accusation in his face. These legionnaires hadn't worn breastplate and pteruges, donning instead black tunics and leathers, but their distinctive sandalled boots had marked them. The same boots her uncle wore with the Legion's crest of laurels cradling crossed swords branded into the leather.

Bruising pressure on her neck had her eyes flying open. Two molten golden-brown eyes stared back. Llion's huge hands had latched onto her neck, like a hawk sinking its talons into its prey, and he yanked her toward him, across the table. Her knees hit the table, ale splashing everywhere, as she struggled to get them under her. Her lungs screamed for air, and she clawed at Llion's hands like a feral beast while his thumb pressed into that delicate hollow at the base of her throat. She gagged, and nearly blacked out.

Distantly, she heard shouting. Someone was beside her

with arms around her torso, supporting her weight. *Thane.* "Let her go!"

The room blurred and darkened. Ty was right about Llion looking for an excuse to get rid of her. If she had demanded Ty's presence with her—

"Let her go, Shade," Halle repeated, voice ringing with authority. The captain was but a hazy spot of indigo at the corner of Seren's vision, but the gleam of silver meant she had her cutlass in hand.

Slowly, the pressure eased up on Seren's shoulder and neck, and she forced herself to take a slow breath even though her body trembled with the pain of denied air.

"I should've let that rockslide bury you alive," Llion growled in her ear.

"Why . . . didn't . . . you?" she gasped.

"Boreal, Drakori, and the prince have plans for you." The gold flecks in his brown eyes sharpened into bright splinters. "Silver had the right of it—I've gone soft, depending on the soothsaying of old women. Drakori convinced them you are the key to saving us, that without you, we are doomed by the gods." An ocean of contempt flooded his voice. "Me? I think you may have doomed us already. If not, you'll be the downfall of my prince. If given time."

He wasn't wrong. Like a hooked fish, she twisted her body in an attempt to free herself.

"Shade, I've never known you to punish the messenger." Halle's voice was quietly furious. At some point, she had edged over to Llion, and her curved blade was poised under her former crew member's jaw. "And that's all this girl is. A messenger for the gods' and goddesses' dreams."

Llion's nostrils flared in disagreement, but his gaze never shifted away from Seren. "You would never use that on me, Halle."

"You're making it easier the longer you choke the life out of my guest and, may I remind you, your recruit."

"One you've sworn to protect," Thane gritted out. "Or was that all for show?"

"She broke that oath of protection when she bloodied her hands against us. But even if she hadn't, I'd damn myself to protect the crown prince."

*Because the prince is his brother.*

Llion's grip tightened, but then slackened; Seren inhaled as much as she could before it brought on a fit of coughing. Now that she could breathe somewhat, she let her hands fall away from Llion's corded wrists as if in surrender. Her left hand hung limply over Thane's arms, still around her waist, while the back of her right brushed the handle of Vindicta. If she reached outright for it, Llion would react to the threat accordingly. Halle was proving a powerful distraction, however.

"She saved you." Halle's voice had a desperate edge to it, though her sword arm did not waver. "You owe her a life debt, Shade."

Ellus had mentioned something about a life debt outside the walls of Luminaria.

"Saving me in Ultima makes us even for the rockslide. But another debt is owed me for the death of the unarmed man whose throat she slit while he was manacled in her uncle's torture room." Llion's lip curled, baring his teeth. "She's Dobhran's murderer, Halle. And if blood runs true, Tarquin Moralis's spy."

Her eyes fluttered shut. *He knew.* But did he have evidence?

He shook her. "Confess!"

Seren stayed limp, trusting that Thane would bear her weight. She didn't need to mimic her earlier dizziness—her head was throbbing, and her hands and feet were numb and cold from the lack of air. *Thane.* Had he stolen her secrets somehow?

When Llion loosened his grip, she couldn't stay silent. "I admit"—she reared up and spat in his face, drawing Vindicta from her holster—"only that the Burner of Gull Harbour deserved to die!"

She stabbed him in his unprotected forearm. A deranged howl bellowed out of him, yet the bastard didn't let go. The pressure on her neck increased, and black spots obscured half her vision. Before she lost all feeling in her fingers or blacked out, she had to pull her blade free and swing again.

Through the ringing in her ears, she heard Halle shouting and boots on the deck above. Suddenly, Vindicta jerked in her hand as her body sagged, and the knife was wrenched free. It clattered to the floor, her fingers too slow and stiff. She truly hung limply now in Llion's chokehold without Thane's support. Tears welled on her eyelashes. She was alone again.

A turquoise blob appeared next to Llion and placed a pale hand on Llion's wounded arm. "Let her go, or I'll rip all your bloody secrets out, Sealgair."

The harsh threat cut through the chaos, bringing everyone to a standstill.

"If you think you will live to utter them, Lock—"

*Crack.* The heavy pommel of Halle's cutlass struck the side of the Llion's head. His hands spasmed open, releasing Seren, and her knees buckled beneath her. As she fell face-forward, Thane caught her, and it was all she could do to hang on to him.

"Enough!" Halle put the sharp end back in Llion's face as he sank down on the bench, blinking. By all rights, he should be unconscious after that blow.

Seren closed her eyes against the onslaught of her strained senses, and her grip on the linen of Thane's sleeves tightened. This time it wasn't Uncle Tarquin's advice, nor Master Kai's maxim, that came to mind; it was the power—the life force—of the stones of the Unkat Axstrida. They had endured much in their ancient lives, and still they stood strong against the currents of Time. So would she.

She reached deep into her soul and found a well of strength she hadn't known existed before, and she slid off the table, away from Thane, to stand on her own before the wrath of a prince.

On the bench, Llion was looking less dazed by the second as well. "Whatever mission Dobhran may have executed at Gull Harbour, he did so at my command. It is I who am ultimately responsible. Now confess whose orders you follow."

"You," she croaked, her throat raw. Lumina and Lleufer, he had almost strangled her. The ringing in her ears had faded, and her vision had refocused. "You . . . are a murderer of hundreds."

"More than you know, Daughter of Morningstar."

It was justice, she decided. Justice from the goddess that the eldest prince deserved to die for the death on his hands. For all who lost their lives in Gull Harbour. He admitted it himself. He was the one responsible. He was the one who should pay the life debts for the massacre.

Maybe the scales of justice couldn't be balanced. But maybe this would tip them in the favour of the dead.

With numb fingers, Seren picked up Vindicta to clean the blade on her sleeve; the blood vanished into the crimson linen as did the shakiness in her legs. Her chin rose. "To avenge my honour and for the Prims who died at Gull Harbour, I invoke the rights and privileges of Aequitas, and I challenge you, Llion Llewyn, to the death."

## 37

U nder the pinkening edges of sunset's skirt, Halle's crew busied themselves about the rigging, their tunics bright splashes of turquoise, orange, and red against the yellowing lateen sails. Seren suspected it rarely took this many to retie tangled lines but that those aloft desired a good view of the duel. After Captain Halle had cleared the lower deck, there was enough open space between the main mast and the bowsprit for decent manoeuvring, though she'd have to watch out for the lines running from the deck to the sails and to the long yard that bent around the triangular sails like the fin of a fish.

While she walked the deck boards to get a feel of the space, Llion relaxed against the starboard railing. He looked damnably unconcerned, whereas Halle fumed beside him. Although the captain's cutlass remained sheathed, her tongue did not.

"Do you understand what you've agreed to?"

A noise of assent rumbled in his throat.

Of course, Llion must consider the match already won. A mercenary with his years of experience against an untried cadet who had pledged a mere month ago? When put like that, even Seren was hard-pressed to bet against him. The sword fight between Llion and Quinton returned to her in flashes. Despite his thigh wound, Llion's skill, strength, and reflexes had been in top form against his younger opponent. While she had observed Llion's technique, so had he seen her moondance. Had he discovered some weakness to exploit?

A seed of misgiving took root inside her. She'd spent most of her time at the Lyceum losing, and she had yet to win a match against Master Kai.

The chatter in the sails quieted. A lithe woman, with her hair wrapped in maroon cloth, approached the duo with a bundle of leather. Although the crew didn't wear uniforms, her tunic was dyed indigo and embroidered with geometric designs like Halle's. Constellations, Seren realized. The tunic and the woman's confident air singled her out as one of the ship's mates.

"Do you expect," Halle continued, glaring at Llion, "your brother will stomach your death because Primordian rules of honour permit it?"

Llion ignored the question in favour of the other woman, who unrolled the bundle on a nearby barrel to reveal Llion's armour and bracers, singed now in places. He took the bracers while she held his cuirass out to slip over his head. With practiced ease, the woman began buckling the sides, much to Halle's growing vexation.

Thane had already helped her with her bracers. After Llion had accepted her challenge, she had retired to her berth to prepare, and Thane had followed her—like he was doing now. Seren had swapped the loose crimson tunic, borrowed from Healer Nemia, with a silver-mesh undershirt from Silver. It was heavier than it looked, and out of curiosity, she had tested it against Vindicta's edge. Like armour ten times its weight, it had held its own. And she was grateful some of Halle's crew had retrieved her pack from where she and Thane had stashed them by the river. Over top of the undershirt went her leather vest, grimy with ash. Last, she had secured her belt and Vindicta on her hip.

"Quartermaster Kamari," Halle barked, finally acknowledging her second-in-command, "tell Shade this is madness."

Not madness. But a way out. Either Llion would die or she would. What was madness was expecting her or him to live on this ship with each other for the next week or so and not kill each other.

"Not for me or you to say, Captain." The quartermaster gave her regal head a solemn shake as she went about her work. "We each walk our own path. The gods end it when they want." A mischievous smile curved on her thin lips. "Unless my dear cousin Nemia tricks Death into waiting longer."

Seren followed Kamari's gaze to the young healer's kind, round brown face and soothing aquamarine floor-length tunic; she perched upon a pile of crates lashed to the side of the ship, and in her lap was her teak medicine box, which had been much depleted in her treatment of their party and the villagers before the ship set sail. If Nemia was in agreement with Halle, she didn't voice her thoughts; her hands, however, clutched the box's handle tighter as if she wished she didn't need to use it again so soon.

Like the craggy shoreline, weathering a spring tempest, Llion took Halle's admonishments in stride. He held his arms out at his sides as Kamari continued her work. The knife wound Seren had given him on his lower arm had been bandaged by Nemia; over top of it went his bracer, so that much of his bronzed skin, burned or otherwise, was now covered by leather or linen.

Halle crossed her arms, her mouth a mulish line. "And if you should kill her, Tarquin Moralis will have your head—"

"He'll have my head anyway, if he can."

"Your oath will be broken—"

*For moon's sake.*

"Aequitas is a sacred pact with the Goddess and supersedes any oath." The interruption earned Seren a scorching glare from Halle and the attention of the entire deck. But she couldn't let Halle talk Llion out of it. Nor did she wish to get into an argument about whether she had broken her oath first. "It allows House brothers and sisters to settle matters of honour without breaking their oath to their House. Even the lowest-ranked member of a House may challenge a patrius."

Halle's brown eyes narrowed to splinters. "This is my ship. Primordian laws have no foothold here. I doubt the regent will agree to Prim law overshadowing a Felinae oath. You needn't do this, Shade."

"By your objections, Halle, one might think you expect me to lose," Llion chided as Kamari resumed tying his bracers.

Good. He wasn't backing down, oath or not. Still, he was far too relaxed and confident for Seren's liking.

"Thoughts of failure don't hound our sealgair, do they?" Thane murmured from beside her, drawing her attention from the bickering. "Maybe choosing knives wasn't prudent."

Every one of her spare evenings in the last four years had been spent mastering what had turned out to be the ancient Felinae art of the moondance. And her unique knife was the sole weapon she'd practised with in the dance. While she was capable enough with a short sword—as Sila had unfortunately learned—she'd never come close to Quinton's skill. And he had barely kept pace with Llion.

"I have faith in this blade," she murmured, pulling it out to admire its one-of-a-kind beauty. The oddly shaped blade gleamed brightly, like moonlight forged into iron by a celestial blacksmith. Her gaze snagged on the glossy black M in the bone-white handle. The inlay wasn't onyx, she realized, but serendium. *Of the stars*. Like Llion's knife. Like the doors. Like the stones.

Something made her rotate her knife-hand until her father's unamkhara ring came into view. Her gut tightened at the sight of the serendium slashed circle on her finger.

*M.*

*Morningstar.*

All these years, she had assumed M was for Moralis and the giver, her uncle. But if the moondance was Felinae, then it followed that the knife she danced with was as well. But how could a dead man give her a knife?

With that question, the edges of her world began to fray. There was no hard evidence that Uncle Tarquin had been the giver of the knife. It had appeared by her beside with a note containing the address of Master Kai's schola, but it had been unsigned. The ascetic hadn't once referred to it or her uncle. Yet he'd smiled when she had unsheathed Vindicta, as if in recognition.

But if Uncle Tarquin hadn't left her Vindicta and sent her to Master Kai to train, who had? Who had prepared her for this day? Whose weapon was she?

Oblivious to Seren's shaken state, Halle made a sound of disgust in her throat to some comment of Llion's. "I should throw you both into the sea. If you enter this foolishness, one or both of you will die."

The argument seemed like it would continue until Thane stepped out from behind her, his dangerous hands tucked in his pockets. "It need not end in death, Captain. Both parties may agree upon a point of rule to decide the victor by first drawn blood."

Thane's detailed knowledge of the finer subtleties of Aequitas seized Seren's attention. When he had followed her to her cabin after she'd challenged Llion, they had discussed his role as her second, nothing further. Not his threat to steal

Llion's secrets, nor her recklessness in challenging Llion. She added his uncanny knowledge of Primordian society to a much-needed future conversation.

First blood, however, wouldn't suffice for her promise to Quinton. And her cousin had put his trust in her, even if Uncle Tarquin hadn't. The turmoil in her quieted. Prince Llion needed to die tonight, preferably regretting how he had underestimated her. Then she would be halfway to fulfilling her mission. Whether Uncle Tarquin had purposefully set her on this path or not, she was walking it now.

*To the end.*

But before she could demand death, Thane grabbed her by the elbow and pulled her to the prow. "*Now* you want him to die," he muttered.

He looked around up at the gawkers and made to sling an arm over her shoulders, in an effort for privacy, but then seemed to think better of it. Instead, he crossed his arms over his turquoise tunic. "Listen, Princess," he whispered into her ear. "You can't kill the bastard—not yet."

Her lip curled. "I can die trying."

"Where will that leave Secundo Attica? If you're dead, he'll do something reckless to avenge you and get himself killed. And if *you* kill the sealgair, the crown prince will retaliate against Attica, and then you and me. I'd rather not lose my head."

The thought of Ty at the whims of the Felinae prince—*Llion's brother*—chilled her.

Thane inclined his head. "And that's if Captain Halle doesn't first feed us to the ice serpents for killing Llion, whoever or whatever he is to her."

Solfire, her desire for revenge had clouded her thinking. Taking Llion out now would be short-sighted. The regent and the crown prince would never trust her afterward. And in Quinton's and Uncle Tarquin's eyes, leaving one prince alive would equal failure at best, betrayal at worst. But her breaking point was that Tyberius would be at the mercy of the younger prince. Who, if he was anything like her, would want revenge.

*We can't settle the debt for the dead—not with more death.* Ellus's words. Unfortunately, he wasn't the prince.

"As much as it pains me to say it, Sionnach, you're right."

He grinned. "Don't be so surprised, Princess. I told you I have no desire to die. Now don't let the bastard get his hands on you. He'll use his size and strength to his advantage. And we still want you to win."

She knew full well what Llion's hands could do; her neck reminded her at every turn, despite the balm Nemia had applied to it. For that alone, she owed him. A liver shot would be ample payback, but there wasn't a chance a skilled fighter like Llion would leave it unguarded. From the scuttlebutt amongst the sailors, she'd picked up that Llion had sailed with Captain Halle before Silver had lured him away to ply the trade of mercenary on the continent. And plied it he had for many years until he been summoned home to the Throne.

Thane returned to the neutral territory of the middle of the deck, and she followed. "Are we in agreement that Aequitas will be fulfilled when first blood is drawn?"

Llion nodded, his expression unreadable. Somewhat mollified, a sour Halle conferred with her quartermaster about the watch-keeping and crew. No one was to interfere in the sacred fight before the gods, by captain's orders. The sailors set about rolling up the sails and dropping anchors to slow their drift.

Meanwhile, a short, brawny sailor in orange had brought Llion a crate, in which the sealgair placed several daggers and knives from his person. From a loop on his belt, he withdrew his claw-like knife. This, he gave to Kamari, and Seren's gut tightened. If it sliced her anywhere, she'd probably bleed out before Nemia could apply pressure.

The same sailor then offered Seren the crate to secure her additional weapons. In it, she placed her dagger from her boot. Using or keeping any other weapons besides their chosen ones would break the rules and cause the match to be forfeited by the transgressor.

As her second, Thane carried Vindicta over for Kamari to inspect, and she handed him Llion's knife. With knives, the most common tampering would be poison. Not that a Prim would stoop so low. Poison was for those too weak to kill by hand or steel. It was said the Marked, however, used all manner of death, and Seren wouldn't put it past Llion.

Once the weapons cleared inspection, Thane approached with Vindicta, tossing it in the air, end over end, before he offered it to her hilt first. "What? Because you marked me that first time, I can't possibly have any skill?"

She scowled, her fingers slipping into the familiar grip. "I prefer thinking of you as an inept jackass, not a capable one." When he chuckled, she couldn't help but ask, "About being a jackass, you're doing a poor effort of it right now, Sionnach. Why?"

Thane's gaze travelled to Llion and Kamari, who had their heads bent together in discussion, then back to her. "Maybe you're not as awful as I thought. Lady Fortunata handed me a raw deal, truth be told. I suppose that's not any more my fault than it is yours." He shrugged, the sea breeze ruffling through his dark hair. "And maybe the future no longer looks so grim."

That was cryptic. However, it resonated with her own renewed sense of purpose.

"It's time." Llion's voice boomed across the deck, and the illusion of a hopeful future she'd been building faltered. This duel would let her know how easy or hard that future might be.

All chatter on the deck ceased as the sealgair took his position in front of the main mast. While the waters weren't rough, it was obvious he had his sea-legs under him. A definite advantage. However, he didn't have the benefit of a moondancer's tutelage.

Thane gave her a searching look before joining Kamari at the stairs to the quarterdeck. From there the captain and mates would watch.

Inhaling deeply, Seren cleared her mind. The ebb and flow of the waves rocked her through the balls of her feet, her knees flexing to compensate for the gentle roll until she could perceive the swirling currents in the dark teal waters below the hull. They called to her, like sirens of Time, and when she reached out with her Eyes, the roaring of Time's Flow returned with a flood of arcane power. It was but an echo of its strength at Unkat Axstrida; yet it engulfed her, body and soul, until it was tempting to forget Llion and follow it.

*Soon*, she promised. With that, the temporal waters receded, but she could still feel them pulsing lightly in her veins with each pump of her heart's flow. Strangely, it was a comfort to feel her Inheritance at the tips of her fingers, not that it could help her in this fight.

In the east, the first star of the night twinkled high in the sky above *Juakali*'s quarterdeck, where Halle stood, surveying her ship and crew under a baleful eye. Seren took her place across from Llion with the bowsprit to her back. In their wake, Lumina loomed, her darkening skirts sweeping across the sky. Behind Seren, into the west, Sol was sinking into a fiery red death below the gentle waves. Two celestial witnesses to mark their challenge: one for the victor, one for the defeated.

It was time.

Raising her knife, Seren locked onto Llion's burnished golden-brown eyes. At last she'd pit her training against the mightiest warrior the Felinae could muster. "Then let us dance under the stars, Llion Llewyn, and see who the Moon Goddess favours."

## 38

Every dance began the same. First, her feet followed one another in a swaying sidestep from side to side. Then her arms arced in protective sweeps, her grip on Vindicta light but firm. All to the beat of her heart. After years of practice, the familiar rhythms of the dance were as natural as the rising and falling of her chest. Her nerves settled into a focused calm, and soon the rest of the ship faded into obscurity.

Except for her opponent. He circled toward her on her left, his hands empty while the wicked, claw-like knife remained on his belt. A coiled ruthlessness had replaced his former nonchalance, and her pulse quickened as she kept the distance between them.

Lumina, she'd missed this. The way her body hummed in anticipation before the world was whittled down to her opponent and herself. A clarity of mind settled over her, turning colours brighter; scents of brine, blood, and sweat sharper; and the soft breath of her enemy as intimate as any lover's.

First blood or not, any fight with a weapon could end in

death, and only a fool thought themselves protected by such rules. If her bruised neck was any sign, Llion was out for revenge. And that made his attack less predictable. The unknown—the risk—enticed the darker part of her nature. Here, in the fight, she could be her true self. What she was trained to be—a weapon.

"Are we dancing or fighting, Seren of the Morningstars?"

In answer, she somersaulted forward into a high-sweeping crescent kick aimed at his face, which he leaned away from, and she immediately followed it with a low swipe at his legs with Vindicta.

The blade sliced through air. He'd leapt clean over it.

By the moon, he was faster than a man his size had a right to be. Before she danced out of reach, he moved in. Almost too late, she realized his hands weren't out to deliver a strike but to throw her down. A ground fight was one she couldn't hope to win against his size and strength.

She twisted away and kicked backward into his unguarded face, clipping his chin with her boot, and he let out a satisfying grunt. Yet the hit didn't faze him. She yelped as he stomped on the instep of her standing leg while pushing her backward, unbalancing her. Pain shot through her leg as she fell hard on her side. As soon as she hit the deck, she rolled. Too slowly, she feared. However, the searing pain of a knife cut didn't come, and she sprang back up to her feet.

Llion canted his head while working his scruffy jaw. "That all your moondancer taught you, Moralis? A few kicks and how to slit the throats of unarmed men?"

He still hadn't pulled his blade. The bastard was toying with her. It didn't escape her notice either that he was using her Prim name as an insult.

"Come closer, and we'll see." She slashed the air in front of her, from her shoulder down to her knees before curving back up to create the endless loop of Celestial Harmony.

Slowly, he moved in, his right forearm raised as a guard. "Why? Do you need me manacled, Moralis?"

Her temper flared. "Are you"—a lightning-quick jab whistled by her ear as she dodged the strike—"offering?"

Another lightning strike. Then another. It was all she could do to dodge and breathe. All with his right, which wasn't his knife hand. In his demonstrations with Silver, he had favoured the reverse stance, which would've made fighting him in an orthodox Prim stance more challenging. Not so for the Moondance. On his next jab, she saw her opening. While his right arm extended past where her head was a moment ago, she dropped her hands to the ground in Half-Moon Over Sunrise and rotated so her right foot exploded toward his unprotected liver. It wasn't a mistake she thought a seasoned warrior like him would make.

Her foot connected under his ribs, but she might as well have been kicking a stone wall. He staggered but didn't drop like he should've. *Solfire.* He must have avoided the full impact by twisting away at the last moment. Still, from the force that reverberated through her leg, she'd done some damage. Not that there was time to celebrate. As her legs spun down, Llion punched her unguarded abdomen. All the air whooshed out of her as the harrowing pain exploded through her. Next thing she knew, she lay crumpled on the hard deck, her body curled inward to protect herself.

*Just like before.*

White light flashed behind her closed eyes—and she could feel clammy phantom hands on her neck, tangling in her hair and dragging her back into the dark alley of her past. From under a hood, Joren's cruel face swam before her as she listened for the heavy fall of boots and waited for the kicks to begin, phantom or otherwise.

"Do you forfeit, Moralis?" The words came from Joren's twisted lips, but the voice was a faint echo of Llion's.

*I thought for every hit your opponents land, you make them hurt. They might win the match, but they don't beat you.*

These crystal tones in her head, however, sounded like Ellus, the words infused with his familiar warmth and quiet confidence. But that was wishful thinking. He was miles away.

But even if her own mind was conjuring his voice, it was enough to shake off the old terror that caged her. Seren reached deep inside—not for the warrior Master Kai had crafted her into, but for the power Ellus had seen as unquestionably hers. She opened her eyes—all of them—to fight back.

Although her lungs spasmed for air, all her Eyes along with every nerve in her body tingled, and she reared up, slashing with a cold, murderous fury that had been building in her since that night four years ago. Llion met her storm of strikes head on, parrying them away with his right arm, his bracers taking the brunt of her blade. As she struck, she saw a phantom of his movements in less than a heartbeat before they came—she saw herself drawing first blood—she saw him drawing first blood. Too many futures overlaid the present, and she couldn't sort the actual attacks from the phantom ones.

A half of breath too late, she realized her mistake. She'd left her torso pathetically open for a blow to the lower right ribs and her liver. There was an audible crack when his fist made contact—

In the throbbing dark, her cheek lay against something rough and hard. She'd lost consciousness, but for how long? Brine and lime oil scented the air, along with the sour stench of vomit. Her entire body was in agony, and she felt like retching with each wheezing gasp. Death probably hurt less.

*Life births pain. The end of one is the end of the other. Embrace them both and rise stronger for it.*

They were the words Master Kai had written in the sand for her on the first evening she stumbled into his one-room schola, her ribs wrapped but still aching and Vindicta on her belt.

As the blackness faded into browns of the ship, blurry boots approached and her mind sharpened. That the pain hadn't ended yet was good. It meant she wasn't dead yet. Nor was the challenge over. Thane and Kamari would've rung the bell if Llion had spilled her blood. It was clear he was avoiding areas likely to bleed, such as her nose and mouth.

The reason was a bucket of ice water: Llion didn't just want to win. He wanted to hurt her. Slowly and painfully. Perhaps, he thought to teach her a lesson.

It was a game she was more than willing to play.

Above where she lay on the deck, the mast creaked as the rising wind whipped the sails and the escaped strands of her hair. Salty spray from over the prow hit her in the face as she forced her body up to her knees, then her feet. Though her bruised abdomen protested each step, a moving target was harder to hit. Even a slow one. She started her swing step, trying to return to the proper state of awareness.

With his hands curled at his sides like beefy mallets ready to wallop her some more, Llion stalked forward, backing her toward the starboard railing. His lower face was swelling, and she detected a hitch in his breathing. Maybe he was done playing. Yet his knife remained on his left side for a same-hand draw.

She scanned him for any vulnerability. Very little of his upper body was unprotected, thanks to his cuirass and bracers. She could continue to kick at his face, or she could slice at his exposed areas or stab through his trousers. But so far, he'd evaded her blade. She considered throwing Vindicta into his thick upper leg. But with his preternatural quickness, he'd dodge it, and she'd lose her only weapon.

Her true strength was in her legs, but her kicks left her open to takedowns. If he pinned her, she'd be at the mercy of his fists, and the fight would end in his favour. Unless she could draw blood before he locked her into a hold she couldn't retaliate from.

When her heel thudded against the gunwale behind her, Llion drew his wicked-looking knife. "Confess you're working for Tarquin Moralis. Let this farce be over."

She couldn't swallow her bitter laugh. It was a question she could no longer answer. Yet part of her longed to rub it in Llion's face, that he'd failed so miserably to uncover her treachery. And part of her yearned to unburden the heaviness of her mounting secrets. But she needed to reach the Felinae Throne and meet the crown prince—and, as Thane had pointed out, preferably not in chains.

Seren slashed at him, more to keep his attention on her knife and not on her feet. "If you want to hear a confession, confess your own secrets, Llion."

His nostrils flared, and she bet he was wondering how much she knew. "You've fooled Ellusander and others with your act, but you don't fool me. It was your plan all along to kill Dobhran—that's why you volunteered to go."

The thought of Ellus loathing her when her mission was completed pained her. Unless she could convince him that accepting the republic's rule would bring peace and prosperity to his people. Perhaps, if the Felinae used their Inheritances for the good of the republic, then all Primordians would see their worth.

See her worth. Like Ellus did.

"Dobhran begged for death," she said evenly. It was the truth.

"Liar," Llion snarled.

Her heart pounded in her ears, and she flushed. *Hypocrite.*

"Your entire life is a lie, *Sealgair*. How many know the truth of who you are? Or what you do? Not even your marriage is free from deceit, I suspect. Or does Lady Llewyn close her eyes to your indiscretions?"

He shuttered his features, but not quickly enough to hide a flash of guilt. "Every word from your mouth is poison. I suppose you learned that from your mother. Did Tarquin send you to seduce Prince Alban like he bade his sister ruin Prince Morningstar?"

For half a breath, she couldn't believe her ears. Forget Aequitas or her mission. She'd cut out his tongue and then his heart. It was Morningstar who had ruined her mother's life and hers.

With a howl of rage, Seren slashed again on his left, high—and he dodged by sliding to his right and closer to her left leg. Just where she wanted him. Her foot spun out from her crouched position, and, as it connected solidly with his recent thigh wound, eliciting a grimace.

But his free hand grabbed her leg and pulled her in close, his claw-like knife swinging around for her neck. She had nowhere to go. Desperately, she raised Vindicta. Blade met blade in a resounding crash. Her arm trembled at the impact. Then, in a blink, the resistance gave way as tiny black shards peppered her face and arms with stings.

Vindicta had shattered his serendium blade.

Llion's roar spurred her into action. Still in his grip, she leaned back to drive her knife below his cuirass, but he punched her in the shoulder. The solid hit reverberated down her bones, and she lost all feeling in her knife arm. Somehow she held onto Vindicta, but her arm hung uselessly at her side and Llion still had her clinched to him by the opposite knee.

A tingle in her palms warned her of the coming headbutt. With her left hand, she punched him in the throat, and his eyes bulged. Without missing a beat, he changed tactics and grabbed her other leg to take her off her feet.

She had less than a breath to turn her position around. Using his hold of her legs as leverage, she squeezed her battered abdominal muscles in an excruciating upward crunch while plucking Vindicta from her useless hand to slice at his jugular.

He shoved her off before her blade could touch him. Someone—her?—howled like a deranged beast. Then her back hit the deck. A war hammer to the spine would've hurt less. *Roll away,* she ordered her body. It refused. Instead, she gasped for breath on the deck like the day's catch while saltwater ran down her cheeks, finding each tiny scratch to kiss.

"I am . . . not . . . my mother."

A shadow fell over her. Instead of the gloat of victory, Llion's eyes brimmed with fresh anguish, his chest heaving. "Maybe not. She killed a prince with her lies, not her hands. I won't let you have the chance for either."

The Eye on her back tingled, and she nearly wept anew—she couldn't afford a wild vision right now. Time's Flow slipped around her, tugging her toward something, a small current in the past.

*Llion, as a young boy, running through a dark wood with a bundled baby held protectively in his arms.*

She blinked at the insight. "You care more about your brother than your own honour or life. But you cannot protect the crown prince from every shadow."

Her forehead tingled, and the silhouette of a needle appeared in her mind, like she had foreseen in the cavern. But why?

"I can protect him from you." His confidence chilled her and made her think of the needle again. Did Llion carry a second weapon, against the rules? That must be it. And she understood he would rather kill her dishonourably now than risk her as a threat to his brother. A part of her envied the fierceness of that love. But she wouldn't die for it.

A wild grin split her face. "Are you so certain of that, Prince?"

At the tingling of her palms, she rolled out of the way, a

hair's breadth before Llion drove a needlepoint dagger into the deck where her heart had been.

Distantly, she heard shouts of outrage and alarm from the quarterdeck. But her attention was stolen by a rogue swell rising over the bow of *Juakali* and blocking out the stars. Seren scrabbled to her feet as Llion wrenched his dagger free, his back to the danger. Some believed Lumina ruled the oceans as well as the skies and earth. If so, the goddess was on her side.

The bowsprit sank sharply downward into the swell, and Llion turned on unbalanced legs. This was her chance. She charged. Right before the wave crashed over the deck, she dropped to the wet deck and slid feet first into him. The wave crashed over them both as he went down, and then she lost sight of him in the deluge. The undertow tossed her back and forth, and Vindicta was ripped from her hand. She kicked, trying to make headway toward the sail; she had to grab it or the yard—something, anything—before she was swept out to sea.

The ship burst out of the swell, and Seren hit the deck again, gasping for breath while sailors shouted in the background. Had Llion been flung over? She had to find Vindicta, but she could barely move. Salt water dripped down her face and into her mouth as she scanned the soaked deck, now in disarray. A few feet away, in a tangled pile of rope, something glinted. *Vindicta*. On her elbows, she dragged herself forward.

Her fingers brushed the handle just as a heavy weight landed on her back. In a blink, Llion had her left arm pinned behind her at an excruciating angle while he reached to pluck Vindicta from her shaky grasp.

It was over. He would slit her throat here on the deck. In his eyes, a fitting death for the murderer of Dobhran. She could already see the blood pooling out around her.

Time was over.

No sooner than she thought it, everything around her slowed to a snail's crawl—the sweat on her brow, the flapping of the sails, the scrambling of the crew. All grains of sand falling through an elongated hourglass. Was this how Vesper moved through the world? Everything else so much slower than herself?

It was as if she were a gull in the wind, gazing down at *Juakali*. Sort of like when she had floated away at the end of her father's execution. Dusk had well and truly fallen; the stars—or bits of Lumina's sister goddess—regarded them from above, unblinking. Up in the lines and on the deck below, the drenched sailors were rooted in place, in the middle of their tasks to put the ship to rights. The bell should be ringing to end the duel. She soared closer to the quarterdeck where a trio of figures gathered, their clothes dripping and plastered to them. Captain Halle, Kamari, and Thane were as still as the marble statues in her uncle's gallery, all in different poses: Halle, in the middle of drawing her cutlass; Kamari, with the bell raised in one hand, her mouth open; and Thane, with one leg over the railing as if coming to her aid.

It was a comforting notion, but the feeling was a distant echo. She would've liked to see those she cared for one last time before she died. A feeling of grief pressed against her, but again it was fleeting and muted and so very far away. She swooped back around the deck, having time now to note the colour variances in the amber teak planks, until she came to where a motionless Llion still straddled her back, her knife in his hand, frozen in the present.

Part of her still resided in that flesh. There was no more fear, however. No more pain of the living. It had to mean she was on the other side. Whatever came before the Vale. Absently, she wondered what Master Kai would think of the release of her soul before death. Of her Inheritance. Of the moondance being a sacred Felinae martial art. Of her knife belonging to her father. Of her failed mission.

Would this moment stretch forever?

There was a soft knocking at the back of her mind, and she could feel the presence of Drakori hovering outside.

*Taibhseir, are we dead?*

Her question seemed to invite the presence inside, and Drakori's brisk but kind voice unfurled around her. *Time's Flow exists outside of death and life, Thrice-Marked. So no, neither of us is dead, but if you stay here, neither will you live.*

She was so tired. *Life is . . . painful.*

*Life is feeling, child. Pain is but one of those sensations. Here in the temporal nothing exists. It's merely an assemblage of what was and what may be. It is not the place for you. Not yet. You must have the courage to choose life.*

*I cannot linger, but make no mistake, if you stay here, out of Time, it is still a choice, and your absence will cause ripples that will affect the future. Yours and many others. If the children of the moons are to fulfill their destiny, you must thread the needle.*

Then, like mist in the morning sun, Drakori's ethereal presence faded, leaving nothing but a hollowness and another vague hint about the future. It was similar to the one Seren had heard from her nursemaid, Nomi. Something about a warrior, a philosopher, and a strategist walking by her side . . . A warrior who wanted a return to bloodshed.

Seren hovered in front of Llion's hardened visage, considering his future with detachment. He would rouse the Felinae to fight tooth and nail against the Legion and her uncle. He would never surrender to a man he loathed, nor would he give her family any quarter. The Legion would slay clan after clan.

Still, it was tempting to stay in this endless moment, without fear and pain, without joy or love, strife or grief.

But it would not stop those she cared about from

experiencing those emotions. Here, she could protect no one. And she very much had to protect someone, her soul was urging her. Many someones.

With a roar, the temporal moment broke.

A sharp pain seared her scalp. It distracted her from the stabbing ache in her chest caused by the crushing weight on her back. Llion's fist tangled in her loosened braid, wrenching her head back to press Vindicta's cold steel under her chin. His lips brushed her ear. "You can't hurt him if you're dead."

Neither could Llion hurt anyone else if he were dead. It appeared she and Llion both suffered from the same logic. A bitter laugh tried to escape, but her breath hitched on her injured ribs, the motion sending another explosion of agony through her. *Focus on breathing*, she told herself. *It's no worse than a wild vision. No worse than what Joren did to you. You survived that. You'll survive this.*

"You think me honourless," she spat. "But you are far less honourable than me, Prince." She didn't dare struggle in Llion's grip. Yet she refused to give up. There must be a way. Her cracked fingernails dug into the deck boards to brace herself. Under them, something smooth, hard, and thin rolled. A forgotten bone-white fishing needle whittled to a nasty point.

*Thread the needle.* Seren didn't think this was what Drakori had in mind, however.

In the distance, a bell clanged and there was more shouting. Thane, Kamari, Captain Halle—someone would intervene before he killed her, wouldn't they? He had a second weapon; he had broken he rules of Aequitas.

"Stay back," Llion warned anyone foolish enough to stop him this time. "I am within my right to dispatch threats to the Throne as I see fit. That's an order, Captain Halle, that as a privateer for the Felinae Dominion, you and your crew must obey."

The bastard wasn't even bringing her to the Throne for a

trial. That sealed her decision. It was a dirty manoeuvre, but if it was her life or his, she picked herself.

"You'll regret this, Llion." Halle's firm and sorrowful voice rose above the din, from not too far away.

"Horseshit. He's broken the rules of Aequitas," Thane yelled from somewhere closer than the quarterdeck. But there was no movement. He wasn't going to—or couldn't—save her this time.

Seren's grip on the long bone needle tightened, as did Llion's hold on her hair. Last chance. "Are you prepared to murder every Primordian in Luminaria to keep him safe?"

"Only the ones I must. Confess or die, traitor."

Before she could hesitate, Seren threw her left hand with the needle back over her shoulder. It sank into something soft and yielding.

A high-pitched cry curdled the air, and Llion dropped her and the knife. She didn't look, just scrabbled forward to grab the blade.

As she turned to defend herself, the weight of a mountain landed on her bruised ribs, and her vision went spotty with the pain. He easily pinned both her wrists to the deck. Her fingers spasmed around Vindicta under the strain.

"Are you so certain that I am the sole threat to your brother, Prince?" It was the last tactic she had to play, but she had to persuade him not to kill her. "Killing me seems *short-sighted*."

Some of his braids had come loose in the tussle, and they dangled down around her in a wet curtain. Blood mixed with tears streamed down his face from his left eye—or what was left of it. The needle stuck out of his ruined golden-brown iris. The sight froze her in place.

"Ellus, is he safe?" he barked. "Tell me what you've seen."

The non sequitur flummoxed her. "Why wouldn't Ellus be safe?"

A tremor wracked through Llion's arms. "Which clan did your uncle and the Legion murder while we were saving Prim lives in Ultima?" He bent the wrist of her knife hand over her head at a tortuous angle, and she gasped. "Was it the Llewyn?"

Vindicta slipped from her numb fingers. "I told you I didn't recognize the clan. But call me a liar again. I dare you."

He chuckled mirthlessly, as if she hadn't taken an eye from him and threatened to take the other, and gathered her wrists together so he could pin her with one hand. Her injuries were catching up with her, and the violent cramping in her gut threatened to pull her under. Above, the sails and stars spun around in a dizzying swirl on the rough sea.

It stopped when the sharp end of Vindicta tilted her chin up, exposing her throat.

She glared up at his one good golden-brown eye. It wasn't supposed to end this way. Would everyone on board *Juakali* —including Thane—truly watch while Llion slit her throat?

"Is this your revenge for the death of your friend? You'll kill me for Dobhran and for whatever future deeds I might commit against your brother?"

"Revenge," he said, so softly it chilled her blood. "That's why you're here. Revenge for the blood that runs in your veins and gifts you a kernel of divinity. But it's not our blood that taints us, Princess. It is our souls that are blackened by the evils we inflict on others. On those we love and those we harm to protect them."

Her heart thumped wildly at the unpleasant awareness that she wasn't that different from the monster above her. Because of Sila. Because she had to live to protect Ty from Llion's wrath.

She gritted her teeth. But they weren't the same either. "I'm here because Devan Morningstar ruined my life and disgraced our House."

"According to Tarquin and Adalyn Moralis." He flicked that topic away. "Where's the Legion hiding? Which clan did they attack? Who is next?"

"I—I don't know." Three pitiful words but the truth.

Doubt crept inside her as she shivered in her wet clothes in the cool night air—or maybe that was the familiar searing pain with every breath. Tyberius was safe. Ellus, everyone. They had to be. *Please, Lumina.*

Then the coldness of the blade was gone. Back on his feet, Llion held Vindicta up in the air, the tip of Vindicta stained red with her blood. Aequitas was over.

She'd lost.

But lived.

Dizziness overcame her. Maybe they'd both lost. They'd both broken their oaths to Aequitas—and to each other.

"You found me in the house." He turned his head to the side; a few loose braids concealed his harsh features. "You will find him."

"Him who?" His brother or Ellus?

Llion staggered over to a barrel to sit. His swollen, ruinous face was barely recognizable, but he waved Nemia off toward where Seren lay on the deck under the stars. So many stars.

Captain Halle was nowhere to be seen. The crew had disappeared from the rigging, and none loitered on deck except for a damp Kamari and Thane, both looking at each other intensely.

"Thane?"

Kamari didn't bat an eye as she lowered her cutlass from Thane's chest. Once free, he strode toward Seren, eyes widening, she supposed, at her sorry state.

On the other side of her, Nemia knelt with her box of supplies, her face composed except for a sad tug at the corner of her mouth.

"Cracked ribs, right side," Seren gasped. The pain was coming on stronger now that she'd survived the fight.

The healer nodded but continued her gentle inspection of Seren's body.

Out of the corner of her eye, she saw Kamari cleaning the

blood around Llion's eye. She felt no remorse—he had tried to kill her. And probably would try again once he was done with her Seersight.

"Use your Eye to find Lady Llewyn and the other recruits," Llion ordered, his speech slurred from the swelling of his jaw. "Just because you didn't see them in your vision doesn't mean the Legion didn't also attack Clan Llewyn. For your sake, they'd best be alive when we reach Caisteal Dìomhair."

Dread overtook her. Frantically, she reached for the roaring waters, Llion's threat barely registering. Lumina, she should've checked to be certain. There might've been multiple planned attacks. How could she have assumed them safe because of one vision?

Arguing voices rose around her, Nemia's gentle but firm one joining in with Thane's acerbic tone against Llion. Something about tending to injuries first. That she needed rest.

But right then, it wasn't Seren's body that was in agony. It was her heart.

## 39

Footsteps dogged Seren as she burst out onto the main deck and into the cool night air. Whoever it was, she didn't feel like answering questions or being ordered back to her berth. The honey-lavender tea Nemia had prepared for her had soothed her injured throat, but it still hurt to speak and move. Cracked ribs, no matter how well wrapped, were not healed in a few days.

At this hour, the deck was empty save the lookout at the top of the mast and a few sailors in the navigator's room. Ignoring her aches and pains, Seren hurried toward the prow of the ship where she might steal a moment of fresh air to herself. The frequent scrying had drained her, but it had been all she could do while her corporeal body healed in bed.

Yet she'd failed to find any of the clans—in the present or the future. The trip to Unkat Axstrida had been a waste; Time's Flow seemed to only show her what it chose. The power that had once thrummed at her fingertips now lay silent. In desperation, she had tried to reach out through the temporal plane to Drakori and Ellus. All her efforts, however, were in vain. Neither answered, and it seemed like she had imagined the entire exchange with the taibhseir during Aequitas.

Ducking under a line, Seren shuttered all thoughts on the matter. She couldn't bear to contemplate any other reason they might not respond. In the morning, she would try again. Maybe she'd have something to report to Llion by tomorrow night. Each time she informed him of her failure, she expected his temper to ignite again. But since Aequitas, Llion had retreated within himself. It was difficult to say if he believed her reports as he spoke to her as little as possible. Undoubtedly, he was regretting sparing her life. By ordering all non-crew members to quarters after the duel, Captain Halle had probably saved Seren from further interrogation or a less hospitable confinement. So Seren was appreciative. But one could only stay inside a box of a room for so long.

The deck pitched downward—the sea had become rougher the farther north they sailed—and she tripped on the steps going up to the forecastle. Despite Nemia's expert wrapping, pain shot through her chest, and a hiss escaped her lips. From experience, Seren knew her ribs would be sore for weeks. By the time she righted herself, her follower was upon her, and his familiar scent of dry leaves and a whiff of smoke betrayed him.

She had seen little of Thane since the duel. He hadn't stopped the duel once it was clear the sealgair had violated the rules of Aequitas. Part of her irrationally held it against him, even though he'd been at the sharp end of a cutlass. But the implicit threat of the Lockpick's presence might just be enough to keep Llion away from her for the rest of the voyage. A prince in hiding must have many secrets to protect, especially if those around him were planning to usurp the crown prince.

As she turned to confront him, Thane reared back from her knife, raising those devastating hands in the air. "Truce, Princess. I'm not here to fight you."

The ship blurred before her, and she fought to keep her balance on the top step. A hazy memory surfaced of Halle ordering him out of her cabin. Yet she was certain he had extracted a promise from the captain that Seren wouldn't be left alone in her vulnerable state. And for the last three days, whenever Seren had come out of a failed scrying or woke from a fitful sleep, the kind-faced Nemia had been there to tend her injuries or offer a cup of tea.

"Then why are you here, Lockpick?"

"You look like hell." At her scowl, he paused, and she sheathed her knife, all too aware of how battered and bruised she felt. "I think you've overused your Inheritance. I bet that's why it's not working. You had visions at the Unkat Axstrida. Then at Ultima. And maybe during Aequitas?"

Using her Inheritance certainly hadn't felt like this at the Unkat Axstrida. The sunken pit had been a bottomless reservoir of temporal water. But then she hadn't scried for days there. And maybe the stones had amplified her Inheritance and her strength. As for scrying during Aequitas, she didn't want to talk about her temporal walk with Drakori, or the way she could sometimes see Llion's moves before they happened.

"I need fresh air, that's all." It came out as a hoarse whisper. They both knew what went unsaid. She needed to find them. Ty. Ellus. Vesper. Kanta. Even Lady Llewyn and Taibhseir Drakori. She needed to know if they had suffered a similar fate as that of the unknown clan.

"You need to sleep, or you won't be able to help anyone."

She knew that, but how could she rest? A noise of exasperation escaped her. "You nag worse than my third nursemaid, Sionnach. And I slept this afternoon."

If falling asleep sitting up while drinking a cup of tea counted as a nap. Besides, if she returned to her bunk, her mind would start searching the temporal waters again. Not because Llion had ordered her to scry for all the clans, but because she felt responsible for their lives after the deaths in her wild vision. If she had seen it sooner, maybe Llion could have sent a bird to warn them. Something. Anything.

"I can't sleep either," he admitted. Did the Lockpick have bad dreams, too? "Mind if I join you?"

She shrugged, too tired to protest him following her onto the deserted forecastle and secretly glad to have the company. *His* company. Nemia was kind but reticent around Seren, and as furious as Halle was with Llion, an aloof distance had grown between the captain and her guests. At the prow, Seren leaned over and inhaled the briny wind. Spray from the waves misted the air, the water taunting her failed efforts in Time's Flow.

Thane leaned back against the railing, his turquoise tunic several shades lighter against the dark blue-green of the rolling sea behind him. "Inheritances. You would think it would make our lives better to be touched by the Goddess." He scoffed. "More like we're marked for cruel punishment."

Her mouth quirked upward at the side. "I didn't need an Inheritance to mark me for that."

But his complaint was not without merit. Ty had said something similar—that she would be ill-used for her gift. Llion had ordered her to locate the clans—which she was willing to do—but what might Regent Boreal ask her to scry for? She didn't care to imagine what the punishment would be for refusing to do as the Throne ordered, or for failing.

Her gaze fell to Thane's pale hands, gripping the wood on either side of him. A Lockpick would be adept at interrogating subjects, gleaning their secrets in a blink of an eye.

She shuddered at the remembrance of his hand on Dobhran. "How many hearts have you picked?"

He flinched and turned to face the ocean. "Despite everyone's revulsion of me, I'm not a pervert who desires people's sordid secrets."

"I didn't mean it like that." It dawned on her that other

Felinae must have shunned him because of his Inheritance. "I thought maybe Llion had ordered you to do it."

"Like he ordered you to scry?" Moonlight reflected off the top of his dark locks while the wind tossed them about. He snorted. "Ever since Istra Boreal foisted me on him, he's wanted nothing to do with me. I think you know why."

It wasn't a direct answer, but she let it go.

Her hand strayed to her bruised throat. "I won't forget how you stood up to him for me."

One of Thane's shoulders crept upward in an uncomfortable half-shrug, like what he had done for her had been nothing. Maybe he had only been driven by his own dislike of the sealgair. But she didn't think so.

"Is stealing secrets as exhausting as scrying?" Her bones felt hollow, her body devoid of substance, as if the life had been scooped out of her.

For a while, she thought he was pretending not to have heard her over the wind and waves, but then his mouth parted. "Although it takes a few blinks in the here and now, I live through each secret as the person commits it or learns about it in what feels like a true passage of time. If they've secretly hurt someone, then I relive hurting that person. If someone has hurt them or secretly loved them, I feel all of it. Pleasure or pain."

The true dreadfulness of his Inheritance shocked her into silence. The horrors he must have experienced as he picked the heart of Dobhran, the Burner of Gull Harbour.

"And while I pick the lock on a heart," he continued, watching the whitecaps, "mine is bare to the one I pick. *Absolutely bare.* You understand? As long as the connection of our flesh continues, they experience my secrets as I experience theirs. Tit for tat, I suppose."

Her heart thudded against her chest, bursting with the selflessness of his threat against Llion and what ruthless acts

Thane would experience if he picked the former mercenary's heart. "But we've touched, and I haven't seen your secrets."

"I can control when I unleash it now. But once I do, it's nauseating. Like seasickness, but a hundred times worse. Imagine inhabiting another's body, feeling their soul in you, and yours in them, where it was never supposed to be."

Sympathy roiled through her at the intimate trespass. It was startling how close their Inheritances manifested.

"Is that how scrying feels?"

"Not when I'm in control." It struck her that no one else had thought to ask her about how her Inheritance affected her. "But a wild vision feels like my spine is being ripped out through my throat before I give in. I used to fight it. But I've found it's better if I don't."

Silence stretched between them, but not awkwardly. Then, without warning, he jumped up onto the railing, which was scarcely wide enough for his bare feet, and landed in a crouch.

"What in Lleufer's name are you doing, Sionnach?"

Instead of replying, he stood up and walked toward the jutting bowsprit, like an acrobat performing at the Amphitheatron. One mistake, one slip, and he'd be lost to the watery depths. The northerly wind whipped his dark locks and his turquoise tunic about as he proceeded along the bowsprit jutting out from the prow.

"Get down!" she hissed.

A swell hit the prow, and the spray splashed his back, upsetting his balance. Her stomach lurched at the thought of him tumbling over, but he hopped over a forestay and smirked.

Seren recognized a dare when she saw one. Climbing up onto the beam was easy enough, even if it pulled at her ribs. Standing was harder. The ship pitched and rolled with the swells, and she had to adjust her weight constantly to stay upright. She closed her eyes to centre herself to the ship. One misstep in this dance, and it would end in a watery grave.

But Lumina, it was exhilarating—freeing—to test herself. Her blood quickened with each step, chasing the lethargy of the past few days out of her bones. Soon she caught up to Thane at the end of the bowsprit, her heart pounding for another reason as they both bobbed up and down in a precarious dance with the ship. "I know about trespassing in someone else's body."

The confession startled the smirk off his face. "You do?"

It wasn't something she wanted others to know, but if anyone would understand, the Lockpick would.

"On the Night of Mair, a wild vision took hold of me. I was inside my father's body, but not in control of it. I couldn't see into his mind or heart, but I was trapped in a cage of his flesh and pain." Her knees almost buckled on a low dip into a swell, but she didn't fall. "It was the day of his execution. It was the first time I've ever felt sympathy for my father."

Another memory of being trapped pushed its way forward. Ice pooled in her belly at the thought of Joren standing over her, and she wondered if her nightmares all these years had been wild visions of her past.

Between her shoulder blades, her Eye rose. She sucked in a quick breath. Not here, not now. She'd pushed it off during Aequitas. But maybe that night wasn't something she could put firmly behind her.

*Ellus, I need you.* She didn't want to face this alone.

"Seren?"

Thane took a step towards her. Panic raced through her as rushing water roared in her ears. Her soul howled loudly against it. She would *not* relive that night again. Yet her spine arched, and she was falling backward into the brink—

A solid arm clenched around her. Thane leaned out over the sea, toes barely on the bowsprit, with one hand wrapped in a line to anchor them. His hair still smelled of smoke from

Ultima under dry leaves, and the scent cleared her head of the last vestiges of the wild vision.

"I got you," he murmured, and her arms wrapped around his neck. So warm. His one-arm embrace tightened gently around her waist, and she could've wept in relief. It was such an odd response, she decided her nerves were still strained from the duel.

Then quick as the cocoon of warmth came it was gone. In a panic, she clenched her arms tighter, stealing the heat from where his neck pressed against her arm, unwary of the danger of losing her secrets.

"Easy, Princess," he murmured, nodding toward the forecastle. "You got this now."

She didn't let go until she realized Thane had released her so they could make their way back.

After sliding one foot forward at a time down the bobbing bowsprit, without further catastrophe, Thane jumped down from behind her and offered her a hand. Deliberately, she thought, and not because her legs were embarrassingly wobbly.

"Most Felinae are afraid of my touch. Others, too, when they know."

She feared what he could do. Who with secrets wouldn't? He could expose her and her mission. But she didn't fear *him*. Maybe she even understood why he pushed others away before they could get too close.

"I've nothing to hide, Lockpick," she lied, putting her hand firmly in his. If he wanted to take her secrets, he could've done so already. She suspected he wanted to keep his own, and it made her trust him more. She grinned. "And I'm certainly not afraid of you."

His grip on her tightened before her feet hit the deck and her knees gave out, but he made no sign that he had saved her from face planting on the deck.

"Everyone has something to hide." He scowled, and as soon as she had her feet under her, he dropped her hand with all her secrets intact. "And maybe you should be afraid, Princess."

She rolled her eyes at the empty threat. She wouldn't let Thane hide behind his surly demeanour anymore. "I can put you on your ass again, like the day we met, Thane Sionnach. Cracked ribs, or not."

Her taunt invoked a round of chuckles from their gathering audience. Light was breaking, and the sailors were beginning their duties. Her remark hadn't been for them, though, and she was pleased to see the dark expression on Thane's face shift into a grin, though it didn't reach his eyes.

"All the more reason to see you back to your cabin before you're forced to make good on your word, Princess."

———

EXHAUSTED from another failed attempt at scrying, Seren tugged the wool blanket tight against the northern chill that had permeated every corner of the ship since Maiden Moon began waning. Tonight, the last sliver of the moon would vanish, and Lumina would retreat from the mortal realm. It was an ominous night aptly called Nomoon. Back in Luminaria, the Amphitheatron, temples, and shops would be closed, and the streets would be empty save for lost souls. It was inauspicious to be out and about on Nomoon, and she prayed Ty and her friends, along with Clan Llewyn, had reached Caisteal Diomhair safely.

She missed them.

For the last week, she'd had little in the way of company. A fever had broken out among the sailors, and Nemia became too busy to tend to her any longer. Not that she needed a nursemaid. Until Thane finished his duties with the crew and joined her for supper in her berth, she was alone. Entertaining herself on deck was out of the question for two reasons: the icy winds and the frequent presence of Llion on the quarterdeck. And despite her weariness, she couldn't rest.

That left the book. The one she'd stolen from Lady Llewyn.

Beneath the thin wool blanket, Seren blew on her chapped hands, rubbing them together to get some feeling back in them before opening the small leather volume. Listlessly, she thumbed through the almost translucent pages to fend off the monotony of staring at the teak walls. Her callused fingers ran over the delicate faded script that filled the pages with words she couldn't read. They paused at the one word that made her blood stir despite the cold.

*Unamkhara.*

Soulshielder. Her gaze drifted to the band with the black slashed circle on her hand, plucked from her father's lifeless finger by Calvus Takkakus, nineteen years ago. Devan Morningstar may have betrayed his queen and king by breaking the Accord, and then betrayed Adalyn and Seren by renouncing her as his child, but he'd been stabbed in the back long before that.

By his soulshielder, Kynden Startaker.

Startaker should've stopped Devan Morningstar from breaking the Accord. Why hadn't he? It was but a small excuse that her father hadn't been born royal, his crown a gift from Queen Ellowyne to her new brother-in-law.

Of course, her parents weren't without blame. Adalyn and Devan must have known full well that their relationship could never be, that a child together was forbidden. Since the Accord had been struck nearly two centuries ago, the lines of succession of the Felinae royals and the nobilis of Luminaria had never crossed. Until Seren was born.

The pages blurred before her as she flipped through them,

faster and faster, until one page stuck to her fingers. It was painted in bold inks of sapphire and crimson and gold. A man and a woman of equal height faced each other, palms held up and pressed together as if speaking a vow. The woman wore a crown, the man none. Slung over his shoulder was a bow and a quiver in the same manner that Lleufer, the mortal consort of Lumina, was often depicted. Around them was a black circle with a diagonal line intersecting it. The unamkhara and Inheritance symbol again.

Above them hung a full moon. Below their feet lay a skeleton, an arrow piercing its bloody heart. From their joined hands, red drops fell onto the bones below them in what looked like some sacrificial rite.

Her mind flashed back to her hand, bloodied by Dobhran's death, clasping Ellus's over Sila's slain body. A sense of dread welled up inside her, and she absently rubbed her forehead. When had it started tingling again?

In a fit of pique, she snapped the book closed, then hurled it at the far wall for good measure. Whatever this ancient ceremony was, she didn't need to know. She had a mission, and it had nothing to do with mystical Felinae claptrap.

The creak of the floorboards and his familiar scent outside her door informed her of Thane's arrival. It wasn't supper time, though. Before he could knock, she opened the door. He wore his wool cloak over his leathers to keep out the cold, and his dark hair curled about his collar.

"I haven't located the clans." It was her standard greeting now.

He waved that off. "They say we should be in sight of the Veiled Isles and Caisteal Dìomhair by supper, if the wind holds."

So soon.

Seren stepped back to allow him to enter, and in four steps, he crossed to the far wall, as far away from her as he could get.

The wall boasted a small desk and a shelf. At his boots lay the tented book. He picked it up with a cursory glance and placed it on the lone shelf. If he wondered why she had a Felinae book, he didn't ask. Instead, his fingers trailed along the shelf, stopping at a stone statue of Sol, a remnant of the berth's former occupant. The god stood bare-chested with a ball of fire in one hand and a bucket of water in the other.

"You know who Llion is."

She hesitated at his cool tone, which she hadn't heard in a long time. It was as though he had steeled himself for this conversation. "He was a mercenary before becoming the crown prince's sealgair."

Thane turned to face her. His nose and cheeks were pink from the cold as if he had lingered outside before coming to her door. "I saw how you looked at him after the fire, and I overheard what you called him during Aequitas. Your Inheritance revealed his true identity to you."

She faltered, but there was no point in denying it. "It did."

As he looked down at the floor, he sucked in his lower lip as if considering his next words. "I've known since picking Dobhran's heart. It shed new light on many things."

"Why didn't you say something earlier?"

"Same reason you didn't confide in me." He gave her an arch look. "I had to be certain I could trust you with this. And I was waiting until the information would be useful."

He trusted her? Useful for what? Seren swallowed down her questions.

"Some say the eldest prince should be the next king," he said carefully. Like Lady Llewyn—who was Llion's wife, she reminded herself—and Drakori. It seemed like Thane had been doing his own spying.

"Shouldn't he be, if he's the eldest? That's how monarchies work." That was neutral, wasn't it? After all, she didn't know exactly where Thane's loyalties lay.

"Dobhran's secrets had some insight on that." He leaned back against the wall, hands in his jacket's pockets, and she settled on the bunk. "On the Night of the Broken, the child Llion disappeared and was presumed dead, but a body was never found. Lady Boreal used her Inheritance to seek him, yet she didn't locate him until a few years ago. When she did, he was rampaging around the continent, a sword for hire, and keeping company with a certain assassin. Meanwhile, Prince Alban, a mere babe when his parents were slain, was raised from birth to wear the crown. After being secretly reunited with his brother a few years ago, Llion stepped aside."

She frowned. This story sounded familiar. Of course, it fit with what Vesper and Ellus had said about the crown prince. "And he became sealgair, protector of his brother."

"I imagine he must command considerable sway over his younger brother because of his noble sacrifice and being the last of their family. To put it bluntly, the man despises us both. If asylum is what you desire, you will not find it in the Felinae Dominion. Not as long as Llion Llewyn has a say in it."

She only desired asylum as a means to an end, but Llion would never allow her to take her place as a princess of the Felinae, let alone permit her to breathe in the prince's presence. She'd be fortunate if she didn't end up slain in her bed at Caisteal Dìomhair.

"You've summed up my position at court. What about yours? Does Llion hate you simply for your Inheritance and delightful personality?"

He didn't laugh like she wanted him to. Instead, Thane rolled something small between his fingers before shoving his whole hand in his pocket. "Those with power often abhor any weakness, lest it bring them down, and Llion Llewyn seems to view his past as just that. I suspect he'd like it and his secrets to stay firmly behind him. We're both threats to that."

Seren remembered Lady Llewyn's empty chair the morning

after the Night of Mair. "Yet he doesn't embrace his future either." As a lord, or as a man who could be king. Few walked away from such power.

"You speak of his pretence of a marriage?" Thane scoffed. "Leeches like him are not uncommon. They'll use anyone for their own gain, then discard them like refuse in the streets."

She didn't argue, but it hadn't seemed like Llion was manipulating his wife, a lady in her own right. As a stranger to the clans, marrying the head of Clan Llewyn was a politically astute move to gain allies. But she honestly didn't think Llion was that ambitious.

"I mean only to warn you of what might await you once we disembark. But enough about him."

Here was the crux of it. Amid the sound of the waves, Thane's voice dropped low and quiet, lapping it seemed against her skin. "What is it you desire at Caisteal Dìomhair, Seren?"

To finish what she started in Aequitas. To get her and Ty out of Llion's grasp. Her hands curled into the scratchy blanket, needing something to do with them.

The thin pallet dipped as Thane sank down beside her. "Or does it matter what you desire? We both have masters, don't we? And their wishes must come first."

Her jaw dropped. It was as if he had transformed before her. Who was Thane Sionnach?

"We do?"

"Don't act coy, Seren. It doesn't suit you, this whole naïve act. My master wishes Llion Llewyn to lose favour with the court and clans, then disappear when the time is right. There can be no peaceful rule while he lives." His attention strayed to her neckline. The blanket around her shoulders had fallen loose, exposing a yellowing necklace of bruises, framed by the V of her leather vest. The largest one nestled in the dip at the base of her throat like a huge oval topaz. "Perhaps the goals of your master and mine align?"

Seren sucked in a breath, the motion eliciting a dull pinch in her wrapped ribs. Ty offered a balm to the pain of her past. An escape. Ellus recognized her need to prove herself and offered acceptance. But Thane alone seemed to understand her darkest desire: *revenge.*

The potent emotion coursed through her. Llion had regretted allowing Quinton to live. And for Lumina's sake, she'd almost died at the man's hands. And he'd try again, as soon as he could, to knock her off the Conquer board. It was as if Lumina sent Thane to her as the key to the problem of the eldest prince. It was on the tip of her tongue to agree, yet she hesitated. Many times she had lost at Conquer because she'd rushed into battle without a full understanding of the players and their alliances.

"Who is your master? A clan lord?" Someone else with power at court? Whoever he was, Seren doubted he wanted both the princes gone for good. And she could not stop at one.

"I think we can both guess who the other's master might be," Thane hedged. "If you accept the offer, my master will ensure you are granted asylum or safe return to Luminaria."

It was tempting. Eliminating one prince might be enough to exonerate her crimes back in Luminaria, but it wouldn't guarantee a smooth surrender of the Felinae Dominion to the Republic of Luminaria. However, she would need allies to take on Llion, especially if Ty wasn't in league with her.

The pallet creaked as Thane stood. "Think on it, Seren. But I must know your decision before you are presented to the Throne."

"And what happens if I refuse?"

"Will you refuse, though?" His throat bobbed like he had more to say, and she had the unsettling feeling that he wished to warn her off. Instead, he gently pried her fingers open and pressed something small and hard into her palm. A gust of wind blew into her berth; then the door banged shut behind him.

Slowly, she opened her hand. In it lay a wooden game piece from a Conquer board—*the assassin*—and around the hooded figure curled a scrap of torn paper with two words scrawled in purple ink:

*Dear Uncle.*

# THANK YOU FOR READING!

If you would like to support me and my books, please consider leaving a review wherever books are reviewed or where you bought this book!

There's a lot of books out there. Reviews help indie books find new readers and help put our books in the spotlight. We also love it when readers recommend our books to others!

If you've already done so, thank you so much!!

OXOXO

# ACKNOWLEDGMENTS

OATHBREAKER is the first novel I've completed from first draft (and many, many subsequent drafts) to published book. It has taken many years to see my dream of holding it in my hands to become reality. On my writing journey, I have been so lucky to have been supported and encouraged by so many.

First and foremost, I offer heartfelt gratitude to my critique partner and friend Anne Wheeler. I fervently believe that this novel would not be in your hands today if I hadn't met Anne in Kristin Kieffer's Your Write Dream Facebook group, where we exchanged first drafts many years ago. Whether I am feeling the highs or the lows of writing, she is there to lend an ear. When I have a plot or character dilemma, she shares her perspective and advice. And when I need encouragement, she sends GIFs that say things like "Gimme, Gimme." The poor soul has read countless drafts of OATHBREAKER, and she's cut my word count numerous times as well. She is a champion. Thank you, Anne, for everything you do, as well as for sharing your stories with me and your friendship.

In the course of these many drafts, I have been extremely fortunate to have had the insight and feedback from a variety of beta readers. Some have critiqued one or more complete version. Others have read chapters and/or blurbs. Some have read for overall plot and character; others for the specific representation of characters who vary from my lived experience. Some have become friends. But all have made me think about my story decisions and, in doing so, they have been tremendously helpful.

My heartfelt thanks (in no particular order) to **Jade, Hope, Julie, Rhiannon, Tauri, Becky, Phoebe, Annie, Monique, Amy, Sarah,** and **Jason.**

If I have omitted any names by mistake, my apologies.

I also owe a great deal of gratitude to the Writers At Work writing group for all of your encouragement and answers to my questions along the way. We met on Twitter or through Camp Nanowrimo, and your presence has made the writing community on Twitter a place I wanted to be for many years. Thank you, **Annie, Hope, Julie, Monique,** and **Steve.** It's a pleasure to read your writing.

I owe much gratitude to my editor, **Ashley Rayner** of Inkwell Editorial. She edited with a delicate but insightful hand and answered my style and grammar questions with patience and generosity. Any mistakes or typos within this novel are completely my fault. My appreciation as well to editor **Bryony Leah,** who edited a portion of a much earlier version.

In the past, other Twitter groups online have encouraged me to keep writing when I felt like the slowest of the slow or helped me explore story elements and concepts with other writers. Thank you to the hosts and participants of **#Turtlewriters** and **#StorySocial** writers for your encouragement and camaraderie.

Many others host/hosted writing hashtag games on Twitter and my participation in those developed my insight into my characters and the story I wanted to tell. Plus, they were a lot of fun!

At home, I have a wonderful family, who have supported my dream; Nonetheless, they've asked the questions writers dread most, such as "What's your book about?" and "When will you be published?" and "Can I have another snack, Mom?"

My parents have always believed in me, and I thank them from the bottom of my heart for all they've done to encourage my creativity and love for writing over the years.

To my husband and children, thank you for all your love and your patience (especially for waiting for snacks because I had to finish a sentence).

A few years ago, my daughter (age 7) asked me what I was writing, and when I explained it was OATHBREAKER, a story she had asked me about before, she was shocked. "You're still writing the same book?"

But the next time she asks me what I'm writing, I can say, "Now I am writing the sequel."

*(Disclaimer: I have written other stories besides this one, but alas, in this instance, it was the same book.)*

Last, but not least, <u>thank you</u>, reader, for choosing to take a chance on this story. I hope you enjoyed getting to know my flawed heroine Seren and her friends/enemies/frenemies as much as I enjoyed writing the first instalment of their adventures. Please consider leaving a **review** on a site of your choice. It is a tremendous help to both authors and readers.

Stay tuned for *book 2* in the Keepers of the Elusive Mysteries series.


Peace, Love & Blue Skies,

*Meghan T.*

# ABOUT THE AUTHOR

Meghan Tomlinson writes fantasy and science fiction stories with a touch of romance. She grew up in a small mining town near Great Lake Superior in Ontario, Canada, reading anything that would transport her to another world. She earned a Master of Arts degree in English Literature at York University. When she's not writing or reading a good book, she's raising two children (and a puppy) with her husband on the North Shore.

# Also by Meghan Tomlinson

"Wild Swan Chase" in *Among Thorns and Stardust*
(a scifi anthology collection of fairy tale retellings)

*KEEPERS OF THE ELUSIVE MYSTERIES*
Book 1: Oathbreaker
Book 2: TBA

*Coming Soon!*
A prequel novelette in the world of *Oathbreaker*

Follow me for updates, sneak peeks, and bookish fun!

facebook.com/MeghanTomlinsonWrites
x.com/ElusiveStory
instagram.com/meghantomlinsonwrites
bookbub.com/authors/meghan-tomlinson